The author was born in East Ham, London, in 1938. He has two sons and a daughter. In 1959 he became a fully qualified electrician after doing a five-year apprenticeship, after retiring in 2006, he moved to Spain a year later with his wife, Josephine. In 2018 Peter and his wife returned to England where they now live in Lavenham, Suffolk, with their daughter, Gemma.

Peter Buckle

THE CRYSTALS

AUSTIN MACAULEY PUBLISHERS™
LONDON * CAMBRIDGE * NEW YORK * SHARJAH

A CIP catalogue record for this title is available from the British Library.

ISBN 9781398407275 (Paperback)
ISBN 9781398416413 (ePub e-book)

www.austinmacauley.com

First Published 2021
Austin Macauley Publishers Ltd®
1 Canada Square
Canary Wharf
London
E14 5AA

Prologue

Some 250 light years from Earth, there existed a similar solar system, a star around which several planets rotated. One of the planets was, although slightly smaller, very similar to Earth. The planet had been inhabited and one of the species was a humanoid genetically but some ten thousand years older than the human race and, because of this their intelligence, was much higher.

The only other difference was their height; they tended to be slightly taller.

They called their planet Umbria and their sun, Radiance. Umbria, came into being as a planet when a dying star came close to their sun and a stream of molten matter was pulled from Radiance and one of those globules of molten matter in the eons of time became Umbria. Radiance was a mature star and now, several billions of years later, was tragically dying and the radiation from it was slowly killing off all life on the planet.

Umbria was already host to a species from another planet. This race was very old, their planet having died millions of years before. They were called Arians and had left their planet in a flotilla of spacecraft. One of the spacecrafts got separated from the flotilla and, close to death, the Arians descended on Umbria. They numbered only a few thousand but were virtually immortal, but had the ability to terminate their lives. They had evolved to a point where offspring were rarely born, just a few, every thousand years. So advanced were the Arians that they could change age and form and sometimes did so to enjoy a younger life again as a different person or creature.

They had a strict non-interference code with other species and only landed on Umbria to survive.

But having been welcomed by the Umbrians, they now felt compelled to help.

They witnessed the radiation gradually killing off all life on Umbria and after many discussions came to the decision to help.

With their great knowledge, they assisted the Umbrians in the building of huge domes over their cities, towns and farmlands. These domes reflected the radiation and after many years, the whole of Umbria was under clusters of such domes.

The radiation, however, had made the majority of Umbrians, both male and female, infertile and their population continued to fall.

Again, the Arians came to the rescue and they developed a drug capable of giving the Umbrians the ability to regenerate. This cure was only for those who had escaped radiation though.

But those who took the drug found their organs bisecting and growing, so all the major organs had replacements as they died. Also, and more importantly, it gave both male and females their fertility again. The regenerating drug did not apply to the brain but like humans, the Umbrians only used one third of their brain and, as one section of the brain became weak another section took over.

All this could only help in the short term however. Radiance in her death throes was expanding and would eventually devour all the planets orbiting her. Initially many Umbrians fled to beneath the surface of the planet. The Umbrians had depleted all the planet's fossil fuels thousands of years previously and this left huge caverns and lakes of water underground. They sealed their underground chambers and lit and heated the caverns with halogen lights suspended from above; this they knew would not prove to be long term and they would have to return to the surface in the future. Those who lived on the surface could now only live under the shelter of the domes.

Fully aware of the impending disaster, the Arians came up with an idea that held many risks but as extinction was the alternative, there was no option.

The Arians planned and assisted in the building of twenty spaceships a mile long and a third of that in breadth. These ships were capable of holding ten thousand Umbrians. They were also interlocking, forming into one enormous vessel. The plan was simple in concept but fraught with danger!!!!!

Away in space, some 470 light years from Radiance, there was a young benign sun with planets orbiting around it, none of which were inhabited.

The Arians' plan was to pull Umbria from its orbit using her moons and the interlocked spaceships as traction.

The spaceships would create a wormhole (vacuum), in space and once free of Radiance's gravitational pull, would start the epic journey towards the young sun with the planets which could possibly support life.

The day came when both the moons aligned, and with spaceships interlocked, and the traction at full power, Umbria started to move out of her orbit.

Disaster struck as Umbria rotated and the traction was focussed on her ocean.

The ocean and its surrounding coastline broke away and came hurtling between the two moons towards the spaceships. The commander took evasive action and the whole mass narrowly missed the spaceships.

All who saw the disaster were horrified, terrified and in shock. The 2500 miles of coastline had more than 700 Crystal Domes some of which were cities, more than a billion souls were lost.

They had also lost their ocean all the fish and creatures within it. Just a small lake of seawater remained. It meant they had lost their main food source.

There were two spacecraft used for transport between Umbria and the main spaceship, one of these disappeared after the mass in the hope of finding some survivors.

Umbria was again taken in tow and began to move away from Radiance.

The remaining Umbrians took stock, a quarter of their population gone and the remaining atmosphere was torn away with the mass.

On Umbria itself, the survivors were those in the Crystals with their own oxygen.

The original plan to move to the benign sun was gone. With the loss of many of the food farms on Umbria the distance and the time it would take was too great.

Now, another plan was needed and, again it was the Arians who the Umbrians looked to.

The Arians knew of a closer sun, where the sun was benign, but more importantly had a planet that could sustain life.

The planet had been probed by the Arians some ten thousand years before but was then in an ice age and was rejected, but it had oceans and a good atmosphere, which made it inhabitable.

Although ignorant of the planet's status, it was decided that this was the chance as its star was half the distance to be travelled.

So, the wormhole was realigned and the great journey began.

At approximately a third the speed of light, the epic voyage would take 800 years.

Manned probes were launched that could travel at many times the speed of light to find out the present state of the planet.

The Grand Council of Umbria ordered landings and so, twenty-five years later, the first probe descended on Mother Earth.

The Umbrians in the probe had detected intelligent life on the planet and the first probe to land on Earth did so in the Atlantic a thousand miles east of Florida. It was 1140.

In the next five hundred years, over a thousand probes were sent and many of these were manned. Umbrians began to inhabit Earth in great numbers in all parts of the planet, gathering information and learning all the diverse languages.

Initially, they kept to their instruction from the Grand Council and built centres where they could stay secluded but being of humanoid form and with the constant mixing of the two species, they started to integrate with the humans. Both male and female Umbrians found the humans exciting as they witnessed their development. Eventually, nature took its course and offspring were born of mixed gender. The result was amazing. The Umbrians were able to keep the secret because the mixed gender was stronger and had the same intellect.

As the intelligence of humans grew, the probes sent to Earth were reduced and only went to isolated locations on the planet. The Bermuda triangle being one of them.

Part 1

Chapter 1

The man moved cautiously amongst the scaffolding that surrounded the bridge. Even at this hour, he could smell the fumes that were suffocating the city. He was at this unusual rendezvous as he had received an urgent telephone call from an informant whom he had known and implicitly trusted for many years. He was there because the informer had warned him that his family was in danger.

It was nearly five in the morning and bitterly cold for June. He pulled his coat tighter around his slim but muscular body. Although in his mid-forties he was still extremely fit.

His head jerked around as he heard somebody approaching, his eyes piercing the early morning mist.

"Is that you Mr Franklin?" Came a hoarse whisper.

"Yes Ivan, I'm over here by the bridge's central support."

The meeting place was Southwark Bridge and, even at five in the morning, would normally have traffic flowing across it. However, the bridge was undergoing repairs which had been promised for years and work had begun.

"Why here, Ivan?" John Franklin enquired.

"Somebody has been following me for days," Ivan said, nervously. "But I think I've lost them for now."

"Well, let's get this meeting over quickly and get off this bridge. What information do you have for me?"

"It's the oil consortium, John, they know about the breakthrough your boy Ben has made and knowing the billions it will cost them, has proved too much for their pockets so they have put a contract out to stop him."

John was shocked!!! He knew the oil magnates would stoop low to maintain their hold on their domination and control of all the fuel markets, but to murder the competition was unbelievable.

"Are you totally sure of this, Ivan?"

"I risked my life coming here," Ivan replied.

John said no more and took out his mobile and called his son. He suddenly sensed other presences. He pulled Ivan into the cover of the bridge support as several shots from silenced weapons whistled through the air around them. Ivan slumped quietly to the ground and was dead before he reached it. John cursed as he was also hit, the bullet spinning him round as it struck him in the hip.

"Hello," came a sleepy voice over the mobile. "Z," said John, and terminated the call.

In his house, Ben leapt out of bed. The last letter of the alphabet meant only one thing, his father was in mortal danger. He flew to his computer and put a trace on the call.

"What the hell is he there for?" He said to himself and, immediately slumped back into the chair and focused his mind.

John struggled against the searing pain in his side as another bullet hit him in the chest.

He slid his hand into his inside pocket and extracted a small tube, resembling a pen. This tube was attached to a wire leading to a power pack. He had not come unarmed. It was a laser and he set it from 'stun' to 'kill'. Like his son, he then focused his mind, and let it drift into the night air. His would-be assassins closed in slowly, like a pack of hyenas, confident of the outcome. Having focused his mind, John raised the laser and instantly a beam of light no thicker than a hair, pierced through the mist. One by one, five of his assailants toppled over, each with a minute hole in his head. With a cry of alarm, the remainder of his attackers slunk back into the early morning mist. From behind them John heard a voice he recognised.

"Finish him off. His battery's…," came the voice with a hint of malicious humour, "His battery's flat."

John cursed, only his friend and confidante would know the amount of power the battery held.

"Freddy Fields, you bastard," John roared through his pain. "You have betrayed us all."

"Goodbye John, old boy," came the reply. "See you in hell."

His killers moved in as John started to slide into oblivion. The air on the bridge was suddenly full of heavy static. Freddy stepped back a pace as his clothes, and those of the remaining killers, burst into flames. They frantically ran around screaming and tearing at their clothes. One of them jumped off the bridge only to hit the scaffolding some twenty metres below. Freddy and two others died of heart attacks. They were the lucky ones as the remaining men were left totally insane, even though their clothes and bodies had not a single burn on them.

Chapter 2

After the attack, Ben had alerted James, the head of his security team and lifelong friend.

Being fully apprised of the traumatic happenings on Southwark Bridge, James had swung into action. He immediately had John and Ivan rushed by helicopter to the Company Clinic in Cumbria. The dead bodies on the bridge were quickly and efficiently disposed of, without trace. The unfortunate survivors were placed in a private institution. They could not retrieve the body of the poor individual who jumped off the bridge. However, it was assumed when eventually found that he was a drunk who had wandered on to the bridge.

John and Ben were now mulling over the awful events that occurred on Southwark Bridge.

"Such is the power of thought," Ben said to his father.

"Only your mind has that much power," his father replied.

"Yes, Dad it is strange that you are unable to create hallucinations as an Umbrian when I have this power and am only part Umbrian. Thank goodness Mum is half human."

John smiled, weakly "I could see the flames myself."

Ben grimaced, "I am not happy with what I did but I had no choice. Now, come on Dad, just how bad are your injuries?"

"Well. Considering I'm in my second life span, not bad for an old man of 139."

"That may well be but we must now concentrate our energies on getting you well. Apart from the damage to your heart, you sustained some very bad injuries on the bridge and you will be laid up on this heart and lung machine for some time."

Ben stood up and looked out of the window. The small medical centre was built by his father many years before within the grounds of their family home exclusively for the use of Umbrians who were now scattered around the world.

It was built in the same style as the house, in the same soft red brick, and stood about two hundred metres from the house thus giving the impression of an annexe or guest rooms for family and friends. In reality, however, beneath the soft red brick facade was a concrete and steel construction. It was solely for the use of Umbrians' close friends and family who needed medical attention.

The view was beautiful, as only the Lake District can be, in early autumn, with the meadows full of wild flowers and grazing sheep. The leaves on the trees in the small wood beyond were turning to many hues of yellow, gold and brown before finally drifting to the ground making a carpet of many colours. Further, still in the distance, was a shimmer of blue which was the lake where Ben had spent many a happy hour fishing with his friends and just occasionally with his father. John was often away, building his fortune in pharmaceuticals.

If only I had been less successful, Ben thought, *we would still have had a good life and dad would not be lying here critically injured.* He suddenly felt really tired, which was hardly surprising considering he had been awake for more than twenty-four hours, coupled with the transporting of his mind to Southwark Bridge. He opened the window by the side of his father's bed and sat down. His father was sleeping soundly now. *I will stay for an hour,* he thought, *and, if Dad is still asleep by then, I will leave and see if I can find the source of the assassination attempt.*

Ben looked out again taking in the beautiful view. The lake shone blue in the sun when suddenly a cloud blocked out the sun and the temperature dropped sharply. Ben shivered and looked in horror at what he now saw. Before his eyes, the water in the lake slowly receded and an icy wind whistled through the window. Ben quickly closed the window and continued to stare out. He could not believe what was happening; everything was disappearing. The lake was now a dry hollow, the meadows had become barren and the trees now stood stripped of their leaves and bark. The sky darkened and then everything turned white and he could see a figure standing alone on the frosted ground. It was his mother; he had to warn her. He pushed open the window, struggling to open it against the howling wind. "Mother, get to cover, hurry."

Quickly the figure spun round and just disappeared. "No, no," Ben roared, as something gripped him hard. He struggled helplessly and felt his mind whirling. In his tortured mind, he heard someone calling his name.

"Ben, Ben," somebody was still holding him, but now gently. "Benjamin," the voice said. "It is alright."

Slowly, he came back to himself and opened his eyes and sure enough, there was his mother looking anxiously down at him. "What the hell happened," he groaned, holding his head which was now throbbing.

"Well," said Louisa, "The mental stress that your mind has endured in the last twenty-four hours has obviously had its toll on you and given you a bad nightmare."

"Oh Mum, it was so real, I really believed it was happening."

"Did something happen to me?" his mother asked, now grinning,

"Well, yes, you disappeared."

"I thought so. I think every sleeping male within a thousand miles had part of your dream."

Ben smiled. "I will have to be more careful in the future and guard, if possible, my unconscious thoughts. Now, I really must get back to the office as I've got Ivan's funeral to arrange and I want to go and pay my respects to Julie."

"Not a pleasant task," Louisa commented, "they were very devoted."

Ben nodded. "Yes, and it will be made worse for Julie as the twins are so young, it will be a small compensation to Julie to be told that she and the children will never want for anything for the rest of their lives."

Louisa smiled. "Do you know the names of the children?" It was a standing joke that Ben, with all his mental capabilities, had difficulty in remembering names.

"There's Ivan junior and the twins, Yvonne and Yvette."

"I'm leaving now," said Ben. "Are you staying with dad?"

"No, I will come back later. I have asked the staff to call me the moment he wakes up."

"Okay, bye for now, Mum, I'll speak to you later." With that, Ben rushed off into the gathering dusk.

Chapter 3

On his drive to London, Ben rang Dennis, one of his security team, and gave him Julie's address in Greenwich. He told Dennis to take one of the surveillance vans to Julie's address and park discreetly at the end of her road.

Several hours later, he stood in front of a pretty terraced house in Greenwich Village. He opened the gate and walked up to the brightly painted front door. Before he knocked, he paused to gather his thoughts. Immediately, ferocious barking could be heard from within. Ben then remembered that Ivan had bought a dog for the children some years before. He struggled to remember the dog's name. Wizards came to mind and as the door opened, he remembered the name "Oz." A dog came hurtling through the open door and rushed towards the gate. Ben was so pleased that he had remembered to shut it when he arrived. A small human form came charging past Ben.

"Come here you little ratbag," it said, and gathered the little Yorkshire Terrier into its arms.

"You must be Ben," said the small girl, cuddling the dog that was now furiously licking her face.

Another face appeared at the door. "Hello Mr Franklin, how is your father?"

It will take a long time but he should make a full recovery," said Ben, briefly studying her face where a brave smile shone through the sadness.

"Julie," Ben stopped and instead motioned to the little girl cuddling the dog. "You must be one of the twins?"

"Yes, that is Yvonne," Julie said softly. "Her twin sister, Yvette, is upstairs in their room. Please, Mr Franklin, come in."

"I insist you call me Ben and may I call you Julie?"

"Of course, you must," Julie countered, and in the same breath said, "Shall I make some tea or would you prefer coffee, or even something stronger? Please, sit down Mr…er…Ben," she said, her mouth quivering nervously.

Ben felt suddenly guilty and realised it must be years since he had been in contact with Ivan's family, although Ivan had been his father's friend. As a youngster, Ben had visited the family many times and had struck up a close friendship with Julie's younger sister, Tessa.

Whilst Julie fussed over making tea, there was a quiet knock on the door and a young lad walked in.

"Ah," said Ben, "You must be Ivan." Ben knew the twins were five but was unsure of Ivan's age and said as much.

"I'm fifteen. How is your dad?"

"Thank you for asking. He is okay, thanks to your father." There was an awkward silence, Ben being at a complete loss of words.

"I'll go now," said Ivan, and silently left the room.

Ben could have wept for him, but at the same time, admired the lad's courage in coming to speak to him.

Julie came in with the tea. "You've met my son then," she said.

Ben nodded. "You must be very proud of him."

"Yes," Julie replied.

Ben looked at Julie, her head was lowered and she appeared to be looking at something on the floor. Her shoulders shook slightly and Ben realised she was crying.

"I'm so sorry," Ben said and took her gently in his arms, where she silently wept. After a few moments, she stopped crying and wiped her eyes dry.

"Your tea is getting cold."

Ben let her free and picked up his cup. "We have things to discuss and a funeral to arrange," Ben blurted out.

Julie nodded. "I know, I have been to the funeral directors already. I want to give Ivan a decent send-off but really the cost is unbelievable and, as you know, my Ivan loved to gamble."

Ben smiled. "Dad did mention it but you have no need to worry about money."

Julie flared. "The last thing I want is anybody's charity," she shouted angrily.

Ben must have looked shocked because she immediately apologised. "I'm so sorry," she said. "I overreacted."

"No, I understand completely," Ben replied quickly, feeling very embarrassed, knowing the lie he was about to tell Julie, was now going to be even harder. "Realizing that Ivan was a compulsive gambler we took out insurance for him and deducted from his retainer."

Julie stared at Ben. "He never mentioned it."

"He did not know," Ben said.

"What exactly do you mean, he didn't know?"

"Well, exactly that. We rightly or wrongly, took it upon ourselves to…" Ben hesitated and then plunged on, "We knew of his gambling habits and because of this, plus the danger involved in his work for our companies and our family, we took out a life or injury policy."

Julie sat there silently for a while trying to digest all this information and the difference it would make for her and her children. Finally, she thanked Ben and said how grateful she was.

Ben breathed a sigh of relief and said, "Right, I'll give you a rough outline of the policy now and fill in the details later. Because Ivan died while actively employed by us, you and the children are entitled to full compensation that has been put into a trust fund. However, I have a banker's draft here for twenty-five thousand pounds that I hope will cover your immediate expenses."

Julie smiled with relief. "It certainly will. I have to admit that things are now rather tight. How much is the trust for?"

"A little over five million pounds."

Julie gasped. "That's an enormous amount."

Ben quickly changed the subject, saying, "I must go now but first I would like to say goodbye to the children. I will put the full details of the policy in the post."

Julie went to get the children and, as she left the room, Ben took out his mobile phone and made a call.

Immediately, a voice said, "Hi, boss."

"I'm leaving now. Is everything okay out there, Dennis?"

Ben's personal bodyguard replied cautiously, "I'm not sure, boss. It's like a ghost town, much too quiet."

Julie returned with the children. Ben smiled and bade them a fond farewell. "You must all come to the Lake District for the next school holidays, which of course, will be Christmas." The children were extremely excited at the prospect and Ben added, "That includes your auntie, Tessa."

Julie smiled, remembering all the great times they had shared in their younger days—the days before her marriage to Ivan and before Ben and Tessa had gone off to university.

Ben gave Julie a hug, opened the front door to leave but then turned to her and said, "Would you take the children down to the cellar for a few minutes?"

Looking at Ben's face, Julie instantly realised that something was very wrong. She picked up her mobile and ushered the children out of the room and down to the cellar. As she left, Ben said, "It's just a precaution and I will ring you shortly."

Ben returned to the front door and, once outside, shivered, not from the chill that was coming with the gathering dusk, but from something else. He could sense static in the air and somebody, somewhere, was trying to probe his mind and it was not a friendly intrusion.

Ben again called Dennis and told him to stay in the van until he called him again. Dennis acknowledged and Ben immediately put Dennis, Julie and the children into a deep sleep.

Ben leaned against the front gate relaxing his body, whilst releasing his mind into the night. His mind was instantly assailed by several minds at once. It was like being beaten up by a gang of thugs but instead of crushing bones, it was his mind that was taking a hammering. Ben fought hard to drive their thoughts back, knowing that if he did not succeed, they would mentally destroy Julie and the children in their efforts to locate Ivan. The thought of this happening created a rage within him that strengthened his mind and he was able to drive them back once more. There was a slight easing on the pressure in Ben's mind and, for just a moment, he thought he had repelled them. However, they returned in greater force and the static around him grew in intensity with bright scarlet streaks of light flashing around his head. Behind him, there was a crash as a window broke under the pressure. In his mind, he cried out for he knew defeat was near. Another window broke, such was the resonance being created and Ben's defence started to cave in.

This is the end, came the thought and Ben cried out with defiance and pain. Suddenly, in Ben's mind, there was a speck of light that grew to a burst of brilliance and he realised he had an ally. The ally joined forces with him, and together they destroyed the malignant attackers. There were despairing screams in Ben's mind then silence. Ben himself drifted in the serenity of the silence.

Eventually, he was brought out of his reverie by the sound of a familiar feminine voice whispering in his ear.

Chapter 4

"Ben, are you alright? Ben, Ben..." The voice came again. Ben shook the remaining cobwebs from his head and looked into a face that was full of concern. The face was freckled and had the most beautiful hazel eyes.

"Hello Tessa."

"Hello Ben," came the reply. "I can see you still playing your silly mind games."

"Where on earth did you spring from?" Ben asked.

Tessa looked sad. "I've come down from university for the funeral and of course, to support Julie." She looked down at Ben grimly. "You and your bloody family. Julie and Ivan were so happy. I wish Ivan had never joined your father's firm all those years ago."

Ben's mind went back to his childhood remembering the happy times with Tessa when she spent the holidays with his family in the Lake District. In those days, both Ivan and Julie worked and lived in London. Tessa was a tomboy and Ben had trouble keeping up with her.

When Ben was still quite young he asked Julie about her parents. Julie sadly replied that she had lost all her family, except Tessa, in her native country Croatia.

A bomb from either rebel or government forces had made a direct hit on her house and killed both her parents. By a miracle or god's will, Julie had been out with Tessa. Julie was only eighteen when this tragedy struck and, had it not been for the love and support from Ivan, her childhood sweetheart and his family, she and Tessa would have been totally alone and destitute. Ivan himself was already a victim of war, having lost both his parents when he was a young teenager. He had been adopted by Michael and Millika Llavinski and had become accepted and much-loved member of their family and friends. It was these good people that he turned to now in desperation. He told them that he must get Julie and her young sister away from this madness, otherwise Julie would surely lose her mind. There was a great family gathering and after much deliberation and heart-rending decisions, Michael and Millika told Ivan that the family had collected enough money to enable Ivan along with Julie and Tessa. England was chosen as Ivan already had a good knowledge of the English language. Ivan was overcome with gratitude. He was fully aware of the sacrifices that had been made by his adopted family as the whole community was suffering from grinding poverty and near starvation in the conflict. He told them that he would remember their overwhelming generosity and kindness and would one day return to Croatia.

Three months later, Ivan, Julie and Tessa were staying with Croatian friends in London awaiting citizenship. Although, Ivan was a fully qualified engineer in his own country, the fact that he could be repatriated at any time, made finding work very difficult. However, he eventually managed to obtain work as a night watchman with Franklin Pharmaceuticals.

Initially, he found it hard to adjust to staying awake all night. Eventually, he became used to the unsociable hours and to alleviate the boredom of the two-hour patrols. He began spending more time patrolling the premises. He was on one of his unscheduled jaunts, standing on top of the building enjoying the view of London when, far below he saw the lights of a large van. He was about to look away when the van stopped. Ivan was immediately alert. Why was the van stopping in a deserted street at the back of his firm's building at two in the morning? The van had doused its lights and pulled up close to the wall. Ivan saw a head appear and a rope ladder snake down on the inside of the wall. Ivan started down the staircase pulling his mobile from his pocket, he rang the police and hurried on down the staircase, not using the lift for fear of alerting the intruders. By the time he had descended the twenty odd flights, the intruders were in. Ivan was on the balcony of the first floor, above the main hall below. Looking down, he saw one of the intruders striding across the floor making his way to the security room. Without entering the man opened the door and slipped a small canister inside, he then closed the door and locked it. Ivan was shocked and worried to see that the man had a key. Ivan ducked as the man turned round and beckoned to his companions. Ivan glimpsed his face and was even more alarmed to see the face of Dean, head of security. Dean then went with his fellow thieves to the door, next to the security room and proceeded to open it. Ivan stood on the balcony in disbelief. The room that the men had just entered, was where the samples of all the new drugs were stored, most of which had not even been patented or trialled. As Ivan looked down, wondering what to do next, he noticed that Dean had left the key in the door. This prompted him into action. He quickly removed his shoes and silently ran down the stairs and across the marble floor to the door. Slamming it shut, he turned the key and, ignoring the banging and shouting that ensued from within, he went to the main entrance to await the police.

John Franklin arrived shortly after the police. He hurried across to Ivan and was horrified to see that Ivan had the key to the drug room. He questioned him and, after hearing Ivan's account of the events of the night, he found it hard to believe, as Dean had been with the firm for twenty years. From that night, Ivan had become indispensable to John Franklin and was often invited to the family home in the Lake District in his capacity as head of security. On these occasions, Julie and Tessa were invited to join him. After the first visit, John realised that Tessa was part Umbrian.

"Are you going to lie there all day?"

Ben suddenly realised that Julie and the children were still in the cellar. He jumped up quickly and John gasped, "Julie and the children..."

Alarm sprung to Tessa's face, "Where are they? With you being in the front garden, I assumed they were out."

They both ran to the house.

"The cellar," Ben yelled, as Tessa was now, way ahead of him.

Tessa opened the door to the cellar, from below a pale blue light shone. Rushing fearfully down the cellar stairs, they were confronted with a strange scene. There they all were, fast asleep on cushions, but, what was stranger still, was that the blue light surrounding them all was being emitted from little Yvette. Neither of them had witnessed anything like that before.

"How is she doing that?" Tessa whispered.

"I don't know but it must be some sort of protective barrier," Ben whispered back. "What enormous power for one so young."

They both pondered on what to do next. Tessa indicated that they should both go back upstairs and, once back in the hallway, Tessa spoke quietly. "I have sent a thought into Yvett's mind saying that I am here and everything is now all right." As Tessa spoke, the blue light slowly faded.

"Thank goodness for that, they will sleep now until you wake them."

Tessa headed for the kitchen, "I'm going to make some tea. Do you want a cup?"

Ben nodded in assent thinking that only thirty minutes ago that Julie was saying the exact words.

As they sat sipping tea, Ben noticed that Tessa was staring at him intently.

"You're keeping something from me," she said.

Ben shook his head but, realizing how tired he was, he knew that he would not be able to guard his thoughts.

"There is something I have been holding back and it's crucifying me." Tessa waited. "Ivan is still alive."

"Upstairs," she grated harshly.

Another time, Ben may have been flippant at that remark but now was not the time. In the loft, there was quite a large bedsit which Julie and Ivan had built for Tessa. It had two large dormer windows, en suite bathroom and air conditioning. It also had modern computers, television and radio. In the very centre of the beautifully decorated room was a double bed placed under the dormer windows where one could look at the night sky. This is where Tessa and Ben now sat.

Ben suggested they both spoke vocally as Yvette might pick up their thoughts. Tessa inclined her head in assent and waited silently for his explanation.

"When my mind reached Southwark Bridge that terrible morning and after I had dealt with the assailants, I went to Dad's aid. He pushed me away, and grasped Ivan. I turned to Ivan only to find that his heart had stopped. However, his brain still showed signs of activity."

Ben stopped talking and Tessa looked at him slightly more kindly and said, "Go on."

"A bullet had nicked Ivan's heart and I believe the shock of that stopped his heart. At first, I was at a loss as to know what to do for the best so I did the only thing I thought would help."

Ben stopped; he was so tired he could hardly hold his head up. Tessa gripped his arm. "Go on," she urged.

"I sealed the nick in his heart before attempting to crank up his brain."

"You did what?" Tessa looked aghast.

Ignoring her outburst, Ben continued. "I took what activity Ivan had left in his brain, boosted it as much as I dared then instructed it to reactivate his heart. Although, his heart responded, I still do not know what damage I have done, intruding into his mind and body so forcibly. Also, because his heart had stopped, there is a possibility of brain damage. Ivan is now in intensive care at our clinic and, before coming to London, I spent time with him messaging his mind from mine with good thoughts of Julie the children and you. Sadly, so far, all I have had back from him is confusion because of the brain damage."

"Who is with him now?"

"Mum, she herself also has great healing powers."

With that thought, Ben collapsed back on the bed, more unconscious than asleep. Tessa lay beside him and, although exhausted, her mind was in such a whirl that sleep was not going to come easy. Ivan was still alive, she could hardly believe it and Ben had left his father to resuscitate Ivan.

Before Ben had fallen into his deep sleep, he had conveyed to Tessa that Ivan knew the names of those who wished the Franklins dead and he had committed those names to memory. Tessa thought that the chances of anybody knowing those names now were very slim but, of course, their enemies were not aware of Ivan's condition. Ben was right to safeguard Julie, the children and Ivan and it was safer for the world to think that Ivan was dead. However, although she now understood why Ben had kept it secret, she felt deeply that Julie should be told the truth.

Ben shivered beside her and she struggled up and found a duvet. She gently undressed him, undressed herself and snuggled up under the duvet with him. Ben continued to shiver so she pulled him close and finally slept too.

Tessa awoke feeling hot and sticky. She threw back the duvet and padded across the room to release the catch that opened the dormer window. She stood for a moment, letting the cool night air wash over her naked body. She then went into the bathroom and stood under the shower rubbing herself down vigorously. Coming back into the bedroom, she examined herself in the long mirror on the wall. She was tall and slim with a good figure but she thought her feet were too large. *Oh, well nobody's perfect,* she thought and trotted back to bed. She looked at Ben still soundly asleep and realised how much he now meant to her.

Her mind went back to the happy days spent with Ben in the Lake District years ago, especially the summer days when they went swimming together in the lake and, afterwards, when they dried off in the sunshine lying side by side. Tessa recalled their intimate conversations about their dreams and aspirations for the future.

She was broken from this reverie when Ben opened his eyes and reached up and touched her. She responded by kissing him and climbing back into bed beside him.

It was hours later when they both finally woke. Ben gave Tessa a quick kiss and jumped out of bed. "We must wake Julie and the children, they've been asleep for such a long time."

"Ben I know we have been blocking Julie's mind regarding Ivan's present state but I feel strongly that Julie should now be told the truth. I fully understand why you kept it from her but I feel we must find another way to protect Julie and the children."

Ben stopped at the door and turned to Tessa in disbelief. "How can I possibly relay to Julie truth now, after all the lies I have said to her?"

"I know you did what you thought was right at the time," replied Tessa, "But I don't think you can possibly realise how close Julie and Ivan are. It is breaking her heart thinking he is dead and I really do not think she will cope with the funeral without having a nervous breakdown and, if that happened you would never forgive yourself."

Ben listened closely to what Tessa was saying and eventually repealed. "I just don't know how to tell her the truth."

Tessa said, "Leave it to me. Now, I think they should all be woken up, including Dennis, who must be roasting in the van, especially now the sun is up."

Ben set off down the street to where the van was discreetly parked outside a timber merchant. He could see the name of the merchant painted on the side of the van. However, on closer inspection, he realised that it was a laminated copy that had been stuck to the van. Amongst all the surveillance equipment, listening devices and computers, there was a tool for every eventuality. The morning sun was now beating down unmercifully on the solar panels that covered the van. He opened the doors hurriedly expecting a blast of hot air to greet him. Instead cool air wafted out from the inside. Of course, he had ordered air conditioning for the vans on long watches on surveillance, making it more bearable. He peeked inside and, there stretched out on a battered Z-bed was Dennis affectionately known out of earshot, as 'Dennis the Menace.' Ben cautiously woke him and in the same instant two massive hands grabbed him by the throat.

"Dennis," Ben frantically yelled. "It's me Ben," the hands hesitated then slowly withdrew.

"Sorry boss," Dennis grinned sheepishly. "I was asleep, what time is it, what time is it?"

"It's okay," Ben assured his minder. "It's around ten, but I asked you to get a good night's sleep," he carefully avoided telling Dennis the reason for his long sleep. "I suggest you go and, have a shave, clean up and have a good breakfast for we have a long day ahead of us."

Dennis was puzzled as to why he had slept so long but, as it was all right with Ben, he did not question why. "I know just the place to fulfil that order, I'll be back within the hour." He gave a quick wave and sped off in the van.

Ben walked slowly back down the street to be confronted by an ashen faced Julie.

"How could you, all those lies and for why? There was no reason on earth for such deception. I wouldn't care if my Ivan was crippled both mentally and bodily. I would still want him here with us." She stopped for breath and continued, "Tessa told me that you had snatched him back from the dead and for that I'll be eternally grateful, but I still cannot understand all the lies."

"I did it to protect you and the children."

"From what? What is it that is so terrible?"

Ben knew that he had to tell Julie at least part of the truth. "Ivan has information about people who wish to cause us harm. These people are extremely powerful and would stop at nothing to keep Ivan quiet, therefore, if they believe Ivan to be dead, they will call off their killers."

Julie started to protest but then stopped herself. She knew from stories she had heard from her own country that torturers could be very inventive and she had the children to protect.

"But what was all that about funerals and pensions and, now that you have told me that Ivan is alive, how safe are we going to be?"

Ben had been busy with regard to their safety and had his answers ready. "I've taken care of everything I can think of at the moment. I know this is going to be an enormous upheaval but we are going to move you and the children to somewhere safe. With regard to the funeral, it must take place. We really need to keep up the pretense of Ivan's death to convince the enemy that he is longer a threat to them. For the same reason, the pension plan will go ahead as planned. We were hoping that you and the children could have stayed here under protection but now, after all that has happened we can no longer be sure of your safety if you stay here in Greenwich."

Julie agreed that it would not be safe for her and the children to stay in Greenwich. She told Ben that she would explain to the children that they would be moving away from London to start a new life somewhere else. Meanwhile, she was extremely anxious to be with Ivan and asked Ben to take her to him. She told the children that she was going to their new home to make arrangements before they all moved.

It was left to Tessa and Ben to stay in Greenwich to look after the children and to see all the arrangements for the move.

Julie hoped one day to return with her children and her beloved Ivan.

Chapter 5

The next few days in London were a hive of activity. Arrangements for the removals were carried out by Ben's security team who hired a huge pantechnicon and the house that had seen so much love and laughter over the years was put on the market for rental.

In the Lake District, work had already begun on one of the cottages which had been set aside for the family. Initially, Julie and the children would stay in the big house with Louisa. Louisa was very excited at the prospect of having a young family under her roof once more. She organised everything, rushing around with the housekeeper, gardener and bodyguard.

After the departure of Julie, the children were left feeling unsettled and, even though they felt content with Tessa and Ben they really missed their mother. To make sure their routine continued as normal as possible, Tessa took the twins every day to their summer school and stayed with them on the pretext of helping, although the main reason for her staying was for their protection against any further attacks.

They returned home each day, with their works of art to be much admired by all. Ben however, found it difficult to recognise himself when he was portrayed in their pictures. He was also mystified as to why there seemed to be more paint on the children and Tessa than on the actual paintings.

Whilst all this activity was going on with the girls, Ben and Ivan junior spent their days packing up, ready for the move, shopping and generally keeping the house shipshape.

When the twins were eventually asleep in the evenings and Ivan was invariably in his room on his computer, Tessa and Ben made the most of this time when they could relax and enjoy being alone together.

In the Lake District, final preparations were being made for their arrival. Louisa was still rushing about trying to appear calm but feeling anything but. The only people not taking part in all this activity were, of course, John, Ivan and

Julie. John was still very poorly and, with Ivan critically ill, the mood in the medical centre was rather sombre. Julie, looking ill herself, spent most of the day and half the night sitting by Ivan's side. Whilst carrying on this vigil, she made frequent visits to the adjoining room where John lay. Julie offered to help Louisa since Julie's place was by Ivan's side. Louisa was pleased that Julie would be able to keep an eye on John as well as Ivan as it gave her more time in the house. Louisa did, however, make late night visits when she administered her own special care which did more good than any medicine by gently caressing their minds with her own life-giving thoughts.

It was on one of these nightly visits when Louisa was so occupied with her thoughts that she failed to notice two people carriers parked in a lane, near to the house.

At first light, Ben was up and waking the rest of the household. Leaving Tessa to organise the children, he checked that the removal van was on its way. Having ascertained that, he was about to ring Dennis when he turned up on the doorstep. He arranged for Dennis to go ahead of the removal van and on arrival at the house, requested him to help Louisa with organizing the unloading of the van. The furniture was being stored at the house until the cottage was ready for the family to move in to.

Ben felt happy that Dennis would be there for Louisa. Over the years, Dennis had escorted his parents around the world on his father's many business trips. He took his position as a bodyguard very seriously and had become fond of them. Equally, they were fond of Dennis and trusted him completely to look after them.

Dennis called the children from the kitchen and installed them safely in his van. He then proceeded to fill the back of his van with the children's clothes, toys, books and games. He also supplied goodies to eat and drink. It was a long way to the Lake District and he wanted them to be happy and enjoy the journey. At last, they went and Ben and Tessa waved them off. Back indoors waiting for the van to arrive, Ben tried to ring Louisa again. He had tried the night before but could not get through. This morning, he had tried to ring the house and the clinic but, again failed to make contact with either. Tessa saw his face and already felt his agitation.

"What is it?" she asked.

"I cannot get through to the house or the clinic."

"Have you tried ringing Julie's phone?"

"I have," Ben replied, "with no luck and what's worse, the children could not reach her last night or this morning."

Ben had also tried several times to contact Louisa by telepathy but also, without success. He made a decision, pulled out his mobile and rang Dennis. When Dennis answered, Ben asked him to use the earplug.

"Can the children hear me?"

"No," Dennis replied. "Trouble, boss?"

"Yes, I want you to get up there as fast as you can but first drop the children off at my Aunt Agatha's; it's a few miles from the house." He gave the address and added, "Get to the house as soon as humanly possible."

"I'm there in an hour," came the reply.

"Good man," Ben said. "I'm leaving Tessa here and flying up."

Tessa looked up at the sound of her name. "What did you say?" she enquired.

Ben repeated the conversation he had had with Dennis.

"Oh, right," she said, smiling.

Ben nodded absently, his mind on other things, and failed to notice the glint in Tessa's eyes. He rang the men in the removal van to warn them of the possible danger at the house, and then rang the head of security. James Cunningham, an ex-SAS colonel, had proved himself many times over and was worth every penny of his extremely high salary.

"James, drop everything. I want you, Peter, Tim, Eric and Maria over at Stamford Rivers airfield as fast as you can."

James hesitated, "Peter and Tim are no problem but I have no idea where Maria is."

"Why no Eric?"

"Well," James sounded embarrassed. "Well, you know young Eric who I recommended…?"

"Yes, of course," replied Ben. "He is a black belt in Judo, I think I remember you saying."

"Yes," replied James. "He started to brag about how good he was to the others and…"

"Don't say any more," Ben said, knowing what was coming next.

"They told him he would have no chance against Maria."

"What happened?" Ben asked.

With just a hint of amusement in his voice, James said "She nearly killed him."

"Bloody hell, James!!!"

"He'll live," interjected James. "Mind you his love life will be severely curtailed for some time and he's finding it difficult to talk at the moment. The jab to the throat she gave him would have killed most men but his fast reaction saved him. Anyway, after that happened, Maria took off and has not been seen since."

"Okay, I know how to reach her. I will call her and meet you at the airfield."

Ben took out his mobile, and scrolled down to Maria. It rang for some time before she answered. "Hello, Benji."

Her voice, with her strong Croatian accent brought back memories of her tragic life and how Ben first met her. "Maria, I…"

"Benji," she interrupted. "How is the young man?"

"He's fine Maria, and he'll be back to work in the near future. You did him a great favour. He'll be much more cautious now which could save him from far worse injuries in the future."

"Benji, I'm so sorry. I could have killed him. I only just managed to pull back in time."

"Maria, forget it. It's in the past now and that is not what I'm calling for."

Ben explained to Maria the threat to his family and proceeded to give her directions to the airfield. He suddenly stopped when a thought occurred to him. "Maria, are you in the flat?"

When Ben fetched her back from Croatia he had immediately employed her as a member of his security team and found her a flat in the now fashionable Islington.

"Yes," came the reply.

"In that case, I'll pick you up, it will be quicker."

Chapter 6

Whilst driving to Maria's flat, Ben's mind drifted back to their first meeting. Ben was just out of university and taking a year out. He had travelled around Europe, visiting places of interest and before returning home, had visited Serbia. His father had business interests there and Ben had promised that he would try to call on some of his business colleagues. As he was so near to Croatia, and had never been there, he decided to go there then.

On arrival in Croatia, he booked into a hotel and then went out for a quiet drink. He found a small bar and found a corner table and sat, where he could observe people as they came and went. Ben had always enjoyed observing people from foreign countries and different ethnic groups. The waitress who had been diligently trying to rub a shine on a nearby table, came over. Ben asked for a beer in his very best Croatian and as she walked towards the bar Ben was fascinated by how she moved. She moved with extreme grace but Ben sensed a wariness in her as if she was being stalked. As she returned with the beer, he noticed her face which was oval with high cheekbones. She had a small straight nose, a sensual mouth and large brown eyes with golden flecks. It was the eyes that took away the beauty from her face and Ben's interest increased tenfold. As she reached his table and placed the beer down, he murmured his thanks. Ben forgot his beer as she nodded and moved away. Those beautiful eyes were completely dead—there was not a spark of life in them.

Ben had to know why. Under normal circumstances, he would never probe into another person's mind without that person knowing. However, so intrigued was he, that he very gently probed her mind with his own. He was deeply shocked as he found he could not enter her mind. Confused, Ben sat staring at her, he had never experienced this total lack of response before. He pulled himself together when he realised the barman was staring at him. Ben did not need to probe his thoughts to know what he was thinking. Ben picked up his beer and took a sip—he was at a loss as to what to do next. He looked at the woman again and wondered what she was doing in the bar and then he thought, perhaps she is a student like myself. He really felt that he must get to know her.

Suddenly, the bar door crashed open and four men virtually fell through it and headed for the nearest table. The barman jerked his head at the waitress to serve them. Ben looked on with interest. She did not move.

"Beer," they shouted.

"Move your arse, slut," said the largest of the four, who looked a really nasty piece of lower life. Still she did not move.

"I do not serve Serbian pigs," she calmly said

Apart from Ben, the woman, the barman and the four men, the bar was suddenly empty.

"I want no trouble," squeaked the now petrified barman.

The big man laughed, turned to his companions and said, "Wait your turn, this is going to be the start of a very enjoyable evening." Then moving surprisingly quickly, he was out of his chair and reaching for the woman. Amazingly, he didn't quite make it. The woman seemed to spin, her hand became a fist and, almost faster than the eye could follow, the fist buried itself in the attacker's throat. He choked and with his hand clutching his throat, sank slowly to the floor. All hell broke loose as the other three chairs went crashing and the men launched themselves at her. The woman took several paces back, and suddenly produced a knife in her hand. The three men hesitated, and at that point, Ben decided to step in. Up to then, the men hadn't noticed him in the corner of the bar. They were very surprised when Ben intervened.

"That's enough…it ends now."

Together, the three men drew knives. Ben slowly rose to his feet but not as a six feet 3 fairly skinny Ben Franklin but as an 8 feet monster with legs like tree trunks and arms to match and, in one of those massive hands was a club the size of a small tree itself. Ben advanced towards the men. The men paled and edged backwards. The waitress looked at Ben in amazement. Due to her complete blocking of Ben's mind powers, she saw Ben stalking across the room with a rolled-up newspaper. As she stared at Ben, her expression suddenly changed and she threw the knife at him. Ben stood rooted to the ground waiting for the knife to strike. However, the knife whirled past his ear and he heard a grunt behind him, followed by a loud bang. Ben turned just in time to see the barman collapsing with the knife protruding from his neck. As Ben turned back to face the woman, a powdering of dust descended on his head and shoulders. Looking up he saw a deep groove in the ceiling directly above him where the bullet had ended up. Ben shuddered. It had been very close; despite his abilities, he had nearly been killed. The woman's speed in reacting had undoubtedly saved him.

At that moment, it was not the time for thanks and Ben yelled at her to collect her knife and anything else that belonged to her and told her they must get the hell out. She did not need a second bidding. She swiftly moved to the back of the bar and retrieved the knife. Wiping it clean on the barman's apron, she rushed through a door to the rear of the bar and reappeared a few minutes later with her coat, handbag and a small suitcase. "Let's go," said Ben.

They were now well clear of the bar when they stopped. She looked at Ben quizzically and said, "What was it you did back there, those men were so scared I thought they were going to wet themselves?"

"I'll explain all, but not right now," Ben replied.

Ben knew he had to get the woman's trust and he also knew instinctively that it was not going to be easy. He smiled at her and, extending his hand said, "My name's Benjamin Franklin. What's yours?"

She hesitated for a moment then, in her husky voice, said, "Maria Anastasia, but everybody just calls me Maria."

"Well what a lovely name, Maria. I like that and you must call me Ben."

From that day forth, however, Maria always called Ben, Benji.

Ben pulled out his mobile. "Maria, I must call Bertram, he's my assistant." Ben started to dial but the noise of the traffic was deafening.

With a jolt, Ben came out of his reverie and was back in the London traffic jam. From behind came an impatient hooting and, looking forward Ben saw a gap of fifty yards had opened up between him and the traffic in front.

At the third ring, Bunny, that was his nickname as he had large front teeth and big ears, answered. "Hi Ben, everything okay?"

"Well, not quite." Ben relayed briefly the events of the past half hour.

"Wow," Bunny grinned to himself and added, "I can't leave you alone five minutes without you getting into a fight and picking up a bird."

Ben smiled to himself, it was typical of Bunny to make light of even the most serious situation.

"The thing is Bunny, I am going to need your room for tonight."

There was a pause whilst Bunny digested this…why? Then he said, "Of course, Ben. As it happens, I was hoping for the night off. See you tomorrow, bye," and he was gone.

Ben turned to Maria who had obviously only heard one side of the conversation. "Well, that at least has your room sorted for tonight."

Maria looked for a catch but could find none and acquiesced. However, although she agreed, she had already decided that she would disappear before dawn.

Once in the hotel, Ben took Maria up to their rooms. On entering, she immediately noticed the communicating door between the two rooms. Ben again hurriedly explained that, as Bunny was his assistant, he was more available when needed. Maria smiled and closed the door to her room. She had, of course, noticed also that the door between the rooms could be locked. No sooner had she started unpacking when the phone started ringing. It was Ben.

"When you have unpacked and changed I would like to take you out to dinner."

Although, she was very hungry, she replied, "I do not think that is very wise as the police are probably circulating my description as we speak." To her surprise, Ben laughed.

"I do not find that very funny," she snapped.

"No, no, of course not. I'm sorry, let me explain about my weird and strange powers. Before we rushed out of the bar and while you were gathering your things, I sort of erased us from their memories."

"But the barman will remember me," she said. "I've been working there for over two months and, as you know, he was still alive."

"Yes, I know he was, but trust me, none of them will remember us at all and the customers that left in a hurry will assume the fight was between the men themselves, and the barman tried to intervene."

Maria didn't know what his game was nor did she believe anything he said about his weird powers, but said, "Okay."

"We'll eat in the hotel," Ben said. "See you in half an hour."

In her room, Maria looked back on the last few hours. She thought what a strange man Ben was and, although she thought he was lying, he certainly did something to those men—the terror in their eyes was very real. Liar he might be, but she still found herself attracted to him. She sighed and shrugged her shoulders and thought that at least she would be having a good meal and would be able to disappear before dawn. After a luxurious shower, she emptied her small suitcase and, taking out her one and only decent dress, she held it up and looked at it in dismay. Creased hardly described the state of it. She searched frantically for an iron but to no avail. With only ten minutes left before dinner, it was also too late for room service. Left with only one option she put the dress on a hanger and with a wet flannel sponged out the worst of the creases. She rubbed it dry as best as she could with a towel. As she slipped it on, still damp, there was a knock at the door adjoining the rooms and Ben's voice enquiring if she was ready. As they went down to dinner, Maria said a little prayer hoping that Ben wouldn't notice that the dress was clinging to her body in places. If he did, he never said and they enjoyed a sumptuous meal, saying little after a rather traumatic day. Ben suggested they retire early as he had a busy day ahead. Maria agreed readily as she intended to be away before dawn.

Ben went to his own room and, as he entered, he heard the key being turned in the door adjoining their rooms. Although, he was very attracted to her he would never have taken advantage of her; he could see it was a one-way traffic situation and no way was he going to pursue a hopeless cause. Ben was intrigued and excited by her, though partly by Maria's complete block to his mind, but also because he knew absolutely nothing about her. As he slipped between his sheets he had one thought in mind—he must persuade her to join his security team. What an asset she would be, not only as a fighter but also as a confidante because no one could be able to reach her mind. Ben realised that she was the only human being he knew with a mind that was totally closed to himself and, as far as he knew, all of his kind. He went to sleep wondering why.

What a beautiful day it was; not a cloud to be seen and a warm and gentle breeze caressed her arms and face as she walked through the long grass. Suddenly, she saw Joseph, the son of the Rostovs who owned the farm a few miles from her own home. He waved and she ran to join him as she often did during the long hot summer days. He grinned as she came up to him.

"Hi, Maria."

"Hi, Joseph," she replied breathlessly—partly from running but mainly at the sight of him. At fifteen, Joseph was indeed a handsome boy.

He was a god to Maria who was only twelve. *If only,* she thought, *I was older.*

"I see you're a shepherd today," she laughed.

"Yes, shepherd today, herdsman tomorrow and milkmaid the day after." They both laughed and threw themselves into the lush grass where they both lay side-by-side, eyes closed, basking in the sun and chattering to one another about everything and nothing.

About an hour later, Joseph whose ears were very sharp, suddenly sat up frowning and silencing Maria with an upheld hand, he listened. As he did so, a cloud drifted across the face of the sun and with it a chill wind swept over them.

"What is it?" Maria asked suddenly alarmed.

"I don't know," Joseph replied, "but it seemed to come from the direction of your home." Seeing her worried face, Joseph answered rather lamely, "Don't worry, it was probably a car backfiring." He listened again and this time he was sure it was gunfire.

"Why don't you come back and have some food with us?"

Before he could carry on, Maria put her fingers to his lips. "It's alright Joseph. I can hear the gunfire myself. I will be back to see you in a few days."

Neither of them knew that what was unfolding would separate them for life.

Maria ran like the wind, her heart pounding and her mind willing everything to be alright—but dread enclosed her soul. She reached the lane leading to her home, looking along the lane she saw a Serbian jeep and lorry right outside her little house. Running up to the house, she noticed that both the vehicles were empty. Too breathless to call out, she rushed in through the front door. Inside she stopped stock still, not believing the sight before her young eyes. On the floor, lay the bodies of her parents, together with Stephen and Jose beneath them. Under her parents and her two five-year-old twin brothers, was a huge pool of blood. Maria swayed and nearly fainted, when from upstairs, came a scream. It was her sister, but why? She should be in college. Maria, her mind numb, was trying to work out why when the scream came again. This time the scream was followed by men's laughter. Maria went cold with fear and stumbled towards her dead father. Tears were streaming down her face as she looked down on her beloved family and then she saw the gun, in her father's hand. She gently removed it and clutching it closely to her, recalled the times when her father had allowed her to use it in their backyard at the little target he had set up for her.

The fear went as quickly as it came. Replaced by a coldness that consumed her whole body and gripping the gun, she advanced towards the stairs. Another scream came from her sister. Ignoring caution and the creaking of the stairs, Maria moved swiftly upward, she held the pistol with outstretched arms, with her eyes level with the pistol sight. Only once before, had she ever aimed to kill. Nearly a year ago, a rabid dog had raced across the field just beyond their garden. Even from several hundred metres, she could see the foam on its jaws and the crazed way it was running. Her father had given a cry of alarm as the poor creature closed in on their small flock of sheep. Maria, as taught, raised the pistol and fired. The dog went down instantly, while her father marvelled at her marksmanship. Maria dropped the pistol and burst into tears. Today, however, there were no tears. As she reached the top of the stairs, she heard a whimper from her sister followed by inane laughter by men gathered around the double bed and she realised that they had taken her sister to her parents' bedroom. Without any hesitation, she stepped through the doorway and started firing. The five men, standing round the bed, dropped dead where they stood. The sixth man, on her sister, grabbed his gun then dropped as he, too, fell back, dead. Her sister stared at her through half crazed eyes and then raised her arm, pointing behind her. Maria whirled round, ducking as she did so. She was then hit herself in the head and blackness enveloped her.

"No, no, no," Ben awoke sweating and shouting. Someone else was also shouting and holding him. He struggled to awareness and realised he was back in the hotel room with Maria fiercely holding him down.

Ben explained to Maria that he had just had the most awful nightmare. He whispered, "Did they really murder your whole family and shoot you in the head?" He then instinctively reached up and ran his fingers through her hair. He gasped when he felt a furrow from the front to the back of her scalp. It suddenly occurred to him that he had been able to read Maria's sleeping mind. "It was you, my nightmare was your reality."

Maria nodded and then began to weep. This was the first she had cried since that day in hell when all and everything she had ever loved had died. It was also the day when her childhood had ended. Somehow, she had survived her terrible head injuries and six months later, had regained full consciousness thanks to the nuns in a convent who had nursed her devotedly. The nuns believed it was a miracle that she had survived.

Ben suddenly felt very cold as the sweat on his body had dried. "I must have a shower," he said.

"Me too," she replied. Hand in hand they walked to the bathroom and showered together.

"Your bed is damp," she whispered, "you may share mine tonight." Holding one another tightly they eventually slept and mercifully, their sleep was dreamless.

Maria woke just before dawn and with all thoughts of disappearing gone, she looked at this strange young man who now knew her innermost and darkest secrets. Feeling a fierce kinship she snuggled closer and felt him respond, even in his sleep. She lay still, hardly daring to breathe. She was now 25 and had never been with a man. She looked at his young face and felt herself go hot and, at the same time, she wanted him so much that she ached with the need of him. At that moment, Ben woke and they made love, slowly at first then fiercely. All the emotions of the past twenty-four hours gathered into a whirlpool which wrenched at their very souls. Twice they ascended to the ultimate limits of pleasure and then they slept. On awakening, they made love once again.

Chapter 7

"Benji, Benji…" Ben looked around dazedly.

"What," he exclaimed. He had just arrived at Maria's flat and there she was standing by his car. She smiled.

"Daydreaming?" she asked and just as suddenly, stopped smiling when she looked at his face.

"It's okay," Ben said, "mostly good memories."

Maria climbed into the car saying as she did so, "I've only packed an overnight bag."

Ben shrugged, "By tomorrow, I hope we have overcome the threat that is facing us." His lips were tight as he said this and Maria felt an element of fear in him that she had never seen before. They drove in silence to the airfield, each of them wrapped in their own thoughts. Ben realised it was over five years since that night and, in those five years, he had seen very little of Maria, although he had kept a discreet tab on her whereabouts and well-being. Ben had asked Bunny to look after Maria. Being in a different country with a different language would not be easy for her and, with her past he felt that Bunny, especially with his easy-going nature, would be of great assistance to her. At first, Ben had been worried as, after a few months in England, Maria had disappeared. It transpired that she had returned to her home country, Croatia. After several months, when she had not returned, Ben sent Bunny to look for her. Within a few weeks, Bunny rang to inform him that he had managed to trace her. When Ben had pressed for explanations Bunny, unusually had gone very quiet and when further questioned had tersely replied that it was to do with family. At the time, Ben had felt hurt his friend's sharpness, but Bunny had explained it away by saying that he was tired at the time. On reflection, Ben realised that everything had turned out well. Maria and Bunny were now firm friends and whenever Maria now went to Croatia, Bunny usually went with her. Although this was a relief, Ben felt a little excluded at the lack of contact with Maria and, even now in the car, she seemed a little distant. He glanced at her, she turned and smiled. On seeing that smile, Ben relaxed as he at least knew they were still friends.

On arrival at the airport, they met up with James, Tim and Peter and went straight through to customs. Ben hurriedly signed the necessary paperwork and then they went out to the plane as the ground staff was making the final checks.

"Lovely day for flying," one of them said.

"Indeed it is and thank you Simon and the rest of your team for the rush job." With that, he tucked a fifty-pound note into the startled man's pocket, and then hurried with his companions onto the Lear. Within minutes, they were taxiing out onto the runway ready for take-off. Having been given clearance, Ben had the plane airborne and heading north towards the airport nearest to the medical centre and his home in Cumbria.

Still worrying about the lack of contact with either his home or the medical clinic, he pushed the Lear to its limit. Far beneath them, the green and brown fields raced passed interspersed with the occasional splash of yellow from the fields of rape. Within the hour, they were approaching the airport.

Circling the medical centre gave Ben more cause for worry; he could not make any mind contact and, he sensed a source of enormous power from below. Looking down, there was also no sign of activity. Hurriedly he cleared with ground control for landing and began to descend. Taxiing virtually to the doors of airport control he and his companions left the plane, cleared customs. Outside was Ben's personal car, with no bodyguard present. Extracting the keys from his pocket, they were in the car and racing towards the house. The house looked deserted as it did from the air. However, once inside they found the housekeeper Betty deeply unconscious. Ben was horrified as Betty was like a second mother to him. Whoever did this, would pay dearly. He silently entered into her mind and very carefully took out the blocks that had her mind frozen.

To his relief, she started to stir and become aware of her surroundings. She looked at Ben with embarrassment.

"Oh dear," she said, "I must have had a turn."

"Are you feeling all right now?" Ben asked looking at her with obvious concern.

"Yes, much better thank you. I must get myself off home, look at the time. Now, where did I put my bag? Ah, there it is," and, gathering it up she rushed off.

Ben turned to his head of security. "James how many men have you got guarding the centre?"

"Seven," James replied. "Five in the grounds and two in the hospital. Jane, my niece, is one of those in hospital in the guise of a nurse."

"Let's get over there and hope that things are not as bad as I think they are," Ben muttered through gritted teeth. "Oh god, where's Maria. Quick, let's get to the centre. On second thoughts, James, I want you three to stay outside keeping out of sight and making sure that no one enters or leaves unless I sanction it."

James nodded but, privately, he was disappointed at being left out of the action.

Ben then asked James if any of his people had met with opposition outside of the clinic.

"None," came the reply.

"In that case, pull out two of your best marksmen and supply them with night sights for their rifles, binoculars and warm clothing. I want them positioned with a clear view of everything that is happening, and in sniper mode. In other words, they don't move unless it's to pull the trigger."

"Give me two minutes and I'll have them where even you can't find them." As James disappeared, Ben smiled, knowing that he would have at least some protection for himself and the rest of his team if things got too bad.

Ben then parked the car, well-hidden amongst the bushes, and moved to the entrance with caution, not knowing what would confront him. He had a small advantage over his adversaries as he knew the grounds surrounding the Medical Centre like the back of his hand. It was pitch black with heavy cloud racing across the sky above him and with not a glimmer of light from the Medical Centre, it made it impossible to see more than a metre ahead. He crouched down, the aroma from the rose beds, and the wisteria that covered the pergola assailed his nostrils. He pushed away thoughts of happier times and gently started to probe with his mind the area ahead of him. There were shadows but nothing he could distinguish. He rose slightly and crept forward across the lawn towards the boiler room at the left-hand side of the centre. Twelve metres from the main building, the boiler had an access tunnel through to the reception area of the clinic. He had only gone a few paces when, from behind him in the distance, he heard rifle fire. He dropped flat to the ground and then, as he did so, there was a buzz above his head like an angry bee. The buzz came from his front. He immediately realised that his enemies were either Umbrians or humans being guided by them to know his position. There was more rifle fire and more buzzing, although this time the buzz came from his earpiece. An anxious voice came over the intercom.

"Boss, can you hear me; are you okay?"

Ben hurriedly pulled out his transmitter and switched it on briefly, whispered urgently, "I'm fine, now, no more contact you will expose your position." There was an immediate click as the transmitter was turned off. Ben gave a shudder thanking his lucky stars he had deployed his team out in the woods. He jumped to his feet and, throwing caution to the wind, ran across the open space towards his objective. As he approached, he slowed down his pace and let his mind drift towards the interior of the boiler room which he found to be empty. He could then see why; outside in a semicircle, lay four bodies. Obviously, they had been sheltering in the room behind them from the cold night wind; warned of his approach they must have rushed forth, only to be cut down by his team. The room was very warm and Ben could almost sympathise with the dead men outside. Had they been outside, under cover, his snipers would not have been able to pick them off so easily. Equally, of course, Ben would have been very dead.

Going through the back of the room Ben unlocked the door and entered the service tunnel. Turning on the tunnel lights to no avail, he retreated back into the room. Of course, the main switch had been turned off to maintain a complete blackout. Moving over to the main switch, he wasted no time in switching the electricity back on. Before the enemy could react, he raced through the tunnel as fast as he could to the cellar beneath the ground floor. Once in the cellar, breathing hard and full of trepidation, Ben went up the stairs which led to the door and opening it slightly he peeked through to find himself looking down the barrel of a gun. His eyes went wide with fear, then he heard a voice he recognised. The voice said, "Hello Benji, what big eyes you have."

There, looking down at him was Maria. Ben looked at her with shock. She looked like a small arms dump with a belt full of holsters, pockets with what looked like stun grenades in them and an assortment of knives and weapons he'd never seen before. "Where did you get so many weapons?" Ben breathed, thinking about her overnight bag which was tiny.

"Oh, I only took them off of those that no longer had use of them." She pointed, the main foyer was strewn with bodies.

Ben gulped. "Ye gods, Maria I see you've come prepared" he said weakly. Maria, her eyes swivelling around, was alert still.

"Benji, we have a war here," she said and started running towards the stairs. Ben, trying to keep up, followed her. He looked down, she had gone through them like a scythe, Umbrians and humans, they had no chance with her skill and her total block on mind control.

Maria slowed and making their way cautiously up, Ben whispered in Maria's ear, "I will go through to the main ward, you follow closely behind."

She nodded then laying her arm on Ben's arm, whispered back, "Be very careful, Benji."

On reaching the door, Ben went straight in. Fortunately, there were only three of them, two with guns and they were already swivelling them in Ben's direction, the third man was shielding their minds. *One of my own kind,* Ben thought. Blocking the man's thoughts, Ben stood aside. He then heard three shots and simultaneously felt a sharp pain in his thigh. As he fell, another shot rang out and the traitor also fell. Ben realised, he was also dead. Maria rushed to Ben's side.

"How bad is it?" she asked. Ben had already pulled his trousers down and was gripping both sides of his leg and, grimacing, he looked up into her anxious face.

"I'm a lucky boy," he said, "the bullet went straight through. But as it did, it nicked the bone." To allay her anxiety Ben gave Maria a weak grin. "See if you can find some bandages, you should have no trouble with this being a hospital."

Maria scuttled off to search for the bandages and soon returned clutching two big rolls, plus felt pads. Maria had also snatched two surgical clips to stem the flow of blood which was seeping through Ben's clenched fingers. Although necessary, fastening the clips sent excruciating pain shooting through Ben's body. Ben gasped with pain as Maria helped him to his feet and, aided by Maria, Ben managed to painfully hop to the nearest dispensary cabinet. Locating a box of pain- killers Ben tore open the box and swallowed the tablets.

Maria held him upright. "Well, your face is like snow Benji," she murmured, her lovely face full of sympathy and concern.

"Give me a few minutes, these are very strong pain-killers and very fast-acting." Ben struggled to keep conscious and gradually the pain subsided until after a few minutes he was able to proceed very slowly towards the main ward. Ben was now feeling very anxious as he could feel something in his mind and, although unable to trace its source, had a terrible premonition of disaster.

Limping along as fast as possible, Maria helped him, they eventually came to the main ward and pushed through the rubber doors. Inside there was chaos as every patient in the hospital was crammed into the one ward. They were being protected by Louisa and several distant relations whom Ben had not seen for several years. Dennis, Louisa's bodyguard, was lying on the floor with terrible injuries. His head resting in her lap and around them were several assailants, quite dead with broken necks.

Ben looked worriedly at Louisa. "Yes, she said he's still alive."

Looking round the ward, Ben could see Ivan but could not see his father.

"Where's Dad, Mum, where is he?"

Louisa lowered her head and her tears fell unashamedly onto Dennis's bruised cheek. "I am sorry," she wept. "He stalled their attack and in doing so enabled us to build our defences." She looked up at Ben, "He saved us all, I didn't know he had so much power." She clenched and unclenched her hands at the thought, "But eventually they overcame his defences and his heart and mind succumbed."

Ben's mind reeled and, for a moment, everything went black. Maria steadied him and the moment passed and things came back into focus. He looked at his mother and with a voice hard and wrought with passion, he spoke.

"I know we are from another world and I know the attack on us was initiated by our own kind. I have no idea why, but I'm going to stop them. It is not revenge but I will stop them."

He heard a whisper. "Take care, dearest child."

"I will," Ben declared aloud. He stood there and his thoughts went back to his past and the good times he had shared with his father. These thoughts were suddenly interrupted by his mobile buzzing. James had to be urgent.

"Ben, you better get out here, we've got trouble and it concerns Tessa."

"But she's in London," replied Ben. "What the hell's going on?"

James spoke quickly and to the point. "After we took out the opposition you were up against, I decided that we should race around to the rear of the centre and that's when I saw Tess. She was heading towards a small corpse but she seemed to be struggling, as if against a strong wind. Two guys emerged from the woods and raised their weapons as if to shoot her, so I took them both out. The strange thing was that Tess was still struggling forward and there wasn't a breath of wind. It was then when I saw a shadow and I shot." James hesitated, "The shadow I mean…I shot the shadow."

Ben interrupted, "James you're repeating yourself, what happened to Tess?"

James sounded unusually hesitant, "Well, Tess fell flat on the ground as if I'd shot her but, of course, I hadn't. I am with her now and there is not a mark on her."

Ben replied, "Stay with her, I'm on my way."

Ben looked at his mother, "Mum, can you manage?"

Louisa nodded, "Just go, Ben." Ben trying to ignore his wounded leg, hobbled after Maria. From the clinic, he could see Maria's back, already skirting the corpse. By the time Ben reached them, Maria had turned Tessa gently over onto her side.

"She seems okay," Maria looked up at Ben with puzzlement in her eyes. "She bumped her head when she fell but that would not have knocked her out."

Ben reached into Tessa's mind and found nothing, there was no response. He went back over his conversation with James.

"I shot the shadow and Tessa collapsed."

"James, go and find that shadow. Maria, go with him. No, on second thoughts, I'll go. James, can you carry Tessa back?"

"Of course," he said and gently lifted her up and started back to the clinic.

Ben added, "Take her straight to Louisa. She's in the main ward."

Ben and Maria approached the corpse and a few paces into the trees, there lay the shadow that turned out to be a young girl. Consciously, she stared up at them.

"Where am I?" she exclaimed. "Why does my chest hurt so?" Ben looked down at her, she looked no more than fifteen and yet this was the source of all the energy that had powered the attack on the clinic. Although wounded, Ben could still feel the power that emanated from her mind.

Looking at the position of the wound, James had pierced one of her hearts. Ben felt no hatred towards her but he had to find out where she had come from and quickly. He very gently scooped her up into his arms and was amazed at how light and frail she was, especially considering the amount of havoc, death and injury she had brought with her. He buzzed for help to carry her to the clinic, with Maria following behind. Maria was still wary and on guard, despite reassurances from Ben. In the clinic, Ben located one of the now empty wardrooms and laid the girl gently on one of the beds.

Maria stayed with her whilst Ben went and fetched one of the doctors. Some semblance of order now prevailed and having located a doctor and given him directions, Ben's next priority was Tessa. Before he found her, he spoke to James who was very unhappy to realise that he had shot a young girl.

"She was a pawn James, you shooting her saved the lives of everybody in the clinic and hers as well. That's presuming she survives the wound."

Muttering to himself and obviously still very unhappy, James hurried off to round up his team and to carry out the gruesome task of collecting all the corpses and transferring them to the mortuary. He, then, rounded up the remaining enemies and escorted them under heavy guard to one of the empty wards. Inside the clinic, Ben stood by the side of Tessa's bed and waited anxiously whilst Louisa examined her. After hearing the facts, Louisa had a very good idea of the cause of Tessa's condition. Louisa turned to face her son and endeavoured to reassure him as much as possible.

"There is no physical damage Ben, but what has happened is due to James shooting the young girl." Louisa went on to explain that Tessa and the girl were in a battle of minds and when shot, the girl's resistance collapsed and left a vacuum which Tessa's mind fell into. Having relayed all this to Ben, Louisa then said that Tessa will recover eventually but she did not know just how long the recovery would take.

Ben was shaken. "Will she definitely be okay and you really have no idea how long?"

Louisa held her son's arm. "Of course, she will, but it could take some time, you must be patient."

"The girl," Ben said. "How is the girl?"

"Recovering," Louisa said. "Her name is Lena and she came through the operation well. The bullet is out and she is awake at the moment which is just as well because she is suffering terrible nightmares."

"Can I question her?" Ben asked, then looking at his mother's face, quickly added, "I will be gentle."

Louisa nodded, "Of course, but not for too long."

Ben pulled out his mobile, and rang James, giving him the good news. James gave a curt thanks, for letting him know, and rang off. Ben gave an involuntary shudder as James was obviously still involved in the gruesome task Ben had given him earlier.

Ben hurried along to Lena's room and was pleased to see a guard sitting quietly outside. She looked asleep but Ben knew differently. She was an Umbrian and she was gently probing the air for miles around and above the clinic for any unwanted mind intrusion coming from the other way. Entering the room, Ben thought the bed was empty but soon realised it was occupied. Her pale face had enormous eyes but her body scarcely raised a bump in the bedclothes. Lena looked at him as he pulled a chair over and sat down close to her bed.

Fearfully, she said, "I cannot help you. I don't remember anything."

Ben smiled. "I know," he said. "You are like me and I know your memory has completely gone with regard to the immediate past. However, beyond that and going right back, you must have a childhood with parents and possibly brothers and sisters."

"Oh, yes," she exclaimed excitedly, her face lighting up and becoming animated. Her bright eyes widened with pleasure as her mind recalled something. "My brother, Jon."

"You see." Ben laughed. "Your memory is still in there somewhere."

Ben did not mention about the slight stimulation he had given her mind, when he had entered the room, and Lena had obviously not noticed. She responded more and more whilst he continued talking to her for the next twenty minutes. He then took her hand in his and told her that she was now perfectly safe and she should relax and get some sleep.

Once outside, he turned to the guard. "Is there someone who can sit with you?"

"I can soon find somebody."

"Thank you," Ben looked down at her. "I want the two of you guarding twenty-four hours a day and needless to say you must both have the ability."

She looked back up at him smiling, "Consider it done Mr Franklin, I'll have somebody with me in five minutes."

"Thanks again," Ben said and then grinning he said, "Let's have less of the formality—the name's Ben". He thought for a long moment, his reputation for not remembering names was cause for laughter amongst staff and friends alike. Suddenly he exclaimed, "Annette".

She clapped her hands, "Well done Mr, er, I mean Ben." Ben strode away, pleased with himself, until she called after him, "Actually, it's Janette, but close."

He reached the end of the corridor, he glanced back to see Janette convulsed in silent laughter. Ben smiled, *well*, he thought, *that is one name I should remember.*

Ben's mobile began to ring. It was his mother, close to tears.

"You had best come and have a look at Ivan. I have put him in the isolation ward."

Now what, Ben thought, as he hurried once again through the maze of corridors leading to the isolation wing. His mother was waiting for him outside.

"You must be prepared for a shock." She gripped his arm tightly. "Your father—your father has entered Ivan's mind and he wants to talk to you."

Ben was totally confused when a whisper of thought entered his mind. "Come and talk with me Benjamin. I will explain."

Ben once again sat by a bed. This time, it was Ivan who was the occupant.

"Let me do the talking Ben. Do not worry about Ivan. Humans only use one third of their brain and I am obviously in an unoccupied section of Ivan's brain. By the time I leave his mind, it will be almost completely repaired.

"The assumption that it is the oil companies who have been attacking us, is probably wrong. I now know, especially after the attack on the clinic, that it is our own kind who are to blame. I believe that the oil companies, although unhappy about breakthroughs with the development and success of all electric vehicles and smaller aircraft, would be more likely to try to buy you out. The attack on the clinic was definitely instrumented and controlled by mind control, channelled through that poor girl; at least she has survived so far. On Umbria, we have what is called 'The Grand Council' who control and monitor all major events and decisions for the whole planet. When we were first sent to Earth, it was on the Council's orders and our mission was to integrate to the best of our ability, into human society. We have successfully achieved this but many Umbrians are concerned that when an Umbrian has a child, that child has enhanced powers, much greater than Umbrians. I now wonder if this is the reason why we are being attacked."

"But the implications of what you have just told me are awful," Ben said. "Surely the integration between us and humans can only benefit both humans and Umbrians."

"I agree with you," replied his father. "But there are many Umbrians who cannot come to terms with all that I have told you. Through the young girl, Lena, I now know the source of the attack.

"Only a member of the Grand Council would have sufficient power to launch such an attack and there is at least one member of the Council here on Earth."

Ben sensed his father's mind probing his own. "Father," Ben reached out with his mind and, for a while they were as one.

"You must stop him," whispered his father. The mind contact with his father was now fading as his hold on Ivan's mind weakened. "The Council member has stolen the guise of a Romanian, Ramon Leopold, who was a great benefactor to many charities in Romania. I'm unaware of Ramon himself, but the council member is obviously using his mind and position to gain information to help him with his plans."

The last thoughts from his father were strange.

"Take Maria with you to destroy him, she will protect you as you must protect her for she…"

Ben suddenly sensed a presence, a mental gasp, the word 'Lena' and then silence. The next moment, Ben was racing down the corridors towards Lena's room. Throwing open the door to her room, he saw Janette and her companion holding on grimly to Lena's hands. Lena, with her back arched and her eyes bulging, was screaming. Ben leapt forward, and gripped their hands throwing his own mental strength with theirs against the unknown foe. How ugly that power was, it oozed blackness and reeked with the smell of age and rot. Its force bore down on him but Ben's own force with that of the two women, overpowered it and it was gone like a switch being turned off. The two women shuddered and, almost as one said, "Thank god you came." Ben said nothing. He searched around for thoughts from his father but realised that his father was now lost to the present world.

Ben turned to the two women. "You two okay?" They both nodded saying nothing, sensing his personal loss. He looked down at Lena and was pleased that she was sleeping peacefully. As soon as they had started, the two women had put her into a deep sleep. Ben thanked Janette and Alice once more and they left the room taking up station outside again. Ben rang Maria who answered immediately.

"Hello, Benji."

"We are going abroad for several days, ring me later and I'll tell you where and why."

After speaking to Maria, Ben then rang James.

"James, I wish to enter Romania quietly. Would you arrange that for me as soon as possible, please?"

"I'm on it," James replied. "I'll get back to you as soon as it's arranged."

Ben went back to the room where Tessa lay. He sat on the bed and took her hands in his and tears sprang to his eyes. She lay as if she was asleep which Ben told himself she was. Despite his mother's assurances, he was still fearful. It was a huge battle Tessa had fought and he was very concerned as to the depth of the void her mind had fallen into, when the opposing force collapsed. He was relieved that Tessa had human blood which gave her the extra strengths and different abilities, unusual and strange as they were. He kissed her beautiful face, peaceful in its unconscious state. He then sought out his mother.

"Mum," he said on finding her. "I have to leave you, will you be okay? If not, I will draft in more security."

"I'll be fine," his mother answered. "Just take great care as the dangers you will be facing are beyond belief."

"You know what Dad's thought transfers were?"

"Yes, and for the record, it was not just you. Janette and Alice, who repelled the latest intruder, and all the Umbrians here in the centre joined their minds to yours to achieve the successful outcome."

"I did wonder," Ben said. "The power against us was enormous and I thought the girls and myself repelled it a little too easily. Was it the council member?"

"Yes," his mother answered. "It certainly was, and as I said, take great care."

The next few days were one big rush but everything clicked into place and, on the third evening, they were aboard the company jet and heading for an unknown destination.

Chapter 8

After a four-hour flight they arrived at their destination. Upon landing, Ben looked around the small windswept airfield and instantly recognised where they were. From the airport near the clinic, they had crossed northern England, the North Sea, across Scandinavia, down through France to the Mediterranean, and then north to Romania. They touched down fairly close to one of the many holiday homes belonging to Ben's family. They were near to the Black Sea. As the communist regime declined, his father had invested heavily in Romania which was beneficial to himself and Romania, as it supplied much needed funds and employment for its people. His father had also built a large pharmaceutical factory in Romania which made him very popular with the government. It was for this reason, that they had been able to enter the country quietly and incognito.

Ben and Maria wasted no time, hurrying to the car which was parked nearby for them. Although a nondescript looking vehicle from the outside, the interior was another story. The interior had been completely stripped and there only remained the two front seats. When folded back these seats converted into two comfortable beds. Where the boot had been, a further conversion was accommodating a small fridge freezer. The back of the seats had also been converted into small containers holding pillows and blankets. Under the bonnet, the old engine had been removed and in its place there was a gleaming monster capable of 250 kilometres per hour. As Ben approached the car, he spoke. "Hello Cari" he said. Maria gave Ben a quizzical look and then stopped dead, her eyes widening as the car spoke.

"Hello, Ben," it replied. Maria grabbed Ben's arm.

"Ben, it spoke to you." Maria knew that computers had voice response modes but she was still puzzled. "How did it know your name? What did you call it? 'Cari'. How did Cari know you?"

Ben burst out laughing at the look on her face. "Cari recognises me through inflections in my voice." He reached the car and cupped his hand around the wing mirror and the car door swung open.

Maria was really curious now. "Why could you not just ask it to open?"

"It's just a safeguard," he replied. "A tape recording of my voice could be used to open her and, although she could not be moved, her interior could be damaged."

They both climbed into the car and stored their gear away. Ben gently touched the steering wheel and the engine started at once.

"How is she powered?" Maria asked.

"There are a hundred high powered solar batteries under the floor which are constantly being charged by the solar panels that make up the car's bodywork.

"Right, let's be on our way," and Ben put the car into gear and they set off. Although he knew of the car's power, he still managed to make the rear wheels spin creating a cloud of dust. Slowing down, he eased the car onto the road. As he glanced sideways, he smiled. "I will have to get used to driving on the right again."

Maria, who was engrossed with map reading merely nodded. "Take the next left, and then second right and straight on for about 90 kilometres, okay?"

"Ms Navigator," came the reply. It was Maria's turn to smile.

"Seriously though, you want to keep on secondary roads all the way to our destination?"

"Yes," said Ben. "No major roads or towns and we use small cafes and service stations for food and toilets."

"Some of these roads are no better than a farm track," muttered Maria, and went back to her map reading.

They proceeded for mile after mile along country roads at a sedentary pace—only occasionally was Ben able to open up the throttle. After ten hours of exhausting driving and with darkness closing around them like a blanket, they called it a day. Just outside a village, they luckily found a lane with a signpost, and on it hung a board that said 'Mallick's Farm board and breakfast'. Down the lane they drove, fingers crossed hoping they still had vacancies. Their luck held and they booked a room with the car safely parked in a barn. They carried their bags up to their room which contained a double bed. After a long and tiring day they did not stop to discuss morals. They undressed slipped into the clean white sheets and were asleep as their heads touched the pillows. They both slept soundly and because their sleep was deep and, because the mattress was old and dipped in the middle they found themselves tangled together when they woke. Ben awoke first and was gently trying to untangle himself from Maria when she stirred and upon opening her eyes, looked at him warily. Ben hastily explained about the bed. At this Maria laughed. "So you say," she said sternly, and then gave Ben an unexpected hug.

Ben felt strongly attracted to her and returned the embrace. However forcing himself away, he said, "It's time we were on the road."

They quickly dressed and with their bags went down to breakfast where it was at least ten degrees warmer. Inside the kitchen, their noses were assailed by the smell of fresh warm bread. On the stove, there were sausages, bacon and mushrooms and in another pan there were eggs. Their hosts smiled.

"Come," said the wife. "Come and join us."

They needed no second bidding and seated themselves at the enormous kitchen table. "Help yourselves to bread and butter. I'll put your breakfast out now and then you must help yourselves to all you can eat." Ben and Maria tucked in, they were ravenous, and did not know how long it would be before they would eat again. Keeping to the side roads had its disadvantages as the deserted roads had very few places to eat. They agreed that the breakfast was the most sumptuous and delicious they had ever eaten, thanked their hosts most profusely, bid them farewell and were on their way.

Within two hours, they approached northern Romania and Maria, studying the map, informed Ben that they would be at their objective which was roughly 130 kilometres north of Cluj-Napoca in approximately two hours. Ben remained silent, his mind too occupied with the forthcoming confrontation with the Council member, in the guise of Leopold. With the member's ability to sense all living things for miles around, Ben had no idea of the outcome. He knew he had to destroy the member, but he had no idea how. Maria put her hand on Ben's arm, knowing by the look on his face, the concern he had for their future.

"It will be alright, Benji, just you wait and see."

Ben, who was negotiating a series of hairpin bends, gave her a quick glance.

"I hope so," he said.

They were now only a few miles from their objective and as they came round yet another bend, Maria exclaimed, "There it is, the castle."

Ben pulled the car over to the side of the road and they both got out. They had stopped at the top of a hill and, all that separated them from the castle was a valley between the two hills. The castle stood on a rocky outcrop and was magnificent and foreboding at the same time.

"We'll take the car down to the valley floor, hide it and make our way on foot."

Maria looked at Ben, "Okay, Benji."

They descended the hill, and at the bottom, Ben searched for a suitable hiding place for the car. Fortunately, the valley floor was well-forested and he turned the car in between the trees which were mostly pine. The car moved silently, over the thick carpet of pine needles until it was well away and almost invisible from the road. Ben turned off the engine and silence descended on them like a cloak.

"We'll stay here until nightfall," he whispered, and then, said aloud, "Why am I whispering?"

"It is a bit eerie Benji, and cold." With that Maria snuggled up close to Ben.

Ben was pleased but slightly bemused by Maria's change of feeling towards him. It must be at least five years ago when they shared that night in the hotel together. Since then he had hardly seen Maria and, when he had, she had always been quite distant and aloof towards him. *Why the change,* he wondered. She now seemed actually protective towards him?

"We must make a plan she said, when the chance arrives, I will go in and…" she crossed herself. "I will go in and deal with him."

Ben pushed her away and holding her at arm's length, said "You certainly will do no such thing. I am not exposing you to such danger."

"We'll see," Maria said.

"No, we will not see," Ben replied angrily. "I will go first and if I fail you must get out fast."

Maria looked at him. "Okay Benji," and no more was said. Although Ben was suspicious of Maria's acquiescence.

Nightfall came and taking provisions for what could be a long wait, they descended through the forest to the valley floor and put on heavy capes as the temperature started to plummet. They took turns at looking at the castle through binoculars. Only a few lights showed through the shuttered windows.

"Nobody at home," Ben said. "I wonder how long we will have to wait." Maria, who was busy oiling her rifle and checking its night sights, made no reply. They waited another three hours and still had no sign of life.

"I wonder if he's staying out all night. I…"

Maria interrupted him. "Listen," she said. "Can you hear anything?"

Ben could not but he could, however, sense a presence which was getting stronger by the second.

"He's coming," he said, and a few minutes later a cavalcade of vehicles came into view. Sweeping past them, the cars turned into the road leading to the castle. They watched the taillights until they disappeared to the rear of the building. Almost immediately the lights seemed to go on everywhere. Ben and Maria continued to wait; eventually the majority of the outside lights went out and the inside lights were doused. On the first floor, one light remained on. Ben could sense Leopold was in that room. "He's in there," he whispered.

Maria raised her binoculars and said, "I can see him." And then more urgently added, "He is coming out onto the balcony."

Sure enough, in front of the full-length doors that led to the room, there was a wide semi-circular balcony and emerging onto it was a tall figure. His eyes glittered as he stared out into the blackness. Ben shielded his every thought, but he knew that the figure was aware of his presence.

"Now's our chance. Let me have the rifle, Maria."

"Benji, the distance is too great." She quietly drew something from her tunic. She stepped up behind him and at the same time Ben's head seemed to explode. Maria caught him as he fell. "I'm sorry Benji," she said to herself and lowered him to the ground. Making him as comfortable as possible, she took off her cape and placed it under his head. She then wrapped his own cape around his body. Then, picking up the rifle, she sped off into the night.

On the balcony, Leopold became puzzled as he could no longer sense anything. It was as if a switch had been thrown. He strained to find the source again but there was nothing. He then called to his bodyguard to join him on the balcony and asked him if he could sense anything in the darkness. The bodyguard put all his concentration into sweeping the area before him and then thought he felt an unknown danger. "Beware," he said.

Maria did not have to go far to reach her ideal spot to fire from. It was still 200 metres but at that distance she could hit a cherry stone. Nestling the rifle into her shoulder, she took aim. She fired three shots, one to the brain and one each for his two hearts. She realised that the bodyguard had somehow seen her and she fired quickly at him. As she did, she was thrown backwards as a bullet hit her in the chest. Her last thought was one of admiration as the shot the guard had made was truly remarkable. She came to a few minutes later with the most terrible pain in her chest and there was something else—her face was being licked. She peeked through half- open eyes into the hairy face of the most enormous dog. The dogs had been released from their kennels as soon as the alarm had been raised. Trained to attack on sight, they were led by two enormous Airedales who, coming upon Maria, hesitated. They were not trained to attack people who were on the ground, more dead than alive. This was different and instinct told them that Maria posed no threat. The Airedale licked her again, and looked on just as perplexed. A small arm slowly raised and a hand scratched the top of his head. It was this tiny kindness that won over the Airedales together with the whole pack. The bitch moved closer and lay down beside Maria. "Good doggies," she murmured and slipped back into unconsciousness. Meanwhile, Ben started to regain consciousness; his head throbbed with pain and it was a few minutes before he could raise his head off the makeshift pillow.

"Maria," he gasped. "What have you done?" He desperately looked around for her and in a daze, staggered to his feet. Once on his feet, he grabbed at the nearest thing to steady himself until his mind and vision cleared. Being sandbagged by Maria put him in a really foul mood and he cursed her stupidity with a few choice expletives. He put on his cape and set off in the direction of the castle. He had no trouble picking his way through the forest floor as all the lights, in and outside the building were now ablaze, with light casting an eerie glow through the forest. With his head aching, he ran on and realised that nobody was trying to enter his mind. He knew then that Maria had succeeded and so wished he could enter her mind. Suddenly, he sensed people moving out of the castle. He used his thoughts to give an illusion of fire. The people stopped as the wall of fire rose before them. He could not sustain the illusion for long but it gave him a little more time. He stopped for breath and immediately felt smaller senses, maybe animals and, in his mind, they were in a circle. Racing forward he came upon a very strange scene. A pack of dogs surrounded a body lying on the ground amongst the bushes. Although, obscured by two huge Airedales, Ben knew whom the body belonged to.

"Maria", he cried in dread and ran to her prone body. In unison, the two Airedales emitted a low growl but allowed him near. Quickly, kneeling beside her, he felt for a pulse. He found one but it was extremely weak. From her back, there oozed a trickle of blood. Focusing his mind, Ben entered the hole that bled. Deeper and deeper he went and repaired the wound. At last, he reached her heart which was damaged and had stopped beating. His mind lurched; he was sure he had felt a pulse. There was no time to be lost and putting his confusion aside, he began to massage Maria's heart. Eventually, he felt it flutter and then beat on its own. He continued through to the exit hole, repairing as he exited. He sat back on his haunches and gathered his thoughts. *I must get her to hospital, as quickly as possible*, he said to himself.

Pulling out his mobile, he rang James who answered immediately. "James, I need a helicopter here in Romania. I will give you directions from the car."

"I'm on it Ben." And James terminated the call. Some distance away in the woods there was a shout as the searchers came closer. One of the Airedales stayed by Maria but the other one, with the rest of the pack, rose and then raced off into the forest. Shortly after, there were shouts and screams and yelps as shots were fired. Then silence. Ben was puzzled. Why would the dogs protect Maria? They obviously came from the castle, perhaps they were badly treated and found an ally in Maria. He gently lifted Maria into his arms and rose into the air and flew. Keeping close to the ground but avoiding the undergrowth below, he flew on between the trees, and back to the car. Eventually, he reached the road, then went on to their small encampment. He laid Maria on to the leafy forest floor and sank down beside her, completely exhausted. From the distance, he could hear the sounds of pursuit, but did not have the energy to move. The Airedale whined and then gave a bark of pleasure as her mate limped into the clearing. Both of the dogs growled at a movement in the bushes near them, then into the clearing burst Cari. Moving closer, the car spoke urgently.

"Ben, if possible, I suggest you enter me and we'll be off."

Ben started to rise but the danger was far from over. A glow of red appeared above them.

From the glow, came the voice of Leopold.

"Found you," it said. It hovered over Maria. "How strange I had no contact with her mind and that is how she destroyed my being. However, I was able to transfer my mind to my bodyguard." The voice became menacing and the glow moved until it was hovering over Ben. "You," it said, "you are on my planet and I can enter your mind and take it over."

Ben looked up, truly terrified, not so much for himself. He struggled to resist but his effort was useless. He felt the mind entering his own, how ugly it was, full of malevolence and intense hatred. As his mind began to submit, he thought he saw a flash of blue then he lost consciousness. The light he saw, grew stronger; a wind suddenly sprang up and the trees moaned under an unknown force. The red ball rose to face the light and from behind it came a further blue ball. The intensity of the two blue lights grew too colossal and smashed into the red ball which exploded under the impact, bursting into a thousand sparks, falling to the forest floor, bursting into flames. The forest started to burn with flames leaping from tree to tree.

"Ben, Ben," the car called.

Maria's eyes fluttered open. "What's happening?" She struggled to a sitting position and realised the danger. Unable to do anything herself, she turned to the car. "You're so bloody clever," she screamed. "Help us."

A whining noise came from the car. From the open doors at the back, two steel plates, slid out. "Stretchers," she gasped and started to try to pull Ben onto one. The dogs seemed to understand and gripped Ben's clothing and dragged him on to the stretcher. Maria rolled onto the other stretcher and both stretchers quietly slid back into the car. She beckoned to the two dogs who needed no second bidding and both jumped in the car with them. Cari slammed her doors shut and sped out of the forest and away from danger.

Through the night, the car sped, and just as her batteries were running low, dawn broke. Across the border they sped, and then southward through Hungary. With Ben still unconscious Maria was giving Cari instructions for their destination. The day was cold and foggy and, although the car was able to negotiate through the mist, her batteries were not charging very well in the fog. There was a hum and a click as Cari switched over to nuclear power. Cari's nuclear pack was the size of a matchbox. It had very low radiation and was undetectable to the monitors that surrounded Budapest. Cari was the only car Ben had built with nuclear power. The danger was too great to have them built as a commercial enterprise. Since the attack by terrorists, all the major cities had such monitors. The attack was aborted and the culprits caught, but the scar had initiated the protective measures that were now in place. Cari raced round the city ring road and then took the road southwest towards the destination in northern Croatia. In late afternoon, they neared the end of their long journey. Entering a village that only consisted of a dozen or so houses, the car came to a rest outside a small inn. As the car doors opened, both dogs jumped out having only been let out twice in the journey. The inn door opened and several people rushed out. The car slid out the two stretchers and Maria and Ben were taken inside. Inside, there was a medical team ready to administer to them. Cari had been sending out messages and receiving signals, throughout the whole journey south; the medical teams arrived along with the security team, around the village and surrounding areas. In charge of all this, was Bunny. Although in great pain, Maria was sick with worry for Ben.

"Is my boy, Samuel, in the back," she whispered through clenched teeth, pain stabbing at her insides. Bunny nodded, his own face taut with worry over the state of the two of them.

"Take Ben through quickly," she said, "there is no time to lose." Still on the stretcher, Ben was carried through to a small room at the back. From the room came a racking cough. Still unconscious, Ben was carried in. On a small bed lay a child, no more than five years old and probably weighing less than a child two years younger. The boy looked up at the man who had just brought Ben in.

"Thank you, would you leave now, please?"

Without a word the man quietly left, shutting the door behind him.

"It will be all right now," the child said, touching Ben's head. From the boy, a brilliant blue light arose and encircled Ben's head. The light dimmed momentarily as the racking cough came again. Ben stirred and was attacked by himself in his mind. Before Leopold was destroyed, some remnants of his brain had entered Ben's mind. This scrap was attempting to take over Ben's mind completely. Ben's face contorted into a snarl as his mind was eroded further. The light came again, intensified and from Ben's head came an ugly crimson red smoke which drifted through the small window in the room. As it went, it dispersed and at last the council member was destroyed. Ben's eyes flew open, the horror of the last twenty-four hours still upon him. He looked at the child before him and wondered how one so young and so frail could take on a council member and destroy him. As he looked the boys started to cough again Ben's look changed to one of concern, and he started to probe the boy's body.

"Be careful," said the boy. "My defences are so acute they may even attack you."

Ben went even more careful and, indeed felt himself being probed. Slowly, he went deeper and deeper, checking the throat and airways down and then into the lungs. Although, the lungs were slightly enlarged, probably due to the coughing all seemed fine. He examined the heart which was also all right. It was when his mind travelled along the pulmonary artery that he found the problem. His mind sensed a blockage; he found it a small flap of skin laying across the artery. Very slowly, he started to destroy the flap. He knew one wrong move and the defences would pounce. At last, he felt the flap come away from the wall of the artery. Ben felt himself being hurled backwards into his own mind as the boy started to cough again. The boy suddenly vomited and then fell back onto his pillow totally exhausted. His breathing, however, had much improved. Ben gave a sigh of relief. It looked as though his healing powers had worked, but it was still early days. Ben eased himself up and when standing, he looked down at the youngster and was struck by something in the boy's face he recognised. Before he could dwell on the thought, there came a tapping on the door. Before Ben could turn to look, the door opened and a girl walked in. He gasped; she was obviously the boy's twin, the likeness was astonishing, but the girl was also a small version of Maria. Ben cast his mind back, Bunny, of course, Bunny was smitten with Maria. Ben chuckled to himself. When Ben had returned to England, he had left Bunny with Maria to arrange for her entry and working visa in the UK. *Bunny, you old devil,* he thought.

"Hello," the girl said. "My name is Fredrika." She looked at Ben, her face wreathed in smiles. "But everybody calls me Fred." Then in almost the same breath, she said, "You must be my daddy."

Ben went white, with his whole world turning upside down, he collapsed, as everything went black. He would have fallen to the floor, but a blue light came from the children, and Ben, with the light shining around him, instead floated gently down onto the stretcher. As he lay there, almost comatose, he remembered that terrible and beautiful night and everything fell into place. It also explained why Bunny had acted so strangely towards him and not to mention Maria's coolness, one moment and protectiveness, the next.

Chapter 9

James took all the men he could spare from his overstretched security and headed for the castle in Romania. There were only two survivors from the council member's force and they hardly knew their own names. Only three dogs survived and these were taken to the local veterinary who promised to treat them and find them new homes. In an isolated wing of the castle, the real Count Leopold and his housekeeper were found and considering their ordeal, were in remarkable health and quite feisty.

Before the arrival of the council member, the Count had huge tracts of land on which there were several farms. The farms had fallen into decline along with the Count's finances. Now, two years later, under the management of the council member the situation had been turned around and the farms were now running efficiently and the finances had now increased considerably.

"He was still a monster," was the Count's only comment.

Next, on the list, was the nursing home where they found Lena's brother Jon and two other Umbrians. There was no trace of the original staff as they had all fled when the council member had been defeated. There was however, one person still working.

This was Bella, the cook who lived locally and although she realised she was unlikely to be paid, stayed on to feed the patients. The feeding of the patients was the easy part as Bella also took on the administration of the hospital that it had now become. When the Count realised how efficient Bella was, he made arrangements for her to be officially employed as the manager. The hospital, which had been a lodge where friends and family stayed, was turned into an exclusive health centre. The remaining Umbrians were taken back to the UK for rehabilitation.

Louisa, meanwhile, had flown to Zagreb. She went straight to the small medical centre which was located inside one of Ben's production units. She went there to prepare for the arrival of Ben and Maria. She had just made up the two beds when Cari called.

"I'm outside," the car said. Louisa went outside to organise the stretchers which were by the car. She almost said thankyou to Cari but could not quite manage it. "I ask you," she said to herself. "I don't care how clever you are I'm not having a conversation with a car." She busied herself helping the solitary nurse and soon had her son and Maria tucked up in bed. Ben was still asleep, but Maria was awake and protesting.

"There is nothing wrong with me," she insisted, and then added, "How is Benji?" She then looked embarrassed. "Sorry," she said. "I mean Benjamin." Louisa took her hand.

"It's okay. I know about the children and I know you call him Benji." She went on, "Mind you, I have not known long and it was a bit of a shock." She then said, on a more serious note, "Without the children, you and Ben would be as dead as Dodos" She was interrupted by a faint rumbling. "What was that?" she asked. Maria's face screwed up and she burst out laughing.

"That," she said, "was my stomach." They both burst out laughing and hugged. It broke the awkwardness between them, and relieved the tension they felt after the close shave with death that Ben and Maria had had.

"I'm so hungry," Maria moaned. "It must been days since we last ate." Then she looked around. "Where are my Sam and Fred? Are they here?"

"Of course, they are," Louisa answered. "They are, at this moment, playing in the unit's crèche and thoroughly enjoying themselves. We are in the medical centre which is situated in one of Ben's business units here in Zagreb."

There was a knock on the door and Bunny's face peered in. "I only have a few minutes I am in the middle of feeding the two Airedales. How are the patients?" he asked. Then he saw Maria awake. "How are you?" he asked anxiously.

"I'm fine but I'll be dead from malnutrition if I don't eat soon."

"I will organize it straight away," said Bunny and started to leave.

Louisa called after him. "Something light, she hasn't eaten for at least three days." Bunny was back in minutes with a tray on which was a huge bowl of steaming soup and a baguette broken in half.

"It's leek and potato" Bunny explained, "straight from the canteen." Maria did not answer, her mouth already full. Louisa picked up half of the baguette.

"Only half now," she said, "and eat more slowly or you will be ill." Maria reluctantly slowed down, enjoying every delicious mouth full. Looking at Bunny's face, Louisa felt sorry for him. He obviously adored her. She hoped, one day, they would eventually get together. It would be good for them and the children. She had already observed that the children had great affection for their uncle Bunny. Bunny saw Louisa looking at him and went red, half-guessing what she was thinking. To cover his embarrassment, he asked quickly, "How is Ben?"

As if on cue, Ben stirred. He had been dreaming that someone was calling him—someone in great distress. He suddenly sat up, shouting.

"Tessa, Tessa."

Anxiously, the three of them looked at him. Sweat was literally running down his face and body. Louisa hugged him to herself trying to comfort him.

"Ben," she said. "Tessa was fine when I left and I made sure she was never left alone."

"I will go up on the roof and make a call," Bunny said. "I should get a good reception up there."

Louisa and Maria looked at each other.

"What now?" Maria said.

Samuel and Fredrika walked into the room. They smiled as they looked at all the worried faces.

"It's all right Mummy, Daddy and Nana. Auntie Tessa's okay. It's just that our little baby brother is beginning to move and it made Auntie uncomfortable," they smiled at the dumbstruck adults.

"If it's okay, may we go back to play now?"

Lost for words, the adults smiled and nodded in assent. When the children had gone, Ben laid back and looked at the ceiling. There was silence in the room which seemed to last several minutes but was, in fact, only seconds. Both women started to talk at once. Ben held up his hand to stop them.

"I seem to have made a mess of everything."

Maria smiled, "No Benji, you haven't. I would never have married you or any other man. Bunny knows this but he will be my companion and friend, as always." She looked at Ben fondly. "What happened that night was written, you dreamt my nightmares…I wanted a lifetime of love and so it happened." Maria smiled, this time from the memory of how it all turned out.

Louisa looked at Ben. "You seem to have been surrounded by women who are prepared to die for you and also to have children by you."

Ben looked abashed and went red. “I never expected this to happen,” then stopped, as he realised the full implication of what he was about to say.

At this point, Bunny came into the room.

“Apparently, she woke and had a bad stomach and when they gave her a scan it showed that she was having a baby.” At this point, Bunny gave Ben a sideways glance. Maria started to giggle, and Bunny who had no sense of humour, stalked out of the room. Ben grinned sheepishly and went red again as he saw his mother’s face.

“As soon as Tessa is well, you will ask her to marry you.” She said more as an order than a request. “That’s, of course, if she will have you. You, Maria, will always be referred to as my daughter and, those dear children as my grandchildren. Whilst the three of us are alone there is another matter I now understand. Maria when I examined you I found you had two hearts, one of which is only on course a few years old.” Maria looked blank and then went quite pale.

“It’s not cancer,” she said fearfully.

“No, no,” Louisa and Ben said in unison.

Ben explained, “What happened is a good thing. When the twins were conceived you inherited from the Umbrian power of regeneration.”

Louisa intervened, “Talking of Umbrians, I left Aunt Agatha in charge of the clinic and to protect Tessa. Did you know Ben’s Aunt Agatha is training to be a council member?”

“My aunt Agatha? Really? Is she really?” Ben exclaimed.

“She is, indeed, and as I was about to say, she has a great knowledge of such matters and, once back in the clinic, I am sure all will be explained. Talking of the clinic, I must return.” She smiled at them. “I have other patients apart from you two. I suggest you stay here for a few weeks and recuperate. The clinic is quite safe and you have Bunny and his two pals to protect you and give assistance, if required,”

Ben thought to talk to his mother about the waste of manpower, but said instead, “Mum, could you arrange for the two Airedales to return with you. The boy dog is suffering badly with his leg wound and our vets there will be able to treat him.”

“What are their names?” she asked. Ben looked blank.

“Oh,” he said, “we never did get round to naming them.” He thought for a moment, then. “Juno and Harvey,” he said in a moment of inspiration.

The next day, Louisa was gone, leaving Ben and Maria alone with Bunny and his friends. After just one day, Maria started getting restless.

"Benji," she declared, "I'm going for a jog."

"Okay, mind you take someone with you and take this mobile." Reaching across, he took a small phone out and gave it to her.

"What is this for?"

Ben smiled. "In case you get lost."

"Okay," she said and was off.

Ben was desperate to catch up on his computer work; after the long period of neglect his business was beginning to suffer. An hour later, all hell was let loose. Maria had disappeared. Knowing how fit Maria was, Bunny had given the task of looking after her to Bert. To give Bert credit, he had managed to keep up with her for ten minutes but then lost her. After an hour of trying to trace her, he rang for help. Bunny was beside himself and the unfortunate Bert got ten lashes of Bunny's tongue. An ashamed Bunny confronted Ben.

"I'm so sorry."

Ben held up his hand. "It's okay," he said.

Bunny stared at him. "Okay?" he said. "How can it be okay?" Ben moved over to another computer screen. Smiling he tapped in a code.

"There she is," he said, smiling. He turned to Bunny. "I was almost sure your man would find it difficult to keep up with her so I planted a bug in her phone."

"Why not tell us." Ben looked at him.

"Oh, you mean the blokes ego."

Ben grinned. "You got it. No way would they have accepted being less fit than a little thing like Maria. The story about the young recruit she nearly killed does not help either." The two men looked at each other.

"I love her to bits," admitted Bunny.

"She is very fond of you," Ben replied. Then the conversation ended and, as if summoned, they saw Maria trotting across the compound looking as fresh as a daisy.

"Next time give your bloke a bike," Ben said, laughing.

For the next fortnight, it became a regular pattern. Ben is working on his computer and Maria is running around the countryside with a young man pedalling furiously behind her. During these outings, they had often seen a young man on a cross-country motorbike who had given them a wave as he passed by. In the second week Maria's escort fell off his bike.

“Damn,” he cried, clutching his ankle.

Maria rushed back to him and gently removed his shoe. Examining his foot, she gave a smile. “I don’t think it’s broken but it’s badly twisted. I’ll call for help.” She took out her mobile. “Oh,” she said, “there’s no signal. I’ll have to walk back until I can get to within range.”

“Here, try mine,” said her escort. He groaned as he moved to get his mobile out but, when he tried to call, he too had no signal. Maria took a note of their position and was away.

She had gone about a mile down the road when she saw the young man on the motorbike. She flagged him down and told him what had happened.

“Hop on, I’ll give you a lift.” Maria gratefully got on to the bike and they were off like the wind. She had to cling tightly to hang on. It soon became obvious that they were going in the wrong direction.

“Stop,” she yelled. The man stopped the bike, but much too quickly and the bike swivelled round. Maria lost her grip and went flying off the bike. She hit the ground hard and banged her head. She lay there dazed and was only just aware of the man approaching. It was only when he knelt beside her that she understood—he was naked apart from the ring in his ear.

“Now, my little beauty,” he muttered, “let’s see all of you.” He pulled off her shorts and pants. She gasped and tried to push him away but was too dizzy. He ripped her blouse open and stared at her breasts. He climbed astride her and leant forward to kiss her nipples as he lowered himself onto her body. Maria lashed out as hard as she could and was rewarded with a grunt of pain, but he was still there. Her eyes focused and she looked desperately around her for something to defend herself, a rock or a stick, but there was nothing near. She lashed out again but he was ready and swung his head away. Then she saw it, the earring, she reached out, grabbed it and yanked it as hard as she could. It tore away from his ear. Screaming, he fell off her with blood pouring from his ripped ear. Still holding the earring, Maria staggered to her feet. Dropping the earring, she picked up his boot and smashed it down on his vitals. He screamed again and leant forward to protect himself. This time, the heel of the heavy boot landed on his head and the young man passed out. She raised the boot again then threw it away in disgust. She slowly dressed, feeling faint. Going over to the bike she stood it up then she picked up his clothes, put them in the saddle box, pulled herself onto the bike and pressed the ignition button. The engine burst into life and she slowly rode towards the base. She stopped once, made a phone call and then drove on until she was back. She dumped the bike and slipped in unnoticed. She headed straight for the one bathroom when Ben walked out.

"Hello," he said. "You're back." He stopped. "My god, what happened to you?" Maria fell into his arms, shaking as if she had a fever. Ben picked her up and carried her into the bedroom. She looked up at him with her enormous brown eyes.

"Benji, I was so very nearly raped."

Ben's eyes hardened. "Who," he said so softly that Maria hardly heard.

"It doesn't matter," she said. "It was just a boy on a bike." Ben looked down at Maria and realised that she had at least stopped shaking.

"I'm going to get you a sedative," and he turned to leave the room.

"No, Benji," Maria almost shouted. "I must wash—a shower. I feel dirty." Ben went back to help her. "No," she said. "I can manage," and she got up. "Benji would you come with me?"

Ben looked startled. "I would have thought that the last person you would want in the shower was a man." She leant against him.

"Will you?" Ben said nothing, but sweeping her into his arms, took her to the shower room where he gently undressed her and stripping off his own clothes, led her into the shower. While she washed her hair, he rubbed soap all over her body, then with a sponge washed it off. Maria turned and reached up to kiss him. Ben gasped and then moaned, as she lowered herself onto him. Ten minutes later, they were out of the shower and dressed, Maria with her eyes shining and Ben looking dazed.

There was a commotion downstairs as the rescue party returned with Maria's injured escort.

"You took your time," he remarked, but was relieved because of what happened a few minutes earlier. Bunny gave Ben a strange look and Ben felt a little uncomfortable. However, Ben was not the subject of Bunny's look.

"The strangest thing occurred. On the way back, we came across this bloke, stark naked and blood all over him and barely able to walk."

Ben looked grim. "And where is this person now?" he asked.

"Well, we were going to bring him back here but he insisted on going to his father's house." Before Ben could speak, Bunny rushed on, "You know him, of course, his father is the industrialist that you have dealings with." Ben asked if the young man's name was Billy.

"Yes," came the reply.

When Bunny had left, Ben turned to Maria. “I’m going to see how that young man is doing?” The hard glint had come back in his eyes.

Maria held his arm. “Leave it until tomorrow, Benji,” she pleaded. “You are too angry now and you might regret your actions.”

Ben relented. “Tomorrow then.” He kissed her lightly on the mouth. He looked at her fondly. “Are you okay now?”

“Very definitely,” she replied, her eyes widening and her face lighting up with that smile she had.

Ben returned to the small isolation room that he was using as his office. The computer looked at him with its grey blank face. Ben grimaced; the last thing he wanted to do was spend several hours at the computer but it had to be done and he was almost up to date with his paperwork. Before he started, he rang a number on his mobile; whilst waiting for a connection he opened up the computer to the file he was working on. A voice came on. “Hello. Lesley here. Lesley Lenin speaking. Is that you Benjamin?” The voice was tremulous.

“Yes it’s me.” Ben hesitated, then said, “I’ve heard the bad news. How is he?” Even over the phone he could sense the emotion. Her only son, beaten half to death by a gang of thugs. Ben had no intention of telling her what a thug her boy was. Lesley broke his silence. “Benjamin,” she spoke with affection. “How are you?”

Lesley and her husband William were good friends. Over the years, they had gone without and worked all hours, making up their business making solar panels. When Lesley had their child, they decided that he would want for nothing. He repaid them by getting into trouble when he was just eleven. He was involved in setting fire to a derelict house. Unfortunately, unknown to Billy and his fellow arsonists, there was a tramp inside. He managed to get out of the building but was badly burnt. Billy was arrested and along with the other boys, faced a long term in a borstal type camp. His parents pleaded, and as he was only eleven, he escaped the imprisonment. At the age of eighteen, Billy forced a girl to have sex with him and she became pregnant. The girl was the daughter of his parents’ best friends and only a minor.

“Benjamin, your men saved my boys life. I’m in your debt until the day I die.”

“Please Lesley, my men just happened to be there.” Ben had to end the conversation. “Lesley, I have to go. I’ll come and see you tomorrow”, and he terminated the call. He was sweating and gripping the phone so hard, he nearly broke it.

He went to his friend's house, as promised, the following day. On arrival, he was warmly greeted by Lesley and William.

"Your men probably saved my Billy's life," Lesley proclaimed. Ben shook his head.

"No, I don't think so," he replied. "It saved Billy a lot of embarrassment though," Ben added quickly. "He would have had trouble getting back to his house unseen in his naked state." They both nodded in agreement.

"I'll go and make some tea," Lesley said.

"And I will take you up to see Billy," William said, showing Ben the way.

"I would like to speak to Billy alone, if that's all right?"

"Of course," William answered as they arrived at the door of his room. "He is in here."

Ben entered alone. Billy lay prone on the bed, unmoving and covered by a single blanket. He stirred as Ben entered and closed the door.

"Who's there?" he whispered. His voice died away as Ben moved closer. "Why Billy?" said Ben, quietly. Not wishing his parents to hear his voice. "You have a beautiful and very understanding wife and two lovely kids, so why?" There was silence and then a whisper that Ben could hardly hear.

"I'm so very, very sorry." Ben looked down at him. Billy's face and shoulders were encased in bandages and Ben could only imagine the damage Maria had inflicted on his regions. Ben found he could not punish him further and turned to leave the room as Billy's wife entered.

"Jayne." Ben said, and before he could say more, she fell sobbing into his arms.

"Who could do this to my Billy," she wept. Ben comforted her.

"I don't know," he said, "but if they can be found they will receive the treatment they deserve."

Ben left shortly afterwards, assured in his own mind that Billy would, indeed, now be a reformed character.

Maria was waiting anxiously for Ben's return. As he entered his tiny office, she closed the door and turned to him.

"How was he? How did he react on seeing you? How were his parents?"

"Slow down," he said. "It was all okay. He has certainly learnt a very painful lesson and both him, and his family will be a lot better off and happier for that lesson."

"Thank god," Maria said. "At least some good came from it." The subject was closed and never mentioned again.

Chapter 10

Ben's work was now completed. All the files were up to date and the outstanding office work was done. Health wise both Maria and Ben were in good shape. The only difference was that Maria was super fit, whereas Ben, who had been stuck in the office, was definitely in need of some vigorous exercise.

Whilst in Zagreb, Ben had some business he wished to deal with and at dinner that night, he spoke to Maria to ascertain her wishes.

"Maria, I have to meet someone on business here in Zagreb. Would you like to accompany me or spend more time with the children?" Maria did not hesitate.

"Ben, I'm your bodyguard. I go with you, Benji. Besides, in your present condition you could not defend yourself against a kitten and the children would never forgive me if anything happened to their weird daddy."

Ben grinned. "You are right, of course. I feel fine but I would be no good in a hundred-yard sprint. However, I'm sure you will not be needed but it will be nice to have you with me. The meeting I'm having is with a woman."

"What does this lady do for a living?" Maria asked,

"Well, she is the Minister of the Interior."

"Oh really," said Maria.

"Apparently, we will be meeting in Zagreb central park because, initially it will be informal."

Ben started to gather up all his paperwork. "We might as well send all the team with Bunny as we won't need an escort to the park and besides I've got you to look after me."

"Behave yourself, Benji." Maria laughed and gave him a playful punch on the arm.

"Ouch," yelled Ben, and staggered against the table.

"Oh, Benji, I am so sorry," and then saw the grin on his face. "You sod," she said.

"Why are you looking at me like that? What's wrong?"

"Nothing," said Ben, not liking to admit that the playful punch had actually hurt.

The following morning, they took off for the meeting in the park. Although it was a glorious day, Maria had a sense of foreboding which she could not shake off.

"Cheer up." said Ben. "We have put the enemy to flight and they are in disarray." Maria smiled; it was hard not to when everything was so bright and cheerful. To cheer Maria up, Ben told her about the banquet they would be going to that evening.

"Ooh Benji, that sounds marvellous but I have nothing to wear."

"No problem, after we have finished the meeting we will go into Zagreb and buy you some clothes. I could do with fitting myself out too."

"I wish now we had not come," she muttered.

"Stop worrying," said Ben, "you're making me nervous." They arrived early, at the opposite end of the park to where the meeting was taking place. Ben parked the car and got out, stretching himself in the autumn sunshine.

"As we're early, let's walk through the park," he said. Maria got out and stood beside him. She said nothing but Ben could see the tension in her face. "Come on, I need the exercise. Even if you don't." Maria put her arm in his and they set off across the park. "What is the Minister like?"

"She sounds very nice," Ben replied as he tucked Maria tightly into his side. "Although I have not actually met her, I have heard that she is extremely efficient and according to hearsay, drives a hard bargain."

"She certainly is. She is married to a professor who happens to be the principal of Zagreb University."

"I know," Ben said. "It's the University your sister attended."

Their conversation was interrupted as Ben's mobile rang. "That will be Bunny calling," he said, he pulled the mobile from his pocket and answered. Bunny's voice came through in a panic.

"Boss, we've got big trouble." Ben knew that something was seriously wrong.

"We are already in the park and will be with you in a few minutes."

"ASAP," was Bunny's reply and the call was terminated.

Ben turned to Maria but she was gone like a gazelle in full flight. She had taken off as she overheard the call, and the panic in Bunny's voice. Ben rushed after her and, as he did so he noticed all the people rushing past him in the opposite direction. They were mainly pensioners and nannies with their charges, but all obviously terrified as they rushed by. Way ahead of Ben, Maria had stopped a young girl pushing a pram. "What's the panic?" she asked.

"There, in the woods, shooting," the girl said, pointing. "Men being shot." With that, the girl rushed off. Maria took off again, running fast towards the woods. In seconds, she was amongst the trees and saw the first victim of the gunfire; a man on his back with blood spurting from a nasty looking chest wound. A woman was crouched down by his side, hair obscuring her face. Maria guessed she was the wife. The woman was shaking from shock and fright. There were four men around the couple, almost hidden, Maria realised the couple must be the Minister and her husband. Maria recognised two of the men as Ben's security and one of his men pointed towards the woods.

Maria raised her hand, slowed her pace to a lope, drawing her favourite throwing knife as she did so. The Minister's two guards' eyes followed Maria as she disappeared into the woods, and then they looked at Ben's two men, their eyes questioning.

"Don't worry, she's the best," came a whisper.

As if to prove the point, a shout, followed by a scream, came from a man in the woods.

Maria withdrew her knife, wiped the blade clean and moved forward slowly. She saw a figure in the undergrowth and raised her knife ready. The figure did not move and with a shock, she saw it was Bunny, blood oozing from a wound to his head, where he had fallen and struck it.

She knelt beside him and with horror, realised there was a far more serious wound in Bunny's chest. *He must be dead,* she thought, and then he opened his eyes. "Maria," he whispered, "there must have been a dozen of them," and then he slumped back.

Maria's mind froze. "Oh no, Bunny, please don't die on me." A tear fell from her eyes as she frantically felt for a pulse. With relief she found one, although it was very weak. She whispered in his ear, "I'll be back, my darling Bunny," and making him as comfortable as possible, she rose and sped off again into the forest.

Earlier.

Many miles away to the north east of Zagreb, Maria's children were on their morning break in their school. For no apparent reason, they suddenly fell to the floor and lay there quite still. Their teacher saw them fall and tried to revive them and called for help. The local doctor was called but he was many miles away attending another patient. The school knew Maria was away on business and therefore contacted who was listed with the school. Agatha, who knew some of the children's strange powers, put the very worried headmistress's mind at rest.

"It has happened several times before," she told her. "They get tired and just fall asleep together. There really is no need to worry the doctor. I'll come myself and take them home. I'm sure after a good night's sleep, they will both be fine." The headmistress agreed, even though she would have felt far happier had the doctor had been able to visit the school.

What nobody saw when the twins fell asleep, were the two small orbs of blue light that rose from their bodies. The lights were the size of tiny marbles that sped off in the morning sunshine.

Travelling at phenomenal speeds, they reached Maria as she rose from Bunny's still form.

If Maria noticed they were with her, she gave no sign. She was on a mission and moving forward again, she came to where Bunny's men were positioned.

She threw caution to the wind and went through the assailants like a scythe. Within minutes, three men were dead and two were running away towards the park exit. Normally Maria would have gone after them, such was her hate, but Bunny was her first priority and she felt she must get back to him. She turned and, as she did so, something from a tree above crashed into her.

He could have just shot her but having seen his men slain by this small figure below, he wanted to physically kill her himself and to let her know why. He dropped down, smashing her into the ground, face down. She twisted her head round.

"This is for my young brother," he screamed, and she saw the knife coming down. Unable to move, she waited for the blow. It never came, instead there was a gasp of surprise and twisting round, she saw the man struggling helplessly as he started to rise above her. Higher and higher he rose, surrounded by a shimmering blue light. His body rose until it was level with the treetops, then it moved slowly sideways until it was hovering above a small clearing. The man screamed as he knew what was going to happen next. The light disappeared and he fell to the ground below. The light had rushed back to Maria, where it paled and was shaking.

Maria hugged the light to her. "It's alright children," she whispered. "He was a very, very evil man who has probably killed many innocent people. Remember that and now you must return. It's not good to be away from yourselves for so long." She mouthed a kiss to the light and it was gone.

Maria lay on her back, the wind knocked out of her. In other circumstances, she would have laughed at her present position. Twice, in less than three weeks, she had been flattened by a man. However, she was far from laughing and terribly worried about her babies. How must they be coping, having killed at their tender age? She shook the thought from her mind and concentrated on getting her wind back. Breathing slowly, she gradually recovered. Struggling to her feet she limped over to where the man had fallen. Surprisingly, after falling from such a height, he was still alive. Maria stared down at him, and as she looked, his eyes fluttered open. She had to know, so she asked.

"This brother of yours, was he one of the murderous squad, who got wiped out about 150 kilometres east of Zagreb?" The man's eyes widened. "Well," said Maria, "it's a small world."

"I do not know why you are here but I am so glad. Your brother and his comrades murdered my whole family and it was me that killed them all, bar one and he shot me and left me for dead."

Maria wanted to kick him and then jump on him but instead, she turned away, saying as she went, "I hope you take a long time to die." And, although nearly every bone in his body was broken, he was eventually found and every effort was made to save him. He died in agony several days later.

Bunny, Maria thought, *I must get back to him.* And she was soon hurrying back to where he lay. On her way, she passed Ben's men and gave them the thumbs up.

"Okay now," she said. "Follow me back." The men just looked at each other and followed.

Maria reached the spot where Bunny should have been, but he was gone. She thought, *surely he would not try to move with a bullet in his chest.* Maria rushed on, sick with worry. Another thought crossed her mind; although Bunny was bleeding profusely from his head wound, she saw none on his chest. *Of course, a laser,* she thought.

She reached the edge of the woods where the Minister and her wounded husband were. Ben was there looking down at the shot man. He was totally unaware of her return, as his mind was deep inside the bullet wound and was slowly removing the bullet backwards away from the heart. Maria guessed what

Ben was about and looked around. The rest of the team were there looking very pale. Was Bunny…

"What is going on?" was all she could say. As she looked and saw that two other men had similar chest wounds to Bunny's. Bunny actually managed a small smile.

"It was the boss," he said. Maria was still perplexed. "Ben made us all wear bulletproof vests."

Maria went to Bunny and hugged him.

"Darling Bunny," she cried. "I thought I'd lost you."

Bunny brightened up enormously. "Oh yes," he said. "I'm pretty pleased I'm still here myself."

"What happened there?" Ben said, pointing to the woods.

One of the men who had just joined the group, looked up with awe and respect in his voice.

"I don't know who they were," he said, "but Maria really hated them. I've never seen her kill." He stopped.

"Well go on," said Ben.

"She killed five of them and it was as if she was enjoying it. It was not like Maria at all."

"I'm still me," piped up Maria, "but they were Serbs of the worst kind. I spoke to their commander before he died and they were the remnants of the secret police, kept together by their sheer hatred of us."

The Minister, who was still kneeling by her husband, looked up and stared at Maria.

"Maria," she said in a whisper. "Maria," she said, shouting this time. "It cannot be you."

She knelt still, shaking her head and staring up at Maria. It was then Maria's turn to stare at the woman addressing her. Maria paled and clutched Bunny's arm.

"Maria," Anna said, "I saw you shot in the head. Is it really you?"

"And you, you were in the house when it was burnt to the ground."

"No, I pulled the revolver from the dead man on top of me and shot the one that shot you in the head. He shot you in the head, Maria. How did you survive? Oh my god," Anna said, her voice breaking, "I left you for dead."

Maria said, "Well, I survived. I could not see or hear anything but somehow I crawled out of the house and neighbours found me and took me to the convent.

A doctor at the convent attended my head wound and there I stayed for many years." Anna got to her feet and touched the top of Maria's head and felt the furrow which ran from the front to the back of her skull.

"Oh," she said, "my darling baby sister."

Everybody around them was now smiling, hardly daring to believe that there could be such a happy ending to such a terrible day. Then, there was chaos as the police and ambulances arrived. Anna walked over to the ambulance to get the paramedics to attend to her husband. She then turned to the police.

"Where the hell were you?" she said, her voice harsh with anger. The police captain held up his hands.

"I'm sorry, Minister, we were told by Mr Franklin that his own team were arranging security but, of course we would have been here as well but the squad assigned to you were tied up by, not one but two bank robberies. We have since found out that both robberies were arranged by the men that attacked you."

"Very well," Anna conceded. "I know we were undermanned. Did you manage to apprehend the two who were trying to escape?"

"Oh yes, and they are singing like canaries. They were scared witless. Actually glad to be arrested, claiming they were attacked by a wraith that moved faster than a leopardess."

The Minister remained silent at this information. One of Anna's bodyguards came to Anna and spoke quietly to her. Clenching and unclenching her hands, she said, "Oh surely not. Are you quite sure?"

"Yes, the paramedics have tried to revive him but I'm afraid he is dead."

Ben overheard the last part of the conversation. Interrupting, he asked, "Where is he?"

"It's no good," the bodyguard said. "He's in the ambulance and he's dead."

"May I just see him?" The bodyguard glared at Ben and stormed off.

"Please, I've a piece of equipment with me that might help if it's in time and there is not too much damage to his internal..." He stopped, and then said, "Well, it might just save him."

The paramedic who did not know Ben, shook his head and looked at the Minister. She looked at Ben and heard herself saying, "Yes, I do not hold any other hope so go."

The paramedic pointed out the ambulance and Ben raced over to it; it was unattended which suited him. Once inside, he bent over the man and using his powers, let his mind drift into the body. It was bad, the bullet had entered the chest cavity from the back, sliced through the lung and exited through the front of his chest near his shoulder. From a small case, Ben took out a surgical knife and a length of tube. Cutting a small slit in the airway, he pushed the tube in. Pushing it further, he guided it to the damaged lung. He sucked the tube until he spotted the pink liquid, withdrawing his mouth, he started to massage the heart; nothing happened. Ben went back to his little case and took out a small pencil-like object with a square end. Placing it over the heart he depressed the end as one would do with a ballpoint pen. The body arched and arched again as Ben sensed no pulse; a third time and then Ben stopped, he felt for and found a small pulse. Gently massaging the heart again, he was rewarded by the heart working on its own. He quickly checked the brain and found no damage, although time would tell more, he felt quietly confident. Pleased, Ben stood back. Sunlight suddenly poured in as the injured man's companion yanked open the ambulance door.

"My god," he said, seeing the tube hanging from the man's mouth. "What have you done to Sebastian?"

Ben faced the man. "What is your name?" he asked.

"Garcia," came the reply.

"Well, Garcia, I have just performed a tracheotomy, and as you can see, it was a success. We now need to get your friend to a hospital very quickly."

The ambulance driver was informed of the emergency. From the ambulance door, Ben yelled his intention of going to the hospital with the patient and the ambulance sped away.

Ben looked at the small jar containing the liquid, it was still trickling through. Ben let his mind drift until he could see the damaged lung then concentrating, he sealed the torn edges, making sure the lungs were drained first, satisfied he withdrew. Coming back from his trance, he heard a voice say, "There is no blood going into the bottle."

"Yes, Garcia, I think your friend will be okay, physically now, the only worry is the length of time he was unconscious but again only time has the answer." They arrived at the hospital and Sebastian was rushed off to the resuscitation ward. Ben stood on the hospital steps feeling quite exhausted. Whilst he stood there, he watched ambulances arriving, bringing people in. Then several cars arrived, Ben's security team and Anna's bodyguards. Word had gotten around regarding Sebastian. Anna came up to Ben and hugged him. "Thanks," she said, and then seeing Maria emerge from one of the cars, she added "for every miracle you have performed for me today."

She was still white-faced from the shock of the attack. Ben touched her arm, "Have you any news from the hospital?"

She shook her head. "No, he is intensive care but progressing well."

At that moment, Maria rushed up and Ben received another hug.

"Thank you, dearest Benji," she whispered. "You have saved many lives today." Ben held her tight for a moment.

"So have you," he responded. He then held her at arm's length. "Are you all right? No aftermath shock?"

The cold blank look that Maria had during the conflict had gone and her face lit up with her smile.

"No I'm fine. I'll probably have nightmares for weeks to come but I'm used to them, and I have Anna back." She said this as if she could not quite believe it, but it was true, the miracle had happened and she had her beloved sister. She went and stood in front of her sister just looking at her. It was still too much for them and they both stood and silently wept.

The men all stood back; they had never seen such emotion, especially from these two women, the men shuffled their feet. Feeling unable to respond, Ben coughed quietly and, talking to no one in particular, said "We best make tracks for the hotel."

Anna immediately responded, "No, you are all coming to our villa. There is enough room for all of you."

Families were informed and hotel bookings cancelled.

On arrival at the villa, Ben, Maria, Anna and Bunny retired to one of the small reception rooms to unwind and recount on the day's traumatic events and, of course, the incredible reunion of the two sisters. Maria turned to her sister and asked her how she escaped from the house. Anna told her again how she grabbed the gun from the dead soldier and shot the one she thought had killed Maria. Anna dropped her head, unlike Maria she felt remorse and horror at killing someone and still felt ashamed of her action,

"He was young," she said and gripped Maria's arm before she continued. "I had to escape and the only transport apart from papa's old tractor, was an army vehicle. The young man I shot was slim, my size, near enough anyway," she added in a whisper "I undressed him and put on his clothes."

Maria gasped, "Why would you do that?"

"Because I would have been stopped a kilometre up the road had I been in civilian clothing. I drove like the wind with my hair tucked under his cap. I just waved at all the patrols and went straight past." Anna continued, "As I neared the city and started to go through checkpoints, I was terrified. I had the gun in my hand and was prepared to shoot anybody who tried to stop me but the men at the checkpoints just saluted and let me pass."

Ben interrupted, "Was the young soldier you shot, an officer?"

"No, I don't think so."

Ben was puzzled, "You were wearing his jacket?"

"Oh no," Anna said. "That was all bloodstained. The jacket I wore belonged to the soldier on the bed."

"Ah" said Ben. "I bet it had pips on the shoulders or stripes on the sleeves?"

"I cannot remember." Anna said, then thinking said the jacket was smarter and had silver buttons on the cuffs.

"Ah," Ben nodded.

"What do you mean, ah?" Maria queried. Ben looked at them both.

"Your sister was extremely lucky—that jacket she had on was an officer and that is how she was able to pass all the patrols and checkpoints."

"What happened when you reached the city?" Maria asked.

"I dumped the jeep, and rang Sebastian. He came and rescued me and I stayed hidden in his house for three years. I had one to one tuition. Sebastian used to set me work in the morning and mark it when he returned home from university. Sebastian was and is one of the good Serbs. After a time, I realised that Sebastian was very much in love with me and when he asked me to marry him I agreed."

"Would you have married Sebastian under normal circumstances?" Maria asked.

"All the girls had a crush on him including me because he was so handsome but, our paths would have parted once I left university. I would probably end up marrying an executive."

Ben was so happy for them, but he was also very tired.

"We will speak again tomorrow," he said. "Right now, I must go to bed before I go to sleep standing." He kissed the two women goodnight and was in his room in bed in ten minutes, and sound asleep. Anna and Maria talked on for a long time after Ben had retired, until overcome by the events of the day, they too, retired.

The next morning, Anna had breakfast served at a large table usually used for conferences. Ben found himself between Anna and Maria—he was still hero of the week on insisting his men wore bulletproof vests. Maria turned to Ben. "Benji, I would like to go back to the children for a while. What they did must have distressed them terribly."

Ben, who was the only one privy to the twins slaying the man in the woods, immediately agreed. "You must go of course," he answered, "and I would like you to take Bunny with you. The children know him as their second dad. I would like to come myself but…" Maria put her fingers to his mouth to stop him going on.

"I know you would," she said, "but I will be fine with Bunny and I know this contract is not only good for your company but also very important for Croatia. I also think that the attack yesterday was designed to scotch the deal."

Somewhat mollified at Maria's little speech, Ben relaxed and enjoyed the rest of his meal. He decided to send all but one of his own security guards back to England, just retaining the young man who was still in hospital with his injuries. His injuries were not serious and he was expected to be discharged the next day. For safety reasons, it was decided to carry on with the negotiations at Anna's house. Anna had all the paperwork sent over from her office and anyone involved with the contract would also work at the house. It was estimated that it would take at least two weeks for the work to be completed, and everything signed.

Chapter 11

The following evening, Ben took Anna out to dinner. Anna, although out for a quiet meal, still had a heavy bodyguard, with two men in the restaurant and four outside covering the entrances. She queried the number of guards.

"You are known to those who would do you harm and I'm not taking any chances; besides Maria would kill me if any harm came to you." He grinned at Anna and she relaxed. The meal passed without incident and soon they were back in the security of the house.

"Thank you, Ben, that was a beautiful evening," and she put her hands gently on Ben's cheek and kissed him. Ben was taken by surprise and instinctively took a step back.

"You do not like me?" Anna said.

"Maria would certainly do me harm if I took advantage of you." Anna turned and walked into her room.

When she was inside, Ben found himself adrift with his emotions and, after a few moments, he tapped on her door and went in. Anna had already slipped out of her dress and turned as Ben quietly closed the door. He crossed the room, took Anna gently into his arms and kissed her. He then picked her up and laid her on the bed removing the rest of her clothes as he did so.

"Why…?"

"I do not know. I have been unable to feel any man, even my dear Sebastian, since that day but you…you are different. Maria told me of your…" she struggled to find the right word and came up with, "abilities."

Anna then reached up and pulled Ben down. Ben could feel the passion rising and pulling off his own clothes, he lowered himself gently down into her. Instinctively, he restrained and slowly built to a climax. Anna had a magnificent body; she was tall with long legs and although in her mid-thirties had a figure of a teenager. She gasped as Ben went deeper and they climaxed together. They held each other tight for a long time before sleeping, still wrapped in each other's arms; in the morning they made love again.

Anna nuzzled Ben's ear, "What made you come back?"

"There was no guard outside your room and I could not leave you unprotected all night." They both laughed and then Ben asked, "Are you okay now?"

"Oh yes, I certainly am. I know I took advantage of you Benjamin but I somehow knew…"

She stopped as Ben put his fingers on her lips.

"It's okay and, if that was taking advantage of me, then I'm the luckiest man on my planet and your Earth."

What Ben did not tell Anna was why he let it happen. He knew that Anna had had no sexual relationship since the day her family was slain, not even with Sebastian and although, he had severe misgivings, had put principles aside knowing it was just the one time and Anna would be free of her inhibitions.

Anna said, "I feel free and myself again. Maria said you made her human again and, so you have with me, also." She blushed and hugged him.

Ben was happy for her and just hoped Sebastian made a full recovery.

Anna said, "Maria warned me that some of the leaders on Umbria were against a peaceful settlement on Earth. Surely that cannot be true?"

Sadly, Ben shook his head. "Not all Umbrians who think that humans are slowly destroying Earth and would eliminate the human race. They are in the minority but some are masters and worse, the leader, The Grand Master, is the main aggressor. They forget that Umbrian's nearly destroyed themselves with contamination in the past. We were sent to integrate with the humans, which we have done but, being of similar genetics, we have had offspring with humans and the children of the mixed parentage have powers beyond that of the Umbrian's. Those who were sent, were instructed to help humans and bring the pollution under control. This is still the wish of the majority."

Anna shook her head. "It's all so unbelievable. So why have your people not attacked Earth?"

"Because they are still a long way from Earth. Let me explain. When Umbria broke free of its orbit and the gravitational pull, the strain was too great and a huge mass of the planet was torn away. Since that time, we have been travelling in space towards Earth. The reason we chose your planet was simply because it was nearer. Originally, we chose a benign sun, much deeper in space. Now, having lost most of our oxygen and our oceans, we need Earth to survive. Also, your sun has two or three more billions of years before it dies. We have been travelling to Earth through a wormhole, that is a projected vacuum in space, which is devoid of all matter. The hole in space enables our small spacecraft to travel at many times the speed of light. Each of these small spacecrafts can hold four or five people. Maria has probably told you that I am only part human myself and although Umbrians have a very similar genetic construction, the main difference is that the Umbrians developed many thousands of years before humans."

Before Anna had time to digest all this information, Ben carried on by saying, "After all that activity last night, I'm ravenous."

After all this extraordinary information, Anna pulled her thoughts together and enquired what he would like to eat.

"Would your staff have heard of a full English breakfast?" Ben asked.

"I'm sure they have." Anna said, smiling. "If not, you can enlighten them. We will have it on the terrace. It is still warm enough."

"Anna," Ben spoke her name with concern, "you and Sebastian are no longer safe in Croatia. I think you should both think about moving to a safer country."

Ben looked at her fondly. "I know what happened last night can never happen again but I am very fond of you and I cannot offer you much protection here. I want this for Maria too; I've never seen her so happy. I have some holdings in Spain and, if initially Sebastian could be persuaded to go there to convalesce, once there, we could possibly get him to stay full time. I could even try to get him a teaching post."

Anna squeezed his arm. "Benjamin Franklin, you're incorrigible."

"Me, never," he said.

Ten days later, Ben had packed and was ready to leave. He left mid-morning but instead of heading west, he went in the opposite direction. He had to assure himself that Maria and the children were okay.

When Ben arrived, Maria, Bunny and the children were about to leave for the convent where Maria had taken refuge many years before.

"You must come with us," she said. "I want the children to meet the nuns and it would be lovely if you were there, too."

Bunny did not look happy, but it was only a short visit and Ben was the father of the children.

Lunch was packed and they were soon on the road. The convent was about an hour's journey and before they realised it, they had parked the car and were at the gates of the convent.

Maria reached up and pulled a chain which rang a bell within the convent. Almost immediately, a robed figure approached the gates as their visit was expected. The nuns' eyes shone as they settled on Maria. From inside the convent, came the rest of the nuns and they all gathered around Maria and the children. A great fuss was made of Maria and the children and Ben and Bunny were greeted with kindness. The nuns were a little confused as to who was the father, Ben or Bunny. They were all welcomed into the courtyard and began to make their way to the massive doors that were the entrance to the main building. Maria looked across at the gardens and stopped to stare intently at a small, wizened figure, busily hoeing. Maria suddenly raced across the lawn and, picking up a stave rushed towards the tiny gardener, the stave raised in attack. Ben and Bunny looked on in horror and, turning to the nuns, Ben was amazed to see them smiling. The children were looking and actually laughing. Ben was beginning to think that he was in a dream. Just as Maria was about to smash her stave on the gardener's head, he turned and with a cry and, hoe in hand, he parried the blow. They both went into the attack and their "weapons," became a blur as they counter-attacked each other. Ben and Bunny then realised that they were evenly matched and had performed the same ritual many times before.

"Now we know," Ben whispered to Bunny, "the reason Maria is so damned good at Karate, or whatever it is they are doing."

The two opponents eventually stopped and bowed to one another.

"You have grown, little one," the gardener said.

"Tey Ling you have shrunk," Maria laughed.

At that point, another small figure emerged and came bustling across to Maria, throwing herself into Maria's arms with a shriek of delight.

"My little angel," she cried.

"My little petal," said Maria. "You are well?"

"Yes, yes," replied Petal Ling and, then looked across to the children. "Yours?" she breathed.

"Yes, indeed," Maria said proudly. "And this is Benji," she said shyly.

Ben was overcome to think that these two tiny people had taught Maria, as a young girl, to defend herself and, together with the nuns, cosseted and protected her.

He turned to the nuns. "Surely you must have condemned the fighting?"

"Of course, we would have condemned fighting," the nun replied, "but what Tey Ling was teaching Maria, all those years, was how to defend herself."

Ben coughed. "Of course," he said. Ben kept his thoughts to himself; the nuns could only see good in Maria and it was best left there. After all, when attacked, one starts off defending and, only as the last resort, attacks back.

They then entered the main hall in the convent and realised that the packed lunch would go to waste as the nuns had laid out a most sumptuous meal for all. After the meal, they were shown the beautiful but severe interior of the convent. Then they came to Maria's room which had been her home for so many years. Maria clutched Ben's arm, almost overcome with emotion. He looked round the room thinking how the nuns had looked after her all those years.

After looking inside, they then went out into the lovely garden that surrounded the whole of the convent. They were magnificent full of beautiful flowers and trees. The vegetable plots were laid out in immaculate rows, containing many types of fruit and vegetables. Tey and Petal followed behind, both of them bursting with pride at the words of praise they received.

It was eventually time to go but just as they were about to leave, Ben slipped into the convent and popped an envelope into the offertory box. He had noticed the state of disrepair of the convent and as an act of thanks and repayment for all the nuns had done, he had left a donation.

The journey back was an anti-climax, after all the excitement even the twins seemed subdued.

At last, the village came into sight and when they came back Ben gave Maria a hug and, turning to Bunny said, "I know they will be in safe hands."

"Yes," said Bunny, "but although I want to stay, what about your security on the journey back to England?"

Ben laughed. "You can drive me to the airport and see me on the plane if you like and of course, I'll be met at the other end."

It was now departure time and Ben knelt and pulled the twins to him. "You look after your mother," he whispered, "and make sure she does not get into too much trouble." Fredrika and Samuel clung to Ben's neck.

"Can't we come with, Daddy?"

"Soon, soon, we will all be reunited." Ben gave them one last hug, rose and quickly entered the waiting car. "Drive Bunny," he said, his voice thick with emotion. With a swift wave, Bunny drove away.

After driving in silence for some distance, Bunny looked at Ben. "You alright, boss?"

"Yes, of course," Ben said. "I am sad at leaving Maria and the children but at the same time, cannot wait to get back to Tessa. I imagine you have a very low opinion of me?"

"No, actually I have not," was Bunny's reply. "I am very fond of Maria but I know she has very strong feelings for you." Grinning wryly, he added, "So I am a little jealous but I realise you knew nothing about the birth of the twins."

Ben just nodded, his emotions torn between two women, the twins and the baby about to be born.

Tessa lay on her back, staring at the ceiling and it seemed to her that she had been this way forever. After the attack by the master, through his medium, although there had been no physical damage, it had taken all this time for her full recovery. Tessa was pleased that the medium also recovering and was now in the bed next to her. They had spent many an hour talking to one another. Tessa's thoughts were interrupted by her baby kicking and she let her thoughts drift to her baby and, once in contact she soothed her child's mind. She turned to the girl who had nearly killed her but now was one of her dearest friends.

"Lena, did you feel that kick the baby gave me?"

Lena smiled, "No, but your mind conveyed the thought."

Tessa began to think of Ben, she knew he was on his way back but his mind was elsewhere, probably thinking about work and she was unable to contact him mentally. Tessa knew of Ben's relationships with Maria and her sister Anna. She chuckled to herself, even Ben had his hang-ups. What Anna did not know, because of her intimate relationship with Ben, like Maria, her body was changing its genetic makeup whereby she would now be able to regenerate.

Tessa's thoughts were again interrupted and she sat up with a jolt; she felt Ben's presence.

"Where are you?"

"About a mile above you," came the reply. "I will be landing in about ten minutes and will be with you within the hour."

Tessa smiled, although Ben had only been away a few weeks, it had seemed like forever and she could not wait to hold him in her arms again. She turned to Lena, "Ben is almost home."

"I know. I think everyone of our kind in the centre knows also."

Tessa laughed, happy and glad that the dramas of the last few weeks were at last at an end.

Tessa and Lena continued to chat happily together about Ben and Lena's brother, Jon.

Time passed quickly and it seemed only a few minutes before the door burst open and Ben rushed in, his arms full of flowers. For the next few minutes, Lena wished she could have disappeared as Ben and Tessa hugged and kissed. Eventually, Ben looked up and said hello to Lena.

Lena looked across at Ben and Tessa and she could not forget that she had nearly caused their deaths and yet here they were treating her as a dear friend. She smiled shyly at Ben.

"I'm so glad you are safely back, Ben. Tessa has been driving everybody mad worrying about you."

Ben smiled, "And when are you two layabouts going to vacate your beds for more deserving people?"

"Well," Tessa answered, "I'm afraid I'm not allowed up until I've had our baby but Lena should be up in a few days and you will never guess who is coming to live in our community."

"That will be Jon," Ben laughed. "I knew he was coming."

The next few weeks were peaceful and Tessa was allowed up, albeit in a wheelchair and she and Ben were given a room to themselves where they spent most of the time, except for mealtimes.

"Ben," Tessa said one morning, "when are you going to return to work?"

Ben looked hurt. "Oh, trying to get rid of me already."

"No, be serious Ben. You cannot neglect your work forever, although you are looking a bit pale."

Ben joked. "Well, it's hardly sunbathing weather."

"Precisely, you need a holiday in the sun."

Ben was staggered. "What brought this on?" he asked.

"It was Aunt Agatha, she arranged everything. Maria is coming over with the children and she will stay with me while you, Julie and the children will be off to Bermuda for ten days holiday on a luxury yacht,"

Ben was shocked, "Who is going to look after the children?" he cried.

Tessa clapped her hands. "The children will be looked after and they will love it," she laughed. "There's a pool on board, deck games and a cinema if they want to relax. Oh, and the two nurses who looked after Lena will be on board."

"Stop," Ben said. "Does this happen to be my boat because if it is, it's a no go, as it's in dock for a refit."

"All done," said Tessa, triumphantly.

Ben gave in, "When does all this happen?" he asked.

"Tomorrow."

Ben shook his head in bewilderment. "I could quite happily wring Aunt Agatha's neck."

Ben knew he would enjoy the company of Julie's children and realised it would be great to spend time with his own two. He was suspicious of Aunt Agatha's motives and, why a cruise? He decided he would ask her himself. There was, however, little time to ask anyone anything as it was a mad rush to pack the cases and prepare in such a short time. The children were so excited, they were hopping around like rabbits. Julie's three had been on a boat but that was a pleasure cruise on the Thames. However, Ben's two had never been near a boat and could not wait for the thrill of actually setting foot on one.

Tessa looked at Ben. "It will be good for Samuel and Fredrika. They have not seen a lot of the outside world and Yvonne and Yvette are similar ages. Ivan, although older, will just so enjoy the holiday, and he can also keep an eye on the young ones sometimes, to give the two nurses a break."

The next day dawned and they were all off to the airport. With all their luggage, there was hardly room on Ben's private jet for all of them. They were soon airborne and this time it was Ben's two who had the advantage as they had just flown from Croatia the day before. After so little sleep the day before, the younger children were soon sound asleep, and tucked up by the two nurses Janette and Alice. Ben turned to his Aunt Agatha.

"Well," he demanded. "Why the sudden determination for us to all go on a cruise?"

Aunt Agatha was noncommittal. "You'll see," she said. "It will be beneficial to us all."

Ben relaxed; he could do with a break and the children would have a wonderful time.

They had been flying for nine hours and the children were now wide-awake and becoming restless. It was a relief to everyone, therefore when the pilot announced they would be landing at Bermuda Airport in ten minutes. On landing, they were through customs and on a coach, heading for the marina where the yacht was moored. Disembarking from the coach, they, with the adults carrying the luggage, walked along the catwalk of the marina. The children were in a fever of excitement. At last, they came to Ben's yacht, and amid a lot of oohs and ahs from not only the children, but the two nurses also, they boarded.

They had a quick meal after which Ben took the children to the stern where the pool was ready and waiting. Amid screams and shouts, the children jumped in. Ben threw in a beach ball and the children immediately started an improvised game of piggy in the middle. The older children were winning easily until the younger ones started to use their special abilities. After that, all chaos broke out, as the ball seemed to have a mind of its own. After a while, Ben decided that they had had enough and pointed out to them that although it was four o'clock in Bermuda, it was actually nine and their minds and bodies needed to adjust. It was not long before they were all in their cabins and sound asleep. They slept until early the following morning. The week continued in much the same vein with deck games and swimming mainly in the morning, fishing trips, sunbathing and the occasional film in the evening. Ben had made sure they had a stock of cartoons and nature films for them. When the children were in bed and asleep it became adult time. Janette and Alice, although keeping a keen eye on the youngsters, were themselves having a holiday of a lifetime.

It seemed to Ben that they had only been on board a few days and yet, here they were, nine days into the holiday and only two days left. The only person who didn't seem to be enjoying the holiday was Aunt Agatha. Ben was still puzzled about her reasons for the holiday. He decided to find her and find out why. He eventually found her in the wheelhouse in conversation with his captain who Ben noticed was looking very agitated. Neither of them knew Ben was there although he was only a couple of metres from them, he was hidden by the wheelhouse door. The captain was shaking his head very firmly, that he had to confirm it first with Mr Franklin. Ben was absolutely shocked when Aunt Agatha said that Ben had agreed with the coordinates that she had given him. Ben had known Aunt Agatha all his life and she had always been an honest and most upright person he knew. Yet, here she was telling a blatant lie. Ben stepped through into the wheelhouse.

"And just when did I agree to these new coordinates?" he asked quietly. The captain turned to Ben. "Ah, Mr Franklin," he said, relief written all over his face. Ignoring his Aunt Agatha, Ben looked at the captain.

"Captain Jones. What is this all about?"

Aunt Agatha had gone white and she looked at Ben shamefaced. The captain looked from Agatha to Ben.

"Your Aunt has asked me to set a course that will take us within the area of the Bermuda Triangle. I'm not superstitious but…"

Ben thought for a moment. The Bermuda Triangle was what many of the Umbrians chose as their destination on Earth because of its remoteness in the Pacific Ocean.

Ben smiled. "Captain Jones would you mind if I speak with my aunt alone for a minute?"

The captain nodded. "We are on auto," he informed Ben as he left the wheelhouse.

"Well?" he asked.

His Aunt shook her pretty little head. It always amazed Ben that someone who was at least 200 years old could look so fit and pretty as his aunt did.

"Well?" he said again. "Who is coming Auntie?"

"Somebody very important."

"I gathered that when you lied. Now, Aunt Agatha, do not take me for a fool. Who is coming?"

His Aunt hesitated and then said, "The Grand Mistress." For a moment Ben thought that his aunt was lying again but there was no reason for this.

"Why? Why would the Grand Mistress come to Earth?"

"She is very ill. She has been poisoned. It is thought that the Grand Master is responsible."

"Why?" Ben asked again."

"Some of the council members are set on ruling the Earth, whereas the female council members would prefer to have a union between the two planets. Now, you know Benjamin you must help."

Ben was still puzzled. "But why now?"

Aunt Agatha looked at Ben intently. "When you and Maria killed one of the council members, it caused an imbalance between the male and female council members and this gave the female members the upper hand. What was even more disastrous, the council member you killed was the brother of the Grand Master, which made him even more determined to wipe out the human race."

"But why bring her to Earth?"

"Because she is close to death and only your skills, added with the protection of the children's abilities, will give her a chance of survival."

Ben was horrified. "You are putting the children in great danger," he said angrily.

"No, no. The Mistress and her companions were not followed to Earth. The Umbrian nurses, who are devoutly loyal to the Mistress are in her chambers on Umbria, giving the impression that they are still attending her."

Ben was still extremely worried, for not only his own children, but also Julie's children.

Equally, he realised that with such a massive threat to all mankind he had no choice and he made his decision. He called for the captain and asked Agatha to return to her cabin assuring her that they would indeed head for the coordinates she had stated. As the captain entered, he looked at Ben.

"Are we heading for the Bermuda Triangle?"

"Joe, it was not prearranged," Ben explained

Joe smiled. "I knew your aunt was fibbing as soon as she said you had agreed. May I enquire as to why?"

Ben looked hard at his friend. "Joe, if I told you the world was under threat from aliens and I was one of those aliens and was attempting to stop the attack, tell me, honestly, your thoughts?"

It was Joe's turn with the hard look. "Ben, you cannot expect me to believe you, but you must have a reason for what you have just said."

"Okay, what if I am going to put everybody on the yacht in danger of their lives including my own children."

There was a long silence, then Joe said, "Well, against my judgment and all I think, I would have to believe you and accept what you are saying."

Would you support me in all I am attempting and would you be prepared to sacrifice your own life?"

This time there was no hesitation. "Ben, you, this boat and your family are my whole world."

"I will never forget the chance you took with me after my troubles."

"Good," said Ben, "now one more thing." He smiled. "The absolute proof for you that I am not a madman. Put your hand on my chest where you think my heart is."

Joe looked at Ben, a bit nonplussed, but did as he was bid. "Right, I can feel your heart beating."

"Now," said Ben, "put your other hand to the left and slightly lower."

Again Joe did as he was bid and, as his hand pressed Ben's chest, he went white and jumped back so fast he stumbled over a chair. Ben helped him up.

"That's just one of the differences," he said. "Are you okay, Joe?"

"No but if I had any doubts before they are gone now."

"One last thing," Ben said. "I told you because we will probably be lucky to come through this unscathed tomorrow. And if we do, it will be down to your skills. On a more serious note…"

"Stop," Joe put his fingers to his lips. "My lips are sealed forever."

Ben relaxed and grinned. "As we are on auto, I think we deserve a drink before we alter the coordinates." Touching glasses, Ben said, "Here's to success tomorrow."

"I'll second that." Joe replied, "Here's to you, Ben."

With the new course set, the yacht moved quietly through the night. Before they retired, Joe had one more question for Ben.

"Would your aunt have made friends with me, to persuade me to alter course?"

"Never in a million years," came the reply.

Joe grinned, sheepishly. "I like Agatha and I think she likes me too."

"I think she does," Ben smiled at Joe's shyness.

At first light, Joe had his crew and Ben's small retinue of staff standing below him on the quarterdeck. Ben stood quietly beside him.

"Good morning, everybody." Joe's voice boomed in the quietness.

"Good morning, Captain," came the response.

"I would assume that the majority of you know our destination today," Joe said, looking down from the bridge. There was a nervous murmuring and a shuffling of feet.

"Yes, we do," the boss replied, acting as spokesman.

"I'm here to say that if any of you do not wish to, or are not happy with our destination, we can have you airlifted off the yacht within the hour." There was silence and Joe let the silence drift on for a minute and then spoke again. "All I can tell you is that we are on a secret mission which could be potentially very dangerous." This time there were some mutterings from the assembly. Joe waited until the noise abated and then repeated the offer regarding the airlift off the yacht.

Again complete silence. Joe smiled, "Thank you for your loyalty and trust; now a little good news. Mr Franklin will be giving all crewmembers and staff a bonus on completion of this voyage." This produced smiles from everybody and there was a ripple of spontaneous applause. Ben's bonuses were always very generous and the element of danger now seemed more remote.

The meeting ended and the crew and Ben's people went about their daily routine. Before long, the children were stirring and before long shouts, screams and shrieks of laughter could be heard from the deck below. As was their daily routine, the children rushed up on deck and hung over the rail to study the sea. "They have gone," went up the cry.

Ben joined them. "What's gone?" he asked.

"The Dolphins," Samuel replied, and sure enough the large pod of Dolphins that had dogged the yachts course since they left harbour had vanished.

"Perhaps they have gone hunting for food." Ben let his mind drift, following the wake of the yacht and there, sure enough, were the Dolphins, but now some fifty miles astern. Ben did not dwell on it but he knew that the Dolphins had sensed the danger ahead and had fallen back.

Chapter 12

The day, however, had continued as usual with the children doing their best to injure themselves and their wards doing their best to keep them safe. It was mid-afternoon when suddenly Aunt Agatha screamed; everyone froze and they all looked round fearfully.

"Sorry," Agatha said and grabbing Ben's arm, whispered, "they are coming." Ben's blood ran cold and he turned to his staff. He asked them to take the children to the lounge and to stay there until he said otherwise. Soon, all was quiet on deck.

"How long," Ben asked. And as if in reply, the air pressure suddenly dropped and so did the temperature plummet. Looking ahead, Ben watched in shocked surprise as a conical shape appeared above the water and although it was at least ten miles in front of them, they could feel the water rising. The cone was causing the sea to form into a giant waterspout. Joe had already turned the yacht around and even with full power, the yacht was making no headway. Turning to face the cone, Ben saw a flash as the sun's rays reflected on an object emerging from the base of the cone. In the same instant, the cone which seemed to stretch right out into space, started to shimmer and then it disappeared completely. Joe swore as he struggled to keep the yacht on an even keel.

"What the hell was that?" he yelled.

Simply answered, "It was a hole in space." As Ben spoke, the object he had seen emerge from the cone, appeared above the yacht. It was itself cone shaped with a completely unbroken surface. It hovered above the deck then, with four feet appearing from nowhere, it settled on to the deck. As it did so, the side of the craft seemed to dissolve and a ramp formed from it, on to the deck. From the craft, two people emerged bearing a litter between them. A third, smaller figure followed. On the litter lay a woman who, although terribly emaciated must have been seven foot tall.

Ben shouted over the rising wind, “Follow me”, and led them down to the yacht’s small hospital. Ben had the woman transferred to a bed and told them to wait while he went up on deck to check on the situation. The only man in the group followed him.

“I must move the pod,” he said.

“That’s madness in this weather!”

The man said nothing but still followed. Once on deck, the man, despite Ben’s protestation, entered the craft. The ramp retracted and the craft rose. Within seconds, it disappeared. Ben glanced up at the bridge, Joe waved at him frantically pointing. Ben looked in the direction that Joe was pointing at, and immediately gave the order to batten down. Ten miles away, where the cone had first been sighted, the sea was now returning to normal, creating a massive wall of water drawing the yacht towards it. Ben joined Joe on the bridge and asked him if they would be able to ride it out. “If any vessel can,” Joe assured Ben, “then this baby is the one.”

Higher and higher the yacht rose on the water and just when the wave started to break over the bows threatening to swamp the vessel, she broke out on top of the wave and, in the next moment, they were plunging down into the trough. Eventually, the waves grew smaller and the sea moderated.

“Joe, I’m going down to see how our patient is. Keep everybody below decks for the time being.”

Entering the medical room, Ben looked down at the Grand Mistress. She was the joint leader of the planet Umbria but, right now she was near to death and was just skin and bone. The older of the two women who had accompanied her on the spacecraft, was bathing her mistress with ice-cold water, her face full of concern.

“What is your name?” Ben asked, as he was probing the Mistress’s body with his mind.

“Sophie,” the woman replied, her head coming up to look at Ben. Ben was surprised that he could not read her thoughts. Aunt Agatha had told Ben that one of the women was, in fact, human. *Of course,* Ben thought; he knew there had been accidents on a few of the landings on Earth resulting in the fear of the Bermuda Triangle. Sophie must have been the result of one of those accidents and, having survived had been taken back to Umbria. With no Umbrian able to read her mind, she was perfect to care for Venus. Also Ben looking at Sophie realised how similar to Maria she was, the same dead eyes and the same lithe and wary walk. He turned his thoughts to concentrate on Venus. Deeper he went, then in her stomach he found it, it was more than a poison, it was a living organism. It may have been minute when it arrived in her stomach, but now it was the size of Ben's hand. The problem now was extracting it from her body. "Sophie," Ben asked. "Her name is Venus," she said. With his mind he spoke her name. The response was immediate.

"Benjamin Franklin, remove that thing from my body. I know I'm too weak for anaesthetic so you will have to do it with your mind." Ben immediately started to enter her body, relaxing it as he entered, hoping he would relax the thing also. "Enough," Venus said. "Now, get it out."

Ben concentrated and Venus gasped as a thin slit appeared on her stomach. She only gasped once and then relaxed into what Ben guessed was a self-imposed trance. Longer and longer the slit grew until Ben was satisfied. He put on surgical gloves and put his hands in the slit then made a small aperture into her actual stomach and gently eased the thing out. Fortunately, it appeared to be in a state of comatose. Ben held it while he spent a few minutes concentrating to reseal her. He whispered to the ship's doctor, "Put her on a high energy drip."

Ben then made his way back to the deck. He looked at the thing he was holding, glad that he had on surgical gloves. The thing looked like a giant slug with six suction pads. Reaching the deck, Ben breathed in the salt air and the spray wet his face. The salt spray also wetted the slug and its skin boiled. Ben rushed to the side to throw it overboard but, from its pads talons appeared, piercing Ben's gloves and his skin. He felt the poison immediately coursing through his body and started to collapse. As he did, a small body grabbed the slug from him and jumped overboard.

"No," Ben screamed. "Agatha, no." He then slipped into unconsciousness. Minutes later, Ben awoke, the doctor standing over him, syringe in hand.

"That took a massive dose of antibiotics," the doctor told him.

"Aunt Agatha?" Ben asked.

The doctor shook his head. She just seemed to disappear." he said, sadly. Ben could feel the boat-altering course and his thoughts turned to Joe.

Ben was carried down to his room where he was told to stay. He drifted off to sleep only to be woken a few minutes later by Fredrika, shaking his shoulder.

"Fred, what's the matter?"

"It's Sam. We heard Aunt Agatha scream and left our bodies to find her and help her. We found her but could not wake her." Fred gave a sob. "Sam wouldn't leave her and now I cannot find him."

Ben hauled himself upright and swung his legs to the floor. His legs felt like jelly but, with supreme effort he got himself up on deck. Going to the yacht's side, he gripped the handrail hard, mainly to keep himself upright. Casting his mind in every direction across the vast ocean, he was unable to sense his son. He must be in Aunt Agatha's mind otherwise, he would have found him. He looked up at Joe and shook his head. Joe understood, if Ben could not trace his son, there was no chance. He opened the bridge door and called down.

"What now, Ben?"

Ben hesitated; he felt so weak. "We will return to port and conduct an aerial search," he said.

Fred was crying. "Surely we should keep searching?" Ben held her close.

"Sam is out there somewhere and we will have him back in no time."

Fred looked at her father. "Daddy, you don't know how, do you?"

Ben said firmly. "We will find him Fred, now go and join the others and let your dad do the worrying."

Ben leant against the rail, the fresh air was certainly doing him good and he was beginning to feel better. He had an idea and called the doctor on the ship's phone.

"Where are you?" the doctor asked. "I imagined you would still be asleep."

"No, I had to come on deck. Is the Mistress responding to the antibiotics?"

"Very slowly. The poison must have saturated her body."

"Right," said Ben, "then let's saturate her body with salt. Put her on a saline drip and try to get a solution of salt water down her throat." Ben explained to the doctor how he was now feeling so much better after breathing in the salt air. "Let's face it, if the salt destroyed the slug it should do the same to the poison."

"I'll set the drip up now and try to get her to swallow some salt water and hope your theory works." It was a very sombre return journey back to port and everyone was relieved when they finally docked. Ben spent a further week conducting a search, but to no avail. He was dreading returning to the centre, knowing he would have to face Maria with such grim news. He had hoped that Sam would have freed his mind long since and freed him of this awful burden. Having left the yacht with everyone still on board, he flew back to the centre.

Maria seemed like a stranger to him. She looked at him with raw hatred in her eyes.

"You bastard!" she shouted at him. "You took the children away on that holiday for the sole purpose of rescuing that woman, knowing you were putting them in extreme danger." Ben tried to talk but Maria stared at him as if he was nothing. "You men," she raged, her voice rising, "you do this to people. You talk of love! So how much do you love Samuel and poor Fred who is breaking her heart for her brother? What are you doing here?" she ranted. "Why are you not in Bermuda, still searching?"

"I returned to explain," he said and then wished he hadn't spoken.

Maria went white and she clenched her fists. "Explain?" she whispered. "How do you explain the complete betrayal of all those that you are supposed to love. You get back to Bermuda and find our son. I cannot harm you, that would be too easy, but I can hate you!!!"

Before Ben could say another word, Maria was gone. Ben had already booked a flight back to Bermuda and was hoping that Maria would have gone with him. However, he knew if things went wrong, he would fear for her sanity. He had already seen his beloved Tessa and promised to return as soon as possible. He set the alarm and lay back on his bed. He had been hoping to hear from Joe who had promised to ring day or night if there were any new developments. Ben fell into a restless sleep.

The next thing he knew, he was staring down at the bodies of her parents and the twins. Maria was standing at the bottom of stairs looking up with hatred in her eyes.

"You," she shouted. "You have stolen their minds." She raised the gun in her hand and started to fire at him.

Ben screamed with grief. "No, no, I have not Maria. I have not."

"Liar," she said, and came over to where he was lying on the floor, covered in blood. She knelt beside him. "You have killed my family," she cried, with her eyes full of hate boring into him.

"Ben," she shouted and started to shake him. "Benjamin, Ben," Ben opened his eyes, and he was staring into his mother's anxious face. He was back in his bed.

"Benjamin," his mother said, "it's all right now." She held him close and Ben clung to her, it was as if he was a child again. After a while, he relaxed and lay back. Louisa looked down at her son. She gave a small smile. "You have woken the whole clinic," she said, "not with your shouting, though that was loud enough but that mind of yours. Nearly everybody in the clinic shared some part of your dream. Are you all right now, Ben?" Ben nodded, unable to speak, the memory of the nightmare still strong in his mind. Louisa turned as there was an urgent rap on the door. A nurse poked her head round the door and beckoned Louisa. Louisa and the nurse exchanged a whispered, quick conversation. Although they guarded their minds, Ben was wide-awake and he sensed Tessa's name.

"What," he said. "What was that about Tessa?"

"She has given birth, Ben, and everything is okay." She hugged him. "You have a baby boy," she said joyfully.

Despite Louisa's protestations, Ben got up and went to Tessa's room.

"Hello you," Tessa said sleepily. "I thought you had gone to Bermuda." Ben kissed her gently whilst looking at his son in the cot beside her.

"Was it my dream?" He asked. She smiled up at him. "Yes," she said, "but he was overdue anyway."

"We have not decided on a name," Ben whispered as the baby stirred.

"Oh yes, we have," Tessa said. "We will call him Mars, the god of war."

"Why?"

"Because," Tessa said, smiling happily, "his daddy is always in conflict with someone or something." Ben smiled despite the weight on his mind.

"You are right. Mars is a good name but let's hope he has more peace than I have had these past few years."

"Ben, you must go and get some rest."

"No, I'm off to the airport," Ben replied. "I will catch up on sleep on the flight back to Bermuda."

Ben kissed Tessa and Mars a sad goodbye and was gone.

"Be careful," Tessa called as he left.

Ben gathered up his holdall and made his way to the airport where his plane was ready for take-off. He managed to get some restless sleep on the plane but felt sluggish as he hurried from the terminal building to meet Joe. All Ben's worries concerning his son Samuel would have disappeared in a trice had he been able to contact him in the first half hour after Agatha jumped overboard.

Samuel was aware that he had to act quickly when he reached Aunt Agatha. She was dying, not from the poison as the salt water had rid her body of the poison. She was, however, immediately in danger of drowning. Samuel let his mind drift into Agatha's and pushed her brain into activity. Agatha coughed, spewed up lots of seawater and began to flounder about. Her eyes flew open and, under Samuel's instructions, began to tread water.

"I have never swum," she gasped. "Is that you, Samuel?"

"Yes, Aunt Agatha. How are you?"

Agatha giggled. "Oh, on cloud nine, thanks to you, my darling nephew." Agatha looked around her, the sea was calm and she could see quite a distance.

"I think we are in hot water," Agatha prided herself on her knowledge of human expressions.

"Do you mean we are in danger, Auntie?"

"Yes, we are."

Samuel let his mind drift; he sensed the Dolphins close by. He wondered why they were not coming closer and then he knew it must be the poison; there must be still traces flowing from her body. Agatha was now tiring rapidly and Samuel was becoming frightened for both of them. Suddenly, as if in answer to their fears, Agatha's body started to rise. Agatha became quite excited.

"Samuel, the clone—it's returned." Samuel's mind relaxed a little. At last their danger was receding. The small spacecraft had risen from beneath Agatha and she was now laying on top of the craft. The hatch beside her opened and the clone appeared. It picked her up and took her into the craft.

"Thank you," she said. Being a clone with no emotions, it did not respond to Agatha's thanks. However it had a brain and intelligence and it was confused. Having deposited the Mistress aboard the yacht it should have destroyed itself and the craft but, it was programmed to protect all Mistresses and Agatha was a Mistress, albeit a novice. Both Agatha and Samuel sensed the confusion.

"What now," Agatha asked Samuel; he did not reply immediately. When in the water, he noticed the Dolphins had returned and now the leader of the pod was circling the craft. Samuel sensed that the Dolphins wanted him to do something and then he understood that it wanted them to follow.

The clone took a lot of persuading, still confused by the conflicting commands. Eventually, though, it agreed but kept the craft well underwater whilst it followed the Dolphins. Agatha fell asleep and Sam, still inside her mind rested. The Dolphins raced through the water following their leader. On and on they went until they gradually started leaving the pod and then there was just the old bull to follow. Soon after they slowed, the clone informed them that they were in shallow water. It told them there was a small island and asked them to leave. Sam pleaded with the clone to stay and told it that there was no need for it to destroy itself or its craft. The clone repeated itself and again asked them to leave; they had no option but to leave.

Agatha conveyed a thought to Sam telling him not to fret, saying the clone is just a computer in a human form. She then splashed her way through the shallow water to the shore. Still weak she sat on a ridge of sand left by the tide. She looked out to sea. The small craft had disappeared but the old Dolphin was still there and it seemed to be looking straight at her. Thoughts sprung into her mind telling her that the old bull had, as a host the Ka of John Franklin and was still living because of this. Inside his mind, Sam had a thought. "He is saying we must contact Dad. Grandfather thinks I've been away from my body too long."

At that moment in time, Ben was sound asleep on the plane. His eyes suddenly opened and his body jerked upright.

"Agatha," he shouted.

The stewardess rushed to him. "Are you all right, Mr Franklin?"

Ben smiled at the young woman. "Sorry, I must have been dreaming. Could you please get me a coffee?" Ben relaxed and let his mind race to find the source of the thought and where it was coming from. The plane landed shortly afterwards and Ben was through customs and out of the building looking for Joe who was waiting with a car. There was a shout and he saw Joe waving.

He rushed towards Joe, anxious to give him the good news. Before Ben had a chance to speak, Joe blurted out, "Samuel is waking up." Ben was so relieved he could have hugged Joe.

"What's your news?" Joe asked.

"I am almost sure Agatha is alive. I have had her Ka visit me."

"Surely, you know if she is alive or not?"

"I'll explain in the car. Has Sam said anything?"

"I don't know. I was here at the airport when the message came through," Joe explained. "The nurse just said that he was stirring and colour was coming back into his face."

Ben desperately hoped that Sam was all right, he knew how long Sam had been away from his body. He tried to explain about Agatha. Joe half understood and, like Ben, just hoped and prayed that they were both safe. Joe put his foot down and they were soon approaching the marina. Parking the car, they ran to where the yacht was moored. Ben jumped aboard and hurried down to his own cabin where Sam was tucked up in the middle of Ben's bed. Ben stopped in the doorway. Sam looked so frail and vulnerable in the big bed. Crossing the room, Ben looked down at his son.

"Sam," he whispered. Not daring to enter his son's mind. Then to Ben's enormous relief, Sam opened his eyes and spoke.

"Hello, Dad. Have I been away from me for long?"

"Long enough. It was two weeks ago when your Aunt Agatha jumped overboard," Ben said grinning.

Sam's face showed concern at the mention of Agatha's name. "She is on an island and she is quite poorly."

"How on earth did she manage to get on an island?" Ben asked, totally amazed.

Sam explained how the clone came to Agatha's rescue.

"Thank god, the clone was programmed to protect all Mistresses." Ben said with relief. "Now to find what island the clone left Aunt Agatha at."

"It was not Bermuda, Dad, it was a tiny uninhabited island and the clone was determined not to be detected. We travelled a long way." Joe was standing in the doorway and overheard what Sam had said.

Joe pondered for a moment then asked two questions; one to Ben and one to Sam.

"Sam, how long do you think you were in the craft and Ben, what speed is the craft capable of?"

He unfortunately only got vague answers. Ben only knew it was fast and Sam said they were ages in the craft. Sam went quiet and held his hand to his head.

"Are you all right?" Ben asked.

"Yes," he said, looking up. "Agatha said we travelled for about six hours."

Joe shook his head in disbelief, "You spoke to Agatha?"

"Yes," Sam said, "and she said to tell you she is okay. She said she thought she was on a tiny atoll amongst the islands of the Bahamas."

Joe already had the yacht out to sea and he now went up to change course.

"How can she be okay?" he asked.

Ben shook his head. "That puzzles me too. It's been over a week since she jumped overboard and she has been poisoned and nearly drowned. Dehydration must have set in due to the amount of salt water she's swallowed, so I've no idea."

With the yacht at full power, they travelled south- westwards at sixty knots. They estimated that it would take ten hours to reach their destination. Whilst Joe busied himself, staying on course and keeping the speed high, Ben lay on his bed next to his son and at last, got a few hours of peaceful sleep. Before he slept, however, he had rung Louisa and told her the good news. He spoke quickly to Tessa, who sounded fine, and was delighted that Sam and Agatha were both alive. Ben did not have the courage to speak to Maria and left it to Tessa to inform her.

Ben slept for ten hours and only woke up when Joe gently shook him.

"Sorry," he said, "we have reached the islands and all we have to do now is find the one where Agatha is." Joe then added that big old Dolphin is back.

Waking with a start, Sam exclaimed, "Dad, that old Dolphin has the Ka of grandfather."

Ben was astonished at Sam's information, but after thinking about it, was not so surprised. His father loved the Earth's oceans and had probably found the old Dolphin swimming aimlessly and obviously close to death and had entered his Ka and restored the old bull's mind and body. Ben assumed the Dolphin must have been swimming close to the yacht when they had started on the ill-fated holiday. The Dolphin was now swimming in front of the yacht, which was almost stationary. Ben tried to make contact with his father but his mind was too reduced by the battering it had received in the battle at the clinic. The energy in his left was used to contact Agatha. Ben looked at the Dolphin and on impulse waved. The Dolphin responded immediately surging up out of the water then dived back again and started to move away from the yacht. Ben turned to Joe and told him to follow the Dolphin. Joe quickly responded and soon they were approaching a small island ahead. Ben and Joe searched the shoreline with binoculars and there was Aunt Agatha sitting on a rock eating what looked like a fish. They were both nonplussed and wondered how Agatha had managed to catch it. They dropped anchor, jumped into an inflatable and made for the shore. Agatha waved to them.

"He showed you the way then," she said, pointing at the Dolphin. There were several more fish drying in the sun and a bottle of water close to where Agatha was sitting. Completely dumbfounded, Ben and Joe just stared at Agatha who now looked quite well and with a nice suntan.

"It was John," she explained. "He threw me the fish and I was able to make a fire. There were numerous glass and plastic bottles and cartons on the shoreline and I found a pool of fresh water, over there," she said, pointing behind her.

There was a squeaking from out to sea and they turned in time to see the Dolphin leap from the water and in a great arc returned to the sea and was gone.

They returned to the yacht, Ben was quiet as he realised his father had helped him for the last time. He was very sad as it could be thousands of years before his father returned as another being. Ben shook himself and put his arm around his son. Joe was insisting on carrying Agatha because she still was looking quite weak from the effects of the poison and only had the use of one arm. The return journey was a joyous one. Ben had his son back and Joe had his Agatha. When they docked in Bermuda, Joe and Agatha had an announcement to make.

"I'm staying here with Joe."

"We are engaged," Joe said happily.

"Good for you," Ben smiled. "I hope you will stay on as my captain Joe."

"I was hoping you would say that," Joe said. "I will happily stay on."

They were back at the dock late that night. Ben had already booked a flight for the morning and they were able to relax at last. Samuel and the two nurses who would be returning with Ben had retired for the night. Sam who was now his old self wanted to stay up but was finally persuaded to go to bed. Ben settled Sam into bed and was returning to the lounge when the phone rang; it was Maria.

"How is Samuel?"

"He is fine," Ben replied.

"That is good," she said and the phone went dead. Ben wondered if he would ever be forgiven. He joined Joe and Agatha for a drink and then decided to retire himself.

Chapter 13

Next morning, although Ben was up very early, the two nurses were already preparing breakfast for everybody. Ben smiled at them.

"Good morning, Janette. Good morning, Alice." They were, of course, the same two who had nursed Lena through that terrible time.

They all had breakfast and then it was off to the airport. Agatha hugged Sam until he squeaked. The bond between them was very strong and for this reason, Agatha's only regret that she would not be returning with them. After all the goodbyes, hugs and handshakes it was time for take-off. With a final wave, they boarded the plane and were soon airborne.

It occurred to Ben that he would be really jetlagged having been back and forth from England in less than three days. It was evening again by the time he arrived home.

Maria was waiting and without a word to Ben she took Samuel to her arms as if he was a baby and whisked him away. Ben was exhausted and miserable. He went to see Tessa but she and the baby were sound asleep. Going to his room, he flopped on his bed and was asleep before his head touched the pillow. He woke to find he had slept for twelve hours. Again he went to Tessa and Mars and this time he was lucky. Both were awake and Tessa held her arms up to him. He held her for a long time and gradually felt the tension leave him.

"I thought you had hibernated," Tessa murmured into his ear, nibbling it at the same time.

"Ouch," he said. "That hurt."

"Well," she replied. "I have hardly seen you since Mars was born and before that you were off slaying our enemies."

"True," he said. "Now, move over a little so I can snuggle up beside you." Tessa obliged, and laid there until baby Mars needed a change of nappy and his tummy a refill.

"Off you go," she said. "I'm sure there are a dozen things you need to do."

Ben grinned. "Well, I want to go to see Mum and the Grand Mistress and they will probably be together chatting." He moved through the corridors and on arrival at the ward occupied by Venus, there was his mother. As Ben entered, Louisa jumped up and hugged him.

"I'll speak to you later, Benjamin" she said and left the room.

Ben looked down at Venus and was pleased to see that now the poison had gone, her recovery was remarkable. Her personal guard Sophie, stood at the bedside and the young nurse was sitting quietly in the corner of the room.

"Is all well with you Benjamin Franklin?" Venus inquired.

"Please call me, Ben."

Venus smiled at her assent, replying, "You must call Venus."

He had many questions to ask and was pleased that if they were informal together it would make the questions a lot easier to ask. He sat by her bed, still finding it hard to believe how different she appeared from the skeletal figure he had seen just a few weeks ago. They spoke vocally and sometimes with their minds, when their throats got dry from so much talking. Ben asked the first question.

"Why did the Grand Master try to poison you?" Venus smiled.

"That was your fault Ben." Ben felt his jaw dropping.

"My fault," he exclaimed. "How could it have anything to do with me?"

"The Grand Master sent his brother to Earth to eliminate your whole family but, instead you managed to eliminate him."

"The Master was the one with the drone, living in Romania?" Ben asked.

"Yes," Venus replied. "But how did you manage to destroy the Master?"

"I was not the one who killed him," Ben said.

"Who then," Venus demanded.

"It was my companion, Maria."

"An Umbrian?" Venus asked.

"No, Maria was totally human but is now, half Umbrian."

Venus was perplexed. "How is that possible against such a superior mind?"

Ben explained about Maria's total lack of reception from another mind. Venus was amazed and found it hard to believe. Ben went on saying, that being unable to penetrate Maria's mind the Master was also unable to detect her presence and that together with the Master's arrogance, that caused his downfall.

"You have saved me," Venus went on, "but I understand from your mother that it has been at great cost to yourself."

Ben shook his head sadly. "I'm afraid so. Maria will not allow me near my children and she now also despises me. In saving you, I put my children in extreme peril, although I did not realise just how dangerous the rescue was. Maria does not accept that seeing the situation through a mother's eyes."

Venus apologised. "I am so dreadfully sorry Benjamin. We can only hope that Maria will eventually understand and find forgiveness."

Ben decided he must ask the question uppermost in his mind.

"What is the intention of the Grand Master and the Grand Council?"

Venus looked at him. "I think you know the answer, Ben."

"Not exactly. Will the Umbrians try to attack Earth?"

"It's very possible," Venus said, "even though the Grand Master suffered a severe setback when his brother was slain."

Recalling the attack on his father, Ben asked, "Would the Umbrians use their minds to control humans?"

"They should not, but we both know the Grand Master's brother was controlling the minds of humans and Umbrians."

Venus said, "I do not know when the attack will come but the Grand Master will show no mercy, he holds sway over the council, mainly because of the way humans are destroying Planet Earth with pollution and destruction of rainforests. But he knows that the Umbrians very nearly destroyed Umbria, thousands of years ago the same way, pollution. I will help all I can as will the majority of Umbrians including half Umbrians such as yourself."

"Thank you for your support, there are questions that I need to ask you but that can wait until you are feeling stronger. My father told me a lot about Umbria and its tragic history but there is a lot of detailed information that I'm sure I could learn from you with regard to the building of crystal domes, for example. Pollution is already very bad here on Earth and we really need to take drastic steps for the future. We Umbrians are fortunate to have that knowledge of the effects that pollution can have and I think even after all those humans know, their reaction to the catastrophe it can cause, has not jerked them into action."

Venus said, "It will be a while before I am up and about but I'm sure I will be strong enough to answer all you need to know soon."

Venus turned to Sophie. "Show Benjamin my legs." Sophie carefully lifted the sheet covering Venus's legs. What lay beneath was horrific. Her legs were almost skeletal, and showed nearly every bone.

"The poison did that?" Ben asked, the horror sounding in his voice.

"Yes," Venus replied. "That is how my whole body would have looked had I not escaped. The poison would have kept me alive until only my heart was beating."

Ben shuddered and looked at her legs again. This time he noticed that new flesh was beginning to show through.

"I will be walking within a month," Venus said, but added with a grimace, "I will be keeping my legs covered."

Ben rose to go. "I will come and talk again," he said.

Before Ben reached the door, Venus asked, "Will you walk Sophie to the village. I would like some papers and magazines and also some bars, that delicious chocolate humans adore."

"I will be fine with Lucy, my nurse and protector looking after me in Sophie's absence."

Ben smiled. Venus definitely had a very sweet tooth.

"I will be happy that the walk will do me good."

With that, the pair of them set off on the mile walk to the village. It was a warm and balmy day and Ben was pleased to stretch his legs. He knew nothing about Sophie and was very much surprised when, on gently probing her mind, found himself totally rejected. Sophie had the same mind block as Maria. He looked her up and down and thought how similar to Maria she was, even to the eyes which, although a different colour, had the same dead look that Maria's had when he first saw her. They soon reached the village and walked along High Street. He could see that Sophie was intrigued by the shops and he let her gaze in wonder at the articles displayed. Ben's curiosity was aroused and he was now sure she was human, although she had come from Umbria. Coming to the paper shop, they entered and Ben helped Sophie pick out the newspapers, magazines and chocolate that he thought Sophie would enjoy. Sophie had some money but Ben insisted on paying the bill and they started back.

Looking at his watch, Ben realised that Fredrika and Samuel would be coming out of school. He and Maria had always picked the children up together but that was not going to happen now. The school was on the outskirts of the village and looking back, Ben could see the cars lined up for the children who had come from far and wide. Closer to the village was The Black Horse Inn where mothers would often gather, having tea and chatting whilst waiting for the children.

Ben also noticed that although it was a warm sunny day, all the tables were empty. He soon realised why. Outside there must have been twenty motor bikes and from inside the Inn there came a loud raucous noise from the bikers. Ben then saw Maria walking towards the school. As he stood watching, she suddenly changed direction and walked inside the inn. The noise inside the bar stopped and after a minute Maria walked out holding a mug, going to a table, she sat and took a sip of the steaming liquid. Ben stopped and waited, sure as he was. Three men walked out, obviously bikers. They walked to her table and sat. One of them touched Maria and a second later was writhing on the floor. The other jumped up and made a grab for her.

"Sophie," Ben yelled, "go back to the centre and get security here," and with that he charged across, waving his arms.

"Enough," he roared. The men totally ignored him. He threw a punch and was rewarded by a grunt of pain. Then Sophie was standing shoulder to shoulder with Maria as more bikers poured out the pub. Maria yelled at him.

"Run, Benji." Wild horses would not move him then and he threw another punch and was then floored by a blow on his jaw. He watched in amazement as the two women floored another three. More bikers emerged from the pub. He also noticed a man in the entrance who was just staring. Ben took out a pencil-like object and twisting it aimed it at the man who turned, looked at Ben and fell to the floor. Immediately, the bikers backed away with shocked looks on their faces. They looked at Ben and the two women who had floored five of them. Their leader held his hands up.

"What happened," he asked. "We never look for trouble and would never attack women."

"I believe that man over there is a mass hypnotist. Anyway, I would disappear. I think I can hear a police siren."

The biker looked at Ben.

"You're not pressing charges?" he exclaimed.

"No," Ben said with a smile. "Let's say you were under the influence and it was not lager."

"Thanks mate," he said and he shouted, "let's move it." and they were on their bikes and gone.

Maria thanked Sophie with admiration in her eyes, and then went to Ben and helped him up.

"Benji, are you okay?" she said giving him a hug as she got him to his feet.

"I am fine, Maria," he smiled and hugged her back.

"Now," he said. "We need to get him," pointing to the culprit, "back to the centre for questioning."

Ben was on cloud nine; his Maria had forgiven him. They picked the children up together and with Sophie, they returned to the centre.

Part 2

Chapter 14

Ben, now in a better frame of mind grinned at Tessa. "I was aware that somebody was reading my thoughts. You know of Andorra situated between Spain and France? Well, what you probably do not know is that we have a holiday home there."

"Really?" Tessa said very surprised.

"Yes, when Dad was younger he loved to ski and Andorra was the place he chose to build a winter holiday home. Mum and Dad spent many happy holidays there. Anyway, the villa is enormous and has several acres of land surrounding it."

"Has it stood empty?" she asked.

"No, it has been well looked after and used as holiday lets, which I have now cancelled. Currently, the whole site is full with my building team who are constructing a new clinic."

"You have been busy," Tessa commented.

"It's a vast project," Ben replied, but refrained from going into detail.

"It could take several different directions," he explained and although Tessa's curiosity was piqued, Ben would not expand on what he had already told her.

"Wait and see," he said.

Tessa was outraged. "Benjamin Franklin is a total secretive monster," and throwing her hands up in mock despair, took the tray and left.

Ben having decided on his initial course of action, rang his accountant Toby Byne.

Toby was a Scot and, with Ben's money lived up to the reputation Scots have with money.

Toby had been with Ben from the beginning and through the hard years when Ben was still developing his various ideas, it was Toby who had kept their heads above water. Toby was delighted to hear from Ben.

"I thought you had retired," he remarked. Ben laughed at the gentle sarcasm.

"Several have tried to," he said.

Toby went quiet at Ben's remark; he knew that behind the joviality of his voice his boss was making a statement of fact. Toby also knew this was not a social call.

"Is this line secure, Ben?" he asked.

"It is now," he said. The call was now scrambled to all bar the two of them.

"Toby," Ben asked, "how much disposable income, have I at this moment in time?"

Toby showed off his genius. "As of this morning," he said, "you could make a cheque out for 350 billion euros."

Ben made a rapid calculation. "That might not be enough," he said. There was a gasp at the other end of the line.

"Are you thinking of buying a country?" Toby choked. Ben chuckled.

"Not exactly," Ben replied and he went on to roughly explain his plans. Toby was awed, dumbstruck and horrified.

When he recovered the power of speech, he said, "You will have us all bankrupt."

Ben spoke to his old friend quietly. "I mean to do this Toby but I think I will need more money at my disposal." There was silence while Toby digested Ben's words.

"There is a way," Toby said, after another long silence.

"Tell me how, my good friend."

"It's as if you know," Toby questioned.

"Know what," he said, puzzled.

"World Wide Motors increased their offer for a majority shareholding in Franklin Motors."

"How much?" Ben asked.

It was Ben's turn to gasp. "That would nearly bankrupt them."

"They are quite desperate," Toby explained.

Ben reflected. World Wide Motors consisted of all the major motor companies before he took the lion's share of the market with his electric vehicles which were dearer to buy but could do 120 miles with one charging, and at a fraction of the cost. Now, the oil companies had joined WWM and they together had the finance to put up the ante. They must be desperate, to offer that sort of money.

"Toby, tell them 800 billion and it is a deal."

"They will not accept that," Toby said immediately.

"I know but they will wonder why, if I do not push for more." Having enquired on a few other matters he said bye and hung up.

He returned to outlining his plans. He then rang the agents he always used for land and building purchases.

"Good afternoon," he said. "Benjamin Franklin here. May I speak with," he looked up quickly at his file, "Mr Collins, please?"

"I am sorry Mr Franklin. Mr Collins is in a conference at the moment."

A man's voice interrupted. "Hello, George Collins speaking, sorry about that we have a temp at the moment."

"Okay," Ben said, and then immediately began to talk to George for over an hour. George's first reaction was one of disbelief.

"Mr Franklin, how much land do you want to purchase?"

Ben chuckled. "Please call me Ben," he said, "and, with regard to the land purchase, what I have told you is just the start. Can your firm manage the purchase? I will expect the prices to be kept tight and that also applies to your good selves."

"We certainly can, although I will have to increase staffing levels in Madrid."

The rest of the call was spent on details of where and the amount of land needed in various locations.

Ben hung up feeling very tired, realizing that the large lunch he had eaten had not helped. He fell asleep and, for once, his dreams were pleasant. He dreamed of Tessa, Maria and, of course the children, with them all relaxing in the paradise he was about to build. He awoke to the sound of the phone ringing.

"Hello Toby," he said, recognizing the number. Yawning. He asked, "Any joy?"

Toby laughed. "They eventually agreed to 760 billion and I said I would confirm the figure with you."

"Well done, Toby," Ben said. They spoke some time on details and conditions of sale, and ended their conversation with Toby promising to send the sale agreement by fax the following day.

That is enough for today, Ben thought to himself, and leaving the office he went to have a quiet chat with Tessa and see his son.

He slept well that night and was up early. He headed for Venus's room and continued his chat with her.

"You heard about yesterday," Ben asked.

"Indeed I did," Venus replied.

"Tell me about Sophie," Ben asked. "If she is a human, is she not?"

"Yes, she is. On one of our journeys to Earth, the wormhole destroyed a yacht and although the parents were lost to the sea, we were able to save the baby and from a tiny bracelet she was wearing, we knew her name and she was assigned to me.

"Initially, I was her guardian but now her roles are somewhat reversed and, and of course she was trained to protect me well."

His curiosity satisfied, he turned to the subject of the Crystals and asked Venus many questions about their construction. When he had gleaned a huge amount of detail from her, she became tired. Ben was ushered from the room by his mother.

"Enough Benjamin," Louisa said firmly. "Venus must rest now."

Ben guiltily conceded and left Venus to have a well-deserved rest.

He went to the canteen for lunch and there he found Tessa and Mars with Maria, Fredrika and Samuel.

"Hello," he said and pulling up a chair, he squeezed in beside them. "I am off to Cornwall," he told them.

The two women looked, stopped eating and stared at him. In unison, they both said, "Where?"

"Cornwall," he said. "You know that place in southwest England."

"When?" Tessa asked.

"Tomorrow, at first light."

"Who is going with you?" Maria asked, already mentally packing an overnight bag.

"Nobody is going with me," Ben answered. "I'm only going for the day. I want to look at the Eden Project."

"You cannot go alone," Tessa said. Maria nodded in full agreement.

"For goodness's sake," Ben exploded. "I am not a child." To his annoyance, they both looked at each other knowingly. He was about to get really annoyed when Venus entered his mind.

"Ben. Lucy would like to go with you. Would you mind?"

After Ben had left the room, they were quite shocked and silent for a while but soon came to the same conclusion. Venus would not put Lucy in danger. This made them wonder about Lucy. All they knew was that she had arrived with Venus, on Earth.

Ben was unsure but eventually grudgingly agreed. Tessa, who had turned into Venus's thoughts, was not happy.

"She is only a child," she said. And enlightened Maria of her thoughts, she had had with Venus.

"I'm only going for a day, and I am taking my plane, what could possibly go wrong."

Tessa and Maria said nothing. As far as they were concerned, Venus was putting the child at an unnecessary risk. Surely she knew the forces opposing them would not miss such an opportunity to attack Ben.

An excited Lucy was up early the next day, walking beside Ben towards his plane.

In a short time, they were airborne and an awestruck Lucy was looking at the unfolding landscape below them.

"Oh," she said. "There are so many different colours."

Ben glanced out of the cockpit window. It was autumn and the scenery was indeed spectacular with its varying shades of gold, brown and green and was enhanced by the early morning sunshine.

Meanwhile, back at the centre, Tessa and Maria were questioning Venus as to why she allowed Lucy to accompany Ben.

Venus raised a hand. "Benjamin will be very safe with Lucy," she answered. Tessa and Maria looked at each other. It was very clear Venus knew something that they did not.

Ben looked at the awestruck Lucy and thought how different her world must be.

In less than two hours, they had touched down and were going to the office, where Ben picked up the keys for the rental car, he had arranged. It was only a short drive to the Eden Project. Parking the car, they walked towards the entrance. Once inside, they began to explore the visitors centre and then entered the dome itself which soared above their heads.

Lucy, who had been scanning the net the day before, turned to Ben and said, "Do you know that the whole Project has been built in an old clay pit?"

Ben smiled and nodded; he did not let on that he had also been surfing the net.

Lucy began reeling off dozens of facts—did Ben know that there were over a million different plants from all over the world, planted within the dome and it was a perfect ecosystem for a world that was now under siege from man's pollution.

"Now that is correct," he said. "Like your people on Umbria, we on Earth might have to start building structures like this to survive. Then Lucy said the strangest thing.

"When are you going to start your Eden Project, Ben?" Ben was taken aback as he has told no one about his plans, and yet this child seemed to know. He decided to tell her the truth.

"Soon, but it will take many years to complete."

Lucy nodded sagely. "Yes, I hope you will complete in time." Ben thought what does she mean, in time? He decided not to question her further on the subject and they carried on with their enjoyable day.

After lunch, they continued exploring with Ben taking notes on subjects he would not find on the net. It was only four o'clock but Ben decided to call it a day. He looked around for Lucy who was rushing around examining every plant she found.

Ben shook his head, where does she get her energy from, he wondered.

"Lucy, it's time to go."

"Okay," she called, showing no disappointment and trotted after Ben towards the exit.

Their car was parked some way from the centre and as Ben strode towards it, his head was full of thoughts and ideas for his project. He was pulled up by Lucy's voice.

"Ben, STOP."

Ben stopped in surprise at the intensity in Lucy's voice. He looked up and found himself facing trouble. There were four of them, three armed with knives and cudgels, the fourth looked very old and menacing. Standing back, Ben immediately attacked the three with his mind, throwing up a barrier. Unbelievably, nothing happened. At the same time, Ben was hurled backwards by the immense power coming from the old man. Ben was frightened, not so much for himself, but for Lucy. He tried again but still nothing. He looked at Lucy and was amazed to see her smiling. Ben looked at her more closely. From her eyes, a soft white light was shining. It played on the men's faces. They looked at her in surprise and collapsed unconscious on the ground. Their weapons rose from them and disappeared down a nearby sluice.

There was a grunt of surprise from the old man.

"Little girl," he said. "You are lost. Against me, you have no defence."

"Jav, you are over confident," she replied.

From Jav came a surge of power so intense Ben was hurled into the air and would have smashed into the nearest car; instead Lucy raised an arm and he sank to the ground, where he stayed and watched the titanic battle between the old man and the young girl. The light from Lucy's eyes never wavered and the old man began to fade.

"Your time has come, Jav," she said. The old man squinted at her.

"It cannot be." he said, staring at her intently. "You are an ancient."

The light from her eyes intensified and the old man began to disintegrate before Ben's eyes. There was nothing left but dust and that blew away in a gust of wind.

Lucy turned to Ben. "We best go or we will be caught in the rush."

Ben, in a daze, looked around him; apart from the three men on the ground there was not a soul in sight.

"How?" he said, then stopped and said, "what about those three thugs."

"They will wake up eventually but with no knowledge of us or what happened," she said.

On the drive to the airport, Ben was quiet. This lovable little girl sitting beside him had more power than anyone else he knew. He shuddered when he thought about it. She had just vaporized that evil old man. Reaching the airport, Ben returned the car keys and they made their way to the plane. As they walked, Lucy took Ben's hand and looked at him intently.

"Ben I did not kill that old man; he killed himself."

"How?" he asked.

"All I did was resist him but he threw all his power against me and it was his own power that consumed him."

"It still scared the pants off me," he said looking down at her.

They boarded the plane and since the clearance was soon given, they were airborne.

Lucy, sitting in the co-pilot seat, turned to Ben. "You will want to know why he called me an ancient," she said, smiling and, knowing that Ben was eaten up with curiosity.

“There are only a few of us and I am the only one who has been born since the Umbrians started their epic journey to Earth. I am from a planet called Arian and I belong to a race of people billions of years old. Our group were explorers who got lost in space and for our survival we landed on Umbria which was in its early stages of development. We were looked upon as gods by the Umbrians because of our superior knowledge but kept ourselves apart because of our strict laws, which was that of non-interference with our host’s natural development.

“I am the only Arian on Earth. When Venus was poisoned, I was asked to become her companion for her protection and to initiate and accompany her to Earth.”

“It was lucky for me you were here today,” he said.

They arrived back at the centre with the understanding between them that their confrontation at the Eden Project would not be mentioned.

Chapter 15

For the next three days, Ben locked himself in his office and only emerged for meals and to say goodnight to one and all. His first call was an attempt to contact George Collins.

George's voice came down the line very faintly. "I'm just north of Oliana. I'm heading for La Seu d'Urgell, I'll ring you when I get there."

Ben sighed and thought for all the modern technology, one only had to drive behind a hill and the contact was lost. He was about to say, "Okay" when it went dead. He then gave up and decided to only ring the hotels where his people were staying and not rely on mobiles. He hoped that once he had established offices of his project in various locations, things would be much easier.

Ben made a call to his accountant.

"Hello, Toby. Is everything going smoothly?"

"Yes, he came back, but I am suspicious. They gave in too easily. I know they are up to something but I've checked and rechecked the figures and they appear to be in order."

Ben laughed. "Don't worry, Toby, it is probably something trivial. As long as they pay up, I'm not worried."

"When will you want to start transferring?" Toby enquired.

"Good point," Ben answered. "I've nearly emptied my Spanish account." He thought for a moment. "Toby, transfer ten billion a week, for ten weeks."

After speaking to Toby, Ben rang George at his hotel and was put through straight away.

"Hello George, I do hope I'm not interfering with your dinner arrangements." There was now a two-hour time difference between England and Europe.

"No," came the answer. "I had a heavy lunch and have done eating for the day. Ben, on your instructions, we have bought every property worth buying and a few that were not. To clarify, some of the properties were virtually falling down but had good potential. I will send you a detailed breakdown by email, but briefly, we have purchased farms, shops, hotels, hacienda, deserted garages, that had sizable plots of land, and two villages," George could not conceal the note of triumph in his voice when he mentioned the last the last entry on his list.

Ben laughed. "How do you buy a village?"

George explained. "The villages were almost deserted and the few families that were still there were more than happy to sell and move to the nearest city. Now, for the bad news, we were unable to purchase any of the national parks."

Ben was mortified, his whole plan hinged on the purchase of parks and reservations.

"But," said George, "I inquired about leasing and they agreed that under certain conditions, this was possible."

Ben's hopes rose. "How long?"

"Not long, considering the money you're investing."

"How long?" Ben said interrupting.

"500 years?" Ben interrupted again. "George that is marvellous. Well done. What are the conditions?"

"The parks have no human habitation apart from park wardens."

"That is fine, I expected that."

George continued, "I did purchase something else; it was not on the list you gave me but I thought it might be useful, in the construction of your project."

"Go ahead; what did you buy?"

"Brass, iron and steel foundry." There was a moment of silence.

Then Ben said, "George you do realise this will affect your salary."

"Of course," George said warily.

"In fact, I will be transferring £5000 to your personal account straight away," Ben said, trying to keep himself from laughing.

"You don't have to do that," said, a now very pleased George.

"The bonus stays, you have saved me a hundred times that bonus. I hope to be in Spain within a fortnight, goodnight George." Ben hung up and retired himself.

Ben could not believe his good fortune, when he thought of the time and work that George had saved him. He realised that George had time wise saved him half a year at least, and some of the purchases were inspirational. Now, he just wanted to be out there with George and looking at all the acquisitions that had been made.

Ben had contacted many engineers he had worked with over the years, some had worked for Ben in the past but now, they either had their own businesses or held posts. When Ben told them of his plans they all thought he had lost the plot and the whole project would turn into a gigantic white elephant. The result was, he ended up with only eight of them to join him; Ben thought that was more out of curiosity. The following morning, he assembled everyone in the Medical Centre and told them of his plans.

I am having a new Medical Centre built in Andorra, although few knew much about Andorra, the small principality that was between Spain and France. There were mixed views regarding the move. Local people who in the village close to the centre mostly decided to stay in England.

They were told their jobs were secure but, for the majority, the excitement was enormous and they were already debating their individual dreams. Ben left them and made his way to Ivan's room.

Chapter 16

In Ivan's room, Ben was greeted by a smiling Ivan. "May I ask why the big grin?" he asked.

"You may," Ivan said. "Today is the day that I am fully recovered. That's what Lucy told me," he added.

Lucy had spent a lot of time with Ivan and with her ancient powers, had finally untied the remaining knots in Ivan's damaged brain. Ivan was full of plans. "We are moving back to our house in Greenwich," he told Ben.

"So I have heard," Ben said. "And young Ivan is off to university."

"Yes, it will be, just me, Julie and the twins. And I've heard that you too are moving."

"Yes, I will be in Spain working on some of my mad schemes but I will be fairly close to the new clinic." Julie came into the room and gave her a hug. Ben made his excuses and left them together.

That evening, Ben had dinner with his extended family and told them of his plans. "I will be off tomorrow and will probably not see you again until you yourselves are in our house as well. Hopefully, that will be very soon."

Everybody was pleased as Ben had been working very long hours and his normally good nature was waning somewhat. Once he had gone, they could get back to some normality. Next morning, having first gone into Tessa's room to say goodbye, Ben was on a flight to Spain before daybreak. On arrival in Barcelona, he quickly cleared customs and trotted along to Hertz to pick up the rental car. Two hours later, he was in his hotel room. George had already booked in and was there to meet him. They greeted each other warmly, although it was the first time they had actually met, they had spent so much time on the phone and emailing each other, it felt as if they were old friends.

George said, "I have asked the hotel to lay on some lunch, it's a little early but it could be seven or eight hours before we eat again." Ben was so keen to get on, he nearly refused but he had missed breakfast and was ravenous.

"Okay," he said. "Let's eat." They enjoyed a good lunch both refraining from drinking the lovely wines offered on the menu. For the rest of the day, they surveyed the land purchases and leases that George had made on Ben's behalf. Ben was impressed as George had been very frugal and careful with the acquisitions he had made. Once he had seen all the land and property, he was keen to see the only commercial purchase, the foundry. Although, he was pleased with the purchase, he did wonder how big it was and how long it would take to extend and modernise it to the requirements needed. He said as much to George. To his surprise, George looked offended.

"Sorry, George, have I said something wrong?" he asked.

George looking miffed, and said, "I obviously know of your project and it did not take a lot of thought to know the type of foundry you would require."

Ben apologised again, asking, "How big is the foundry?"

"We will be there soon enough and then you can see for yourself," came the curt reply.

Ben kept quiet as they entered the industrial estate. They drove on until Ben thought they were in the wrong place.

"Here we are," George said. Ben gasped; it was like entering an aerodrome.

"What the hell did they make in this foundry, aircraft?"

George chuckled. "I think they did actually, but mainly the foundry was used for the construction of ships keels. Apparently, they had moulds the length of the building."

"George, I am really impressed—for the money it cost, it is one hell of a bargain."

George grinned. "I thought you would be pleased."

Ben looked around, there was not a soul to be seen and it was as quiet as a grave. He turned to George, saying, "It seems deserted and although it is siesta time, surely someone would be about?"

"Well, I have, a set of keys so we can have a good look around your premises," George said.

They did a complete tour by car, so vast was the area. Looking round the offices, Ben was again impressed by how modern the offices were. He said to George, "I think we have seen enough for today. We'll go into town and try to find out why the foundry is deserted."

As it turned out, they did not have to, because as they emerged from the office block, several vehicles drew up, one being a police car. People stepped from the cars looking very serious.

Ben assumed correctly that they wanted to know who they were. They strode up to Ben and George and demanded to know if they were the new owners.

"I am Ben," Ben said smiling, but sensing that something was seriously wrong. "How can I help you?"

One of them stepped forward. "My name is Francis Claude. I am a solicitor and represent the workers who were employed by the foundry." He looked at Ben and turned to the Guardia who were still inside their vehicle. "You may go," he called out. "I know these gentlemen." The Guardia driver looked relieved and drove off, no doubt to continue his interrupted siesta.

Francis looked at Ben. "I recognize you." He said, "You're Benjamin Franklin." Ben nodded, wondering what these people wanted as the purchase was all above board. The workers and staff were all guaranteed continued employment. It was obvious that something was amiss, however, he guessed that somehow money was involved and, just knew it was his pocket that would suffer.

Ben was right; the previous owner just pocketed the money for the purchase and vanished. Francis added, "He never even paid the wages that were due."

Ben immediately made assurances that no one would be out of pocket. Francis turned to the waiting crowd repeating Ben's promise. "I will arrange for your outstanding wages to be paid and those who wish it, will remain employed." This caused a small cheer and applause from all there. Everybody went their ways, apart from Francis, Ben and George who went first to the band to make all the financial arrangements to reimburse the unpaid employees, then to a delighted Francis's home for a meal and after, to finalise the deal.

Chapter 17

It was some twenty months later and Ben was standing on the base from which one of the huge steel arches would eventually rise up, to form part of the first Crystal Dome. The base, almost the size of a football pitch, that looked from a distance like a giant Wellington boot, was one of many needed for the Dome. Occupying the heel of the boot was a huge chrome structure into which one of the arches would sit on massive hydraulic cushion, which would enable movement of the whole arch; the shoe part of the boot that housed the controls of that section was, at present one mass of cables waiting to be connected to the various terminals. When finished, the Dome would measure twelve kilometres across and seven hundred metres high at its apex. When completed, the Dome would be one of the greatest single projects ever undertaken. The base would cover an area of approximately thirty-seven square kilometres. The Dome was being constructed just north of Trago, in northern Spain and spanned the river Grau. A massive dam had been built and the reservoir which would eventually serve the main dome and several smaller domes housing farms. Once full, the water would flow through driving turbines which would be one of the sources of power, before going through the sluices and into the dome serving the thousands who would eventually live there.

Ben looked north towards the dam where the water was already flowing through the sluice gates, feeding the river once more. He climbed the service steps on the inside of the boot, climbing through the hatch at the top. From there, he could see the reservoir, now full, and he could see the sparkling waters within it. The dam stretched way beyond his sight shimmering in the evening sunlight. He felt a surge of excitement as he looked from left. He could see the areas where other boots were rising from the earth. There would be fifty boots to support the Dome, each supplying its own section.

Ben was delighted with the progress and was looking forward to the completion of the first boot. Soon the girders would be in place and the sections of the unique glass plastic would be resting on them. Ben, nevertheless, knew it would be many years to build the thousands needed to house the human population throughout the world. The Glasplas, as Ben named it, was one of the many formulae that Venus had given him. The covering would give the interior of the Dome complete protection against pollution and had the strength to withstand all the elements. The Dome completely resembled an egg and, with its shell, made it virtually indestructible. The Domes would eventually be all over the Spanish mainland and would be linked by six covered-causeways, four lanes for electric motor traffic and two-way lanes for electric trains.

When Ben first started the project, he was subjected to much ridicule from the media.

'Franklin's folly' appeared on the headlines of all the world's press and, and of course, television sets. This continued until it became second hand news. Not long after, he started to get inquiries from other countries who were becoming concerned at the amount of pollution.

The countries who mainly used fossil fuels for industry and transport were finding that their population was dropping, not hugely, but worldwide the population in a year had dropped by approximately one and a quarter million. Such was the concern; petrol vehicles were being banned from the majority of cities throughout the world.

Eventually, a world meeting was organised and representatives from around the planet attended it to learn more about the project. Around a thousand reps turned up, each accompanied by technical experts. They were all given a full set of plans and drawings to pore over before the meeting was convened. Ben obviously headed the meeting accompanied by George; cost was the biggest issue, many of the smaller countries would need help from the World Bank. On the technical side, Ben answered. "Yes, there would be no fossil fuels allowed for any source of power. The source of energy would come from either water or air turbines. There would also be solar panels on the sides of the Domes facing the sun. As an alternative, there would be a nuclear plant some two miles through an underground tunnel and at a depth of five hundred metres. These sources of power would be converted to electricity and would also power halogen (SUNS) within the Domes." George took over and with the architect, detailed the building plans. Stressing that the base of the dome and some of the buildings would be constructed, where possible, with waste plastic. Lastly, all present were invited to tour one of the sites being constructed.

With the meeting drawing to its end, Ben slipped away anxious to get back to the hotel; it was late, and he had hardly eaten since breakfast. He hurried along the path towards his car, thinking of food and the lovely wines that went with it. His thoughts switched to Tessa and Mars who were visiting Julie, Ivan and the children in Greenwich. Tessa was hoping to get Ivan and his family to move to Andorra, away from all the fumes and pollution of London. As he walked on, he heard dogs barking, and then he gasped and fell to the ground. What the hell was his last thought? Blackness enveloped him and his mind was torn from him. He then found he was looking through Mars's eyes. In Greenwich, Tessa had been shopping along with Mars who was in his buggy and a security guard who was carrying the shopping. The guard suddenly fell over.

Tessa turned to see what, when she felt a sharp pain in her head and she too fell. As she did, she turned to shield Mars who she was carrying, as all the shopping was in the buggy.

Mars woke with a jolt. "Mamma, Mamma," he cried out. There was no response. Although, Mars was only two years old, he sensed danger and looked to see six hooded men in black, fast approaching him. Mars was very frightened and angry, being Umbrian he had the intellect of a six-year-old. The thought flashed through his mind that these men would hurt his mummy. He screamed at them. "Dadda, Dadda."

Ben was suddenly there in the mind of Mars. After pacifying his son, he looked through his eyes.

What he saw shocked him to the core; the car park in the near vicinity was strewn with cars, one unfortunate woman was standing rigid, staring at her car which was upside down wheels still spinning. Fortunately, she was the only shopper in that area. Other cars were either upside down or smashed into adjoining vehicles. There were two masked bodies impaled against the perimeter fence. And Ben could see three others, who were obviously in the same group of attackers, crushed under vehicles. Ben looked at Tessa and the guard laying on the ground. Reassuring himself that they were not seriously injured, he looked down. Mars was standing very still with his tiny hands clenched tight. Ben could see the white bones of his knuckles.

It was then that Ben's mind went cold with shock as he realised that the carnage before him was caused by his son. Ben sensed the presence of Lucy, the thought came from her, are you okay Ben, then added security will be here soon. Ben looked and saw her or rather the golden orb that she arrived as.

"My god," she said, seeing the scene before her. "How did this happen."

Ben immediately sent the thought. "I overreacted when I saw the attackers." He knew just as quickly that Lucy knew it was Mars. Tessa and the guard started to regain consciousness.

"Ben," she said, "what happened?" As she spoke, Mars rushed into her arms. As he did so, Ben was back within his own mind.

He opened his eyes and found himself looking at the muzzle of an enormous dog. He looked around, he was surrounded by about twenty very hungry looking dogs. The dogs had found Ben and the Irish Wolf Hound was about to take a bite, but then sat on its haunches as a wisp of white breath came from Ben's mouth. The other dogs moved closer and got snarled at as the Wolf Hound decided it had to guard Ben. Ben could hear shouts and through the bushes, his Airedale appeared; it exchanged growls with the Hound and settled on the other side of Ben.

The shouts got nearer and led by Maria, several guards appeared.

They stopped and gaped at Ben laying there surrounded by dogs.

Maria suddenly giggled. "Your turn, Benjie," she said laughing.

Ben raised his hand. "Hello all," he said weakly.

Maria took charge. "Benjie, are you okay? I've got transport coming for the dogs." Looking at Ben's face, she added, "Lucy appraised us all of what happened in Greenwich."

"I'm fine and my cars are just on the other side of this glade. I will take my Airedale back with me though." He stood and smiled at the dogs.

"Stay," he said, and strode off. "Come Juno," and the Airedale trotted after him.

The whole pack was enticed into the truck that came and was taken back to the centre. Eventually all the dogs were found homes.

Ben's car was near the glade of trees and as he approached it, he heard a snarl followed by a faint whimper. *Now what,* he thought, and looked to see where the sounds came from.

He saw an old pallet at the edge of the glade, beside it, digging, was a wolf. His dog was already bounding towards the wolf. Ben saw the wolf was obviously starving and a bitch, by the size of its stomach.

"Stay," Ben said, and his dog hunkered down. Ben walked across; as he did so, he subdued the wolf. The wolf wanted to flee but found itself unable to move, it did manage a snarl as Ben approached.

Ben peered through the slats of the pallet, underneath there was a slight depression and there lay a small dog and three pups.

"Ah," Ben said to himself, and pulling out his mobile, rang Maria. When she answered, he told her what he had found.

"Oh, Benjie, you are impossible, we will have to open up a boarding kennel for dogs. And one wolf," she giggled. "I will come by myself to help. Will it be safe to have them all in your car?"

"Yes, I have subdued them all. Mind you the puppies look more dead than alive."

Maria was with him in a minute and Ben moved his car to the pallet.

"Cari, put out stretchers, please."

"Yes, Benjamin," the tinny voice answered.

They laid the dogs on the stretchers and then carefully picked up the puppies.

"Oh no," Maria said. "Benjie, this little chap is dead."

He took the puppy from her. There was no heartbeat. Ben gently massaged its little body, with no response.

"Oh, Benjie," Maria wept. "Poor little thing." Its little body was still warm though. Ben tried one last thing; he softly blew into the tiny mouth, it coughed and something came out of his mouth. It yawned.

Between the hugs and kisses he was getting from Maria, he managed to say.

"Whatever that was that came out, must have choked it," he said to a grinning Maria, who took the puppy and cuddled it all the way back to the clinic.

The vet had been called and took the wolf away to have her puppies looked after until she could tend to them. On Ben's instructions, the wolf would be kept in captivity, its chance of survival in the wild with her pups was nil. Hopefully, it could be eventually domesticated. And the pups certainly had every chance of being tamed.

Ben had a very late dinner and several glasses of the hotel's very best wine, and decided to have an early night. He had rung Tessa, and she, Mars and the security guard were quite recovered from their ordeal. The carnage in the supermarket car park was put down to a rebel group whose bomb had exploded prematurely, the sixth man was found in the road outside, and he too was quite dead.

Ben took it easy for a few days, during which Tessa and Mars returned from England with marvellous news. Ivan, Julie and the children were selling up and moving to Spain.

Ben was hoping they would have come to Andorra but Ivan junior was transferring to the University of Barcelona. *Well,* he thought, *it's only an hour's drive from us.*

While Ben was in the house, he rang George every day for updates.

George had completed the buying of land that Ben required and was now organizing the construction of Domes. So successful was he at his new task that it gave Ben a thought.

He rang George a few days later and asked him if he would like to become solely employed by Ben only. His reaction surprised but also pleased Ben.

"I am terribly sorry but the company I work for has hit hard times with the recession, which as you know, is worldwide at this moment in time. The truth is Ben, your project is keeping us afloat."

"Okay, George. Leave it with me. I'll be in touch."

Ben rang the managing director of George's firm; the secretary put him through immediately.

A strong northern accent came over the phone.

"Hello, Mr Franklin. Robert Lyon speaking. How can I help you? I hope everything is satisfactory?"

"I will come straight to the point," Ben said. "I wanted Mr Collins to leave your employment and come to me."

There was an "Oh" from the other end. "Needless to say George refused, so I purchased a majority shareholding in your company. I did some research and found you were about to make redundancies, as I do not want this to happen. I took the action I deemed necessary."

There was silence from the other end so Ben continued, "Everybody remains employed, however I will require staff to work abroad at times and would be grateful if you could take control of that, i.e. passports, medical cards, security checks and of course they will need to have the language of the country they are in. I will need George at my side from this day forth. Sorry to spring all this on you but as I am going on a short holiday, I want to be able to relax whilst away."

He came off the phone and, from his computer sent Bob Lyon all the details appertaining to the construction of the Domes. Then he went back on the phone to appraise George, who was amazed, speechless and very grateful, especially when Ben informed him he had a 10% share in the company.

"I am off tomorrow, George, so everything is now in your capable hands."

"Thank you, and enjoy your holiday," said a very happy George.

Having finally finished with the phone, he sought out Tessa.

"Where would you like to go?" he asked. "Anywhere in the world," he added.

Tessa was dubious. "The trouble is." she said, "everywhere is so polluted now. I know we could go on a cruise in that yacht of yours."

Quite animated now, she went on. "It will be good to see Aunt Agatha again and meet Captain Joe," she said laughing. "Also I've never seen your yacht, let alone sail in it."

So it was settled, and a few days later they were on a plane to Miami where the yacht was moored. It was just Ben, Tessa and Mars. They did ask Venus to join them but she declined, saying. "I will stay, George might need my advice". So they included Lucy and Sophie who had been aiding Venus in her recovery.

"They all need some good fresh sea air," Tessa said to Ben.

Whilst in the air, Tessa, who was looking out the window, remarked on the colour of the clouds. Ben looked and sighed. "I'm afraid, it's the pollution," he said. On landing they went through customs and as they came out they could see Joe first, who was much taller than Agatha, they were both waving wildly. As they got closer, Ben was amazed at how well they both looked. Agatha had really filled out from the last time he saw her. He said as much to Tessa. She smiled and said, "Look again, Ben."

"My god," he said, "she is pregnant, she must be." Tessa put her hand over Ben's mouth.

"Hush," she said. "It's rude to discuss a lady's age."

Ben thought to himself, *Agatha must be 200 at least.* A thought came into his head. "Actually, Benjamin Franklin, I am 237 and I would be very grateful if you kept that to yourself and never let slip to Joe."

"Sorry, Aunt Agatha," Ben thought back to her. "I'm forever getting Earth and Umbrian ages mixed up." Then they were all together greeting each other with hugs. They had their luggage taken out to the taxi and once it was loaded, they all piled in for the short ride to where the yacht was moored. The luggage was transferred to the catwalk, Joe then got his crew to carry it all to the yacht's deck where it was left to await its allotted cabin.

"Now," Joe said, "would you all like a shower first or food?" Unanimously, it was agreed to be a shower first. Once refreshed, the whole assembly enjoyed a sumptuous meal set before them. By the time they had finished eating, it was quite late, and Mars having fallen asleep was put to bed. The adults then, all caught up on their various activities and adventures. Joe talked about the exotic places he had sailed to in his lifetime, and they all listened fascinated. While Joe talked, Agatha just sat and stared at him. Ben and Tessa could sense the love that poured her mind. Tessa reached for Ben's hand; they relaxed, enraptured by the locations that he and Agatha had visited. Joe finished by saying they would revisit some of them.

For two whole months, they were able to forget all their concerns and worries that had beset them in the past. The weather was beautiful and with the clean air and the smell of salt from the open sea, they just lazed. On many occasions, they just dropped anchor, got the fishing rods out and just sat in deck chairs waiting for the tug on the line. On good fishing days, they would down the rods and enjoy a swim, either in the sea, if safe or in the yacht's pool.

On the very last day, before sailing for home, Joe eased the yacht between a narrow channel of coral reef. The yacht entered a lagoon. Being totally enclosed by the coral reefs, the water was calm. "This is the place to swim," he said. "The water is shallow and being so, it is also quite warm."

Agatha, who up to then had declined swimming, lowered herself into the water and thoroughly enjoyed herself. Being unable to swim, she laid on her back and paddled. The salt water keeping her buoyant, she paddled herself a short distance from the yacht. She was suddenly shocked to find a Dolphin swimming alongside her, but only for a moment.

"John Franklin," she shouted with delight, "how do you like being a fish." The Dolphin squeaked with its high-pitched voice and swished its tail angrily.

"My dear sister, I must remind you that Dolphins are mammals." Agatha, of course, only heard the squeak, but was able to understand the thoughts of her brother quite easily. They conversed with their minds for some time. Agatha was the first person he had spoken to since he had taken over the mind and body of the ancient Dolphin. Although Ben sensed his father's presence, he had never been able to exchange thoughts or converse mentally.

After Agatha had told John what Ben was doing, John said it will be too late, there will be a long darkness for Earth and the survival of the human race will be limited.

When Agatha repeated those words to Ben, he shook his head.

"No," he said. "There will be great loss of life but I am sure that humans and Umbrian will survive, although I do not understand, THE DARKNESS father is talking about." Ben would say no more, but it left a shadow on his mind. What darkness did his father mean? Pollution, yes, contamination and global warming…he stopped himself, speculating was no good, his father knew something though.

The next day was again beautiful and the previous night was soon forgotten as the yacht slipped anchor and eased her way out of the coral lagoon.

"What now, Ben," Joe asked.

"I would like you to sail us back," Ben said.

Joe grinned, "I thought you would say that, I've already plotted the course."

"Mind reading now, are we?" Ben asked.

"Well, you know, live with grow alike," they both laughed.

After two weeks, they had crossed the Atlantic and were under sail in a gentle south-westerly.

Joe called Ben to the bridge; when Ben entered, he saw the frown on Joe's face.

"Trouble?" he asked.

"I'm afraid so. There is a really nasty storm further north and it is heading our way."

"Can we avoid it?" Ben queried.

"Well, we can double back or head south and go around the southern tip of Africa and up its east coast and through the Suez Canal."

Ben laughed. "I'll tell the girls their holiday's just been extended."

So Joe put the yacht on a southerly course. A week later, after passing Cape Town and the Cape of Good Hope, they were now under sail and, and cruising up the west coast keeping close to the coast so they could enjoy the beautiful scenery. It was extremely hot and they were thankful for their air-conditioned cabins. At Durban, they put into port for fresh water and supplies. After spending the night in one of the best hotels, they all took breakfast and boarded the yacht at midday. They set sail. Again they were in the light south-westerly and travelled on mainly under sail. They passed South Africa, then Mozambique, Tanzania, Kenya and Somalia. Then rounding north Somalia, they altered course to pass through Gulf of Aden, then across the Red Sea and through the Suez Canal. Being so close to shore, it remained very hot and they even suffered the occasional mosquito. Ben was feeling jaded and after dinner decided to turn in. "I'll send Sophie and Lucy up. It will give them a break from looking after Mar," then he was off to his cabin.

At first light, Ben was pacing the deck. Something was troubling him, it had to do with North Africa. A movement by his feet distracted him, he looked down and there it was, a Gecko. He bent down to pick it and as he did so, he experienced a sharp pain in his head and everything went black as he fell against a stanchion. Aunt Agatha, who still wanted to talk to Ben about what his father had said, saw Ben laying there and rushed to his aid. Joe, who was on the bridge unaware, heard Agatha scream. He swung round in time to see Agatha being cudgelled. Flicking the yacht onto auto, he raced down from the bridge. He came armed, he always kept a rifle on the bridge and he came with murder in his heart.

Although Joe knew of the dangers on the Somalian coastline, he only had a crew of five including cook and they were soon overpowered. Below decks, Tessa heard the sound of gunfire, and grabbing Mars cautiously, opened her door. At the same time the door opened and Sophie and Lucy stood there. "What was that noise?" she asked yawning and stretching.

Tessa said, "I think we have trouble. That was gunfire."

Mars started crying. "Daddy's hurt," he cried.

Sophie was very suddenly, very wide awake.

"Go back to your room," she commanded, "and lock the door."

Tessa objected. "Sophie, you will get hurt."

"Just do as I say."

"Behind her," Lucy said, "We will be alright."

The two women raced up to the deck.

All her dear friends were laying on the deck and they were bound head and foot.

"What have we here?" a big black man asked. Sophie stared at him with hatred.

He was obviously the leader of the pirates.

"Put that gun down," she said.

"I might just lower my gun and put another bullet in your captain," he said and laughed at the look of hate in her eyes as he started to lower the gun.

There was a shot but the gun was pointing at his own head, he fell, his dead eyes staring at Sophie.

"Now, all of you, drop your guns." They did so and then they were in the air and dropped into the sea. Sophie turned to see the silver light coming from Lucy's eyes.

"Thank you, Lucy."

"Is that all of them?"

"Yes," Lucy said. She was now kneeling by Joe who was now laying in a pool of blood and beginning to lose consciousness. "Hang on, Joe" she whispered and ripping open his shirt stared at his wounds, the silver light pouting over Joe's body. The wounds slowly sutured and gently, turning Joe over, she repeated the process on the bullet's entry holes. As she eased him into recovery position, Joe squinted up at her, a grin on his pale face.

"That is quite a good trick you have there," he said, then promptly passed out.

Sophie grabbed a knife from the deck and released the crew. The doctor ran across to tend to Agatha and Sophie, then rushed to Ben. Lucy joined her and attended to the head wound. Meanwhile, Agatha had started to regain consciousness. She looked around her and saw Joe lying flat out on the deck, with blood all around him.

"Joe," she cried. "My Joe, what have they done to you," and pushing the medic aside she staggered over to where Joe lay inert.

Lucy called out. "He is alright, Agatha, I have seen to his wounds." Knowing of Lucy's powers Agatha relaxed a little and sinking down, put her arms around him. He opened an eye.

"That's nice," he said and snuggled up in her arms.

Agatha was helped, but Ben and Joe were carried down to the ship's small hospital. The bosun went to check on the yacht's course and the others started to clean away the mess on deck.

Sophie was on the point of going down to give Tessa the good and bad news, when she noticed a movement by one of the yacht's lifeboats.

"You there, come out," she called. She glimpsed a face, and a figure running to the yacht's deck rail. "Stop," she ordered and strode across. When she had had that glimpse of a face, something had stirred inside her. She reached the figure, it was just a young lad barely in his teens, she judged. He was obviously petrified of her and cringed away.

"Look at me," she commanded. "Let me see your face."

He looked up at her. It took Sophie's breath away. Although, he was just skin and bone, covered in sores and filthy dirty, his face was like looking in a mirror.

"Come," she said and held out her hand. Taking his hand, she could feel him trembling.

"It is alright. I'm not going to hurt you, you must have a good shower and then we will get some cream to put on those sores."

“Thank you,” he said. Sophie’s heart started pounding. She tried to dismiss the thought but, no, she had to find out somehow.

While the boy was showering, Sophie went to see how the injured were responding to treatment.

Agatha was okay, considering her pregnancy. Joe was still unconscious but safely out of danger.

“How is Ben?” Sophie asked.

Tessa was talking quietly to the doctor.

“I think he is okay, the bullet just grazed his head. The doctor is more concerned with the bad bruising he sustained when he fell against a stanchion. What I fail to understand was why he was clutching a Gecko in his hand?”

Having satisfied herself that all seemed well apart from Ben remaining unconscious, she went to see how the boy was faring. In her hand, she had a tin of salve for the sores.

She applied the salve to his back and watched and talked, while he applied, the rest of the salve.

“Are your parents still running Somalia?” she asked.

He nodded and then said, “Yes, they are.” The boy continued, stammering badly, “But they cannot leave…well they could have but in the end they were forced to stay.”

“Were you captured?”

“No,” came the reply. “Initially, we were rescued and held to ransom. But the money never came. My father was forced to work in the fields and the big man who shot himself took my mother as one of his wives.”

“What is your name?”

“Jack,” he said with a little more confidence, although he had no idea why he was being treated so kindly.

“Will you come with me?” Sophie held out her hand. After a moment of hesitation, he held out a painfully thin hand up to her and taking it once more Sophie took him to her room and sat him on a chair.

“Wait there,” she said kindly. “I will not be long.” She walked in the direction of Tessa’s room and after knocking, went in.

“Tessa could you do a DNA test for me?”

Tessa was extremely startled. “And for whom is this test?” she asked, “and why?”

"Come with me just for a moment," and she led Tessa to her room where Jack, all cleaned up and tidy, was sitting with a small smile.

Tessa looked at him and gasped. "Ye gods!" she exclaimed. "He is your double."

"Am I being stupid?" she asked. I know nothing of my family, but we were shipwrecked and it was the same time I was rescued by the Umbrians, if there is a slightest chance…" She went quiet for a moment then burst out, "I must know."

Tessa took swabs from their tongues and told Sophie she would contact her later on in the day.

Sophie was on tenterhooks, her emotions going from delight one minute to depression the next. In her mind, she was already planning to go ashore and rescue her parents.

At last, Tessa called for her on the intercom. Sophie was so pent up, she nearly fell down the gangway steps.

"Well," she said, "have you got the results? No, do not tell me." Seeing the look on Tessa's face, she drooped, in despair, "Well there was a chance he could have been my brother."

"Were all the tests negative?" she whispered.

"That is what I find hard to believe." Tessa answered. She took Sophie's arm. "They were all positive," she announced.

Sophie collapsed into Tessa's arms. "Are you sure?"

"Absolutely," came the reply. "I double-checked. Jack is definitely your brother. All we have to do now is rescue your parents."

"I will go by myself," Sophie said. "They're my parents and with Ben and Joe out of action, and you and Lucy looking after everything else, that only leaves me, anyway." Sophie stopped talking and froze as a deafening clattering came from above.

"What is that?" she yelled above the noise. Her voice edged with fear.

"That," Tessa laughed, "is your other choice."

They went up on deck, arriving just as a Lynx helicopter landed, the rotors stopped, the doors opened and out jumped six very tough and very tired men, looking bleary-eyed as if they had just jumped out of bed. This was actually true; some fifteen hours before in the earlier hours, they were scrambled. Knowing it was an emergency they had tried to get a few hours' sleep. They had their guns cocked, as they looked around the deck.

Tessa raised her hand. “It’s okay,” she called out. “All is secure,” she assured them.

One of the men smiled and turned to help a very tall woman down from the helicopter.

Tessa and Sophie stared at the slight figure. “Venus,” they said in unison.

“Venus?” Tessa asked, the shock showing on her face. “What are you doing here?” Lucy piped up.

“We had a mind chat. Venus decided that the men cannot look after themselves, let alone the women.” The men grinned and John who led the men, asked how Ben and Joe were. Tessa made light of their injuries.

“They will both be okay given time.”

“What now?” John asked.

“Well,” Tessa replied, “if you feel up to it, there’s a rescue attempt to be made.”

The men grinned; after being cooped up in the copter for so long they were raring for action.

Jack, who had recovered from his flight, was questioned by John to get some idea of where the rebels were camped and the size of the gang.

The yachts maps were fetched and, after looking at them for a long time, Jack suddenly pointed. “There,” he said, “on the side of that range of hills.”

John looked at himself. “That range of hills is thirty kilometres long. Can you be more accurate?”

Jack thought. “There’s a split in the middle of the hills,” he pointed, “just there” and he again pointed at what looked like a line running from top to bottom on a cliff.

“It’s about two miles from the beach, hidden and easy to defend,” one of the men remarked.

“We will survey first and then plan our tactics for the rescue.”

Sophie was so pent up, she wanted to scream, such was her desperation to rescue her parents from the hell they must be living in.

But she thought these men are professionals, and so she kept quiet.

The chopper was refuelled and took off into the evening.

There were four men on board including the pilot; they also had Jack and Sophie on board.

Sophie had insisted on going which was just as well. Jack was petrified of the helicopter and would have jumped off, instead he shut his eyes and clung on to her.

In a matter of minutes, they were hovering in front of the fissure. It looked formidable. There was a deep crack in a buttress with a ledge which led to a huge cavern. Jack, who was still clinging to Sophie, peered out and then screamed. "There they are, Mum and Dad." Sophie nearly fell out herself as she tried to see. All she saw were stick people, down below.

John shook the boy who was almost hysterical. "Are you sure Jack?"

"Yes, YES," came the answer. "I recognize Mum's kaftan."

John swore under his breath.

It looked like a trap, and they, if not very careful, would be walking into it.

"Arm up," he said. "We are going to attempt the rescue." He ushered the children to the comparative safety at the back of the copter. Then, moving quickly, he armed himself with a long tube that he took from a box. He braced himself against the fuselage and shouted instructions to the pilot and the helicopter swept towards the cliff. It was met by a hail of bullets, that whizzed past his body. He raised the bazooka to his shoulder, took careful aim and squeezed the trigger. Ducking back into the relative safety of the fuselage, he gave a small prayer of thanks.

The helicopter swung away amidst a hail of bullets. Behind them, there was an enormous explosion, the helicopter turned again just in time to see the whole cliff shiver and then collapse in a cloud of dust.

"That was a result," John said grinning at the success.

He turned to his team, there was a silence, looking he saw one of his team cradling a companion in his arms.

One of the bullets had struck him in the head. The one holding him, looked up, with tears in his eyes. He said, "Gerald did not deserve that."

John let out a stream of expletives. It was bad enough losing one of his best men but these two had always worked together, which had been acceptable, as they were brothers.

John gripped Tom's arm. "Sorry mate," thinking sadly there would be no more jokes about Tom Gerry!

He turned angrily to Jack. "I hope, for your sake, that it is your parents down there."

The copter landed close to the couple. John's heart melted when he saw the state they were in.

They had been badly beaten and were both unconscious probably in that state to stop them from warning their rescuers. John turned to Tom.

"Sorry mate, I'll need you to carry them back to the chopper."

Sophie moved to Tom's side "I'll hold him."

Tom looked at her, "It's alright love. I'll just lay him down."

"No," Sophie was insistent. "I will hold him. He's not quite dead," she whispered.

A glimmer of hope flickered on Tom's eyes and he gently laid his brother in her arms.

"No promises," she said, as Tom moved away to join John.

He did not answer and jumped from the copter as soon as it touched ground and then, running hard towards the parents, John yelled, "Keep low." They did not hesitate in their approach, hoping that the rebels had laid no mines near the unconscious couple. Holstering their guns, they scooped up the prone parents and legged it back to the helicopter. This was no easy task as they were on rough terrain and running in a crouched position. Then, what they had feared, the crackle of gunfire. They both dropped flat, bruising their elbows as they tried to cushion the prone pair. The closest the helicopter could get was two hundred metres and they had only covered half that distance. The gunfire was coming from the base of the cliff. Too close!!

There was a sudden clattering coming from the Lynx and then silence.

"Now," John roared and they rose and pelted to the safety of the helicopter.

As they clambered aboard, John shouted to the pilot.

"Go, go," and they soared into the air.

Sophie was still holding Gerry, and she looked across to where her parents lay. She searched, with her mind to see if they had any serious or life-threatening injuries. She breathed a sigh of relief, there were none. She returned her attention back to Gerry; with her powers, she removed a blood clot from his brain and then stopped the bleeding both inside and outside of his head. One of the bullets that had come through the fuselage, entered his head and travelled round the inside of his skull.

He had been fortunate that most of the bullets' energy had been spent coming through the fuselage. Despite her prowess, Sophie could not find out what damage had been done to the brain. That would be discovered when he regained consciousness.

Chapter 18

The Lynx rose and sped back to the yacht. John stuck his head in the cockpit door.

"Thanks, Andy."

"No problem. I landed facing the cliff just in case they still had fire power."

"Well," John laughed, "your covering fire saw us to safety and the rocket you launched, finished them."

Andy smiled grimly. "Shame about Gerald." John nodded. "Sophie's keeping him alive but I do not hold out much hope." Andy looked over his shoulder to where Tom was sitting, hunched up, his hand covering his face.

"Are they actually brothers?"

"Yes," John replied, "and that makes it worse. They are inseparable and if Gerry does not pull through, I think Tom will leave the team. I know I am being selfish but they are two of my best men." Andy shook his head, sadly.

"I've not seen Gerald but I have been told his face is a mess," but he added in an attempt to cheer John up, "at least you rescued the parents and got them back safely."

John retreated back into the cabin as Andy concentrated on bringing the Lynx safely down on the deck. Having radioed ahead, there was already a stretcher to take the desperately injured man to the yacht's small hospital room. Two more stretchers were found for Sophie's parents. They were carried down to a cabin adjoining, the hospital being now full. Fortunately, they were not badly injured, just badly bruised from the beating they had had.

John lowered himself from the copter, wincing as he jumped the short distance to the deck.

"Not you as well, boss," Tom said as he followed him down. John shook his head.

"No, a couple of bullets hit me but my flak jacket stopped them. I'm just a bit bruised."

Louisa examined him much later. And although the bullets had not penetrated the jacket, the heavy calibre bullets had broken three ribs. One of the broken ribs had nicked a lung, but by some miracle, there was no internal bleeding.

The three most seriously injured still lay in the hospital room. Ben and Joe were out of danger but Gerald's condition continued to give grave concern; his breathing was ragged and he was too ill to have the bullets removed. Another helicopter flew in as Andy left in his. The copter had another three security men, but even more importantly a plastic surgeon and a whole pallet of medical supplies and equipment. The surgeon wasted no time; firstly, he looked at Gerry's x-rays and having studied them immediately scrubbed up. He then got Louisa and Venus to lay out his surgical tools. Lucy sat ready to be called upon if required after setting up an intravenous drip for Gerry. Four hours later, he stepped back and nodded to the women he left, leaving them to re-join the skin. Obviously no needle or gut was required. Louisa and Venus joined minds and the skin came together leaving an almost invisible scar which, with time, disappears completely.

The surgeon had made no attempt to remove the bullet but, had rebuilt the bone structure of Gerry's face. The two women then scanned his brain but could find no bleeding. Sophie's efforts earlier had paid off and the bullet, although it remained, posed no threat. They then focussed their attention on Ben and Joe. Louisa looked anxiously at Venus. "I do not understand why he is still unconscious," she fretted.

Venus, who was examining Joe, said, "And I do not understand how this one is still alive given the number of bullets that struck him."

As if he heard, Joe moaned and started to stir, his eyes fluttered open and he looked at Louisa and Venus. He stared at Venus.

"What are you doing here," he asked, "and how," he added. He looked again, saw Gerry, and looking totally puzzled asked again what was happening.

Venus smiled, "Well, at least his brain is working." Looking down at Joe, she asked, "Do you remember the attack?"

"Of course," he said, then his face contorted, and he struggled to sit up. "Aggie," he gasped, "where is she? Is she alright?"

"Of course, she is," they said in unison.

Louisa added, "She has been ordered to have complete bed rest and we have virtually had to tie her to it, she's been that worried about you." Joe sank back; if Louisa said Aggie was alright then she must be. "My god," he said, "the baby."

"Baby is fine," said Lucy, from the corner of the room.

"Oh hello, Lucy," Joe said wondering how many more people he had aboard his boat.

He settled back only to stiffen again.

"Ben," he said. "I saw him get shot in the head."

"Yes," Louisa said, "but he should be okay. It was just a flesh wound."

What she did not say was their anxiety over Ben's failure to regain consciousness.

Joe looked around the ward, saw Ben, and said, "Sorry," unaware of Ben's state.

"Who is that," he whispered, seeing Gerry.

"That's Gerry, one of the security team." Venus informed him. He got quite badly shot up.

"Now, get some rest. Joe we will come back later. You ring the bell by your side, and someone will come immediately." Joe layback. Louisa was not telling him everything about Ben's condition. He had noticed the tone of anxiety in Louisa's voice when talking very quietly to Venus. It was obvious they were talking about Ben, by the way they kept looking across to where he lay.

Joe thought back to his first meeting with Benjamin Franklin junior. Ben was six foot two, just turned sixteen, and fresh out of school, and on holiday.

His first meeting with Joe was more of an encounter.

Joe was drunk, which in those days was pretty much the same every day.

He had been the successful captain of his own ship. He was also a joint partner with his best friend, in the import export trade. They had orders to transport cargo to ports all over the world. Sadly, on reflection, he had been too successful. He had a beautiful wife who he worshipped, at first it was mutual, but he was away too long and too often, and she left him for someone else. To make matters worse, that someone was his business partner.

After two years of drinking, delivering cargos to the wrong port in the wrong country, and several near collisions with other vessels, now his ship was impounded against bad debt and worse, he had been summoned by the marine tribunal and was likely to lose his captain's licence.

Joe was not only drunk when Ben first saw him, he was also being mugged, because he resisted when he saw a knife coming towards him. The knife seemed to slip past him and the same thing happened to the cudgel, which was brandished. Then he heard Ben's shout, he took heart and started to fight back. Joe was big and when sober, he would have annihilated the three men attacking him. As it was, he landed a couple of hard punches and the men turned and fled.

As Ben walked up to him. Joe limped to a nearby hydrant and sat on it.

Through swollen eyes, he squinted up at Ben. "Thanks," he said.

Ben smiled. "I did nothing sir," he said.

That one word 'sir!' put Ben into a different category in Joe's mind.

Ben went on. "Can I walk you back to your place?" he enquired.

"I have no accommodation at the moment."

"Well, tonight you can be my guest."

"You live here?" Joe was astonished, it was quite a rough area.

"Well, sort of," Ben said and helping Joe to his feet lead the way through the narrow streets.

They set off exchanging names and weighed each other up.

They hadn't gone far before Joe stopped.

"You okay?" Ben asked.

"Yes, but I know this area."

"Oh, do you work in the port?"

Joe said, "No, but I'm the captain of that ship over there, or to be correct I used to be captain of that ship." Ben heard and sensed the bitterness. But said nothing.

"That's my yacht over there," Ben said, as they reached the catwalk.

"Bloody hell," Joe exclaimed. "What's your surname Ben? Franklin!!!"

Ben burst out laughing. "How clever of you," he chortled. "It was Dad's but he signed it over to me for my sixteenth birthday."

Joe suddenly became very sober. "Are you sure I'll be welcome?" he grunted.

Ben became equally serious.

"My father trusts my judgment in the friends I keep."

Well, Joe thought, *I'm a friend now.* Little did he know what Ben suddenly had in his mind.

Ben got Joe to shower and taking his clothes he got one of the crews to launder them.

As Ben was a similar size to Joe, he got some of his own for Joe.

He shouted to Joe. "I've got some coffee on the go and there are some fresh clothes outside the shower."

Joe appeared a few minutes later, pale but quite sober. He gulped down the first cup and held out his mug. Ben gave him a refill and asked about food. Joe grimaced, saying, "Maybe later."

Ben questioned Joe. "Are you unemployed at present?"

Joe gave Ben a quizzical look; he found it a little daunting talking to a sixteen-year-old about his business. *But what the hell,* he thought, *the boy meant well.*

"I'm unemployed, broke and probably about to lose my captain's licence. Why…have you got a job for me?" he challenged. Joe then got one hell of a shock.

"Yes," Ben replied. "I want you to become captain of this yacht." Joe leaned heavily against the galley sink.

"You want what?" he choked on his coffee.

Ben carried on. "I know it's tiny compared to the boats you're used to but it's a job, I think, you would enjoy and I have a very good reason for asking. We are, at present, without a captain. Our present captain had to leave," he added. "Sadly, his wife had a stroke. We were sorry to lose him but he was due to retire in two years anyway."

Ben rushed on. "Do not worry about your captain's licence. My father will vouch for you, so what do you think?"

Joe, by this time had a broad grin on his face; if this was really true his whole life would be turned round but he hesitated on the side of caution.

"I think we will wait to see what your father says and the result of the tribunal. If that all goes well, then yes, I would be pleased to be your captain."

His thoughts were interrupted by a moan. He looked across; Ben was coming to. He rang the bell to summon Louisa. "Hang on mate," he whispered to Ben.

Then Louisa was there, leaning over and talking to Ben. He opened his eyes and spoke quietly to his mother. Joe heard Louisa. "Oh, no, no, no," she cried.

Joe felt terror rise like bile in his throat.

"What is wrong?" he said.

Louisa turned, tears streaming down her face.

"He is paralysed," she wept and turned back to her precious son, hugging him to her breast.

The cause, it was found out, was the support post on the yacht's railing. When Ben was shot, he fell heavily against the post and cracked a vertebra at the base of his spine.

He had already been inside his body and welded the bone together but the nerve ends would not knit. He put on a brave face, saying it would probably be only a few days before he was back on his feet, but he knew that having a part human body, the paralysis could be permanent. Everyone on board rushed to see him and wish him well. The following morning, Ben and Jerry were taken off in the remaining helicopter. Tessa, Louisa and of course, baby Mars left with them. Joe stayed, one, he was the captain and two, there was no way he was leaving Agatha, and until he was back on his feet, he could be found by her bedside, where she was ordered to stay by the doctor. Everything returned to normal and once clear of Somalia, tensions eased, although the mood was very sombre.

Ben and Gerry were in the same ward, and with Gerry still unconscious and Ben unable to accept his enforced immobility, and refusing to talk to anyone, the morale was low for visitors.

Gerry was receiving a lot of attention and physiotherapy and had at last come out of danger.

He began to show signs of waking up which was good news for all. Ben, though, remained in his reclusive state.

Ben did gain Gerry's attention though, when in the middle of the night Ben was woken by a shout.

"I cannot see," he shouted. "I can…NOT SEE." Ben pressed the emergency button and a nurse was there in seconds. The room became crowded as a doctor, optician and the physiotherapist all turned up. Gerry was sedated and it was suddenly just Ben and Gerry again. Next day, Tom came in and sat by Gerry's bed, he asked how Ben was and was met by silence.

Gerry still sluggish from the sedation, woke.

Tom grabbed Gerry's arm. "I am so sorry, bro," he said and burst into tears.

There was a stunned silence. Tom was renowned for being one of the hardest on the security team. The silence was broken by laughter.

"Jesus, Tom," Gerry said. "It should be me with the tears."

Tom took a deep breath, blew his nose and managed a grin.

"Sorry, I'm just so happy you are still with us."

"Talking of being with us," Gerry said, turning to face Ben, "why are you here, boss?"

Ben, having been shaken out of his reverie, told him and was again given sympathy.

"Bloody hell, I am really sorry mate."

Ben had no reply, here was a very healthy, active young man who was probably blinded for life and here he was wallowing in self-pity.

From that morning, he agreed to physiotherapy and a regime of exercises that left him exhausted. The weeks passed and although he was still paralysed, he felt much healthier in mind and body. One morning, he had an idea.

"Why are we laying here like a couple of zombies. We should get out and enjoy ourselves."

Gerry turned to Ben chuckling. "I like your optimism mate but how do we achieve this expedition of yours."

"Ah, wait and all will be revealed." Ben took his mobile out from under his pillow and dialled in some numbers.

Gerry who was listening, remarked, "That's a very short number."

An old friend came to reply to Ben.

The connection was made and a disembodied voice said, "Hello, Benjamin."

Ben smiled to himself. "Hello, Carrie, where are you?"

"I'm in the car pool, three floors below you," came the reply. Ben could have sworn he heard a sigh before Carrie added, "Where I've been for the last three months." There was a pause of a few seconds while, as Ben guessed, Carrie searched her vast store of vocabulary. Sure enough, Carrie finished her sentence, "Since you went on your expedition."

"Well, Carrie, I am going on another expedition and I would like you to meet myself and my friend outside the main entrance of the clinic at nine o'clock tomorrow morning."

Again, Ben sensed an emotion. But this time it was one of expectancy.

Not this time Carrie, Ben thought, *it will just be a trip I will be going on with Gerry.*

Gerry was bursting with curiosity. "Who is Carrie?" he asked.

Ben smiled. "It," he said, "is a car albeit a very clever car."

"But," Gerry stuttered, "but you were having a conversation with him." He searched for a word, "IT!!!"

"A voice programmed computer, Gerry," Ben said laughing at the expression on his friend's face.

Ben pulled his own computer out from under his pillow, asked a passing nurse if she could plug it in, thanked her, turned it on and booted it up. He thought it unbelievable, but the date proved it, he had not used it for two months. Fortunately, everything had been transferred over to George.

Ben felt a wave of guilt, George had run the whole show with no help from himself.

He rang George on his mobile.

The call was picked up immediately. “Hello Ben, how are you? Silly question but hopefully you will be up and charging about soon, and before you ask everything is fine at my end.”

Ben thanked him, and promising to see him the following day, rang off.

Early next day, Ben was up at the crack of dawn. When up, it was with the help of two nurses who having got him in his wheelchair took him off for a shower, under their coveralls, they both had swimsuits on. Bathing Ben tended to be hazardous, as Ben kept falling off the shower chair.

Back in the ward, he stayed in the chair and as soon as breakfast was finished and they were alone, he pushed his chair to Gerry’s bed. Helping each other to dress, they then vacated the ward, with Gerry pushing and Ben guiding. Reaching the lift, they went down to the car park.

Carrie, on Ben’s instructions had parked close to the lift.

“Good morning, Carrie.”

“Good morning, Benjamin,” the car responded. Gerry giggled.

Opening the car’s driver and passenger doors, Ben guided Gerry in and got Carrie to turn and move the driving seat so he was able, with the use of his arms, to sit in it.

“Back to driving position, Carrie,” the seat moved smoothly back to face the steering wheel.

“Carrie, I am unable to use any of the foot controls so would you make the adjustments.”

There was a humming, a few clicks and Ben was informed that the car now had control of the foot controls.

Ben, from his computer, had given the car’s sat nav a detailed map of northern Spain so they were ready for the off.

Ben had one more thing to do.

Gently easing into Gerry’s mind, he asked, “Can you see the cars around us Gerry?”

There was a gasp. "Yes I can. How?"

"Sorry," Ben said. "I've put our minds in parallel so what I see, you see. I did not tell you because you might have not been receptive"

Gerry was over the moon. "I can really enjoy our trips now."

Exiting the underground car park, they set off.

Ben felt as if he was actually using the foot pedals but of course, he wasn't.

They drove along, both enjoying the scenery, golds, blues, greens and yellows and the myriad of hues in between.

When they went on a stretch of motorway, Gerry's sight started to fade, he realised it was his concentration that was getting the images from Ben's eyesight.

Two hours later, they were approaching the first completed Crystal.

Passing through two massive doors that swung shut behind them, they drove down what appeared to be the high street. Carrie stopped outside two buildings, both restaurants, but so completely different. One was a typical English pub, right down to the oak beams and plastered walls, whilst the other was Spanish with just a bar and kitchens inside. And all the seating was in the open, under cover, hanging from the overhead covering were thousands of plastic pots which made a sighing sound as the breeze passed through them. The pub was actually called The Olde English Inn, but the Bodega was called The Yoghurt Potters. "Well," Gerry said, "do you want a pint or a bottle of wine?"

That got a smile from Ben. "I imagine you can get either from either."

"Hello," said a voice, "they told me you had managed to escape."

It was George. Ben who was now in his wheelchair pumped his hand.

"George, am I pleased to see you. How are you coping with all the work I've landed you with?"

"No problem Ben, you giving me a free hand has made everything so much easier. I've obviously employed more staff, and with this Crystal completed, I have started on the foundations of another five. I have booked you both rooms in the Inn," he said smiling, "so we can talk later. Now, who is this friend of yours?"

"Sorry, this is Gerry, and he unfortunately, is blind," Ben then whispered, "at present."

George raised an eyebrow but said nothing.

George taking Gerry's hand, shook it warmly.

"Pleased to meet you, Gerry. Now, what sort of a host am I? Please come inside and we will have some lunch."

Before they could move, however, an ambulance pulled up behind Carrie. Ben groaned. "I wondered how long before the troops arrived." He turned to George. "George would you ask that ambulance driver to turn around and return to the centre."

Dutifully George went across. As he did so, a figure emerged from the back of the ambulance.

"Mother." Ben breathed. "I might have guessed. Hello mother, why are you following me?"

Louisa smiled. "I was at a loose end and thought it would be nice to come and see you and your first greenhouse."

Ben winced. "Mother," he said, a trifle tetchy, "it's called a Crystal."

Louisa smiled even more sweetly, "Yes, my dear boy, but we can't have you running round the countryside in your present condition."

"Mother, I am not a child. Do you really want me to lay in that hospital bed all day and every day?"

The last thing Louisa wanted was Ben moping in bed, so she conceded.

"Very well, Benjamin, just be careful."

"I will take care of them both," a tinny voice said.

Louisa shuddered. *Oh no,* she thought, *that vehicle was talking to me again.* She rushed back to the ambulance and was gone.

Ben and Gerry stayed with George for a week. Gerry was left rather to himself as the other two had their heads together most of the time. But with a few pints and a barmaid to chat to, he quite happily whiled away his time. The following morning, Ben found George downstairs at breakfast.

"Good morning, George,"

"Morning," came the amiable reply.

"I'm taking Gerry to my lab today. There is only a small chance but I am going to try to restore his sight, even if he only has partial vision."

George expressed his surprise, from what he had heard the bullet had done irreparable damage.

"I will forewarn him and he can make his choice, but knowing Gerry, I know the answer."

And so it was, even with only a 10% chance, Gerry grabbed at it.

They set off shortly after, thanking George for everything he was coping with.

It was about a two-hour journey to the lab, but it started to rain and being Spain, it turned into a monsoon, reducing them to a crawl. It stopped eventually and within minutes there was a bright blue sky and the air was so fresh they wanted to take great gulps of it.

"Wow," Gerry exclaimed, "look at that."

Ben, who at that moment in time, was negotiating a series of hairpin bends said, "Look at that." He slowed and looked ahead; in the sky was a brilliant rainbow and below it, a second rainbow, the colours were vivid.

He smiled, "Wow, indeed,"

Soon after, they were approaching a copse of trees, Gerry looked, the road ended before they reached the trees. "Ben," he yelled, and instinctively slammed his foot down onto the floor as the trees loomed upon them. Gerry shut his eyes bracing himself, nothing happened.

"Sorry," Ben said, as Gerry cautiously peeped. The road was there again.

"Hologram, I should have told you, oh and there is another one coming up."

Sure enough a cliff was ahead and they were about to run into it when it too disappeared and they were in a brightly lit tunnel.

They drove for another ten minutes and stopped.

"Right, we walk from here or rather I sit in my chair and you walk," he said grinning.

Having got Ben into the wheelchair, they walked to yet another wall that dissolved as Ben operated a remote. Ahead now was a door and passing through that they entered the lab.

It lit up and Gerald the images Ben had sent him. He gasped; the lab looked more like the control room at Houston. Gerry was truly amazed.

"I never knew this existed."

"Very few people do."

After a moment's thought, Gerry asked, "So why bring me here?"

"It is also a medical centre and I have built some extremely advanced technical and surgical equipment and apparatus, at the moment untested, so you will be my guinea pig. I am telling you this again because there is only a slim chance of full vision but a reasonable chance of partial."

The response was immediate. "Please, boss let's get on with it."

"Please, you might call me a lot of other names after the op but for now, call me Ben."

"Yes boss, oh sorry." They both laughed nervously.

With Gerry pushing, Ben led the way to the shower room.

Guiding him into the shower room, Ben said, "Have a shower, when you're done tell me and I will bombard you with antiseptic ensigns, then when you leave the shower you must don the suit which is hanging outside the door."

Five minutes later, Gerry emerged looking like a spaceman in his plastic suit.

Having scrubbed up himself, he then got Gerry to the adjoining room and told him to lay on the operating table. He then gave him an injection in the neck.

"Count to ten Gerry." He got to six then his voice trailed off and he was under and sound.

Ben got to work immediately, taking both eyes out and laying them very gently onto the sterilised pads he had laid on his cheeks. Ben used a laser which not only cut but also sutured to microscopic detail. An hour later, he was finished. *Only time will tell now,* he thought. Although, he was quietly confident of the outcome, having taken a scan and looked at it through a microscope. Another hour passed and Gerry began to stir. Ben waited until he was fully awake.

"You okay, Gerry?"

"I cannot see," he muttered drowsily.

"That's okay, your eyes are covered with bandages."

Gerry breathed an audible sigh of relief.

"I have done all I can here so we need to make tracks and get you back to the medical centre. The mobiles are useless here so any calls will have to wait."

They made their way back to the door to the tunnel.

Closing up the lab, they moved towards the car.

Gerry stopped pushing. Ben, thinking he was still not quite with it, said nothing.

"Did you hear that?"

Ben listened and after a moment he heard it too, a faint drumming sound, and getting louder.

Ben, concerned now, gave Gerry vision of the tunnel, pulled a revolver from the bag on the chair and handing it to Gerry told him to take cover. Gerry scuttled away and disappeared behind an archway that protruded. Ben moved his chair so it was half-hidden by Carrie. Pulling out his remote, he doused the lights in the tunnel. The drumming slowed, then stopped. Now with no sound, his worst fears were realised; this was no search party, this was enemy.

He configured the remote into a laser and moved the chair sideways to get a better view as he was unable to penetrate their minds. The chair creaked and all hell was let loose. Carrie became a glow of light and at the same time Ben's chair was struck by an enormous electric shock. The pain was terrible, his whole body convulsed including his LEGS!!!

Gerry got struck by a splinter of rock, a bullet had struck the rock that sheltered him.

As Ben slid into unconsciousness, he heard Carrie open fire with its own heat seeking automatic weapon. The bullets obviously found their mark because it became silent.

Gerry crouched behind his rock, still clutching his laser gun. He sensed more than heard a presence and a voice spoke and took the gun from his hand.

"It is alright, Gerald," the voice said.

Only one person called him Gerald! Maria! He gave a sigh of relief and passed out.

Maria made him comfortable and ran over to Ben who was actually smouldering.

"Benjie," she cried. His clothes were charred in places with wisps of smoke coming from them.

The wheelchair was a wreck. The thick rubber tyres were burnt to shreds, right down to the rims.

Frantically, she searched for a pulse, and to her great relief found one, very weak but a pulse.

"Oh Benjie, what have they done to you," she felt like crying, not knowing his condition.

In fact, he had had a massive electric shock and the thing that saved him were the tyres on the chair, they had stopped the current passing through Ben to earth. Otherwise, he would have been just charred and burnt to death.

There came the sound of running feet again and Maria stiffened.

"It is alright," a tinny voice informed her. "I asked for help."

Maria gave a small smile. "Thank you, Carrie."

Within a few minutes, Maria was surrounded by several of the security team.

They informed Maria that just one of the assailants was alive.

"Stretchers," Maria said. The men looked at one another, they had just run a mile down the tunnel and not one of them were thinking of stretchers.

"Again, Carrie came to the rescue. I will take Benjamin and his companion to the entrance. There are blankets under the back seats." And with that the two stretchers slid from her rear.

Maria commandeered two of the security; one was already with Gerry. "Can you carry him to the stretcher Tom?" He nodded. Maria pulled the blankets out and laid them on the two stretchers, then got the other man to help her carry Ben to the car.

Once on the stretchers, they retracted back into the car.

"Right, you two in the car with me." Maria turned to the other men. "Could you clean up here please and make it secure? Oh and bring the one that survived to the medical centre." She gave them a smile. "And thank you for coming."

"Hope the boss and Gerry will be okay," one of them said and they all added the same.

Arriving at the tunnel entrance, Maria found there were now two helicopters and from the second one Louisa and Tessa emerged.

"Will they be alright?" they asked.

Maria assured them that they would both be fine, only she was far from sure about Ben.

While the two were being transferred to the helicopter, Louisa asked Maria how she had managed to get to Ben and Gerry so quickly.

"I was following them," Maria said shyly. "Once I knew they had planned their little escapade, I put a bug under the wheel arch on Carrie, and I followed them on that," she pointed to a motorbike by the side of the road. "Mind you," she sniffed, "I nearly got drowned in that rainstorm earlier."

Maria got a hug from the pair of them.

"Thank you, yet again," they said.

"Now," Louisa started, "let's get these two back to bed where they belong." She winked at the other two. "I think I might strap them to the bed. Especially this one," she added bending down and giving Ben a gentle hug. They all laughed.

"What a good idea!" Tessa commented, half-serious.

Ben woke feeling really awful. Here he was in the same bed aching even more, he started to remember them!! TRIP!! And swung his head round: more pain, and there was Gerry.

"Gerry," he whispered softly.

The response was immediate. Gerry turned over to face him.

"Ben, you're awake," he shouted. Ben stared at him.

"I told you those bandages had to stay on at least five days," he said accusingly.

Gerry laughed. “Ben that was over a week ago.”

“Oh, have I been out of it that long.” Gerry nodded. “Well, are you going to tell me can you see anything?”

“I can see. I am now looking at a very serious boss, I mean Ben. Yes, I can see even better than before, thanks to you, boss.”

Ben was delighted that it was worth waking up for, he thought happily.

The room was suddenly full. Ben had three women trying to hug and kiss him and Tom trying to shake his hand. He was beset by pain. “Ow, ow, ouch,” he yelped.

Everyone jumped back.

“Ben, Ben, what is it?” Tessa said, wanting to hug but not daring to.

“My whole body aches.”

The room emptied then filled again with doctors who asked questions and pushed and poked him. Then, he was sent off for a scan and when all the results came through, it turned out that the shock Ben had received was similar to that of a shock for cardiac arrest, it jolted the nerves in his spinal cord into action.

“That may be,” he said, “but I can’t feel my legs now.”

The physiotherapist worked all day on his legs and Ben was still unable to put his feet to the floor. Maria came in to a grim-faced Ben.

“I thought I might be able to walk again, so far no luck with that.”

Maria sympathised and after chatting for a while, trying to cheer him up, she left. She was back within a minute.

“Ben,” she screamed, “it’s Mars. Something terrible happened, you must come.”

A terrified Ben jumped out of bed, took a step and crashed to the floor screaming.

“Ow, my legs are on fire, what has happened to Mars,” he yelled.

Maria rushed to help him and with a nurse, got him back in bed.

Maria hugged him. “Mars is fine and Ben you took a step.”

He looked at her in horror. “Maria, you lied to me, you of all people, how could you?”

She hung her head in shame.

“Oh, Benjie, I’m so sorry, it was Venus. She said it was the human side of you that stopped you from trying to walk, Louisa and Tessa agreed, saying it was the only way to galvanise you into moving your legs.”

He looked into her eyes, they were close to tears.

"They're unbelievably evil, them and their Machiavellian schemes."

He pulled her close, gave her a hug and a light kiss on her lips.

Maria sighed, not so much with relief, more for the kiss.

As if on cue, Venus, Tessa and his mother came in, bearing gifts.

Flowers, chocolates, strawberries and a big tub of Tiramisu ice cream. All the food he adored but was seldom allowed.

The following weeks were hell for him. He had a physiotherapist every morning and in the afternoon he was walking, or rather trying to walk between parallel bars his arms bearing most of the weight, with his hands clenched and feet moving slowly along the floor.

After six weeks, he was able to walk the whole length of the 30 feet ward unaided.

He then started to go on short walks, gradually increasing the length day by day.

Maria always went with her, she okayed with Tessa first. Tessa just laughed at Maria's asking.

"I trust you more than anyone and besides, without you there would be no Ben. How many times have you saved his life? And risking your own into the bargain."

Soon he was running. Well, stumbling was a better word but it was worth it. After each session, Maria would give his whole body a vigorous rub down, and that Ben really enjoyed even though he got a slap once or twice when he misbehaved, but he was feeling fit and well. *It's time I started pulling my weight*, he thought.

Maria, for her part, was happy. She kept Tessa informed of Ben's progress and struggled with her conscience being so close to the man she loved but should not love. Tessa would tell her she was too old fashioned but in her mind that still seemed wrong. What would her sisters at the convent say?

On their run one morning, Ben turned to Maria. "What happened to that woman?" he asked.

Maria looked at him. "What woman?" she asked.

"The one you shot in the tunnel."

"Oh, her. She is in Lucy's care and Lucy is slowly getting more information from her. Her name is Azel," she added.

The same evening, Ben entered the medical centre and made his way to a secure ward where he was admitted by a profile recognition sensor.

Seeing a light on in a small office, he entered. Lucy sat there her fingers flying over a computer keyboard, without stopping, she said, "Good evening, Benjamin."

"I thought so," he said. "You put the thought in my mind to pay you a visit."

This time Lucy stopped typing and turned to face Ben.

"I thought you would like to know that was the last attempt by the Grand Master to kill you, even though he fears you and your ability to survive. You should have been burnt to a cinder by that shock you received," she added.

"Why me," he asked. "In fact, why my family, the attacks have been against all of us, even baby Mars."

"It's because you're a throwback, Benjamin."

"A what?"

"A throwback. When we, the Arians, settled on Umbria we had a strict dictate. We were never to integrate or interfere in any way with the Umbrians. Many hundreds of years ago the impossible happened. An Arian fell in love with an Umbrian against all odds, and they had a child. But all ended well. The child was pure Umbrian and the offspring up to this time have all been Umbrian, until now."

"Mars," Ben said, immediately. "He is part Arian. That is why they attacked him and Tessa in London." He shuddered at the carnage Mars had caused in the car park, and the power Mars had, to be able to drag his own mind to there.

"Yes," she said. "Mars has some of your powers, but you." She hesitated. "You are the direct descendant of three worlds, which makes you most vulnerable and also the most dangerous enemy of the Grand Master. With the combination of your triple genes, your power," again she hesitated, "your ultimate power is unknown even to us Arians."

"That is ridiculous, without Maria, I would be dead, um, well I have lost count, how many times."

Lucy smiled. "True," she said, "you have kept your skin just because Maria was always there to guard you."

"But why can I not defend myself."

"Your genes are pure Arian which binds you to the dictate of the Arians. You must not defend yourself or harm another species".

Really confused now, Ben said, "but when I went to my father's and Ivan's aid people died then."

"You were defending and the hologram you set against them, would have been harmless if they were innocent." Your human body is protected too, you should have burnt with that electric shock. Even if your Umbrian and Earthly bodies were destroyed you would still survive albeit as a globe of pure white light, which is our natural state. This body I have was chosen for me when I was created or born," Lucy stated.

Lucy let Ben take in all that she said, and then carried on.

"The human race is in grave danger Benjamin. After hours of questioning, Azel told me that the Grand Master will destroy the majority of humans and she, as the Grand Master's leading Mistress will rule Earth. Apparently, he has already sent the Masters he trusts to Earth to welcome him in his victory. They are dispersed now but will gather when the Grand Master arrives."

Ben was in the depths of despair, it was true since the industrial revolution, the contamination has grown slowly at first but now in a few decades even with the Crystals the population would be decimated. Before then, if that madman was not stopped. Some small steps have been taken in the 1950s; in one year, 10000 people had died in London. The burning of coal fires was banned, a drop in the ocean, he thought gloomily.

The developing world, with its billions of human inhabitants, had ignored all warnings and good intentions in the race and name of progress.

Years earlier, he had learned of the development of a filtration plant which took in the contaminated air and expelled pure oxygen. Some of the worst affected cities had them installed in the worst areas, mainly in hospitals and medical centres. Alongside the air conditioning plants, the air was virtually 100% clean. He had them installed in his own workshops and his father's pharmaceutical factories the cost was high but this was largely offset by having a much healthier workforce.

Making a decision, he started making phone calls to everybody he knew in the industrial world, plus politicians and friends who had influence in high places. Thirty hours later, his staff rang Tessa. Lucy answered. Tessa, she explained, was away working in a field hospital, the injury rate was high in the building of the Crystals. Lucy, who was now the nanny for Mars when Tessa was away, relayed the message and Tessa then rang Maria.

She found him slumped over his desk phone in hand, dead asleep.

It took her ten minutes to wake him, another ten to drag him to the shower. And half an hour later, he was in bed asleep. Maria rang Tessa on her mobile and said she would ring again when he was woken by Maria. She has a tray laden with food. Smelling it made him realise just how hungry he was. His stomach gurgled.

"I see we're a mite hungry," she said, laughed and nearly dropped the tray.

"Whoa," he said, grabbing the tray. "God, I am so hungry. What have we here, maid?"

"I think it is called A Full English breakfast, my lord."

She spoke with a plum in her mouth. "If that is all, I'll be off," adding "I've never seen so much fat on one plate before."

"Back to the scullery maid," Ben managed to say between mouthfuls.

She was back in ten minutes, just in time to see him wipe his plate clean with his last piece of bread and empty his mug of tea.

Seeing crumbs on his pyjama jacket, she commented, "Oh dear, I should have given you a napkin."

"Ah," said Ben, "that filled a whole maid. You may take my tray and brush those crumbs off me."

"Of course," she said, "how uncouth," she added brushing off the offensive crumbs, her nose, so much in the air she failed to notice the glint in his eye.

She went to put the tray on the side table and as she turned to straighten the bed, he grabbed her.

"Oh what are you doing, unhand me," she struggled furiously to no avail.

"You, too, are punished for your rudeness to your lord and master," he said, smugly.

"Oh no," she wailed as he started to kiss, she felt as if she were floating and looked down at him and she was floating, her body was several inches above his. He rose to her and they slowly spanned above the bed. Finally, coming to each other, they climaxed. Afterwards, they both lay side by side. For the first time in days, Ben felt relaxed, his worries in the background.

Maria, despite her scruples and guilt was on cloud nine, ten and eleven.

"Well," she said. "I've heard of mile high club but not six inches," she giggled.

They slept and both woke feeling rejuvenated. Ben never told her why he was so distressed and Maria, knowing Ben as she did, never asked. They showered and decided to go for a run.

It had rained overnight and the air was fresh and clean. At times like this, Lucy's predictions seemed impossible.

Maria who was way ahead of him, suddenly shouted out, “Look,” she said, pointing north. He did and although it was early autumn the Pyanees had a sprinkling of snow on them. They ran on, mainly on the abandoned roads. Spain, as it developed and built new straight roads, just left the old twisty ones. They had an abundance of undergrowth on either side of these roads and a profusion of brightly coloured flowers some of which were growing through the cracks in the road.

He was breathing easily and considered himself really fit. Catching up with Maria, he informed her that he would be working during the week, but would still like a run on weekends.

Maria nodded. “As long as you don’t mind me being around. I promised Tessa,” she added quickly.

Ben teased her. “If you want to be around me, I will be more than happy,” he said.

Maria gave him a gentle punch which nearly sent him flying and had him rubbing his arm.

“Behave yourself or I’ll abandon you, you sod,” and laughing, she ran ahead.

“I will, I will.” They ran at a steady pace enjoying the breeze when they reached the higher ground which was fortunate because as the morning progressed the temperature lower down was rising. After a ten-kilometre run they were back at the place where they were stripped off and had a shower and then flopped into rattan chairs on the shaded patio. Although, they had had a good breakfast they were both starving again. Then the maid came out and Ben looked up and smiled, she felt her legs go wobbly such were her feelings for Ben.

“I have just made a paella,” she stammered. Ben and Maria both said, “Yes, please, a paella would be very acceptable.” The maid with Ben’s smile still focussed on her, went red and rushed off in a fluster.

“Benjie,” Maria chided, “you have that poor girl tripping over her own feet and the paella will end up on our laps instead of our stomachs.”

Ben helped himself to a glass of fresh orange juice which was on the table. Having taken a long thirst-quenching drink, he laid back in the chair and contentedly closed his eyes.

“There,” he said. “I will keep my eyes shut until the paella is on the table.” Again they both slept well and early the next day, they were in the car driving to meet George.

Maria had been up very early packing their things and getting together all the paperwork Ben would need. Hence she was now sound asleep stretched out on the back seat.

Ben had his wrist mobile on as he was driving, and it was on loudspeaker.

George's voice boomed out. "Hi Ben. Hi Maria." Maria started suddenly, very much awake.

"Bloody hell," was her only response to the very cheerful greeting.

"Sorry," came a much-subdued voice.

"It's okay, George," Maria muttered, rubbing her eyes.

"Problems, George?" Ben asked.

"No, just change of meeting place."

"Where to now?" Ben asked.

"Not much further. Zaragotha instead of Lleida. About forty minutes' drive."

"Ok, bye for now."

Ben fed the new destination into the sat nav and continued on. Maria said, "Bloody man," and promptly curled up again and went back to sleep.

Two hours later, they had arrived and Ben was gently shaking Maria.

"Come on sleepy head, we are here."

Maria yawned and stretched and said, "I'm hungry."

"Well, you're in luck, it's lunch time." Maria shook her head to straighten her hair and jumped out of the car.

"Come on lazy bones," she said laughing as Ben struggled out of the car, stiff from the drive. They had stopped on the forecourt of what looked to be a very nice hotel.

"I hope the food is as good as the hotel looks," Maria commented.

In front of the hotel, George appeared through the revolving doors. After hugs and kisses for Maria, George took Ben by his shoulders and surveyed him.

"You do not look too bad."

"Thanks," Ben answered with a grin on his face, pleased to see his good friend again.

"You look a bit frayed round the edges yourself."

"Well," George replied, "when your boss decides to take a six-month sabbatical and you're left holding a project of a few hundred billion one can reasonably expect to get a few grey hairs." They both laughed and then went all serious.

"I'll never forget the effort and work you have put in George."

George almost blushed, such was his pleasure at the praise. Even Maria looked surprised, Ben was never one to give praise normally.

"Come on in the hotel," George said. "I want you to meet someone and besides it's getting bloody cold out here." Inside, he led them to the bar.

"Ben, Maria, may I introduce you to Romilly, my girl Friday." Romilly smiled and shook their hands. Romilly was striking, nearly as tall as Ben, with tawny golden hair with eyes to match, a high forehead, high cheekbones with a large nose which seemed to fit well on her attractive face, under the nose was a sensuous mouth. She was slim, he thought, but well-proportioned and her legs seemed to go on forever but ended in a pair of incongruous boots. Ben's survey had only taken a few seconds but it earned him a cool look from Maria. Romilly slipped her hand into George's and bending slightly, she gave him a kiss. *Well,* Ben thought, looking at George's face which was rapturous. *Well,* he thought, *not only about girls Friday but all week too.*

George gently disengaged himself from her embrace.

"Romilly is from Israel and she is my chief engineer."

Ben suddenly remembered George going on about a really brilliant engineer, but never realised it was a woman. His thoughts were interrupted by Maria.

"If I do not eat soon, I'm going to pass out." George overheard her.

"Maria, I have a table for us, follow me." So all four proceeded to their table. Much later, after a five-course meal, they retired to the lounge to discuss the progress on the Crystal Domes.

Maria, after five courses of excellent cuisine and half a bottle of a very nice Cava, had a blissful look on her face.

"Do you mind if I go to our room and have a little rest."

"Of course, you must," George said. Noting she had said our room, he added, "I have actually booked two rooms but they have an adjoining door." Maria took the key and disappeared.

Finding her room, she opened the door and nearly fell. She was very, very tired and the Cava had not helped. She took a quick shower which helped a little and then flopping on the bed, she was asleep in seconds. Much later, Ben slipped into her room and gently covered her naked body with a duvet. Before he went up to his room though, he wanted a progress report from George.

George pulled out a battered briefcase which was stuffed full of plans and specifications relating to work done, work in progress and plans which were still at the drawing board stage.

Initially, he laid out a map of Spain. On it, from Barcelona across northern Spain to the borders of Portugal were a line of Crystal Domes connected by what looked like a silver thread, but were in fact a four-lane road and a two-lane rail track. Ben could see at a glance that only a few were near completion, but was also staggered at the amount of work that had been done.

"George you have created miracles to have accomplished so much." George grinned.

"Thanks, I'm quite pleased with myself but I have a good team" and his eyes wandered to Romilly who was busy sorting the various plans out. For the next few hours, they worked mainly on prioritising future construction, Romilly was proving herself to be a huge asset when it came to engineering problems on the sites themselves, especially where the terrain is mountainous, which caused structural headaches. Finally, they were finished for the night.

"How about a nightcap," Ben prompted.

"Not for me, I'm bushed," Romilly answered.

Ben stood up and kissed her.

"Thanks for all you have done. It made things easier for George having you on board."

Romilly laughed. "It's a pleasure and shopping area, besides you are paying me for it."

George stood up also. "Goodnight darling," and he gave her a hug and a kiss. She gave him a hug back and left them.

Ben noticed that George was a bit slow when he stood up.

"You okay?" he asked

George grinned. "Just a bit stiff."

Ben looked more closely, he did not look fine. He ordered their drinks and settled in the very comfortable armchairs. While waiting for the drinks to arrive, he examined George. His mind is as sharp as ever, he thought. He started to examine internally, he didn't have to go far; damn he has cancer. Fortunately, it was still in its early stages. Their drinks arrived. George took a sip.

"I needed that," he said, relaxing.

Ben asked quietly, "When did you last have a medical?"

He grinned wryly, "When I joined you."

"Well, you're going to have one tomorrow and I want you and Romilly to go on a course of injections. There is a nasty virus going around and you are both exposed to all sorts of diseases when you're on site. Some of the workers from abroad have not had proper medicals and you both need to be protected." George looked at Ben astonished.

"What was that outburst about?" he exclaimed. "I might be a bit stiff and tired but that is all."

"Nevertheless, I'm the boss and that is what I want, you wouldn't want Romilly becoming ill, would you?" George scrutinised Ben.

"There's something you know, something you are not telling me."

Ben laughed. "I know nothing, now drink up so I can order another."

The pair spent another half hour drinking, then George, yawning, declared he was ready for his bed.

"See you in the morning, sleep well." Ben looked at the clock at 12.

He had a quick shower and crept in to where Maria lay; she was sound asleep. He crept out; *let the girl have her rest,* he thought. Once in bed himself, he was asleep in seconds. He woke up only minutes later. It was, however, early morning. He could see the light filtering through the curtain. He heard a slight rustling sound. There he heard it again, then he realised someone was in bed with him, he swung round and found himself looking into two enormous eyes.

"Maria, I thought you would still be asleep this time in the morning."

"Well, I was but you left the communicating door ajar and your snoring woke me."

"I do not snore" he protested.

"You do," she insisted.

"Liar," he said and he added, "you know what happens to those who tell porkies."

"Not that," she squeaked as he started.

"Yes, I'm afraid so, death by tickling."

The screams from Maria gradually faded into moans and gasps of pleasure.

Much later, when they were both utterly exhausted they lay side by side.

"I hope you feel your punishment was justified."

"Oh, yes, master," she gurgled. "I feel completely punished. Shall we have a shower now?"

"Yes," he said, "but just a shower."

"Oh tired, are we?" she giggled.

She made a mistake, saying that, because just as she was stepping into the shower, Ben turned the cold tap full on.

There were more loud shrieks as she jumped out the shower and Ben got called many names that he had never heard before. After their shower, they lay on the bed and quietly talked until the sun slowly rose. Ben told Maria of the conversation he had had with George the previous evening.

"Did you tell him what the injections were for and what they did," she asked.

"No, I did not," he said. "I'm not sure what the reaction would be, but George will need surgery for his cancer, anyway. His heart is in poor shape, so the injections will eventually help there, and it will help Romilly and the baby she is carrying." Maria was surprised at this new information.

"Will the baby benefit?" she asked.

"Of course, he or she will inherit Romilly's extra genes."

"Well, I hope they go ahead with it. I like George, and now I have met her, Romilly, I find I like her. George is obviously very much in love with her and she is with him. They make a fine pair."

"Invaluable," Ben murmured wondering how the hell he was going to explain to George and Romilly about having double organs and long lives. To Maria, it was simple. Although you could die by accident or, especially in her profession, by being slain, you could live for a thousand years and should wipe out anyone's doubts. George and Romilly appeared finally just before noon looking very happy and pleased with themselves. Ben asked them what they would like for breakfast-cum-lunch, they both saw the waiter hovering to lay tables and settled for a sandwich which George asked to be served in the lounge along with a jug of coffee. He said all this in fluent Spanish. Turning to Ben and Maria, he asked if they wanted anything else, as they had already eaten. He also asked for a jug of warm milk. George speaking in Spanish obviously pleased the waiter and surprised Ben.

"Who taught you Spanish?"

"Oh it was Romilly. Spanish was one of her languages at university."

"George is an excellent student, he has an ear for languages," she added smiling.

Ben watched quietly while they ate, pouring himself a coffee, he came to a decision, which, if went wrong, would be a disaster if they rejected what he asked of them.

Seeing the tension in Ben's face, George asked, "Is everything okay?"

"Nothing," he lied. "Now if you have stopped stuffing yourselves like two hungry wolves, I suggest we will ask for a packed lunch and then go and look at our latest project." George immediately looked pleased.

"It's coming along very nicely."

"I know, I have seen the satellite photos," Ben told him.

They all wrapped up. It would be quite chilly at the altitude where the latest dome was under construction. George insisted on driving, knowing all the twists and turns, plus all the ruts and potholes on the minor roads. It was not long before they reached city number five, simply named as it was the fifth under construction. George had taken them on a route that led to a mile above the site so the site was spread out below them from their view on the mountainside.

Ben gasped, even though it was in early stages of development and was just showing its bare bones, it was breath-taking. The city consisted of twenty domes and the whole site measured at least 15 miles across, some 225 square miles. Although uncompleted, its different structures could easily be identified by its areas. From the city in the centre with its shops and commercial buildings and a park with a large lake to the outskirts with its suburbs, with houses and moving out further, the outer ring of domes were all dedicated to the production of food. Maria's eyes were popping out of her head.

"My god," she said, "it's magnificent. No, it's better than that, it's beautiful and stupendous." She had a thought. "There were no factories, where is everything made?" she asked.

"You're standing on top of all the industrial production businesses," Romilly told her. "Over the course of time, the whole centre of this mountain has been eroded, so it's ideal for production, all the fumes and gases etc. are passed through a filtration system within the mountain so it's ideal."

"Oh," Maria said, quite lost for words, "it's amazing."

"It's bigger than I comprehended," Ben commented.

"Yes," Romilly said, "to supply and feed a million people it will have to be even bigger than what you see."

"You have been doing your sums," he said looking at her with new respect.

"Is that okay, Ben?" George asked. "We have gone over budget."

Ben just smiled. "That is why I gave you free rein," and he pointed to the city below. "Now, before we go down to have a closer look, there is something that is very important and very serious I have to discuss with you and Romilly."

"I thought so," George muttered, "when you started talking about injections last night."

Romilly turned to George. "What's this about injections," she asked.

George told her of the conversation he and Ben had had the night before.

Romilly went pink. "I'm not sure I want to have any injections," she exclaimed.

Ben thought, *I'll have to come clean.*

Turning to Romilly, he asked her outright, "Does George know." She went a pinker shade.

"Know what?" he asked startled.

Before Ben could say anything, she said, "I'm pregnant, George." Then turning to Ben, she shouted, "How the hell do you know?"

Ben sent calming thoughts over them, *this is it,* he thought.

Turning to face them both, he said, "I have certain powers, or if you like, abilities. To put it bluntly, I can see into people's minds and bodies."

Both George and Romilly paled.

George looked at Ben, often he would think of an idea or plan and Ben would question him about it without George saying a word. He now knew Ben could actually read his mind, scary.

"What are you telling us, Ben? Are you a genetic experiment, bionic or on some sort of super drug?" He then said this jokingly, "Or are you an alien?"

"You're wrong on all counts, although the last guess was close. I'm part human and the other part of me is from another planet."

"An alien?" they gasped.

"No," he said, smiling, there shocked faces more like a foreigner but not from another country, from another world.

He then told them, as briefly as possible, his and his family's life history. He hoped he had done the right thing in telling them and in the next few minutes, he would know. He also informed them of the benefits of the injections. Leaving the worst to last, he told George about the cancer.

George just smiled.

"I did wonder, I was getting pains, and just took pain killers. I hate going to the doctors," he confessed.

"Just one other thing, I have only told two other people. Maria being one of those." George held his hand up to stop Ben.

"I know I speak for the both of us Ben, our lips are sealed to the day we die."

"Well," Romilly said, "these injections will not harm our baby. George will be cured of his cancer and," she added lightly, "we will all live to a thousand years."

"At least," Ben said, now really happy he had told them. "The oldest recorded age for an Umbrian stands at 1457."

George grabbed Ben's hand and shook it, "Thanks Benjamin." Romilly kissed him lightly on the cheek.

"Thank you Benjamin, for your concern, of our wellbeing, telling us has put yourself and your fellow Umbrians at risk. It proves to me that you think of my George," she added looking at George's shell-shocked features. "I now think we should return to the hotel and get my George booked in for surgery for his cancer, and I leave it to you Ben with regard to the course of injections."

Ben smiled, "There is no panic. The cancer is at an early stage. But I have to admit I'm hungry, must be all this fresh air. We will go and say hello to the site manager. See if there are any problems and then go back to the hotel for some good food and wine."

"No wine for Romilly," George said grinning from ear to ear. He looked at Romilly and said, "I can hardly believe it. Me, a dad at my age."

Romilly smiled, "I am very happy." Suddenly the smile left her face. "My god," she gasped. "What is that…" They turned to see what and gasped themselves.

In the distance, racing, it seemed towards them, was a black column which was half a mile wide.

A tornado, rare, but there it was racing, it seemed straight for them sucking up a maelstrom of dust leaves, powerful enough to uproot small trees and bushes. "Back in the car," George shouted. "We'll all get blown off this ledge." Ben remained motionless.

"It's okay. It's moving to the west of where we are," and so it was but the wind was increasing and as it reached the site below them, building materials and site rubbish were swept into the air.

"Oh, no, no," Maria screamed as a figure was swept off the top of one of the buildings under construction. Down came the tiny figure, arms and legs flailing helplessly as it fell to certain death, hundreds of feet below. The others all turned away, but Ben continued to stare at the falling figure. The dome where the tragedy was about to happen was the pleasure and a hundred yards from the building, the figure that was blown off, was a lake. The wind, a surge in power and the poor sole was hurled towards it and then with a mighty splash, disappeared.

George who was now standing beside him said, “That was impossible.” Down below, tiny figures raced from where they had been sheltering, one dived in and dragged the body out as he lifted it out and put it down. To everyone’s surprise, it stood and staggered into the arms of, one assumed a relative, there was a faint cheer from way down below and sighs of relief from Maria and Romilly.

“How could he survive that? The impact on hitting the water from that height should have killed him.”

“One will never know,” Ben said. “Especially those down there, we best get down there must be damage and the site will need cleaning up.”

Romilly’s eyes were shining. “I know it was you Ben and I salute you,” she shouted.

They made their way down and walked into a major row.

“What is going on,” George demanded. The site manager saw who had descended on him and went white.

“This girl has managed to get employment here,” he spluttered, “illegally.”

“So it was a girl,” George thought.

Addressing the manager who was on tenterhooks with his job on the line, George said, “I thought it was your job to oversee all new employees.”

“I am sorry for my fault but when she came for the job her hair was cut short and she was dressed like a lad. And she gave her name as Stephan but her name is Stephanie.”

George had no choice. “I’m sorry but the law had been broken; the three of you will have to be dismissed.” He was going to add, and face possible prosecution, but Ben interrupted.

He had been observing the young girl and gentle probing saw high intelligence.

“Sorry George, you are right of course, but I want to know why, and put the question to the girl’s father, why not?”

Crestfallen, he explained, “She is a student and the fees are high and the extra money was needed.” He held up his hands. “I’m sorry for the deception senior Franklin.”

Ben smiled at the girl. “What are you studying Stephanie?”

"Physics and engineering senor," she answered, her eyes bright with unshed tears at the thought of her dear father losing his employment.

In Spanish, Ben said, "George would you mind if I altered your decision."

George was obviously pleased at Ben's intervention. He hated sacking anyone.

"No, of course not, Senor Franklin."

Ben continued. Addressing the workers, he said, "What happened today bar the miracle, could have been a tragedy, not just for this father and daughter, but for all of you. The site would have to be closed while an investigation was made, you know the consequences of that. However, although Stephanie must leave the site immediately, I will not be dismissing her father." He was interrupted by a burst of applause. "I will however be paying for all his daughter's university expenses if she accepted."

He turned and had a quiet word with George, then turning back to face the manager he told him he still had his job. "I am told that you are very busy so we have agreed to overlook your error. To make light of the whole matter, perhaps you could employ Stephanie during her gap year." There was a roar and everyone involuntarily ducked as the scaffolding collapsed from the side of one of the buildings. George took over. "I want a dozen volunteers to work the weekend to clear the debris and make repairs to any damage."

A sea of hands went up. "Pick your twelve best men," he told the manager." Addressing all the workers again, he said, "We are leaving now and as the site is dangerous you can all go apart from the twelve volunteers." More applause and the workers dispersed. The girl threw herself into Ben's arms much to the horror of her father and the manager, but to the amusement of Ben's friends.

"Thank you, so, so much, Mr Franklin. I accept your very kind offer, you will not regret your trust in me." Ben gently disengaged himself.

"Good luck with your studies and ask for Ms Romilly when you leave university and start work."

Once back in the hotel, having enjoyed a late lunch, the girls went off shopping and Ben, with George, discussed the future.

"I noticed the solar panels on the south facing side of the dome, brilliant George. However for all future Crystals, forget the sealed road and rail links, those you have already started on leave until last. They are too time consuming. Now, how about you any questions or info for me."

"Yes, the Spanish government is chipping in quite a lot with the city domes with regard to the nuclear power source. I think it is about national security, mind you but it saves you a few billion."

"No nuclear power for the domes everywhere else though. We have come up with an alternative, oil driven generators."

"What did you say?" said a shocked Ben. That is not good at all. What? Are you thinking of using fossil fuels?"

"Well," George explained, "you know the breakthrough they've had with oxygen producing plants?"

Ben shook his head, so George told him. "They have now found the DNA and it is now possible to simulate certain plants entirely so all the toxic gases will now pass through a distillery plant which is full of growing algae which is fed and watered so when the carbon dioxide and other gases pass through it, it comes out as oxygen."

"That is brilliant, George. Well done you have probably saved us a few billion with that and the solar panels, plus the boost it will give domes with regard to the power supply."

George smiled, saying, "They were both Romilly's ideas, and the saving is good however," he coughed nervously, "I have plans for twenty domes more discounting the cities, and we are going to run out of money. Sorry the costs were higher than expected."

"May I butt in?" Romilly said. "I think we will be okay if Benjamin is willing to invest more."

"Of course I will," came the reply. "If I have any left," he said, grinning.

Romilly smiled. "Oh you have," she said. "Your shares in the WWM come to 1.5 trillion."

"How do you know that?" Ben gasped. He always left his finances to Toby.

"Um, she follows the markets, especially yours as we're spending your money."

"Will that suffice, will it be enough George?" Ben asked.

"Ample," came the answer.

Ben looked at Romilly. *A truly remarkable woman,* he thought.

"Romilly, when we were at the site, you said I salute you, now I must say the same. I salute you," and he bowed his head to her. She went pink again.

"Thank you," she answered.

“One last thing. How long do you think, roughly,” he asked not wishing to put pressure, “to the completion date.”

“Twelve to fourteen years max,” George answered. Ben had hoped earlier but hopefully it would be in time.

He raised his glass to them. “George, Romilly, to the future and I will never be able to thank you both enough for all the work and effort you have both put in. Now, off to bed with you, I will see you at breakfast and then we will get you both sorted, injections first and then the cancer scans for George.” It was hugs and kisses and then saying goodnight, they were gone.

Ben had one last drink and then retired himself, thinking Mars will be 17 in 12 years.

Everything went well that year. Nearly; George recovered well from surgery but although Ben was now helping, all the technical and construction problems fell in Romilly’s lap.

And through overworking, whilst she was pregnant weakened her physically and she, from the dust and contamination on site picked up a virus and had to be rushed to hospital.

For a month, things were desperate for her and the baby, who was born premature. Louisa and Lucy nursed her and with time she and the baby recovered. George was virtually living at the hospital, so Ben had to cover for both of them. Nevertheless, when Romilly left hospital, he insisted that she and George take a six-month sabbatical, despite their protests.

The following years seemed to fly and George’s prediction of twelve years was spot on.

The Crystal Domes were completed and the cities with their surrounding parklands and farms were almost developed.

Also at that time, observatories around the world were discovering a strange anomaly in space. There was suddenly a hole in space where there should have been stars. Although it was many light years from Earth it was there, or rather not there? The military worldwide went on full alert and probes were launched towards the mysterious ‘HOLE IN SPACE’, as the world papers displayed. Of course, there was one group who knew exactly what the hole was, the Umbrians and their human confidantes. They were equally worried and were also preparing.

Ben looked at the headlines, had it not been so serious one could have laughed at the contradiction in the headlines. Following his train of thought, he calculated the world to be eight light years away which meant it would be circling the sun in roughly 12 years. The Grand Master was planning, but what, he had no idea, which just made everything worse. Away in space, the Master was putting his plan into action. Over the years, many thousands of Umbrians had taken refuge in the Ark from their damaged planet, but now through rebuilding and repairing their Crystals, they were able to return. This, the Master did; he then vacated all from the lead ship apart from the clones, such was his distrust of his fellow Masters and ships' officers. Then, giving orders he had all the magnetic ties disconnected and his ship left the Ark. He had consulted with no one, which led to great consternation amongst all the Umbrian people.

Once, he had the total support of all the Umbrians. He had eliminated poverty, united all of the Umbrians with all their different religions and beliefs, and by doing so, eliminated all conflicts and wars on his planet. That was many centuries ago. He had total power over the planet and against advice made many mistakes, the worst being when the Umbrian planet was taken out of orbit.

Instead of evacuating his people to the side, not under traction, against all advice, he had decided not to. The result was a terrible disaster. A huge portion of the planet had become dislodged and was torn away. Over two billion of his people had been in that portion of the world and now they were gone. One of the captains followed the track of the lost section in case of a few survivors but it was a forlorn hope. Since that time, hundreds of years before he had lost the trust and became isolated from his people, even the majority of his ministers no longer trusted his judgement. He was now never called by his birth name which was Irexl that alone was considered a great insult on Umbria. On Earth, once the initial panic had subsided everything settled down; defence preparations were made but whatever and why the planet suddenly appeared, it was still in deep space some eight light years' distance. Once he was clear of the Ark, Irexl reconfigured the star positions that had been beamed from the planet. On Earth, scientists decided the planet must have been hidden by a huge cloud of cosmic dust. They were however aware that it would come close to the sun and Earth's orbit. Deep beneath the Pacific Ocean in its tiny spaceship the clone that had rescued Agatha and borne Venus to Earth knew what the Irexl was planning. Being a clone, he was privy to all the commands given by Irexl. Although he was deep below, he was able to monitor through radio and satellite signals all that was happening above him on the Earth's surface. The clone also had friends down in the depths of the ocean. The school of Dolphins led by the big old bull often used to visit him, the old one though, the clone realised was holding the intelligence of an Umbrian and with the Dolphin's nose pressed against the hull of the spacecraft, they conversed. The clone, over the years, had slowly gained the ability to think independently. It was breaking away from its origins and developing its own mind, it was all very confusing for it at first, but gradually after a period of dual personality and with the Dolphin came Umbrian's help, it eventually developed a mind of its own. The clone, John decided, needed a name of its own. "We will call you Colin." John conveyed, as he thought the name, the clone sensed amusement.

"What is it?" he asked, "why are you so amused."

Just my senile old brain, John thought back. *Colin the clone*, I thought it funny. That was many years ago. But now there was no time for light hearts. The clone after much thought had broken the yoke of its other self and had told John of Alexl's plans for Earth.

John listened and as he did so, a great fear came upon him. If he carries out his plan, virtually all humans will die, he thought. Yes came the answering thought, they will. Is there no way to stop him? No, he is too powerful inside his spaceship. His defences are insurmountable. I must leave you, look after yourself my good friend and thank you and with those thoughts, he left. The clone looked at the Dolphin on the other side of the shell that encased his craft, which acted as a one-way window. He could see and sense the terrible distress the Dolphin was in. I thought, why thank me when I told such awful news?

He watched as the school of Dolphins slowly disappeared. John led his school of Dolphins across the southern Pacific and, on reaching Atlantic waters, headed north towards the Med. All through this long journey, he was trying to contact his son. Eventually he did, a fellow Umbrian in South Africa picked up his thoughts and being a friend of his son simply picked up the phone and rang Ben, telling him his father wanted to contact him urgently. Ben was himself in the Atlantic. Ben went to his cabin relaxed in a chair and let his mind drift. What his father conveyed to him made him give orders to change course back to the Med, then on to the north of Spain docking eventually in Barcelona. Whilst sailing north, he sent messages all over the world and although not daring to say why, he urged all people of all countries to prepare for a disaster of epic proportion. When pressed, he replied he did not know the facts but hinted that there should be several meteor strikes in the Earth's oceans, in the very near future.

He hoped this would have the effect of encouraging the world's populace to seek high ground for safety.

Deep in space, Irexl was preparing for his journey to Earth. The wormhole was the biggest ever attempted for a spaceship the size of Irexl's. He had timed his arrival above Earth to coincide with the full Moon. Now that the time had come, he started to create the wormhole in front of his spaceship. At first, it seemed impossible, the vacuum kept collapsing, then joy, it held. He did not hesitate, sending his ship surging into the wormhole. Faster and faster his ship went until his image was left behind itself. So fast, many times the speed of light, he thought his very soul was being torn from his body, then after time had become irrelevant, he felt the ship slowing. During that epic journey, the clones had control of the ship and now as they approached the planets circling the sun, they turned off the massive antimatter cyclops machine and the ship came back under its own power. As the wormhole evaporated, the clones guided the spaceship until it was in front of the moon, then Irexl turned the cyclops back on and waiting until the Pacific Ocean was below, he created a wormhole. When Venus had arrived the wormhole had created a huge wave. But now the wave would be a thousand times greater. Using the moon's gravity for his ship he increased the intensity of the wormhole and the ocean waters rose and rose, half a mile and they still rose, he laughed a maniacal sound, the clones looked not knowing the source of amusement. When the waters reached a mile high, he turned off the cyclops and waited until the Earth span and the waters of the Atlantic were below. He had decided this was the best way to get rid of the humans and the treacherous Umbrians. This way, he would drown them all without damaging the land. And once more, he thought, with his deranged mind he would be the hero of his people.

In the weeks prior to the arrival of Irexl, Ben had been frenetically working, sometimes twenty hours a day. He had contacted his scientific worldwide and given them vital information. His warnings, it appeared were working, people all around the world had or were moving to higher ground and the Crystal Domes were full and totally sealed. As soon as the spaceship was found by Earth's monitors, Ben rushed off to his laboratory beneath the mountain. He refused point blank when first Maria and then Tessa begged him to let one of them go with him. "Look after the children and yourselves," he cried as he rushed off from their home in Andorra. Ben settled himself in the car.

"Carrie my lab, as quick as you can."

"Fasten your seat belt Benjamin," came the tinny voice and the car took off at breakneck speed. Ben could only imagine the number of calculations the computer must be making as they hurtled along the shortcut with all its hairpin bends, he reached the tunnel and was soon at the airlock to the lab. Jumping out he approached the airlock, it was open.

"What the hell, ANYBODY THERE?" he shouted. Silence. He went slowly forward, having retrieved a laser from the car and entered the lab. He failed to notice on the other side of the car a battered old bike. At the clinic, Tessa and Maria were having a counsel of war.

"Ben said look after the children," she said with an indignant snort. Her indignation was justified. All the children were now virtually adults. Maria's two at university in Madrid and Mars in the newly formed space academy in the USA. The academy was for training in spaceflight. Ben and Tessa has reservations about Mars being so far away.

"He is only seventeen and I'm going to miss him terribly." Ben knew what she meant. Although, only seventeen he was far beyond that in intelligence and had gained a place at the academy's university. Mars pleaded with his parents, morning, noon and night and they had finally conceded. They agreed mainly because Lucy was going with him. "I'll go with him!" she said.

Mars was over the moon; not only had he got his own way, he had Lucy to accompany him.

He had a terrible crush on Lucy even though he knew she was several years older than himself. What he did not know was Lucy being an Arian could have been twenty or two thousand and had the ability to act or change, her age.

"Well," Tessa said, "at least there is one child we can both look after in our little family."

Maria looked at her.

"You're not, are you?"

Tessa grinned, "Afraid so."

"When?" asked Louisa.

"I've known for about a month," she replied.

Louisa asked, "Does Ben know?"

"No and please do not say anything, he has enough problems at the moment and they could carry on for weeks, months or even years to come."

"Congratulations," Maria said, giving her a hug.

"We have two each, now," she said, laughing.

The laughter died on her lips as the tea cups started to rattle and doors creaked.

"It has started," she whispered. Everything went quiet outside, the birds stopped singing and chirping and the dogs whined and came indoors with their tails between their legs.

"It's all right," Louisa said, patting their heads, "it is just a nasty devil making the Earth shake. Benjamin will sort him out." The dogs wagged their tails slowly at the mention of Ben's name.

Ben was attempting to do so, 'The sorting out', at that moment at that very moment in time. He too had felt the slight tremor but fortunately no damage was done, and he continued on his computer. Around the world and in space were signal stations. Ben had hacked into these and reconfigured the whole signalling system. Now, the stations were sending out a gravity repulse beam. It worked slowly at first but then the wormhole wavered and the oceans stopped rising. Irexl at first could not understand why. He put out probes, found the source and laughed aloud.

The clones again turned and looked at him. Going to the bank of computers, controlling the ship's weaponry he punched in the coordinates and pressed the fire button. Below on Earth, the mountain that housed Ben's lab disintegrated, inside as he felt the first shock, Ben put all the stations on automatic, the trouble was that the signal was no longer being coordinated. He lost control after that and although his lab was cocooned in ten metres of reinforced concrete and a miniature Crystal Dome, it seemed as if the whole lab was being shaken to pieces. A piece of equipment struck him on the head and his last thought was of the billions of humans and creatures that were about to die. Then he lost consciousness.

Irexl, way out in space, smiled; he would not have to use his weaponry again. He started to raise the oceans waters again so sure was he that he would be acclaimed once the Earth was rid of the humans that had already badly polluted his new home. It did seem there was little that could be done to stop him. Every available pilot was in the air and the craft designed for space were heading to the spaceship knowing they would be lucky to find somewhere to land if they themselves survived. Mars and Lucy were also in the air, albeit in a trainer spacecraft with no weaponry. The only capability it had was to reach the edge of space which was to give astronauts training in weightlessness. Mars thought it was helpless, Lucy explained if we can get far enough into space I might be able to influence Irexl's mind. They looked down at Earth. It was truly terrifying; the ocean was like a mountain, so high had it risen.

"He must be totally insane to do such a thing," Lucy said quietly. "If he is," she added, "I doubt I will be able to have any control over his mind, we are too far away." Below they watched as the water surged towards the land. They failed to notice a tiny spacecraft rising beneath them.

"Hello," said a voice. "I'm Colin." They both turned, saw the craft that was now beside them.

Mars spoke first. "I've heard of you. Dad spoke of grandfather's friendship with you. You are an Umbrian clone."

"Yes, I am now. You must come aboard my craft immediately."

"Why should we do that?" Mars asked. His question was directed at Lucy. She knew immediately.

"Colin's craft has the ability to create a wormhole," she said.

"What are we waiting for?" he said, unbuckling his harness. "Let's get aboard." The airlock from the trainer was a simple tunnel and Colin had to make minor adjustments before they could board, and get strapped in. In minutes, the wormhole was created and slowly at first then whoosh they were near the moon and more importantly, Irexl's spaceship. Mars was feeling a bit light headed from that journey but Lucy was in deep concentration and seemed to go into a trance.

Aboard his ship, Irexl's had not even noticed the arrival of the tiny craft such was his attention on the rising waters, his face radiant with the pleasure of his success, slowly the smile faded and then clutching his head he screamed and fell to the floor, the clones looked on helplessly as his whole persona collapsed. The vacuum disappeared and with it the wormhole. One of the clones took control of the spaceship and it started to turn and when it had the vacuum was re-established and the ship moved slowly towards it then disappeared. For several seconds, Lucy stared as if following the progress of the ship; she turned to Colin.

"Return us to our craft please, Colin." Before they left him, Mars thanked the clone along with Lucy for literally, he had saved the human race. Colin did not quite understand because what he did was the logical thing to do but nevertheless he did sense a feeling of pleasure. Back inside their own craft, Mars was bursting with curiosity.

"How did you control Ireland? He added the clones."

"It was as I feared," she said. "He was completely deranged, and as for the clones they were created to obey. Irexl will recover eventually and the clones will look after him until that time."

"Why did you not destroy him, he has murdered half of the world's population and virtually all other creatures that live on Earth."

She bowed her head.

"We have vowed to never interfere and I have done just that."

"Lucy, the people of Earth, of Umbria and I'm sure your own race will be your case," he said gently.

"One last question. Irexl will never return, will he?"

Lucy, lifting her head, answered, her voice barely a whisper.

"After a period of time the vacuum will cease and his ship will be several hundred light years away. He is already a thousand years old so his life span will soon end, so no, he will never return." Mars put his arm around her.

"Let us return to Earth, or at least try to," he said and kissed her. She said nothing but when on the flight back, he gave her a glance and her eyes were now shining.

They managed to land but when looking for a place to land they were horrified by the devastation which they assumed must be all over the planet. Even worse was the damage done to the Earth's tectonic plates. Under such enormous traction, the plates moved and cracked causing volcanoes of titanic proportion along with the eruption of many dormant ones. The dust and ash spewed into the air and soon covered the planet with a noxious cloud, those who had survived drowning were now being choked to death by the fumes. It was estimated that a million died that day and many millions more in the following years. Virtually, all wild life became extinct, the survivors, humans and animals that survived were in the Crystal Domes which worldwide now numbered over 25000, half of these of course housed farms and farmland. In heavily populated areas, food became so scarce that deaths became numerous through malnutrition. With no sun, day by day, the temperature started to drop.

Ben, when Mars and Lucy were looking for somewhere to land, was just regaining consciousness his head, ached from something hitting it but worst of all a huge steel cabinet had fallen on top of him and would have crushed him but for one of the draws shooting out and jamming. He was pinned tight and his ribs were near to breaking. The drawer creaked and he cried out in pain as his ribs were squashed further. He heard a rustling noise. *Oh no,* he thought. Rats, he knew they existed in the tunnel, but he himself often left the outer airlock open. The rustle came again, his skin crawled, they must have smelt me, he thought. He looked round as much as he could and although only the emergency lights were on, in the semi-darkness he saw two eyes, that is an enormous rat he thought.

"Hello," said the rat. "You seem to be stuck."

"Who the hell are you?" Ben groaned.

"I'm Molly, your cleaner," came the reply. "Wait there. I'll be back in a moment, oh sorry."

She scuttled away and Ben thought, well at least it's not a rat but why has she rushed off; there is no one else with her and even with a lever, he stopped thinking the pain was too great.

In the distance, he could hear a rattling and banging, more rattling and Molly reappeared huffing and puffing, dragging an enormous pallet truck, she slid the steel arms under the cabinet and began pumping the long handle up and down. After a while, the weight started to lift off his chest, the relief was enormous.

"Hold on," she said. "This might hurt," and with that she put her hands under his shoulders and pulled him out. The pain was terrible, he thought he was going to faint but at least he was free.

"Thank you," he gasped. "I'm so glad you chose today to do your cleaning. I wondered why the airlock was open?"

"Oh sorry, I dropped my key in here once and thought I would be locked in here forever. I managed to find it obviously but, that's why I leave it open," she finished lamely.

Ben was puzzled. "So come here now. I shut the airlock when I came in but after what happened I would have thought you would have been long gone by now. You haven't lost that key again, have you?"

"No, you're right. I would have left last night but it is jammed, the airlock is stuck. I've been scared silly, but after a few hours, I heard you groaning, I thought you were a ghost." She giggled.

"Well, let's see if we can get out now," Ben said, and with Molly helping him they got to the airlock as she had said it was well and truly stuck. He took a small key from his pocket and then inserted it into a door at the side of the airlock. There was a click and a hiss as the air from the lab escaped into the tunnel.

"Ugh," Molly croaked. "I can hardly breathe." It was true the tunnel was filled with dust, Ben guided her to the car and painfully eased himself in.

"Are you all right, Carrie?"

Molly thought that bang on the head has made him lose his marbles.

Then, she got the fright of her life when a voice answered.

She went to jump out of the car, Ben gently stopped her.

"It is okay. It was the car who answered me."

She paled, "It must be me. I must be the one going mad."

Ben started the car.

"I have turned the air con on, Benjamin."

Molly screamed.

"Molly." Ben said, realizing why. "It is okay the car has a voice generated computer," he smiled to himself, remembering when Maria had first got in the car.

Carrie edged slowly forward. *Thank God,* Ben thought. The tunnel seemed to be okay. Everything was fine until they neared the entrance. Ben could see nothing but Carrie's sensors had picked up a large obstruction, a boulder in fact.

"Expect a loud noise," Carrie announced.

Ben put his hands over his ears. Molly followed suit and for good measure squeezed her eyes tightly shut. A thin beam came from the front of the car, from a third headlight a thin beam shone, there was a whoosh and a bang, a lot more dust and Carrie went forward through to the entrance.

"I'm glad, we're back in the open again," Ben said, no answer. He turned to look, Molly still had her eyes shut and her hands firmly clamped over her ears. He pulled her hand away.

"It's okay now, Molly."

Only it was far from okay, the roads were badly damaged and in parts had gone completely.

Carrie, on Ben's instructions, was cautiously making its way to Molly's home. When they got there where the home had been, there was now a pile of rubble. Molly screamed and burst into tears. Carrie turned on her sensors. "The house has no occupants," she announced. While consoling her, Ben noticed a scrap of paper pinned on a gatepost, retrieving it, he read it and handed it to her.

She was still in tears, "Where had they gone, how can I trace them," she wailed. "Where am I going to live?"

"You will come and live with us and we will eventually trace your parents, so stop your crying and cheer up," he encouraged her.

She mopped her face with a rather wet handkerchief.

"Sorry it's all getting rather too much," and gave a small smile.

Ben himself was desperately worried about the centre and all those in it. He had tried to contact by phone in the lab and now mobile but had no joy with either. The computers were down also.

They drove into the capital Andorra La Vella. At first, there seemed little damage but as they went through the older part, many of the old buildings had collapsed. There was confusion and the road was blocked. Ben got out, telling Molly to sit tight when he went to find a way through. By a miracle nobody was killed, all had evacuated the older buildings at the first tremor, but the local police who knew Ben well told him an old couple probably too frail to get out in time were trapped in the basement of a house. Ben looked at the problem; it seemed impossible. They would have to be dug out and with the amount of dust in the air, they would probably be dead in the time it would take. He turned slowly, his chest was aching. As he turned, the manhole cover he was standing on moved, from when they used coal, he thought absently. Then it dawned on him, "See if you can get to them through that?" he asked. It worked, a young man, the couple's grandson volunteered and went down the hole like a rabbit. Two minutes later, he was back.

"They are alive but they have swallowed a lot of dust. I will need help." In another ten minutes, they were in the ambulance.

"Take them to our Medical Centre," Ben instructed. "They need treatment and its near."

Five minutes later, he was home and Molly was helping him out of the car.

Upstairs in his house, a curtain moved, there was a shriek and Louisa, Tessa and Maria rushed out the front door all tried to hug him at once, that is until he yelped.

"We thought we had lost you," Louisa explained. "All the communications are down and when you never returned we feared the worst." Ben looked at the drawn faces of the three women. They looked as if they had been up all night which was probably true.

"I had things on top of me, literally," he explained how Molly had rescued him, and found her family and had fled. Louisa looked up.

"Oh you poor thing," she said, going over to her. Molly burst into tears again. Louisa consoled her. "We will trace them. I'm sure they're safe and sound and you must stay with us until we find them."

"She is a very resourceful young lady," and she went on to explain how Molly had rescued him.

Louisa put her arm around her shoulders, and with Tessa and Maria taking an arm each of Ben they all went inside. Ben looked up as they walked up to the house. The house and clinic, the city and surrounding farmlands were all under a Dome, but as he looked up, he saw a thick layer of dust had settled on the dome, already with no sun it was feeling colder. Once inside, the women sorted out some clothes for Molly. Having been the latest person to save Ben's life, Molly was overwhelmed by the gratitude of everybody, such was the relief for his safe return.

"I hope Mars and Lucy are okay," he said, "and where are George and Romilly. I've not seen them."

"They're not back," Louisa explained. "The two engineers who were coming from England ran into trouble when the earthquakes started. They were just on the border of Andorra and a tremor caused a cliff fall blocking the road as their wives and children were with them. George and Romilly insisted on going mainly to get them the children and as much of their belongings as possible. Obviously I have been unable to contact them or the pilot, even the Chinooks radio was out." Ben pondered for a moment.

"They might be okay," he said. "Phil is a damn good pilot. And with all the dust and fumes in the air he might have decided not to risk the flight back. Please, God, they make it back."

The southern hemisphere had been worse hit by the waters being over a thousand metres on landfall. By contrast, in the north at three hundred metres was bad but less damage, the worst was still happening the tremendous pull on the Earth's crust which was causing volcanoes worldwide. Two million people died on that first day, along with most of the world's wildlife.

Another 1-5 million would die from the effects of dust and pollution. The Crystal Dome saved the near annihilation of humans, with over 3 billion packed into the thousands that had been built, a few were destroyed and badly damaged but most and their inhabitants survived. The Earth's sea creatures also suffered great losses but mostly they breathed air from the seas, plants and without the huge amount being fished they recovered their species a lot faster. The one small grace was a two-thousand-mile belt which varied in width. This went right around the Equator here from time to time and had weak sunlight and the temperature was although close to freezing, did allow some growth of plants and some wild life. The Crystal Domes were built at frenetic speed and the gigantic dust extraction plants were doubled in number. After many years, the volcanic ash and the clouds of dust began to clear and the loss of life decreased but the fear of the unknown was great. Earth went into a mini-ice age. It could have lasted hundreds of years but the crystal domes along with technology developed, decreased the winter of the world to ten years.

The Winter

Mother Earth, screamed and roared as her body was pulled and her bones were cracked.

The earth's tectonic plates were cracked and broken in many places.

She roared as the volcanoes erupted and bled when the lava flowed.

Her body was scarred and her green mantle burnt.

Then she wept and her tears were of water, dust and ash from the eruptions.

Finally, she drew her tears around her body and got colder and colder. Her tears turned to black snow and then many other colours before, after many years it finally turned white.

There was a loud yawn from behind the door of the adjoining cabin.

"Alison come, and look." Alex banged on the door of her door, impatient such was his excitement. It's the sun come and see for yourself." The door opened slowly and a head appeared hidden behind a mass of auburn curls. Alex reached out and grabbed her hand.

"What is the fuss," Alison mumbled, "and where is all that light coming from, I can't see a thing, it's so bright"

"Just come and see for yourself," he begged. Alison pushed back the mass of hair to reveal a pixie face on which there was a small but perfect nose, a wide and generous mouth and two enormous eyes which turned up at the corners. Also ears that were definitely pixie like.

"Ow," she said, "Let go, you're hurting my hand."

"Sorry," he said, "but come and look." Alison squinted her eyes.

"Just a moment," she said and dived back into her room. She returned wearing what looked like enormous sunglasses but in fact were goggles to wear against snow blindness. She looked out through the observation window in the revolving turret; she stood for several minutes taking in the scene before her. Far to the east, she could see the clouds that had given the heavy snowfall overnight.

They had left behind them a brilliant blue sky and a contrasting white snowfield. Glancing sideways at the outside monitors, she gave a small gasp.

"Alex. Alex," she said stumbling over her words. "The temperature out, outside it's only minus two Centigrade." (Which considering the normal early morning temperature was normally minus twenty degrees), made it quite clear almost spring-like in fact. Alison looked again at the monitors, the oxygen levels were normal and were showing no signs of contamination. Alex nodded.

"I know," he said, "I've already checked."

He looked at his friend fondly. "Go and get dressed," he said. "But not the normal stuff." The normal stuff was something akin to a space suit. "Just wear something warm, it will still be quite cold and you best get the snow shoes, not knowing how firm the snow is." Within minutes they were togged up. Opening the airlock, they jumped a few feet to land in the snow. He scooped up a handful. "It's firm," he exclaimed and threw it at her.

"You sod," she screamed, as it splattered all over. Laughing, she retaliated and it grew into a full-blown snowball fight. Within a very short time, they were out of breath and red in the face.

Calling a truce Alison said firmly, "we must keep up our exercises more diligently."

"Well, we can," he said, "but now we can do them outside. Let's go for a walk, but we will take the snowshoes just in case" he added. Turning their backs on their little craft, they set off.

"Look, see that rock we'll head for that. I want to see if there is any plant life?"

"I doubt that very much," Alison said, "but the rock is quite a long way so the exercise will be good."

The rock was indeed some distance away and Alex was again out of breath. He sat on a small rock. "You go ahead I'll catch you up in a minute." Alison went ahead, pleased she was fittest of the pair of them.

Back in their little craft, an urgent message had come through. "Do not leave your craft and return to base immediately. The sudden change in temperature is causing many problems."

Alison was nearly at the base of the rock which towered up into the morning sky, its side almost vertical. She looked up seeking a way to climb the cliff. As she looked, the snow started to move beneath her. She half jumped, half fell onto the rock, desperately seeking and then reaching out to a small spur of rock, she managed to haul herself onto it, sitting astride it and leaning into the cliff face, her hands splayed out gripping the edges of the spur. The snow fell away into a chasm that seemed to go down forever.

Alex thought she had fallen and ran to the edge of the ravine and saw her clinging to the cliff opposite.

"Hang on," he yelled. "I'll get our craft and lower the rope ladder." He discarded the snow-shoes and pulled out two short boards with straps for his feet. Putting them on, he leant forward and pressed a button on his chest. A small rocket ignited on his back and he was hurtling back. Just a few minutes later, he was opening the airlock. He opened up the intercom.

"Dad," he yelled, "Alison's in terrible danger." Back inside the Dome, his father paled. He knew there was little that could be done to help. It would be an hour before they could reach the two youngsters. He felt a hand on his shoulder. "Ben," he said. "Did you hear that?"

"Yes," Ben replied. "Organise the rescue party and I will see if I can speed things up." Ben left and went to his office.

Once inside, he locked the door and slumped into his favourite chair. Fifty kilometres to the south, Alison was still astride her little sanctuary. How long before help arrived, she shivered with fear and although she had only been there a few minutes the cold was already seeping through her clothing.

Her mind drifted back to nine or was it ten years ago. Then it had been cold but not inside the Crystal Dome. The Dome was in England on the outskirts of London, although warm inside, outside the dome the temperature was freezing in winter and barely warm even in mid-summer.

The CO_2 emissions, mixed with the carbon monoxide and many other equally contaminating gases had, as many environmentalists warned caused global warming and then with the loss of the Gulf Stream extreme cold for some parts of the northern hemisphere. The sky rarely showed the sun and going outside of the dome without a mask and thermal wear was hazardous. The dome they were in was terribly overcrowded and her father Richard, an electronics wizard, was worried not so much for himself, he had a good job with a ridiculously high salary, but his concern was for his wife Elizabeth and his daughter, they deserved a better future than the one that was stretched out before them. His best friend Jack who was an electrical engineer was of the same mind and he had a wife Jenny and his son Alex, who felt the same with all the robberies, often just for food. Food was scarce and there was strict rationing. His father told him it was worse than what it was in the Second World War. Both children were eight and the overcrowding was so bad their playground was now the school roof. The parents met to discuss their future, there was a glimmer of hope though. Both men had worked for Benjamin Franklin before the huge salaries had tempted them away. He had been a good friend as well as their boss and when they left, he told them if they ever needed a job to e-mail him. This they did, after agreeing that whatever salary was offered they would be happy to accept. With the email sent, they were now waiting on tenterhooks for the reply. It came quickly and it was a yes.

Celebrations were short with the few friends and colleagues they had, most of their other friends had already left years before. After frantic packing disposing, of their worldly goods, they sold their tiny apartments for astronomical prices and purchased tickets on the Euro Express which would take them to the south of France, from there they would drive through the very south of France then over the Pyreanees to Andorra and the future. They both had similar vehicles, both space wagons, obviously large, which was very fortunate as every inch of space of the roomy interiors were used to hold their most precious possessions. Before they could blink, they were driving to Euston station and boarding the train. Driving onto the train seemed so strange and they had to stay with their cars until they were underway.

Eventually, they were off and in their respective cabins. Again they were surprised the cabins were more like rooms in a hotel or on board a ship. Apart from the usual tea and coffee there was enough food in the fridge freezer and cupboard above to last the whole journey. In forty minutes, they were speeding through France, still inside the tunnel that stretched now from London to Paris. Unable to use nuclear power the, train was being driven by hydrogen fuel which was feeding the massive engines. Once clear of Paris, the scenery was still bleak, but improved slightly the further south they went. “How boring,” Alex commented, as with chin on elbows, he stared out of the window.

“Oh what is that?” Alison asked, interrupting Alex’s gloom. In the distance, ahead of them looking like a giant glowing mushroom sparked off all the colours of the otherwise drab landscape, albeit it being mainly the colour of the chemicals in the snow the light was reflecting.

“It’s enormous,” Alison breathed, almost holding her breath as she looked at the enormous Crystal Dome.

"It covers the whole of Lyon," wife Jenny explained. She looked across at her friend Elizabeth, adding, but I have no idea how they feed the populous inside the dome. Do you know Liz?"

Elizabeth returning the smile told her, "To the west and east of the main dome, there are many more domes which are used for agriculture and farming, with all the farms animals you can imagine. I could go into more detail if you want to be bored out of your mind."

"Ok," Jenny said. "Another time. I am interested though." Soon they were entering the dome, they could actually hear the note of the engine change as they went back to hydrogen fuel. It was like entering another world. Unlike the dome over London, this was spacious with neat rows of houses, although they were ten storeys high and held twenty luxury apartments in each block.

They really did look like French houses, even having the traditional shutters. The train was stopping overnight to restock and clean the cabins, so although they would be returning to sleep on the train they had the day to explore and enjoy Lyon.

"This beats walking up and down the corridors for exercise," Alex shouted as he ran down the street, he stopped suddenly.

"Oh," he exclaimed, "a park and it's got swings, seesaws and roundabouts." He was gone.

"I always thought Alex was so grown up," Alison said with a sly smile, before she took off to the delights they only had in a very limited way back in their old home. Near, where the children were now happily playing, was a small bar from which the parents could hear music. They all looked, thinking, *shall we?* Richard took the initiative taking Jenny's arm. He said pompously, "Come my girl, I am taking you to lunch."

"Flirt," Jack and Elizabeth cried.

"I know, it's the French air. Now, what would you like to drink my dear," he asked, grinning at Jenny and at the same time turning his nose up at the other two.

"Oh," she said making her eyes roll at Richard, and half turning to wink at the others. "French champagne of course and only the best." Richard paled, champagne of any sort cost a small fortune now, all the vineyards were a distant memory and what was produced under the dome was very limited and only affordable to millionaires and Richard was not one of them.

"Of course," he said and headed towards the bar.

"You best stop him," the others said laughing. Jenny put her finger to her lips and pointed to a small notice in the corner of the bar. It said owing to the shortage, champagne will be unavailable until further notice. All three then collapsed with laughter when they saw the relief on his face. Richard joined in the laughter.

"That taught me a lesson," he chuckled. They sat at the bar and really enjoyed a champagne substitute which they all agreed was as good as the real stuff. They sat there some time watching the children enjoy themselves.

After so much exertion, the children finally tired and almost had to be carried back to the train.

They managed to stay up for dinner then were in bed and asleep in moments. The parents spent the evening talking about their future plans, taking turns to check on the children although the cabins were locked. As the train proceeded south, the countryside got greener and they even had a sunset to look at. Unfortunately, there were still industrial areas and the poorer atmosphere was almost visible when the smoke and fumes rose. They all agreed on one thing: the human population was slowly but surely destroying itself. They retired themselves and were soon asleep with their good dreams and some bad ones. They woke refreshed and ready for the last leg of their journey, which would take them through the far south of France then into the Pyrenees and towards Andorra, gathering their belongings from their cabins, they boarded the cars and drove off the train and started on the last leg of the journey. As they continued south, the sun appeared and it became warmer. In the fields, there was greenery and they saw sunflowers with their heads facing south.

"Why does that happen?" Elizabeth asked.

"It's a growth thing," Richard explained, "they turn their heads to get sun all day."

The journey was uneventful and they were able to enjoy the open countryside as they started to get to higher ground, which was still free of contamination. Along the side of the road, wild flowers grew in profusion. On the other side, there was a tumultuous stream, which because of recent heavy rains was now akin to a river. "Let's stop," the children pleaded. Richard flashed his headlights to the vehicle ahead and Jack slowed to a stop.

"Problems?" he asked as he walked back.

"No, not at all, the children wanted to stop and we could have a picnic and the lovely fresh air," he added.

“Jack, hmmm that is nice,” he said, taking a deep breath. As he spoke, he felt the ground vibrate beneath him. Richard rushed past him and took a flying leap across the split that had appeared in the road, taking Jack’s car with it. Landing by the car he pulled the door open and the engine roared as he put it into gear to try to drive the car back on the road. But it was too late and the car started to slide into the stream. Jenny screamed and tried to open the car door.

“No,” Richard shouted and pulled her back as the car went into the rushing water. Bobbing along in the water, it disappeared in seconds.

“Back in the car,” Jack yelled to Elizabeth and the children and jumping in himself his intention was to go past the split, but there was a rock fall in front and further back behind them. They were stranded. Thinking fast he pulled his mobile out and rang Ben.

A panic-stricken Louisa answered, “Oh no,” she said, when Jack told her of their situation. She herself thought for a moment. “Is there anywhere a helicopter could land?” she asked.

“Yes, there is a layby twenty yards away. It could land there.”

“Give me your coordinates,” she asked. He quickly looked on the sat nav and told her then the line went dead. He tried to contact Jenny. Nothing, there was no signal on any of their phones.

There was another tremor, he looked fearfully at the cliffs above him as a few rocks dislodged and came tumbling down. “Stay in the car,” he told the children who were crying copiously having both lost a parent. Elizabeth hugged them both with tears streaming down her face.

The next ten minutes were the worst of Jack’s life. Grim-faced, he scoured the skies searching for their life line, and then there it was. He waved the red blanket furiously and was rewarded when the helicopter turned and headed towards him.

“All of you, out of the car.” Liz essentials only and he grabbed his friend’s battered old briefcase and two suitcases, Elizabeth did the same, taking just her handbag, a suitcase and a small box with some of the jewellery Richard had bought her over the years. The two children grabbed their favourite toys and stood there shaking. They moved towards the layby as the helicopter came in to land. As it landed, two figures jumped out and ran towards them. It was George and Romilly, knowing they would want help, they had insisted on going. The pilot stayed in the cockpit its rotors idling ready for a quick take off. While he had been waiting Jack noticed it had gone very quiet; not only had the birds stopped singing, the stream had stopped flowing. *A rock fall upstream,* he thought. It was all rushed as the children and their two parents climbed into the copter with the help of Romilly and George. They were about to climb in themselves when Alison screamed, "My puppy," she cried, "he's in the boot." Romilly jumped back down again and rushed to the car, throwing open the boot saw the little box with holes, grabbed it and charged back. The helicopter was starting to rise, she threw the box on and jumped. She just managed to get a hand on the rim and George grabbed her other hand that was flailing the air. There was a roaring sound and it became clear why the pilot took off. The stream had burst through the cliff fall and was coming down on them in a wall of water. It hit the wheels of the copter and then nearly swept Romilly away, she lost her grip and it was just George holding her and he was being dragged out himself. His other hand found a small ring on the copter's floor, used probably for tying down equipment, he held on grimly. "George," Romilly cried out. "LET GO. Tell our daughter I love her but you must let me go, she must not lose the both of us."

George knew they were both going to die, he was getting weaker but just refused to let go of her. He sensed rather than saw movement by the hatch, a hand went past him and grabbed Romilly's arm another hand grabbed him by the collar and then they were both dumped on the blankets that lay on the deck. George was almost comatose, *the hand of God,* he thought. Romilly although shivering with cold and fright, was alert. *How,* she thought; *whoever he or she was they should have been sucked out of the copter.* Through half closed eyes she saw their saviour, having slammed the cabin door shut. He was releasing himself from the restraining harness he was wearing, many years previous had been a volunteer air sea rescuer, the harness was part of the gear used to rescue mariners and mountaineers naming just two for that purpose. As he went back to his sad little group, she spoke.

"Thank you," she whispered, barely able to speak through the numbness that beset her whole body.

His grim face softened a little.

"There have been enough losses for one day," he muttered.

Romilly hugged George and wrapped him in the blankets they had actually brought for the others.

"George, it's all right, we are both alive and safe." George was gasping for breath and only half conscious, squeezed her hand. *Well lady,* she thought, *I lost a few of my cats lives today.* Her lower body was soaked and she was, even with a blanket wrapped around, still freezing. The woman came across a suitcase and started rummaging amongst the clothes within, pulling out some items she handed them to Romilly.

"My friend is," she could not bring herself to say, was. "She is a similar size to you," and she handed Romilly some clothing and underwear. She turned and went back before Romilly could speak. The helicopter was still rising and the pilot called Jack to the cockpit.

"Trouble?" Jack asked.

"Yes. Take a look at that." All around them were clouds of dust that seemed to be rising with them. "Can you look for a landing place for us, all my concentration is needed to fly, the winds are so turbulent." Jack peered through the glass for several minutes.

"Over there," he said. "Sorry, 30 degrees to your left, there is a plateau on the side of that cliff face." A few minutes later, the copter, with the wind buffeting it, landed on said plateau.

"Thanks," the pilot said. "My name is Phil." They briefly shook hands and looked at the terrain. They were on a small area of rock with a cliff face towering above them.

"I'm afraid we will be here some time," Phil said "and we best tie the copter down, if this wind gets any worse it could blow it over."

"Can you move the copter closer to the cliff face," Jack asked. "Only I think there is a cleft in the rock face and if it's big enough it could give us more shelter and there are probably spurs of rock we can tie the copter down with."

"Yep, no problem, I can use the tail rotors to get closer."

This was done and the cleft, although, not big enough to house the copter, it gave it a lot more shelter from the rising wind. As it got colder inside the helicopter, they decided to check out the cleft. Jack volunteered and it was certainly a large split in the rock face and it went quite deep.

There were a few stunted trees which were very dead. *They could be useful,* he thought.

They were there for three days before the dust started to settle and using a knife and brute strength they used the wood plus two pallets stored on the copter, to keep themselves warm, by lighting a fire. They put George nearest to the fire, the children slept with Elizabeth, snuggled up and exhausted from the trauma. Jack paced up and down or sat with head in hands, sleeping a little. Romilly when she was not napping by the side of George, kept the pilot company taking turns to keep one eye on the lifeline. The helicopter. George dreamt of Romilly. The first time they met was in his office. Desperate, for more staff he put an ad on line, then wished he hadn't. He got dozens of applicants most of which got binned. He took on a few who had sent their CVs and had one from Israel with an excellent CV. He was a bit wary why anybody would need to travel that far. Nevertheless, he offered an interview and agreed to a date with, he checked the name R J Bryant. *I must ask him why he wants a job here,* he thought. Perhaps he is an environmentalist. The day dawned and the applicant marched into his office. George rose and came from behind his desk. Before him stood a tall slim woman with long legs that ended up in a pair of incongruous boots. Her face had clear bright eyes that were smiling beneath arched eyebrows and a high forehead that was topped with light auburn hair.

A neat ponytail was keeping it in place. She also had a generous mouth above which was a prominent nose. He had already decided that she had the job. But, being George, he went through her CV. It told him nothing he didn't already know apart from two things; one she was a woman and the second came out in their conversation; she had just come away from a very messy divorce, he noted. *So also independent,* he thought. He offered her a lot more than she was expecting and said he needed an assistant and she met all the requirements of that post.

Romilly was over the moon, here she was assistant to the big chief who was the right-hand man to the legendary Ben Franklin. Also in a very short time, she knew that George really liked her, he insisted on first names and although he never tried it on, he sought her company a lot. She enjoyed the attention and his company, they got on well together. *I'll have to discourage him,* she thought, *he must be twenty years older than me.* She had a few dates with other men and kept her distance socially, just having the occasional meal with George. Neither of them was very happy, George because he just wanted to be with her and she, because she really liked George and could sense his disappointment. The crunch came when out with a man she had dated a few times, tried and very nearly succeeded in raping her. She had invited him back for a late-night drink and he had dragged her into her bedroom and threw her on the bed. She fought back but was losing, as he mauled her she smashed him with the bedside light and managed to turn on the house alarm.

"You cow," he yelled and punched her. She screamed more with anger than pain. The door burst open and her would be rapist was lifted bodily into the air.

Jim, the porter, headed with the struggling man to the window. Seeing his intention, Romilly shouted, "No, Jim throw him out the door." This he did and crashing into the wall opposite, he slumped to the floor, the reason she stopped Jim throwing him through the window was her flat was on the second floor.

"You all right Miss R?" he said. Romilly thanked him and he left to deal with her assailant. She just got into bed and nursing her bruised body, fell into a restless sleep. Next morning, she looked in the bathroom mirror, looking at her bruises, she dreaded the thought of seeing George.

Feeling like death, she walked into his office. He took one look at her white face and the bruises on her neck and shoulders, and turned his back, saying over his shoulder.

"You look ill. I suggest you have a few days off to recover. I'll see you in a few days' time."

George went to his desk and sat down feeling sick to his stomach and being so fond of her, sick with jealousy. Of course, he knew nothing of the circumstances, but he knew Romilly well enough to know she would not have welcomed such brutality. He found out who it was soon enough. Romilly as his site engineer had constant contact with the workers. When he told the foreman that she would be off for a few days, the man looked sheepish.

"Who?" George said, knowing his own job was in danger, the foreman told him. Giving his name he went on to tell George how the individual had been boasting about his conquest to his workmates. George looked hard at the foreman. "Get rid of him permanently," he got a nod in reply and the following day the man was gone, apparently to a relative's funeral. George let things go for a few days to let his dear friend and colleague get over her traumatic experience.

But then, to his great dismay, he had an email from her. "Sorry George." it read, "I had no option and I've returned to Israel for the foreseeable future. Please, do not try to contact me."

George worked hard and drank harder for the following few weeks and nobody, not even Ben, dared go near him, let alone talk to him. Then one day, he packed a bag and disappeared. Ben was informed, but knowing what the cause was did nothing, but he certainly hoped it would be resolved. George booked the first flight he could get to Israel, having found her address before he left. When he left the plane he went straight to the said address. Arriving very late, he looked for signs of occupancy, there was, a light in a small window that gave him some hope. Ringing the doorbell, he waited. He saw a shadow above, peering down from behind a column on the balcony.

"George," said a surprised voice, "hang on. I'll be down in a minute." He waited and moments later, the door opened a crack.

"Come in," she said. "I've just had a shower." He entered and there she stood with just a towel wrapped around her. Not knowing what else to do, he put his arms around her and hugged her.

"Come back," was all he could think to say. To his surprise and delight, she nodded. Slowly, she became more and more fond of him and, although not marrying, there was always too much to do, they became partners, or an item as the modern trend said. George opened his eyes.

"Romilly," he whispered weakly. She grasped his hands firmly.

"Hang on George, hang on. We will be home soon."

Alison was watching them and listening. When she heard the words hang on, she started to get colder and colder and suddenly she was sitting on her tiny spur of rock. Another voice inside her head was saying, hold on, hold on. Ben had reached her semi-conscious mind. Hold on, he kept repeating to her. Alison stirred, shivering feverishly, she muttered, "What's happening? Where am I," she was startled as two shadowy figures appeared before her. *I'm hallucinating*, she thought. *I recognise you*, her mind told her, *you're Mars and Lucy.* Mars moved closer and started to lift as Lucy used energy from her mind to heat Alison's body. The heat moved around her and the ice that was now actually holding her to the rock face melted and she was in the arms of Mars. He was carrying her up the cliff face heating her from his body. Lucy rose with sending more heat to the near frozen girl. Alison, now more aware, thought she must be in heaven. Here she was in the arms of the young man; every girl in the dome would have sold their souls to be where she was now. Through her euphoria, she heard the sound of swishing blades. *Damn,* she thought as the helicopter landed. *As I thought,* she moaned to herself as Mars lowered her gently onto the stretcher.

Snug under the blankets, she looked up and all thought of Mars disappeared. There stood Alex, tears streaming down his young face, "I thought I had l...l...lost you, too." He was referring to his mum and her dad, they had lost, although years ago. Even then they had had a narrow escape, but eventually the dust had settled to lower levels. Phil, their pilot had checked the altimeter in the copter, it showed 3000 ft. The Crystal dome was higher, so taking a calculated risk, he packed them all into the helicopter and they got back safely. The landing pad on top of the dome was covered in dust and grime, but knowing roughly its position, Phil hovered over and the rotors downdraft cleared the pad enough for him to land. They were lowered still in the copter and were met by Ben who was worried sick up to that point. She looked up at Alex and the normally serious Alison broke into uncontrollable sobbing. In a moment, she and Alex were in each other's arms.

"Steady," Alison murmured. "I will end up with cracked ribs." There was another surprise as the pilot came back to check on her new passengers.

"Romilly," Alison exclaimed.

"Yes, me again. You two just cannot keep out of trouble," smiling down at them as she replied.

Alison asked quietly, "How is George?"

"Virtually 100%," she answered, "and moaning because he has to do physiotherapy daily." She winked at Alison. "You will certainly have a tale to tell all your friends." She left them. Alison blushing and Alex looking puzzled. In a few moments, they were airborne and on the way to the safety of the Dome. Alison was whisked off to a hospital albeit under protest.

"I am fine," she insisted.

Romilly who had taken her in, said quite firmly, "We will let the doctors make that decision." She smiled at the girl laying on the stretcher as the ambulance took them to the hospital. "I'm no expert but in addition to the bruising on your thighs while sitting on your little perch, you are probably suffering from hypothermia. You might also have a touch of frostbite, it will all have to be checked out. Your Mum, Alex and his dad are already at the hospital and I will ask George to pop in and say hello when he is in for his physio appointment." Alison snuggled down in bed enjoying the warmth. Before long, she was sound asleep. Romilly went to the department where George had just finished some strenuous exercises and now after a shower was relaxing. He smiled as she entered and jumped up to give her a hug. Having been in touch with Ben he knew of the exploits of Alex and Alison.

"Are they both okay?" he asked.

Romilly smiled saying, "Alison has to stay in but she is glowing in the glory of being rescued by Mars."

George laughed. "That will keep young Alex on his toes." Romilly held her love at arm's length.

"And you, my love, how are you?"

"I am fine really another week and I will be finished with the physio and just have monthly check-ups."

"Well, I should be able to see you every day," she responded. "Mind you, I am rescuing lots of survivors, I am amazed at how many did manage to survive. The air is much better now but the storms are still raging." George said nothing. He hated Romilly flying but knew how much she felt the need to help now they were no longer rushing around building Crystal Domes.

The Recovery

Mother Nature was recovering for a long time. She was back on her feet and shaking her skirts.

Although the earthquakes and eruptions had ceased, the rise in temperature was causing another set of problems. There were floods and landslides and storms, hurricanes tornadoes and torrential rain. Nobody could leave the domes, if they did it was at great risk. Through all the demise of so many creatures and humans, there was one species that flourished. The fish and some of the mammals that lived in the sea. They were no longer fished by the thousands of tons daily and their oxygen was there below the seawater in the plants that grew there.

Alison was in hospital for ten days. Where she had gripped the rock between her legs, there was severe frostbite. She was now totally bored. Although, she was in total luxury, there was little she could do having been told on no account must she leave her bed. She was even taken to the bathroom in a wheelchair. The insides of her thighs were still red raw, however once in the wheelchair she was able to roll out onto the balcony. Alison looked glumly at the monitor that showed the outside of the dome. Whereas she was, when out on the balcony bathed in the soft sunlight of the domes, halogen sun outside the dome was a nightmare. Ever since her rescue, there had been one continuous storm, not a normal storm. But one which was accompanied by torrential rain, hail, sleet, snow and hailstones the size of tennis balls, which she could hear drumming on the domes skin. Even now as the dome's 'sun', faded into the evening mode, Alison could still hear the drumming. Slowly, the noise lulled her senses and she drifted off to sleep. Much later, she woke with a start. *Why*, she thought and then realised it was the silence. She looked up at the dome's roof and gasped. She was looking at millions of pinpricks of light. "They are stars, of course," she murmured to herself "and there is the moon." Having not seen the heavens for ten years, it was a beautiful revelation. Slightly behind her on the edge of her vision, she saw a light brighter than that of the moon. Alison swung her chair round. "Oh," she exclaimed. "Oh my goodness, what is that." There, hanging above her, was another moon or so it seemed. Slightly smaller than the Earth's moon it was to the eye. But the light was a hundred times brighter. *The light came from what?* she thought. It was like looking at a thousand diamonds reflecting the sunlight, she turned away the light was too bright to look at. She turned and rolled to the monitor and focussed on the, star-like moon. Then, increasing the magnification she stared at the image before her. "The Crystal Domes," she breathed. She had heard rumours of course and unfinished conversations when entering a room unannounced, only snatches but enough to make her realise that something was heading to Earth and needed Earth's assistance. So it had arrived. *What now,* she thought. It was very obvious that a being from that planet had caused the devastation on Earth and the death of nearly half the population of Earth's populace and nearly all of Earth's wildlife. But she had also heard that Mars and Lucy had destroyed the alien and his ship. So she wondered what the members of Earth's newly formed federation were going to do, how would they react to these aliens that really can be called the enemy. Earth's leaders were at that moment doing that but with communications still very limited and the defences mostly in ruins, the logical and actually only thing they could do was to sue for peace. Most of the world's population were unaware of either the attack or the response of their leaders. The majority were under the impression that Earth had suffered a major earthquake and those that survived wanted just that, survival.

Alison sighed, she really wanted to get out of hospital. She wheeled her chair back to her bedside and selected a book to read from the bedside table, and eased herself back into bed.

Barely had she drawn the covers over herself, when the doctor walked in, accompanied by her mother, Alex and his dad. "Good news darling," her mother said, making it a statement. "You're coming home today, now, in fact." Alison actually squealed with joy, and Alex was grinning from ear to ear. The doctor however was serious.

"You must take it easy. You nearly lost most of your thigh muscle in that escapade, and," he added, his eyes crinkling, belying his serious expression, "make sure you keep up the exercises and renew your dressings regularly."

"Yes, doctor," Alison replied meekly, "and thank you." It took a little time for her to dress, but then she was wheeled out to the waiting vehicle and gently lifted in. home at last she breathed.

"You are very lucky," Alex said, squeezing her hand. Alison's head came up.

"And why is that?" she asked.

"Well." Alex explained, "People are coming in from all over. Many Domes were damaged and apart from the loss of life, there were a lot of injuries also…" Jack's voice drifted back to them.

"There are a lot of injuries coming in now," he murmured. "God, look at the state of that vehicle."

The vehicle heading towards them had certainly seen better days, how it was still running beggared belief. It had no lights, no windows apart from the windscreen and that was badly cracked, different wheels on which were bald tyres and the bodywork was completely rusted. Alison peered through the window as it passed. The driver looked like a tramp. His face barely visible behind a huge beard; beside him was a woman with greying hair who seemed familiar. She looked at the man again and screamed, then screamed again as Jack slammed on the brakes and she was shot forward, jarring her legs.

"What the hell," he said. "Why did you scream?" Alison could hardly speak, she was so agitated.

"It's Daddy," she half sobbed, and turning to Alex, she said, her voice choking, "your Mum."

Jack stared at her, hardly daring to believe, but hoping she was not mistaken. He swung his vehicle round and followed it to the hospital, where the wheelchairs and bed trolleys were waiting. He stopped and jumped out of the vehicle. Running to the dilapidated vehicle, he yanked the door open.

"Jenny," he shouted and dragged her from the vehicle into his arms. "I thought you were dead," he cried, the tears rolling down his face

She stared at him, it was as if she was staring at a ghost.

"We saw a mountain fall on you how…just how did you survive?"

The bearded man looked across at Jack's vehicle and he too jumped out and rushed across, opening the door, he too stared. "Alison," he said and went to grab her, but then saw the bandages on her legs. He too, wept.

"My girl," he choked, "and Alex," he said as he saw him sitting white faced at Alison's side. "You best go and say hello to your mum." There were a lot of tears and hugs while the hospital staff looked on bemused.

Jack came across and had a quick word with a porter. Slipping a fifty-euro note into his hand, he said, "Once you have got all the patients out, would you get rid of this vehicle; the keys are in the ignition." The porter grinned seeing what was happening, although not quite knowing and nodded. With Richard beside him and Jenny in the back with the two youngsters, the only things Richard and Jenny retrieved from their vehicle was his battered old briefcase and her handbag. On the way back, they each told the other of their escapes. The land rover had been swept downstream in the torrent of water, when it suddenly stopped and the car was sitting on the riverbed, thanking God that Jack had left the keys in the ignition. He tried to start it, and after a few bangs and belching of exhaust fumes it had, they drove along and there it was, a slipway, obviously used for launching canoes as there were several on racks by a small building.

Richard was no fool, the cliff fall was only blocking the water temporarily and when it did come, it would not be a gurgling little stream. He made for higher ground, found shelter in a cluster of rocks and waited until the dust had dispersed enough for them to continue, eventually gaining access to the Crystal Dome in Barcelona. Jack told him of their narrow escape, explaining the landfall that he and Jenny had seen was a few hundred yards away. "Mind you, if I had been quicker to follow you, we would have been buried alive."

Looking sideways at his friend he said, "Elizabeth will never recognise you with that beard." Richard was too overcome with emotion to reply.

Jenny, in the back, was hugging the two youngsters. She suddenly spoke. "As soon as we get back could I have a shower or even a nice long bath?"

"Of course, you can," Jack laughed "You do pong a bit."

Arriving back, they were greeted by a shocked Ben, who wondered who these two very scruffy people were. When told he was even more shocked and hugely delighted. He made a joke of, "You're a bit late arriving," he scolded with a big grin. "Elizabeth is baking a pie you best come and say hello to her," he said, addressing Richard. "I'm sure she will be pleased to see you."

They went through to the kitchen. Elizabeth was up to her arms in flour as she mixed it with butter for the shortbread pastry she was famous for. Looking up, she saw a bearded tramp.

"You bastard," she screamed and threw herself at him.

Richard, beneath his beard, paled and backed up, the room was a cloud of flour as she first beat him on the chest and then hugged him, saying, "Why didn't you contact us, where have you been?" He looked into her lovely tearful face.

"There were no communications, we were not trapped but in a dome and outside, well you know, how bad it was and lastly we thought you, Jack and the children were dead." Having said that he burst into tears, hugging his daughter and wife close to him.

"We will have a party," Ben declared. "But only after," he added smiling, "you and Jenny have had a chance to spruce yourselves up."

"Oh yes, please!" Jenny exclaimed. "Mind you I've nothing to wear."

Elizabeth looked at her friend who was once 4 sizes larger than herself and was now probably thinner.

"You can raid my wardrobe after you have had a bath," she added, grinning. Then taking Jenny's hand she took her off to her room.

Ben, who was the nearest to Richard's size, told him where his room was and offered the same.

"I am sure Ben will not mind you using his razor," Elizabeth called out to his back as he disappeared. Before they reappeared, Louisa, Tessa and Maria with her children came in. They were again all amazed and delighted at the reunion of the two families.

"Jack," Ben said, "after the party tonight and a good night's sleep, I think the four of you should take off to a hotel for as long as you like all expenses paid. It will give you a chance to catch up. Alex and Alison will be fine with us." This brought a storm of protest from the pair named.

"We are not letting our parents out of our sight ever again," they said in unison. So that was decided and the two families went off on a week's holiday.

The following morning, after the party, the house seemed quiet without Alison and Alex who were always up with the larks. Ben walked into the lounge to find George walking up and down like a caged lion.

"One more week George and your physio will be finished. As long as you do your daily exercises."

"It is not so much that," George grumbled. "I am bored I cannot play any strenuous sports and I miss Romilly terribly. And some of the places she has to land puts her at great risk. Mind you, do not tell her I said that, she loves what she is doing and she is saving lives and rescuing people on a daily basis." Ben patted his friends shoulder.

“She does love flying but if you feel that way, tell her. But to put your mind at rest, she is good. Phil the one that rescued you, tells me she could land on a sixpence if need be.”

George shook his head. “I will be glad when it is all over this rescuing.”

At that precise moment in time, Romilly was thinking the same as George. As the rescuing of survivors was becoming less the places the poor souls were sheltering were becoming further and further afield. This latest mission was at the limit of her helicopter range. Having got the seven aboard, she was heading back. It was no easy journey, the turbulence was bad and eating up the fuel as she struggled to control the copter. She shot another glance at the fuel gauges. Damn, damn, she said to herself, we are not going to make it. As if to prove her right, the engine spluttered. “Shit,” she said to nobody in particular as she was alone in the cockpit and switched to the reserve tank hoping it was full. Obviously not, the gauges were still showing empty. Home was too far away, she started scouring the landscape below for a possible landing place. Although her big helicopter could normally land on a sixpence, with her load of seven people and they insisted on bringing all their luggage, she would need a short landing runway. The helicopter had two short stubby wings to facilitate such a landing but she reckoned she would need a hundred metres of runway. Looking down, she saw a field but going lower she could see the reflection of water albeit in patches. Romilly started to panic as the ground rose and as she topped a small bluff, there it was, a plateau. It was hardly big enough but she didn’t hesitate; she stabbed the mayday. She landed right on the edge of it and started to apply the brakes and prayed it would be long enough. It was not. “Oh no,” she gasped as the further edge loomed closer, she said another prayer and as she did one of the wheels hit a rock slewing the copter round. It stopped with one of its stubby wings hanging over a ravine. Clutching her chest, her two hearts pounding she thought, *I must be out of lives now.*

There was silence for a few moments then a cheerful voice called out from behind the cockpit door. “Are we there?”

It was at that point she decided her flying days were over. “No,” she called out, “but somebody will be along soon.” She nearly added ‘to rescue us’ but stopped herself in time. Saying instead to pick us up. “I did not have quite enough fuel for the journey back due to turbulence.” She was glad the cabin door was there as she started shaking with the trauma of it. “Thank you God,” she whispered. Checking to make sure the mayday was still sending and giving the coordinates of their position, she rang George; of course, no signal. She then tried the copters radio to send a message, again nothing, she swore again, then stopped. We are still alive. Be thankful, she told herself.

Romilly made her way to her passengers. They all looked up as she entered through the cabin door. The one she recognised as the leader, named Jeremy, asked what was happening.

"I'm afraid we just ran out of fuel," Romilly answered. But then hastily added to reassure them, help is on its way, so make yourselves comfortable, it could be several hours before it arrives."

She went to the small fridge and took out a handful of pre-packed meals which she gave out.

'"I'm afraid I cannot heat them," she explained, "but the fuel we have will be needed to us in case there is any delay and we're not refuelled by nightfall." Jeremy smiled at her.

"This is a banquet compared to what we have been living on," he explained and ripping off the foil, joined the others and started to wolf the contents down.

"Eat it slowly," Romilly instructed. "It has a very high energy content and if you have been on a poor diet, it could make you very ill. If anyone thinks about going outside," she added, "please don't it is far too dangerous." Again she returned to the cockpit and settled down on the small bunk she had had installed for the times when she was away for longer periods. Romilly and her little group were unlucky. Although, the mayday was transmitting, unfortunately it was not being received. The signal that did however get through, was the one she sent when they were still airborne. Her position was pinpointed and a Chinook was dispatched and was already halfway there. Romilly was unaware of the concern she was creating as the only contact with her was while she was still in the air. George was sitting in his favourite chair watching an old film. It was suddenly cut to allow a broadcast about a missing helicopter. George jumped up and rushed to the phone just as it rang. Snatching it up, he heard Ben's voice.

"Hello, is that you, George?"

"Yes," he gasped. "George she will be okay, a helicopter is on its way to her now." In his mind, George thought differently. No his mind said, I knew this would happen. He collapsed to the floor unconscious and the phone clattered down beside him.

"George!! GEORGE!!!! Are you okay?" No answer. Ben cancelled the call and rang the Medical Centre, giving them George's address, he explained he thought it was a heart attack, he then got his call transferred to George's consultant. He told him his fears. "I will ring the ambulance and instruct them," the consultant assured him. Within the hour, George was in the hospital on a heart bypass, Ben was at his side along with Louisa.

"How bad, Mum," he asked.

"Not good," she said. "He had stopped breathing by the time they got to him and both hearts had stopped. They got the new one going again but it is still too young and he will have to stay on the bypass until a donor can be found to replace the old heart." She put her arm around her son's shoulders.

"I am sure a donor will soon be found." Louisa said consoling him.

Ben shook his head.

"Romilly's going to be devastated, she is devoted to him."

"Let's wait and see what the scan shows first," Louisa said.

"Do you think she is okay?" Ben asked. Louisa nodded vigorously.

"I would stake my life on it. I have flown with her many times when visiting other Domes. She can fly upside down while waving to someone on the ground."

In spite of the way he felt, Ben grinned saying, "I hope you're right for both their sakes."

Six hours later, Romilly was standing by George's bedside, tears streaming down her face.

Brushing away the tears, she held his hand and leaning over, gently kissed him.

Easy to say that, she thought, *now it's too late.* Ben who had read her mind, sent the thought, *you don't know that.*

"Please god, you are right," Romilly said. And he was; his mind was undamaged and through another tragedy a donor was found. The man working on the repairs to one of the Domes was killed in a fall. His family donated his body to the Medical Centre and when they were told who it was, it lessened their grief a little. George was much admired by all who worked for him. In a letter, they expressed this writing, that they hoped it would give him a long life. Christmas was suddenly upon them and the man's wife and children were invited to what George and Romilly called their extended family. George was now fitter than he had been twenty years ago, although his replacement heart had only been transplanted two months previously and his second heart was getting stronger by the day.

The Orphan

Umbria was in a steady orbit parallel to Earth at a distance of 1.5 million miles. There were many problems and disasters to overcome but that was for the future and although both planets had suffered heavy losses of population, the outlook was good and they would eventually flourish.

Lucy and Mars were both pouring over the data they had gleaned from their computers. Averting her eyes, she glanced across at Mars; he now knew her true age which was young for an Arian but way beyond that of a Human or an Umbrian. His only sadness was he would only be with her for a thousand years, it was fortunate he had the Umbrian gene. Lucy loved him greatly but when they made love they had to seek complete isolation, because the air became full of static and around them was a display similar to that of the northern lights which obviously they found extremely embarrassing. The information they sought was the loss of life on Earth. Now that communications were getting back to normal, it made their task possible. They were surprised, although most of the land animals were lost. The human losses were only a fraction of what was first surmised. The sea mammals were of the same numbers but the fish had multiplied greatly in numbers. The Umbrian losses were greater although they lost less than a hundred million on their planet, but the loss of life when their ocean was torn away with the coastline was over 1.5 billion. This was from the cities that were on or near the ocean. Ben came bursting in.

"Great news, the dust and fumes and gases have dispersed and the air is pure. All the plants and trees are growing again and people are moving out of the domes and back to their towns and villages."

"How is Alison?" Lucy asked. "Is she out of hospital yet?"

Ben smiled. "She is fine and glowing in the glory of being rescued by the Adonis Mars."

There was a snort from Lucy.

"The Adonis has been basking in fame somewhat himself," she said hiding her face and winking at Ben.

Mars actually blushed and rising to his feet, grunted, then said, "I am hungry. Let's go and eat." Lucy gave him a playful dig in the ribs. Then the three went off to see what delight the canteen had. As they walked, there was a drumming sound and looking up they saw the cause. Huge hailstones which were more like rocks were hammering down on the dome's roof, the noise was tremendous. They hurried on and were soon inside where it was much more peaceful. Finding a table, they sat and looked at the menu. Food was still scarce so there was little choice.

"How is Louisa and Tessa?" Lucy enquired. The two of them were several hundred metres away to the west tending to those who had sustained injury in the hazardous work of repairing the domes.

"They both are fine," he said. "Mind you, I will be glad when they return. It can be dangerous but they do have Dennis with them and he often helps when someone gets trapped in rubble." He went on to explain that during the tremors there had been a massive landslide and although the domes are virtually indestructible; the fall had nudged the dome and the foundations were damaged. The workers were replacing and reinforcing the foundation when there was further movement and some were unfortunately killed and many more were injured ranging from cuts and bruises to broken bones and wounds needing stitches. To make matters worse, the hospital's senior surgeon had injured himself when the hospital suffered damage when part of its foundations collapsed.

"Let's hope Mum and Granny are missing this weather," Mars said.

Ben nodded, looking round to see how the queue for food was diminishing. Then he saw them. "Well, I'll be damned, it's George and Romilly." He called them over and Mars found two more chairs for them. They had hardly sat down before George and Ben were discussing the damage and aftermath to one of their domes. Romilly, being an engineer, just listened, interjecting when she had a point to make. Mars and Lucy, who knew virtually all that was happening worldwide, went to join the queue, asking first if they could get the others anything. Romilly turned to George.

"I think you should eat now darling. You know what the doctor said about keeping your strength up and all this talking is making you agitated." She cast a warning glance towards Ben.

"Yes, we must not wear the old chap out," he said giving George a wicked grin.

"Less of the old," George retorted. "I've worked you to a standstill many a times and drunk you under the table afterwards."

"True, true," Ben surrendered laughing and holding his hands up. "How good or bad do you really feel in yourself, my friend?"

"I will feel a darn sight better when this second heart starts working properly."

Two women on the next table looked across at George's remark. Ben smiled across at them.

"He means his new heart," he gave as an explanation.

"Sorry," George whispered. One of the two women sent a thought into Ben's mind.

"My name is Eva. May we talk with you?"

Ben laughed out loud.

"Well," he said, "it would be a lot more suspicious if we all sat here in silence nodding to each other."

"Of course," Eva said, smiling.

Ben smiled back saying, "How can we help you both?"

"We have just come here from Umbria and we entered the Dome as refugees." She bowed her head. "I am sorry for the deception."

Lucy and Mars had returned. Lucy who had been looking at the two intently, suddenly spoke, "You are members of the Supreme Council, are you not?"

The two nodded. "We are and my name is Adele," she added

"Why are you here?" Ben asked. "You must know there is much hatred for Umbrians especially for the Council members. The loss of life on Earth has been terrible. I know," he went on, "it was just the one that caused it but the majority of Earth's people do not know. They think it was the pull of your planet's gravity that caused the disaster but that does not lessen the hate."

"We of course know that we are reviled by our own people for our and your losses."

We were pursued here though by those still loyal to the Council and only have a slim chance of survival."

"So," Ben asked. "What is so desperate to induce the Council to send you to almost certain death?"

It was Eva who spoke just saying one word, "WATER." She said putting much emphasis on the word. Ben and Mars looked at each other in amazement.

"Water," they said. Not having a clue as to why.

Lucy knew though but she let Eva explain.

"Water is virtually gone from Umbria," she explained. "When Umbria was pulled out of the orbit round Radiance, it lost a huge amount of land and also her main ocean. We now have little water on our surface and have to rely on what is underground and what we have left in our shelters, I believe you call them 'Crystal Domes'."

Ben and Mars were stunned. To be without its oceans, Earth would become a desert and then surely all life would cease.

"But how can we help?" Mars asked.

"Earth has an abundance of water, seas and oceans overflow with water and many die when you have tidal waves or tsunamis." Eva spoke with passion. "You could spare us some and not notice the difference."

"Impossible." Mars and Ben said in unison. "You're saying that if we somehow could give you our sea water in great quantities, it would lower the level of our oceans."

"Yes, it would benefit both planets."

"But, surely you realise it would take a thousand years to transport a small lake, let alone a sea."

Lucy cut in a small smile on her face.

"Actually, it would be quite possible." The smile got bigger when she saw the look on their faces.

Then it dawned on them. The wormhole, once started it would be like taking water from a bottle with a flexible tube, the flow would be continuous.

"Is that what you mean," Ben asked, "a wormhole."

The two women nodded excitedly. Then they both started to talk together. Ben held up his hands. "Whoa, back a bit. How, if it was possible, would it be implemented?"

Glancing at her companion, Eva spoke.

"In the South Pacific, there are vast areas of ocean which humans never go near and with so many of them destroyed now it a surety, but we would set up a force field, say 200 kilometres enforced by a matter barrier." Ben had heard of such barriers but he still had strong reservations about the whole scheme.

"What about the sea creatures that are living below the waves?" he asked. "And there are some fully armed nuclear submarines roaming the seas and they could be anywhere in the world and you definitely do not want to suck one of those up."

"There are no ships either above or below the sea in that area." Adele said, earning a warning look from her companion. Not to be stopped, Adele added, "and all the fish, amphibians and crustaceans and other life forms would be herded to safety. Also, if they were sucked up, their chances of survival would be quite good because of the oxygen that is in the water."

"Well," Ben smiled at the young woman's enthusiasm. "You have certainly done your homework, a human word for research," he added seeing the confused expression on her face. Eva looked anxiously at Ben.

"Do you think Earth's Council of Nations would agree? It would be very beneficial to Earth. All we would need is literally, *a drop in the ocean*," she said, smiling at her own knowledge of one of the sayings. Ben nodded.

"It sounds feasible. There are a lot of cities on Earth which are on estuaries and are vulnerable to flooding. Although up river, even London has flood barriers. There is a good chance they will agree. Umbria being much advanced in all fields has already, on the medical side, given Earth the cures for many of our diseases and life-threatening conditions such as cancer, stroke, and of course the life prolonging gene. In the meantime, I suggest you come and stay with us, so we will be able to discuss this crazy project further." As Ben stopped speaking, a car stopped just outside the canteen and two people got out. Lucy tensed, staring at the man and woman.

"There is danger, Benjamin" she whispered. Ben pulled out his mobile and spoke rapidly into it, rising from his seat along with Mars and George.

"No Benjamin," Lucy cried out. But it was too late. Ben's three guards were approaching the pair, the woman smiled at them and then everything seemed a blur. The guards were on the floor and the assailants were through the canteen doors heading towards Ben and his friends.

In one swift movement, Lucy was on her feet and raising her hand she cried.

"Stop." They did, in mid-stride they stopped and a puff of smoke came from their ears.

"Sit," Lucy commanded. This they also did, stumbling into chairs, but then they fell to the floor.

They fell just a few yards from their table. Lucy started to shake and leaned against the table, gripping it hard with her hands. Mars caught her as she seemed about to collapse.

"Lucy," he lowered her into the nearest chair. What is it?" he asked, his voice cracking with anxiety. He felt a great emotion emanating from her body.

"Please," he said. "Let me help you. Tell me what it is?"

Lucy looked up into his eyes, she could feel the love he had for her, it was that tangible.

"I have committed the ultimate sin of my race," she said. "We are not allowed to interfere. It is an oath we made eons ago. I have broken that sacrament."

Bowing her head she whispered sadly, "I could not let them kill you all, especially you." Then Mars saw tears fall from her eyes. Almost weeping himself, Mars said, "What you did was not bad nor evil. You did not stop them to save yourself even. And they are not flesh and blood, they are clones. I saw the smoke come from their ears."

"No, my dear, kind Mars, they are Umbrians who have been conditioned and implants inserted into their brains. They have obviously also been given muscle building drugs hence the speed and power they had. It would have been part of the conditioning program."

With tears still falling, she lowered her head. "Mars I have interfered and I have killed two innocent Umbrians. I must eliminate myself."

Mars shook his head in disbelief.

"If you do," he said, "you will have a third death on your hands. If you do that, my life would be nothing without you. But you know that." Then it happened. It was as God was giving Lucy a reprieve. One of the two assailants stirred slightly. Lucy jumped up and rushed to the pair. Placing a hand on their necks, she felt for a pulse. Her face broke into a smile.

"They live," she shouted out, "their pulse is weak but steady." Mars was euphoric, near to tears himself, having been on a roller coaster with his emotions in turmoil. Lucy turned to ask Ben for his help, then realised she had put him in a comatose state when she had shouted. "Stop!!!"

She went to him and gently held his face between her hands, she told him to awaken.

He shook his head saying, "What a strange feeling. I knew all that was happening, but was incapable of lifting a finger to do or stop anything."

"Sorry, Benjamin, I knew your men would suffer injury or death and tried to stop you calling them. Could you get help now, though I think your men are probably concussed and I would like to get these two to the Medical Centre ASAP."

Ben picked up his mobile from the floor and made a call, doing as Lucy had asked. He asked for medics and back up security. Eva and Adele sat white faced, not only because they had been close to death themselves, they had exposed Ben and his friends to the same danger. So sure were they that they themselves were the target.

"We must leave now," Eva said rising.

“You just stay where you are,” Ben said, gently putting his hand on Eva’s shoulder. She sat but looked up at him.

She said, “If we stay, we will be putting you in great danger. There are still many on Umbria that do not want anything to do with humans. They are mostly the male members of the Council. They held sway after Venus disappeared. We know she must have died, because we found out she had been poisoned with one of the most deadly poisons on Umbria.” She hesitated and then went on, “It’s like a living virus” she explained.

Before he spoke he looked at Lucy. She shook her head. Ben, of course, knew that Lucy although was in the guise of being Venus’s maid, she was in fact her protector and still wanted the knowledge that she was still alive to be kept secret. Lucy put the thought in Ben’s mind. “I will tell them when they are safe and secure in the Complex.”

All conversations ended then, as a helicopter rose from behind the adjacent buildings and as it lowered down to land in the square, men and women spilled out of it. The men and women who were heavily armed, deployed themselves round the square. Some entered the now empty canteen, apart from those who were with Ben. The medics followed with stretchers for the injured security and the assailants. There were many faces at the windows of the surrounding buildings but they disappeared as the security swept the roofs looking for any snipers.

“Let’s get the hell out of here,” Ben shouted to the two commanders. Within minutes, the square was empty as the helicopter rose and was gone.

“To the Medical Centre,” Ben ordered the pilot.

“I am already heading in that direction,” came the reply. Ben thought for a moment.

“No, on second thoughts, head for the house first. I want as few people as possible to see our guests,” he said referring to the two Umbrian women. “It will only take a few minutes,” he added.

Speaking now to the medics, he said, “How are the patients?”

“The security men are badly concussed, but they should be okay, the other two are in need of the attention of a neurologist, and that is not in my field.” They landed near the house and apart from the pilot and the five injured, they stepped from the helicopter. Lucy whispered to Mars.

“I will go with the patients. I need to examine the two Umbrians who attacked us.”

To thwart any objections from Mars she added, "You go to the house with the others, I want you there to help protect the Umbrian women. There might be further attacks."

Although Mars doubted what Lucy had said and was worried for her if one of the assailants died, he agreed knowing she would have good reason for not wanting him there.

"You take good care and promise not to harm yourself because of your conscience," he said, taking her in his arms and hugging her fiercely. Fortunately, no one was looking in their direction as static started coming from the pair of them and they were encased in a blue light.

Mars released her from his arms and hurried away to the house. Lucy and two of the security team re-boarded and the helicopter lifted away into the evening sun, landing again almost immediately as the Medical Centre was only half a mile from the house. Once inside the centre, the injured security men were whisked away for assessment and treatment. The two Umbrians were taken to an isolation ward with Lucy following. In the ward, she put a no admittance sign on the door and locked herself in with the pair and waited. In a few seconds, she began to sense his presence and there he was, a golden globe of light which hovered just above her.

"Father," she asked with her mind. "I want to know what is it, what is happening. These two should be dead and me also," she added.

"They should have died but you saved them somehow. In doing so, you broke our vow of non-interference." Lucy felt the warmth of her father's love as he spoke to her, his thoughts of information surprising her.

"We Arians gathered and decided that after all our honourable non-interference vow had no meaning. After the deaths of so much life, both on Earth and Umbria, we came to the decision, it was a hard decision after all the millennium we have held it, but it was made. The two here should have died as you said but we interfered with the implants and took out the self-destruct mechanism of the implants before they were inserted." Lucy started to speak but was stopped by her father. Her eyes were drawn to the corner of the room where there was, of course, CCTV sensor. Of course, she thought in an isolation ward there had to be a monitor. Lucy sent thoughts to her father.

"Can the monitors see you father?"

"No, they just see you and the two Umbrians." Lucy asked her about the implants.

"You interfered with the implants. But they were rendered unconscious."

"Yes, but had we interfered too much it would have been noticed," came the answer.

Lucy wished her father could adapt to his body form but with the monitors that was impossible; there were many humans at the centre and at the present time it was dangerous. Her father went to the female patient and a golden glow surrounded her head. After a few moments, she started to stir, moaning she tossed her head from side to side and then her body started to convulse, as it did the glow intensified. Lucy looked on anxiously. She is only a young girl, she thought to herself. The girl gave one last convulsion and lay still.

"Father is she going to be alright?" She was worried now. As she spoke, the girl's eyes fluttered and opened.

"What is happening?" she asked. And then looking round and seeing Lucy, she spoke again.

"And what gives with the glow around my head?" Lucy almost laughed, wondering who had taught the girl English. Lucy answered her. First she, with a thought, demobilised the monitor.

"The glow around your head is my father, he is one of the ancients as am I."

"Does Daddy have a name?" The girl asked boldly. Again Lucy smiled at the girl's English.

"My father's name is Axcelor and may I ask what is your name?" The girl opened her mouth to speak and then closed it again. She paled screwing her face up as she tried to remember. She put her hands to her head but to no avail.

"I do not know. Why do I not know?" Tears sprang to her eyes and she shook her head, really frightened by now. Lucy held the girl's hand.

"It is alright, it will come to you soon. You have had an accident," she said telling a white lie.

The glow was now centred round the young man's head. He responded well and was much more alert. When asked he gave his name as Jacob. That is why the girl cannot remember. They erased their memory and gave them Earth names, while the girl was trying to remember her birth name. Whoever groomed the young pair is a dangerous enemy. The young man is still confused about his identity whereas the girl is trying to remember. Axcelor looked down at the two youngsters from his host planet wishing the Arians had abolished their non-interference vow long ago.

"I have done all I can for them. They will recover in time but it will be traumatic for them. Lucy, I will leave them in your hands. I must leave you now. There are things we, the Arians, must do to stop Earth and Umbria coming to war with each other. We must achieve this for we have to right our own wrongdoing." Lucy had a feeling of great love and then nothing as her father's glow disappeared. She looked at the sensors and found them working again. She looked at the pair of young Umbrians. *I will get you back to normal,* she thought, *you see if I don't.* Lucy called the consultant and then the doctor. When they came to the room, she asked the consultant if he could monitor the two patients, and got the medic to give them a strong sedative. She promised to return the following day to start the treatment they needed. Basically this was a program of psychological repair of the damage to their minds. Going outside, she used her mobile and called Carrie using voice recognition. It was not the original car that had taken Ben and Maria on that perilous journey when they both nearly died in their conflict with the Grand Master's brother. It was, though, a duplicate of the original apart from the nuclear pack which was considered too dangerous.

It was there in a few minutes and in its tinny voice it asked, "Where to Miss Lucy?"

"Take me to the house please, Carrie." Like everyone, Lucy was amused that she used the word please when talking to the car's computer.

Arriving a few minutes later, Mars was at the door waiting for her.

"I hope those two did not cause any more trouble?" he asked.

"No," Lucy answered. "The victims of their patriotic fervour and it nearly cost them their lives for what they thought wrongly, the defence of their homeland. Now they are in a confused state. Their minds will need unravelling, which, given time and with the help of psychologists and myself, this will be achieved. I am sorry but I will be spending a lot of time at the centre for the next few weeks, but I will come back every evening. I promise," she added giving him a hug,

"How are Eva and Adele?" she asked.

"Extremely happy to be alive," Mars said, thinking to himself, the memory of the trauma the two women went through.

"At present they are enjoying some peace and quiet and," he added, "waiting for their dinner as we all are, but now here, we can all relax and enjoy the meal." They both hurried to the dining room which was capable of sitting, sixty people. On the walls were many beautiful paintings by some equally famous painters.

Also there were lovely wall hangings and along the edge of the room were outstanding sculptures. Dominating the centre of one wall was a huge roaring fire with warm air ducting to ensure it heated the whole room.

Everybody turned as Lucy and Mars entered, Lucy feeling extremely embarrassed at delaying everyone's meal started to apologise but Ben stopped her.

"Lucy, no problem we have all been enjoying a nice glass of wine in your absence, and," he added, "we are waiting for Venus to join us." As he spoke, both Eva and Adele turned to stare at him, shock showing on their faces which were blanched of colour. Ben felt, rather than saw, their agitation.

"What," he asked, "what have I said." Lucy knew of course, there had been much secrecy surrounding Venus's survival. She, of course, should have died. So no one was informed to the contrary, to protect her from further attacks.

Lucy had also used her powers to cloak the existence of Venus. And Venus realizing the importance of her anonymity, had agreed to keep a low profile and stay within the confines of Ben's huge house.

Without alerting all of those seated, Lucy transmitted her thought to Eva and Adele informing them of the tacit facts. The two Umbrians visibly relaxed, and smiling at Ben, Eva said, "It was nothing Mr Franklin. We just had some good news and were rather shocked."

Ben grinning with relief said, "Well, thank goodness for that. And please you must call me Ben." There was a ripple of laughter and everyone at the table smiled, knowing how Ben hated being referred to as Mr Franklin.

Romilly sat and stared. She was sensing something but was frustrated not quite knowing what.

I must be almost reading everyone's minds, she said to herself.

Everyone was busily chatting and Romilly let her mind drift back to the last few hours.

She and George had come back early after lunch with friends, partly because she did not want George to be overtired, but now she wanted him to herself.

As they entered their room, Romilly declared, "I must have a shower," and proceeded to rid herself of her clothing.

George helped her undo her dress, then slipped it from her shoulders. He then kissed her neck, at the same time he also undid her bra, turning her around, he kissed her tenderly on her mouth.

"George," she murmured, "I think you", she was unable to say anything else because their tongues had suddenly become interlocked.

"Hmmm," was the only sound she was able to make.

They took a shower together, and afterwards slowly and carefully dried each other.

Romilly took his hand and led him to their bedroom. They lay and kissed.

George started at her neck and slowly worked his way down her body, kissing it as he went, right down to her feet and started back up again. Romilly was in heaven it seemed, and he was still kissing; he got half way up and the kissing got more intense.

"George, no you must not do, oooh, aah," she climaxed, her body spasmed and she sank back into the soft mattress. "I think we best have another shower," he said, a huge smile on his face.

He started to apologise for not making love properly.

"George," she almost wept, "that was beautiful. I am wicked to let it go that far my darling."

She was, of course, referring to George's slow climb back to full health.

'I am fine,' he said. "Both hearts are beating well. I just need my physical strength back."

Romilly looked at him fondly. She had had quite a few lovers in her life but was unable to recall any heights that George had just taken her to. She asked him if he had taken his medication.

"Yes, I have. Now, you go and enjoy your dinner, I," he said dramatically, "must rest my poor body."

He said it with a pained expression on his face, then burst out laughing when he saw the expression on hers. She hugged him, bit his ear for revenge, kissed him and left to have dinner.

Romilly, now back at the table, flushed at the memory.

"Oh George," she murmured to herself.

"Sorry, what did you say?" Turning she found Maria looking at her now deep pink face.

"Oh," she said, "just a happy memory." Maria gave her a bemused smile and raised her glass.

"To George," she said and then with a grin added, "and you."

Ben looked at the gathering around him, pleased to see so many friends. He looked again, no George, he thought he let his mind drift and it found George sound asleep in bed. Looking up then, he found Romilly staring at him. "Sorry," he thought and she smiled back.

His mother and Tessa were missing. At present, they were at the other side of Spain tending the injured after a massive landslide came down on a Dome. Normally, the hospital could cope but the landslide damaged the hospital and with the injuries to the staff and patients, there was chaos. Louisa and Tessa renowned for their (healing powers), decided to go and offer their help. Dennis went with them. He was never away from Louisa's side for long, an arrangement Ben was very pleased with. *When they have returned, I am going to take all gathered at this table, plus George,* he thought with amusement, to where… To England; now the air was clean and the storms and winds abated it would be an ideal venue. A small cloud crossed his mind. He shook it away, and decided to retire for the night. Once in bed, he was asleep in minutes. He suddenly awoke, looking at the bedside clock. One o'clock, he remembered in his dream there was a sound and it was that, that woke him. He went to the window and looked out where everything had been coming back to life, it was gone, all the land before him was barren, trees were leafless, their branches bent in a howling wind, the lake had gone and the earth was black. He saw a figure straining his eyes. He saw who…Mother.

"Mother, take cover, get inside," he screamed. Then she disappeared "NO, NO," he screamed.

There was a loud banging now and he heard his name. "Ben, BEN, DAD." He woke sweating as his door burst open and Mars, Maria and Lucy rushed in. He looked up at their shocked faces.

"Dad, you were shouting," Mars said, his face showed concern for his father.

"Your mother, Tessa and Dennis, they have all disappeared," he corrected himself. "That is, in my dream, they disappeared. They must be in danger."

Lucy closed her eyes and after a moment said, "No, they are still there but I cannot place where they are."

Ben jumped out of bed and pushed numbers on his mobile phone; not available, the voice said.

"Right," he said, pulling his clothes on. "I am going to find them."

Maria said, "I will be ready in ten minutes, Benjie." Lucy was still treating the two Umbrians and Mars and was loathe to leave her until she had. Ben told them both not to worry, he had Maria.

In ten minutes, they were in the car heading for the railway terminal. At the terminal, there were no trains due. It would take forever to travel there by car, with the roads still under repair there were diversions and hold ups every few miles. Ben tried the heliport not really expecting any joy; he was right, no helicopters. It was the terminal manager who came to the rescue, having overheard part of the telephone conversation, the bit where Ben said it was vitally important. He turned to Ben, "Mr Franklin, we do have the maintenance engine in the sidings, however, it is not meant for travelling."

Ben shook his hand. "Thank you," he said, "that will be great. Lead us to it." The manager took a key from its ring and led the way to a very decrepit looking engine with a trailer. Unhooking the trailer, he handed Ben the key. He showed Ben the basics of driving the thing then he climbed back out, wished them luck and went. The next four hours were hell in the bone shaker as Ben pushed the train to the limits of its speed. Arriving at the dome, Ben enquired of the whereabouts of his wife, mother and Dennis only to be informed they had left two days before. Ben was surprised they had left, thinking they had gone missing inside the dome.

"Where the hell are they? We will have to retrace our steps." They re-boarded the boneshaker and started back, after a mile Ben slowed to a crawl, then stopped.

"Here, this is where they left the track." Maria looked at him surprised. They were in a long dark tunnel of solid rock. But if Benjie said here, then here is where to look. A faint blue light from above shed an eerie glow in the tunnel.

"Let's get out and look," she said. Then as Ben climbed out she stopped and lifted the lid of the hard wooden seat they had sat and suffered on, grabbing a huge torch, she climbed down again and turned it on.

"Well, at least it works," she said nervously as a bright beam lit up the wall. She shone the torch along both sides of the tunnel.

"There," she exclaimed. Ben peered at the wall and sure enough there was a uniform crack from floor to ceiling. They examined it and brushed the sand away at the base, and there it was, a lever. Ben put his head against the wall, yes, they were behind it, he knew.

First Ben, then both of them, tried to move the lever, it refused to budge.

"Give me a minute Benjie," and she rushed off to boney, their nickname for the engine, returning with a hammer and a long lever. After a little persuasion, it moved and as it did, they watched a whole section of the tunnel slide away.

Into the lion's den and she shuddered at the thought.

Part 3

Chapter 19

Ben and Maria moved cautiously forward. It was a barren landscape inside the huge cave. No sign of life or vegetation, and a there was huge concave base which had obviously been a lake. Ben exclaimed, "It's my dream, when mother just disappeared." Maria shivered, and it wasn't from being cold. Buildings came into their view on their right, Ben knew then it was where Louisa and Tessa were, he also sensed an immense power emanating from the same building.

Maria yelled, "Look out Benji."

Then fell to the ground as large rock struck her head. Ben twisted round. "NO, NO," he roared, and threw himself on top of Maria as a hail of stones and rocks pummelled into his back and head. He started to lose consciousness; as he did, his last thoughts were of the ones most dear to him. Louisa, Tessa, and Maria, who could be dead beneath him, and of course Dennis, who nearly gave his life guarding his mother, and all the patients when the clinic was attacked.

A silence came as a white light started to drift from Ben. It was a soft light like the one that came from Lucy at the Eden Project. The missiles were now floating away and settling on the ground.

The power coming from the buildings intensified and for a moment the light from Ben dimmed. But then it got stronger and brighter, so bright it covered the whole cavern and it still increased in its intensity, until from the mountain through every crack and fissure, it shone, even where the water was still trickling into the vast barren lake.

The light pierced through the trickle, pushing aside all the rubble that was blocking the river, the trickle became a torrent and then with a deafening roar the water poured into the lake. It resumed its natural course filling the lake, then into an underground river that bypassed the inhabited dome and flowed through the domes where the crops and animals were. The reservoir's dam which had been near to collapsing through the pressure of water, slowly returned to its normal level. The domes would have been washed down into the valley had the dam burst, and the inhabitants looked to the light that saved them all as a miracle. Back at the clinic, Mars looked shocked.

He had felt the power that was pouring through his father; what also shocked and surprised Mars was the distance from which the power had travelled. Was it a call for help?

"Dad," he said. Lucy looked calm.

"Your Dad's okay." she said and then shook with fear.

"What is it?" Mars said.

"'The power he has is enormous," she answered.

Ben was totally unaware of anything around himself. He sensed Maria was with him and okay, well nearly okay. The light played on her and already the deep gash on her head was healing. He wanted to do something but could not remember what. His mind drifted in the light, what was it!!! He drifted on. Someone was calling him.

"'Ben, Ben," the voice became more insistent. "Benjamin, WAKE UP."

"MUM," he shouted in his mind and struggled to come from his comatose state, as he did, the light retreated back into his body. His eyes fluttered and he found himself in his mother's arms.

"Benjamin Franklin," she whispered. "We thought we had lost you." Ben hugged his mother.

"Thank god, you are here. Are you all okay? Tessa and Dennis."

"Yes and Maria, if you can manage to get yourself off her," she said, managing a smile.

Ben twisted round. "Oh," he said, looking into Maria's enormous and now laughing eyes. "Sorry."

Maria looked up. "I forgive you," she whispered.

Ben slowly got to his feet and got a hug from Tessa.

"Tess," Ben said, "the baby."

"Baby is fine," she said.

Standing behind Louisa, Ben saw Dennis. In the short time they were missing, he had lost a lot of weight. Still 6 feet 7 but so slim, almost skinny.

"Hi boss," he murmured, obviously embarrassed.

Louisa interrupted, "Dennis was on a rescue mission and they overpowered his mind and held him captive. We thought he was lost or injured and went to look for him."

"But," Ben said, "we were told you were on the way back."

"That's what was put in everyone's mind, by them," Tessa said.

Ben's face hardened. "Who is them?" he demanded.

"They are all very dead." This time, it was Louisa who replied.

"'Dennis, are you okay?" Ben asked.

"Yes boss, they put me in irons and used me for bait." He looked down at the ground as he said it.

"Dennis, it is not your fault. They used Louisa and Tessa as bait also."

"Next question," Ben asked, "is why I thought all the council were against that maniac?"

Louisa answered, "Not quite. There was a hard core who thought along the same lines as the master. He sent them ahead to be rid of any major obstacles and they still thought, even with the master gone, that they could gain control. Their power was immense they were of course responsible for those two who are in Lucy's care at the moment."

"How many?" Ben asked.

Louisa spoke again, "23 masters and 15 Umbrians who were fanatics and they also had brain inserts."

"What killed them?" Ben enquired puzzled.

There was a long silence; nobody wanted to tell Ben. In the end a voice piped up. Maria whose scar from the rock almost completely healed, said the word, "You Benji, but you saved us all."

Ben looked at them all. "Impossible," he said, shaking his head in disbelief.

I have not got that sort of power. Lucy and Mars maybe but never me, never."

Louisa put her arm around her son.

"My darling boy it was Lucy who told me, that driven hard enough, your power is insurmountable, even more so than the ancients themselves."

Ben shook his head.

"Then why, right from the beginning, have I always needed protection from the master," he exclaimed. "Maria slew him, and he almost took over my mind."

"Almost," Louisa said. "It was always almost what happened here when there was nobody to rescue you. It would have been the same result. They knew this and took a chance; by using no weapons, they tried to stone you and Maria to death, then they would have slain Tessa, myself and my dear Dennis."

Digesting those words, Ben found some solace, but was still horrified at the number who died. Mars and Lucy, Samuel and Fredrika appeared as two blue lights giving Ben and Maria a mental hug, then disappeared again.

Mars said, "Some good news…those two Lucy was healing are okay and better still, they were just two rebels and disposable by those who sent them. They have certainly seen the error of their ways. Oh and I've organised a clean up here."

Ben had a thought about the stone throwers."

"They were clones and you turned them all off." Mars said with a smile. What he did not say was "permanently".

They all went through to the tunnel where a train was waiting and boarding, travelled back to the terminal where Romilly and George were waiting with a helicopter.

"Just this once," Romilly said smiling, referring to her flying.

Then they were back in the medical centre where everyone anxiously waited and after hugs and kisses all round, it was back to normality or as close as they would ever get.

Ben was trying to come to terms with the power that came from his being. Looking back, the only humans he had slain were those that had attacked and nearly killed Ivan and his father. He had always been protected by his mother, Tessa, Lucy, and Maria.

He had lost count of the number she had killed protecting him.

"Ben, I must tell you why you never used those powers you have."

Ben looked at Lucy but remained silent.

"You're a throwback," she said.

"A what?" he said, shakily.

"A throwback," she repeated. "Many eons ago an Umbrian and an Arian or as you call them, 'Ancient' fell in love. You, my dear Benjamin, are a product of that love for a reason only known to the gods. The mix of Human, Umbrian and Arian has given you powers that are beyond those of us Arians." And she went on, "Being ancient, your instincts stop you from intervening with other races. Hence your inability to defend yourself."

Ben, in that instant, realised all and just said, "Oh I did wonder and now I know. Thank you Lucy."

Often he had spoken with Maria about the times she had defended him and now he knew.

He saw it in her eyes, at times when they talked of the past, and now he had killed and he hated himself and the power he had inherited. But he also realised, what was done, was now hopefully the end of a very traumatic era.

Eva and Adele were safe and also excited and pleased with themselves. After a few hitches, the main hitch being the transport of water from Earth to the surface of Umbria, the waterspouts caused by the wormhole were far enough from land and only caused higher tides on landfall.

After several months, it had to be halted though, 'Earth's wobble' had started to increase, as some thought wrongly, it was the extraction of billions of tons of water.

As scientists investigated, the cause was the meteorite strike of several million years before. It had made the earth top heavy, and now the effect of the gravitational pull had ceased. The Earth was now reverting back to the original wobble of 23 degrees. This meant longer winters and the freezing of the ice caps.

Fortunately, the storms were not as severe as anticipated and earth retained her 23-degree wobble after a few years. Also, the Earth was spinning slower.

The slower rotation was also less severe being only slight, amounting to slightly less than 4 minutes a day. When calculated it was just 1 day per year, almost exactly. This time difference was easily overcome by adding a day on the month of February. The saying now went, 'thirty days hath September, April, June and November, all the rest have thirty-one, except February which has twenty-nine and thirty every leap year.'

Ben went to see Eva and Adele. "You must be disappointed," Ben said.

"We are, but also very grateful," Eva said. Adel nodded, "You have given us time," she added. Ben looked puzzled.

"The water from Earth, although an enormous amount, was only enough to form a lake a mile round, and a lot of that water will seep back into the subsoil."

"So what can you do now."

The women both smiled. "We have looked at the other planets in your solar system and a few have water; extracting it will be very difficult though."

"Of course," Ben said. He could not remember the name but knew one of the outer planets was covered completely with ice.

"You would have to shatter the ice to pass it through the wormhole that would be nigh on impossible," Ben said, after giving it some thought. "Also, you do not know the quality of it. What gases and waste matter it might contain."

Adel sniggered, and went red. Eva gave her a sharp look.

"What," said Ben, wondering what he had said to cause amusement.

Eva, embarrassed, said, "It was the word waste, Benjamin."

Ben thought for a moment then it dawned on him.

"Oh, the plastic waste. Did the water from Earth contain much of it?"

He was then, staggered by the reply.

"300,000 tons," she said. "But," she added quickly, "we were grateful for it. We were able to build another dome."

Of course, Ben thought to himself. The barriers at the exclusion zone were there to keep all living things, shipping and aircraft out. With the billions of water being sucked up, the currents would obviously move the plastic towards the wormhole.

He smiled at the two women. "Well," he said, "beneficial to both Umbria and Earth. I wish you success with your project."

He still had serious doubts though.

On his way back to the centre, Venus came to his mind. "Ben," came the thought, "you are right to be worried. The two planets in your solar system with water that is easy to extract have huge gravitational pulls and we have little time to spare."

Tessa greeted him with a hug. "Say goodnight to your daughter and perhaps we could retire early." This she said with a mischievous gleam in her eyes. Ben found Victoria reading and told her not to stay up too late. He took late and promised to go riding with her the very next day.

"Okay, Dad, just swatting up for the exams," she answered, giving her father a big smile.

Victoria, at eleven, was the image of her mother and just as beautiful, like her father and Mars. She was a mixture of three species and was super intelligent. The exams she was referring to was for her entrance to university. Ben bid her goodnight, kissed the top of her head and went to join Tessa.

"Well, wife, why early night?" he said this with his back to her so she would not see the grin. "Oh," she said faintly. "There is a film I wish to see but as I'm so tired I thought I'd retire early."

"I think you're telling me those little white or rather grey fibs again," Ben said.

She then shrieked as Ben picked her up and dumped her on the bed.

"Now, how can I punish you woman," he said grinning evilly.

"Oh master, not that," Tessa replied, stifling her laughter.

"'Fraid so," he said. "You are to be kissed into oblivion."

"Ooh please, mercy master."

The next hour was intermixed with shrieks, moans and groans of pleasure and then a dreamy decline into a deep sleep.

Ben, as he fell asleep, was thinking of ways of getting water to Umbria before the planet died from the lack of it.

His mind drifted away into space, his mind searching. He knew as a fact that many meteorites consisted solely of water, on and on his mind drifted and then deep in space his mind sensed it. 'WATER' His thoughts rushed on and he knew he had found it.

His mind sensed something else, but it must be wrong? What he sensed almost felt in his mind, as if it was a living thing.

Not just one but many. He let his mind go even further, but then all went black and he was falling into a hole so deep, it was cold and then there was nothing but a tiny thread as fine as a cobweb.

Something was gripping him. He had no will or power to stop it. Far away, he heard his name, "Benjamin, Benjamin."

Only one person called him by his full name. "Mother," he breathed. There was a rush of sound and his mind was back in his body.

His eyes fluttered open.

"I cannot see," he cried. "Mum, I cannot see."

He felt and smelt his mother and slowly his vision cleared. Through a mist behind Louisa were other people.

"What happened?" he shouted.

"Hush, Ben, it is all okay now."

Ben thought *that is Lucy's voice.* His vision cleared and over his mother's shoulder there was Lucy, Mars, Tessa, Victoria, Maria and Venus.

He looked at them all.

"You look as if you have not slept for a week." That drew a faint smile from them all.

"Well," Louisa replied, "that is roughly how long you have been away from us."

Louisa gave him one more hug and released him.

"Where have you been this time," she demanded. "You were hanging on to life by a thread."

Ben looked shocked. "I cannot remember but I must remember, it's vital."

Lucy asked everyone to leave the room, "Just for a short while, please. Oh Venus, would you stay?"

Venus sat in a chair while Lucy put her hands on Ben's head. After a short time, Ben exclaimed, "Venus, we have little time. They are coming."

Venus looked at Ben. "Who are coming Ben?"

"I do not know," he shook his head in frustration.

"But they told me. Or did I sense it?" He went on. "I could feel their presence."

Lucy held up her hand. "Ben, stop. You're rambling."

Lucy thought about what he had said and she realised who 'THEY' were.

"But that is impossible," she said more to herself than anybody else.

"What, what do you mean?" Ben and Venus said.

"Well, I looked for where Ben's mind could be and when I finally found it, it was drifting in space, deep space and then he or rather his mind vanished. Now, I think I know where, but," she repeated herself, "it is impossible."

Ben and Venus shouted as one. "WHAT IS IT OR THEY?"

"I think, Ben might have had contact with Umbrians."

Venus looked shocked. "How and where," is all she said.

Lucy explained, "The trajectory where his mind was drifting was where Umbria came from. I know, think, hope, even believe maybe they somehow survived when the massif aqua (ocean), was torn from the planet."

She went on. "A lot of the coastline was ripped away as well and along its several thousand miles there were, as the humans call them, crystal domes. Somehow, some survived the catastrophe."

She added, "Only time will tell us how and how many."

Ben crossed himself, he never believed in any religion but his human side always believed that there was a god.

Venus's face glowed. "Please let it be so," she breathed.

"Ben seems to think the meteorite will arrive in our solar system soon," Lucy explained.

"I hope so," Venus exclaimed, "we have no ecosystem and the water is nearly gone again."

Ben interrupted, "Sorry Venus, but we must send probes to know the speed and distance."

"It is vital to know otherwise it could crash into Umbria's surface or just miss completely and be irretrievable. When it gets close, we have to put it in orbit."

Ben collapsed back onto his pillow white-faced and totally exhausted.

Lucy, went to Ben again and laid her hand on his forehead.

Ben went to sleep, deep deep sleep. Lucy then called the others back. As they entered, there was a gasp of shock from them all. Ben's face was as white as chalk, but worse, his lush thick brown hair was the same snow white.

Louisa swayed and collapsed. Dennis caught her and picked her up, carried her to the sofa and laid her down.

Tessa burst into tears and Maria found she was crying too. Mars just set his jaw and said nothing. Victoria put her arms around the two women and consoled them, saying, "It is okay. Dad will be okay."

Lucy did her best to explain. "Ben went beyond the powers of the ancients and the strain on his mind and body were too great. The white hair just shows that some of that power worked against him"

Tessa, ashen-faced, asked, "Will he recover?"

Lucy was slow to answer. "I do not know," was her reply. His body still functions but I worry about his mind." She went to Mars and held him close.

"I am sure he will recover," she whispered."

Mars took control. "If he does or does not, he is looking to us to carry out what seems impossible. Louisa and Tessa, you stay with Ben and nurse him, and you, Dennis, I want you to make sure they're not disturbed." He relented, "albeit, apart from Maria and the children."

Lucy faced the problem once more. "There is a way," she said, "it is what nearly destroyed Umbria."

A whisper entered her mind. "Well done, Lucy, traction."

Lucy smiled. "His mind is okay," she proclaimed but it will be a long wait for mind and body to come together.

And so, while Ben hopefully recovered, the mammoth task began.

All the spacecraft that could be spared were fitted with the massive traction drives and were readied to go into space.

Everything was timed to the second to get the meteorite into orbit around Umbria. It had to be at the correct velocity and distance, and also have the right orbit.

The years flew by and then it approached, although it was only a fraction of the size of Umbria, it was massive, virtually solid ice.

The fear was that the domes might be torn away under traction, but they were now deep within the ice, so quite secure.

The domes within the ice numbered close to 1500, being on the coastline that circled the ocean, some twenty domes were cities.

Contact was made with all, bar 5 domes, and they were small, the inhabitants already housed in the city domes.

The loss of life was enormous, initially mainly from the coldness of space. But being powered by nuclear plants, the heat of the domes was quickly adjusted to compensate for the extremes of space.

Most of the planet's oxygen also was sucked into space and the gravity of the freezing ocean drew the air to it.

Food was no problem as most was grown in domes attached to the inhabited domes. There was little meat, but mostly they ate fish, all domes having fish farms of various sizes.

Venus was overwhelmed with joy, possibly almost a billion more survivors once they were able to get the frozen meteorite into liquid form back on Umbria along with the domes and inhabitants.

Venus often called in to see how Ben was. One of the women was always with him, although Lucy tried to keep their spirits up, they were missing Ben and his funny ways as Maria put it.

Louisa was with Ben that day, when Lucy called.

"He still sleeps," she said. "But I always talk to him, and I am rewarded sometimes with a smile or better still a thought from him."

Venus, was delighted. "This man," she said, "saved my life and is the saver of the majority of Umbrians." She looked fondly at Ben, and exclaimed, "Look his hair…its growing back to its natural colour."

"Yes," Louisa replied with a good sign. In her heart though she just wanted Ben to awaken, she thought sadly it was now nearly four years since he went into his comatose state.

The meteorite, now within orbit was changing, the air round it warmed by the sun's rays was drifting clear and by gravitational pull was returning to Umbria.

The water was a greater problem, being still in space it remained in its frozen state although slightly defrosted.

A satellite was put into a parallel orbit with halogen suns, as they were called, and the slow process of thawing started; too fast and the meteorite would shatter.

At last it started to rain and there was much jubilation by all Umbrians. After a 100 days, the smiles began to fade and fifty days on and all were miserable with the rain, the floods and general disruption.

With traction, the Domes, with the inhabitants safely evacuated, were lowered onto the surface of Umbria albeit actually onto the water with mighty splashes.

They were then towed to the coastline and anchored. The traction held the domes virtually to the surface, so there were few injuries of those who stayed mainly to safeguard against accidents to the vital services, i.e., the nuclear plants etc.

The old coastline was a greater problem, but again the gravitational pull of the spaceships held it. Then with traction, it was coalesced into a single mass leaving Umbria with a small moon twenty thousand miles across.

At last, after nearly two hundred days, a watery sun appeared. The hurricanes, typhoons etc. at last after several more months receded into gales and storms.

'WARM SUNNY WEATHER Umbria is getting,' were the headlines splashed across the majority of Earth tabloids.

The Umbrians on Earth and Umbria itself were euphoric.

After many centuries of thinking their race was to become extinct, they now had a future of billions of years, well three or four at least.

They had millions of seeds, and plants stored and propagating inside their domes. Although the air was too thin to go out, now the waters had subsided and were able to drive out in their adapted vehicles. The seeder's as they were called did just that, drill a thousand holes at a rate of thirty a minute and plant a seed in each hole.

Within a year, the land on the planet was turning green and the air in parts was already breathable.

Back on Earth, Ben still slept, four years, a long time!!!

As Lucy explained, "He is hibernating."

He needed no food, and was on an intravenous drip.

A tiny chip was placed in his brain to keep the vital organs functioning and a pacemaker in his heart to keep it at a steady rate. After all that, the girls still went to him daily but spent the rest of the day normally. Nurses washed him and put him through a gentle physiotherapy routine a few times every day.

Lucy spoke with her father. "Is it possible for him to recover?"

Her father replied, "As an ancient, he would have died, your mind had drifted to its limit when you found his, and when it went from you, his mind was lost to his brain at that point.

"His mind did find where it left yours and finally returned to his body. His brain is fine but all his thoughts are still lost."

It was at this time that Tessa was with Victoria, now nearly sixteen, like her brother Mars, was super intelligent.

She looked up, "Mum, I am going to sit with Dad."

Tessa was not sure. "Your father is still asleep darling."

"I know, I want to wake him up," Victoria said.

Tessa stared at her. "I do not think your father is ready to wake up," was the only reply she could think of.

"But of course lets go and see him," Tessa and Victoria went to the hallway and there they met Lucy.

"I thought I'd come with you," Lucy said, smiling. Tessa smiled weakly in return realizing Lucy had listened into their thoughts. In the room, they let Victoria go to Ben. Tessa had the wildest thought. "Could she? Could our daughter bring Ben back?"

A thought came from Lucy. "Do not build your hopes too high Tess, even if she can bring Ben back to a conscious state, his mind has been dormant too long."

Lucy stopped and spoke, "Victoria is aware of my thoughts. You do have, power young lady, is it enough though?" Lucy sighed and like Tessa hoped.

Victoria put her hand into Ben's and looked at his closed eyes, as she did, the same soft white light that Lucy had, came from hers, only this came in pulses, slowly at first then faster until it shimmered all around Ben's head.

Time seemed to stand still, Lucy and Tessa felt sleepy. Falling asleep on their feet, instead of falling, they floated to the sofa and lay there.

Victoria was taking Ben's mind back again slowly minute by minute, hour by hour, day by day, then faster; days became weeks then months and finally slowing to first one then two, three and finally four.

The whiteness around them was so bright they both appeared part of it.

Like a switch being touched it went out.

The sun shone through the window. Ben yawned and woke.

"Oh," he said, looking at Victoria. "You could be my daughter," he laughed, "she is only eleven though."

"I must alert everyone. Umbria's ocean is returning."

"It is okay, Dad, you told Mum before you went to sleep. Everything has been completed."

Ben shook his head and stared at the young woman sitting on his bed. She said, "DADDY!"

"Victoria," he whispered.

Victoria wrapped her arms around his neck. "Time is not important. All the time you were asleep. It is only what happened before and after that is."

While Ben was trying to digest this, Victoria woke Tessa and Lucy.

The pair of them spoke as one. "Ben, you're awake."

Ben smiled, "it appears so, I cannot quite believe I have been that way for that length of time," he added.

The door flew open, in came Mars, Maria and Venus. After a group hug, where Ben was nearly rendered unconscious again being smothered, Victoria intervened by saying, "I think Dad needs to rest now."

Everyone, including Ben, burst out laughing, nevertheless quietly left, leaving just Tessa and Victoria. Tessa burst into tears.

"I thought I had lost you, Ben," she wept through tears of happiness.

Victoria explained how she managed to wake Ben. Tessa shook her head in disbelief, giving her daughter a hug, she laughed, "You are your father's daughter. There is no doubt about that."

Ben was, of course, a hero having saved Earth from near extinction, he had now done the same, for Umbria.

Ben would have none of it. "I just pointed everyone in the right direction," he insisted.

"Most of the time I have been kept alive by others and they have also done most of the work to realise the ultimate result.

"And," he added, "it was the captain of the spaceship who went back and rescued the billion Umbrians."

Venus became the grand Mistress of Umbria having fully recovered, and was again the beautiful woman as before. In addition, Colin the clone became a Grand Master, which amazed all, but his logic was infallible, earning him his position. All the Earth leaders formed a council and made a reluctant Ben adviser to that council.

All the crystal domes on both planets were left, and the city and town domes became the premier place to live, with their constant temperate climate through winter and summer, the population enjoyed life completely.

Many smaller domes became holiday resorts and again with the controlled climate you could ski in one and sunbathe on the same day in another.

The population on both planets slowly recovered and travel between the two took little time due to the advantage of the wormhole set up between them.

Ben, back in the house, had all his family and friends either with him in the house or living close.

Two were missing however Joe and Aunt Agatha. Fifteen years ago Joe with Aggie and their baby who was yet to be born were in the Atlantic heading to Spain.

On board were his crew and their families. Bermuda was unsafe and when Ben told him to get out as fast as possible, Joe either misunderstood or decided to do so. He discussed it with Agatha and she agreed, in fact, insisted they would flee in the yacht with the crew and their families. Ben tried to dissuade him telling him the danger was imminent but Joe would not listen due to his loyalty to his crew and the fact that he thought the safest place was on Ben's unsinkable yacht!!! He had sailed and Ben had no news of his whereabouts or even that of the yacht.

Two days later, he had a visitor. Dennis came in and told Ben that this weird bloke had been asking to have a council with Mr Franklin.

"I told him to get lost but since you have been awake, he keeps coming back."

"Does he have a name?" Ben asked wondering.

"Colin," Dennis answered.

"Send him to me please."

A minute later and there he was, Colin.

"Where are they, Colin, and call me Ben, please."

"The Canary Islands," came the answer. "I found the Mistress on the big island."

Colin went on. "She refused to leave with me here." He sought for the right word. "Her mate is injured, she told me to come to you." After more questioning, it transpired that Joe saw the wave coming and had put Agatha with the crew and battened down the hatches. He then attempted to ride the 500-metre-high wave in the hope of beaching the yacht in Spain or Portugal. He nearly succeeded but the wave swung the boat round and it beached backwards in a gully halfway up a mountain. The crew and Agatha survived with a few broken bones and bruises. Joe had not been so lucky and from Colin's description it sounded like a bad back injury was sustained when the wheelhouse got smashed into splinters. With no communication and no other boats they had all been stranded and survived on what food was left in the evacuation of the inhabitants and fishing.

Ben sat listening mesmerized, but only for a moment. He called Lucy and Louisa to a council of war. They returned to the islands with Colin and took drugs to sedate Joe for the journey back in Colin's space pod. Mars and Dennis went with Ben in three Chinooks to rescue the crew of his yacht. He only had two pilots available. Romilly came to the rescue, George being more than happy knowing Ben would be with her. Ben gave the two other pilots a quick briefing, giving them the exact location of the yacht.

"From here," he said, "head out to the Med and then switch to hydrogen power; just use bio power over land, have a safe journey see you there. Hopefully, we will have enough room for all the crew?"

One by one the three huge Chinooks took off. Giving Romilly the same instructions, they headed down the east coast of Spain then west to the straits of Gibraltar and following the coast of North Africa before going west again to the Canary Islands. Over flying Ben surveyed the scene below before telling Romilly to land. His yacht was in a sorry state, she was wedged bow first, in a gully at least 200 metres above sea level. Ben marvelled the way Joe had managed to keep the boat afloat and save all on board. Looking at where the wheelhouse had once been, he was surprised that Joe was still alive. Landing alongside the two Chinooks, he took stock of the task before them. There were sixty-five of the crew and families, a tight squeeze and Ben had to be firm about their luggage. "Only your most treasured possessions," he insisted. They acquiesced gladly. Just happy to be rescued after what seemed like a lifetime. They were mostly healthy with a tan, Ben gently jostled them saying they could have been stranded in the Arctic. Then, with them all aboard, they had an uneventful return journey. Maria and Tessa had been busy arranging temporary accommodation for them and with Mars and Dennis helping, soon had them in their homes. Romilly rushed off back to George and Ben went straight to the Medical Centre to see how badly injured Joe was, and to give his aunt Agatha a big hug. Joe was in a bad way. Louisa and Lucy were either side of his bed and Ben could sense that Lucy was seeking out his injuries with her mind. Louisa motioned him to where she was, moving aside so Ben could assess Joe himself. Ben let his mind wander and once inside, Lucy guided him to the worst injury. It was his back, of course. When the yacht struck the bow first he was hurled backwards through the wheelhouse that alone should have killed him. His back was broken in three places and he had two broken ribs, his left arm was obviously badly broken and he had a deep scar on the side of his head. Amazingly, he was conscious. He looked up.

"Sorry boss" he whispered the drugs were obviously doing their job in sedating him. Ben realised what he was talking about.

"Joe, for god's sake, sod the yacht. You have saved nearly seventy people, they all would have died had they stayed in the Bahamas. Now, relax and count to ten and Lucy and I will see what can be done."

Joe laid back and in seconds was asleep. After five hours, an exhausted Lucy and Ben sat back. "We will give it forty-eight hours and then physiotherapy for a week before we get him to try to walk," Lucy said. Ben agreed. He had, like Lucy, had no sleep for over a day. He just wanted to lay down but he had one more thing to do. He turned and looked. Agatha smiled and next moment, Ben had scooped her up in his arms. Aggie, I thought I had lost you and Joe. She shook her pretty little head.

"No," she said. "He has been so ill Benjamin. I hope you and Lucy can cure him." She turned to a young girl standing quietly beside her. "Ben this is my daughter, Josephine." Ben was in shock. He nearly fell and the girl caught him.

"Thank you," he said.

"I am so terribly tired I had forgotten how long you were stranded." In his mind, he thought, *my goodness she certainly has Joe's strength, she was tall like Joe and has broad shoulders for a girl.*

"You must tell me of your unwanted adventure later," he said and leaving them, flopped on his bed and slept for twenty hours. A year later, Joe was at Ben's side.

"Only you could do it Ben". He had salvaged the yacht, he never told anyone but had organised it quietly approaching a boat builder he knew in southern Spain. After repairing the bow, the yacht was made watertight and a giant slipway was built with cranes. They eased the boat onto the slipway and released it. Down it went, gathering speed every metre it went. It hit the water causing a mini tidal wave and disappeared. All watching held their breath for long seconds, then up it popped, it was towed to the shipyard and there it stayed in dry dock for nearly a year whilst it was repaired and refitted. She now stood on the slipway ready to be launched, her name hidden by a flag. Ben turned to Joe.

"You best launch her," he said handing him a bottle of champagne.

"I…I don't know her name," he stuttered. He nearly said you should do it, but said nothing.

Ben pulled a cord and the drape fell away revealing the name. JOSEPHINE.

"Carry on, Joe, name your yacht." Joe stared at Ben totally bemused and then taking a deep breath launched the yacht. Joe's crew already aboard shouted and waved as the yacht was towed out to deeper water, the bosun at the helm ready to steer her back to her berth.

"Can we all come for a cruise on your yacht Joe?" Ben asked. Joe was speechless again.

They did go on the cruise for five months and all of Ben's family, who included Maria and her children, with Bunny, Ivan and his family, George and Romilly plus their daughter Rose.

The yacht was packed and the poor chef and his team were running off their feet and the crew were run off their feet but they did get respite. Every major port, they stopped at for supplies etc. Ben's whole entourage stayed for a few days at the best hotel in town or city while they took in the sights and so the story, against all odds, had a joyous ending until the next time.